INDISPUTABLE PROOF

GARY WILLIAMS AND
VICKY KNERLY

SUSPENSE PUBLISHING

INDISPUTABLE PROOF
By
Gary Williams and Vicky Knerly

PAPERBACK EDITION

* * * * *

PUBLISHED BY:
Suspense Publishing

COPYRIGHT
Copyright 2012 by Gary S. Williams and Vicky W. Knerly Partnership

PUBLISHING HISTORY:
Suspense Publishing, Digital Copy, September 2012

Cover Design: Shannon Raab
Cover Photographer: iStockphoto.com/sculpies
Cover Background: iStockphoto.com/7io

ISBN-13: 978-0692259610 (Suspense Publishing)
ISBN-10: 0692259619

THE NOVELS OF
GARY WILLIAMS & VICKY KNERLY

ADVANCE PRAISE FOR "INDISPUTABLE PROOF"

"Dan Brown better look over his shoulder – Williams and Knerly are here for his crown. *Indisputable Proof* is an edge-of-the-seat thriller with great storytelling backed by brilliant research."
– Greig Beck, best selling author of *This Green Hell* and *Dark Rising*

"The more I read by Williams and Knerly, the more I fall in love with their writing style, genre, characters, and most of all, their solid plotline. It amazes me how seamlessly everything falls into place in their novels, especially in *Indisputable Proof,* and it's obvious that Williams and Knerly put in a great deal of time and effort researching Biblical history while writing this amazing novel. Not only are the authors historically accurate and able to work in even the smallest of historical details, but they also use historical accounts to their advantage, filling in holes with their own added imaginings that cause the reader to stop and wonder, "what if?" It's an age-old mystery unfolding before the reader's eyes, giving a different perspective based on recordings and findings of the past, and the way Williams and Knerly present their novel, pulling the reader into the story and causing them to question all they know, is amazing.

"If you've enjoyed any of the Dan Brown's books, or the movies *The Da Vinci Code* or *Angels and Demons*, then you'll love *Indisputable Proof* (and all Williams' and Knerly's other novels as well)."
– A Book Vacation Review

DEDICATIONS

Gary dedicates this book to his children—Josh, Jeff and Kristin.

Vicky dedicates this book to Kathi and Leanne, who know her secrets and keep her sane at all times.

ACKNOWLEDGEMENTS

Gary and Vicky would like to thank their families and friends for their continuing support and encouragement.

The authors would also like to commend the following people for their efforts with this book: Janice Lake, Maryanne Pease, Susan Parker, Les Williams, Sonya Guess Ashton, Mille & Mark Sorger, Dalerie Fisher, Bob Campbell, Dot Esh, Deborah Wall McGraw and Tony & Margie Hawkes. We value your feedback, and thank you for your scrutiny.

Thanks to Lori Wiggin for her expertise with medical laboratories.

Also, kudos to our publicist, Diane Buckner. We continue to function as a well-oiled team.

With each book, we have gained a larger audience, and our ardent followers have been instrumental in getting the word out. We appreciate your support more than you'll ever know.

Lastly, we would like to thank all the readers. We hope you enjoy this story and follow us on future adventures.

INDISPUTABLE PROOF

GARY WILLIAMS AND
VICKY KNERLY

SUSPENSE PUBLISHING

CHAPTER 1

August 30. Thursday – 6:33 a.m. Oviedo, Spain

Father Juan Carletta gazed upward as he approached the Cathedral of San Salvador, admiring the white stone bell tower silhouetted against the Spanish sky. Daylight broke on the far side, gilding the top of the edifice and sending orange-yellow light streaming through the slitted openings. The elder priest moved with urgency today. The security guard, Javier, had failed to check in at 6 a.m., and he was anxious to know why.

He hurried through the plaza toward the large square abutting the western end of the church. The dew on the grass dampened the bottom edge of his cassock as he went. He reached the central door and pushed it open. As usual, Javier had unlocked the cathedral before the priest's arrival, and the guard's adherence to routine brought a small measure of solace.

Father Carletta entered the cathedral and glanced ahead at the cavernous space. The lofty eight-sided dome stretched high overhead. Unlike the bright brick exterior, the lack of natural light here cast a forlorn gloom over the interior.

"Javier?" Father Carletta called out into the shadows.

He received no response.

"Javier, where are you?" he continued more loudly. His words echoed softly.

The smell of cinnamon from the candles stacked at the ambulatory hung heavily in the air. He moved up the center aisle toward the main altar where the image of the Divine Savior spread across a four-column baldacchino. He carefully surveyed the pews as he went, looking for any sign of Javier.

At the transept, he turned left, moving down the north aisle, straining to see in the dim light. An uncomfortable and unexpected aura filled the cathedral this morning.

"Javier, are you here?" Father Carletta's voice tightened.

He reached the opening off the north transept leading to the Capilla de Nuestra Señora del Rey Casto. Ornate buttresses and regal columns remained cloaked within the shadows. The longer his calls for Javier went unanswered, the more concerned he became. He turned and retraced his steps.

The priest hurried past the apse at the altar and aimed toward the south transept connecting to a spectacular cloister filled with monuments and pilgrims' gravestones. Father Carletta's footfalls on the hard surface sounded close and distant at the same time, causing him to look back over his shoulder more than once as an uneasy feeling continued to well up inside him.

He paused, listening intently for any sound. The prevailing silence sent a cold shiver down his spine. He took a deep breath and shook the feeling away, chiding himself for being foolish.

He moved to an adjoining cloister where an elaborate, full-scale diorama depicted Roman guards leading Jesus away from the Garden of Gethsemane. Father Carletta had viewed this diorama many times, yet today, something seemed odd about it. Nevertheless, he continued on.

One more place to check, he thought, although it was a long shot. After that, protocol required him to notify the archbishop.

Father Carletta exhaled a troubled breath. He liked Javier. The thought of the guard losing his job was disconcerting.

The priest returned to the apse. Here the south transept opened on a stairwell with steps leading upward. He took them quickly and turned left, stepping into a rectangular ante-chapel known as a *cella*. Although fitted with sconce lights on either side, he unexpectedly found himself in a pitch-black room.

Father Carletta paused. A prickle at the top of his head caused him to shiver again. The light bulbs were changed monthly. It would be nearly impossible for both to have burned out at the same time. Then he forced an inward smile. Surely it was just a coincidence.

He retreated from the darkness and returned to the main cathedral to retrieve one of the many votive candles that lined the ambulatory. He found a book of matches inside the pulpit, lit the squat red candle, and returned to the *cella*, carrying it by its glass holder.

Once inside the long room, the meager candlelight proved ineffective in reaching either the side rubble-masonry walls or the barrel-vaulted ceiling which soared twenty feet at the crown. Ahead, somewhere in the darkness, the two aisles overlapped into a slightly elevated chamber. There, a barrel-vaulted entryway secured by iron bars and an iron, prison-style door shielded the upper sanctuary.

Father Carletta moved slowly. Warmer air blended with a strange odor, masking the normal, musty smell of aged stone. The fact that he could not account for the peculiar stench was troublesome. He swung the candle from side to side, eyes wide and nerves on edge. The smell grew stronger as he proceeded. His footsteps sounded unusually loud, and he became wary of the noise he made. No matter how hard Father Carletta tried, he could not fend off the overpowering sense of foreboding.

"Javier, are you in here?" he called once more tentatively. A bead of perspiration ran down his cheek. The annoying smell turned rancid. His pulse quickened.

It suddenly occurred to him what had been wrong with the life-size diorama back in the cloister. One of the Roman guards was missing his weapon: an antique halberd on loan from an Italian museum. He tried to remember if it had been there the day before, but he could not be sure. The archbishop had a tendency to rearrange the dioramas often. Still, the thought was unsettling.

He continued to pitch the candle back and forth as he went, as much out of fear for what might be waiting in the darkness as to search for Javier. The candle flame flickered and receded, casting ghostly shadows along the walls. Father Carletta swallowed a dry lump.

Suddenly, two pale men leapt out of the darkness. Terrified, Father Carletta clutched his chest. He could not breathe, could not think. Several long seconds passed before he finally registered the statues of the two Apostles. The stark figures carved on a pilaster had been brought to life by the darting candlelight. With a flood of relief, he exhaled slowly. He crossed himself before continuing.

His heart was now beating in his ears. He raised a section of his cassock to cover his nose. It did little to mask the vile odor. When the iron cell door finally materialized in the dim candlelight, Father Carletta stopped with a sharp gasp.

Please let it be another trick of the light!

He eased closer and realized his worst fear: the door stood slightly ajar. He looked through the iron bars and saw the array of religious reliquary items on display. A jolt of nausea struck him. The centerpiece of the room, the Arca Santa—a large, black oak chest—stood open.

Nearly breathless, Father Carletta rushed forward and yanked open the cell door, almost dropping the votive candle in the process. The flame flickered light into the chamber. His overwhelming concern was for the contents of the Arca Santa. He hurried over to it, ignoring the repulsive stench. The items were kept in strict placement surrounding the central relic. Father Carletta conducted a frantic mental inventory of the contents. To his horror, the Sudarium—the very cloth that covered the face of Jesus Christ immediately following his death on the cross—was gone!

"Ay Dios mio! *Oh my God*!" he gasped. He staggered, lightheaded. Father Carletta regained his balance just before he crashed into the glass case to the side. The jostled candle flame sent light dancing madly across the Arca Santa. His vision blurred, and he struggled to catch his breath.

Moments later as his world slowly came back into focus, he spotted a dark mass on the floor nestled between the back of the Arca Santa and the rear wall: an amorphous form, partly shielded by the chest. His mind could not comprehend what he saw. All he could make out were two long, dark horizontal shapes on the floor. A third, thin linear shape floated parallel six inches above them. The sight was further convoluted by the unstable candlelight casting the unknown objects in shadow on the near wall. His thoughts ran incongruently, spinning with the tragic repercussions of the missing

Sudarium from the Arca Santa and now grappling to make sense of the scene before him. Only when he moved to the rear of the chest and held the candle lower did the entire ghastly image solidify.

A man lay on his back, the axe blade of the missing halberd buried deep in his chest. The shaft of the long weapon hovered horizontally, stretching down the length of his body and beyond. The large axe had caused an enormous gash, and tattered flesh spilled out through the blood-soaked material of his shirt. Dark blood saturated the floor near his chest, and droplets splattered the rear wall behind the Arca Santa. The dead man's unseeing eyes were open, and his lips stretched apart as if his last mortal act had been to scream.

Through his horrified confusion, Father Carletta recognized Javier. Terror infected his mind as he felt his body go weightless, then all went dark.

CHAPTER 2

September 10. Monday – 5:28 a.m. Jacksonville, Florida

Maria Varchin sat patiently at the nurses' station on the 4th floor of Memorial Hospital. To her side, Susie Hampton looked down at the desk. The halls were quiet at this hour. Both nurses pretended to busy themselves with paperwork.

Susie glanced up at the clock on the wall. "T-minus two minutes and counting," she recited aloud with a ghost of a smile.

Dr. Tanika Sager happened to be passing by and overheard her. "Shift ending?"

"Better than that," Maria remarked.

Dr. Sager glanced down at her watch. "Oh, it's *that* time," she said with a wide grin. "You know, normally I'd consider this type of behavior unprofessional, but I have to admit…" she shook her head as if censoring herself. "Do either of you realize how rare it is for an African American man to have blue eyes?"

"Those eyes could melt Antarctica, Doctor," Maria said.

For almost a week, Samuel Tolen had arrived on the 4th floor at precisely 5:30 a.m. At first, Maria had assumed the man was either a prominent doctor or someone high up in the hospital administration. He had an undeniably warm nature with virile good looks and a commanding presence. She had since learned he was some sort of federal agent and that his father was a patient on the floor. The circumstances of his visits were disheartening. On the flip side, his daily appearance brought an injection of life to the women working the floor. To Maria, Samuel Tolen was like a strong cup of coffee that jump-started her morning.

"You know," Maria said, turning to Susie, "He's probably old enough to be your father."

"My kind of daddy," Susie responded, buffing out her long, blonde ponytail.

"T-minus one minute," Maria said, impatiently eying the clock.

Even Dr. Sager seemed anxious to get another glimpse of the man. She hung around the desk for no particular reason, shuffling and stacking some pages in an open folder on the counter.

At precisely 5:30, the elevator swished opened. Samuel Tolen emerged, dressed impeccably in a white, long-sleeve dress shirt covered by a fitted jacket, dark slacks, and black polished shoes. He casually ran a hand over his close-cropped hair as he strolled up the hallway. He looked to the nurses' station and smiled, gazing at all three women with those wondrous blue eyes.

"NASA, we have *no* problem," Maria said in a song-like whisper as he passed by.

"Liftoff," Susie giggled.

Seconds later, the man disappeared inside Room 438 at the far end of the hallway.

****

Samuel Tolen sat beside the bed reading the various instruments which emitted a chorus of clicks, hums, and beeps in the otherwise quiet hospital room. The ventilator huffed and hissed its rhythmic cadence. The usual confluence of smells filled the air: disinfectant, rubbing alcohol, fresh sheets.

His 73-year-old father lay motionless in the bed. The sheet was pulled up to his neck and then folded neatly down. His gaunt features were a drastic departure from the robust man Tolen had known to be so vibrant and full of life. As always, the sight of the feeble man who had been so prominent in Samuel Tolen's life stirred deep sadness.

When the opportunity had arisen several weeks ago for a leave of absence, Tolen had seized it. For the last six days, he had stayed at his father's house on the St. Johns River in Green Cove Springs on the outskirts of Jacksonville. While there, he had busied himself with minor home repairs and dock maintenance to keep his mind off his father's condition. Each morning, he drove to Memorial Hospital in Jacksonville to visit his father. Every day, he battled with the decision. All the while, Jaspar Tolen lay in the same position, eyes closed, with no hope of ever reviving.

Tolen looked down at the paperwork in his hand. There could be no disputing the document's authenticity or intent. His father had ensured it was written in such precise detail that there was no danger of ambiguity or misinterpretation of his instructions. Legally, it was solid as a rock.

He looked back at his father, the man who had single-handedly raised him after his mother died when he was ten. The man had been his role model, dispensing inspirational quotes at every opportunity and, throughout his lifetime, Tolen had soaked them up like a sponge. Now, there would be no more intellectual sharing, no more comforting words. Now, his father's dark skin was flaccid, his cheeks hollow. His once-solid muscles showed initial signs of atrophy.

Tolen looked again at the paperwork in his hand. Then he pushed up his sleeve and stared for a minute at the long scar on his right forearm. With an exhale, he dropped his sleeve, folded the document and tucked it inside his coat pocket.

He rose silently, bent down, and kissed his father on the forehead. Just as he reached the door, his cell phone went off. He closed the door behind him and answered in the hallway.

"Vakind," Tolen said, recognizing the number, "can I call you back in a few minutes? I'm at the hospital."

"You're booked on the next flight to DC. Do you have a bag in your car?"

Tolen thought for a moment before responding. "Enough to make do."

"My apology for cutting your leave short, but this is an urgent matter. I'll brief you when you arrive at the office. To clarify, I mean the office at your new assignment. Oh, and by the way, I'm now the acting Director of Operations." There was a click, then silence.

Tolen returned the cell phone, and at the same time pushed the paperwork further inside his inner pocket. *Acting Director of*

Operations? What happened to Carlton Tannacay?

CHAPTER 3

September 10. Monday – 1:56 p.m. Washington, DC

The elevator doors opened to the third underground level at the Smithsonian Institution. Samuel Tolen followed a banal hallway past a warren of offices, most with their doors closed. He emerged into a tiled foyer where a no-nonsense, fifty-something administrative technician with a bored expression stood filing manila folders in a cabinet. He asked for directions to conference room L311 and, with a drastic change in body language, she offered a remarkably friendly smile. "You must be Dr. Tolen," she said with an informed nod. "This way, please." She gestured for him to follow her down a side hallway, leading him toward the far end.

Upon reaching the conference room door, the woman knocked, opened it, cordially motioned Tolen inside, and closed the door behind him. He was greeted by four pairs of eyes belonging to two men and two women, all dressed professionally. Seated at the far end of a long, polished mahogany table was acting Director of Operations, Morris Vakind, with his signature strong chin, dirty-blond hair (longer than would have been expected of a CIA director), and a deep skin tone which rivaled any California surfer's tan. He was dressed in a charcoal gray suit and sported a blue tie; his hands firmly folded before him. To Vakind's right, Tolen recognized Dr. Sheila Shaw, the prim and proper, yet very personable, director of the Smithsonian Institution, whom Tolen had met prior to starting his leave. To her right sat CIA Analyst Tiffany Bar. She was as much an enigma to Tolen as any woman would ever be. Brilliant, witty, short, with her own unique style, she was in her fourth year with the agency, although she had yet to reach the age of 24. On Vakind's left was a man Tolen did not recognize. He had stubby black hair and looked to be in his early forties with classic European features. He wore a white shirt, dress slacks, and a sports jacket. Tolen noticed the slight swell of a pistol secured in a holster underneath his left arm. The man was obviously law enforcement.

Vakind silently motioned for Tolen to take a chair next to the unknown man. As he approached, the diminutive Tiffany Bar gave Tolen one of her trademark smiles as she brushed her long blonde bangs back over her ears. He returned a nod and then looked to the unknown man, extending his hand.

Vakind began the introduction, "Agent Tolen, this is Spanish Inspector Pascal Diaz with the Cuerpo Nacional de Policia, the National Police Corps of Spain. He reports directly to Spain's Ministry of the Interior."

Diaz took Tolen's proffered hand, gave it a curt shake, and wheeled back toward Vakind. The Spanish inspector's posture was rigid. Whatever business was to be discussed, Diaz was anxious to get under way and did not wish to waste time exchanging pleasantries.

"Tolen, I know your work as a liaison with the Smithsonian was to commence upon your return from leave, but a situation has arisen. As such, since you technically now report to this Institution, I've invited Sheila to sit in on this briefing so she'll be aware of your activities," Vakind paused, appraising those present in the room with a sweeping glance. "This discussion is to be kept in the strictest confidence."

Vakind turned to Tolen. The acting director's expression had been noncommittal up to this point, but now his face hardened. Tolen noticed a folder on the table before Vakind. "Have you ever heard of the Cámara Santa in Oviedo, Spain?"

Tolen's curiosity waxed as he quickly searched his memory, nodding. "It's a small building attached to the Cathedral of San Salvador, a Gothic church built in the Middle Ages. It houses numerous reliquary items of religious significance."

"Correct. Eleven days ago, on August 30th, someone broke

into the Cámara Santa. They breached the inner sanctum, picked the locked gate, and stole the Sudarium from inside a medieval reliquary chest, known as the Arca Santa."

"What's a Sudarium?" Bar asked with a perplexed look.

Tolen explained. "The Sudarium is a shroud. It's the cloth that was purportedly wrapped around the head of Jesus Christ immediately following the crucifixion while he was still on the cross."

"I thought it was called the Shroud of Turin?" Bar remarked, still confused.

"They're two different relics," Dr. Shaw added. "The lesser known Sudarium suffers from little-brother syndrome to the more famous Shroud of Turin, which was said to be wrapped around Christ's entire body after He was removed from the cross." She smiled patiently as she tented her fingers on the table and leaned in slightly. "Whereas the Turin cloth is large and finely made and has an imprint of a man, the Oviedo material is much smaller and rougher, and has no discernible image. Instead, there are blotches of what is thought to be human blood and lymph on the Sudarium."

"Not thought to be, *is*," Diaz cut in sternly. His English was crisp, with a moderate Spanish accent. "Analysis has confirmed it is human blood, type AB positive. The same type found on the Shroud of Turin. The Sudarium is also mentioned in the Bible. It is truly a magnificent object."

Tolen noticed that the CIA director averted his eyes away from Diaz as he continued. "During the theft, a security guard was killed. He was stabbed with a knife, then struck with a first-century Roman halberd—an axe blade topped with a spike mounted on a long shaft. The halberd had been on display in a diorama in one of the nearby cloisters." He exhaled with a remorseful expression as he pulled a photograph from the folder and held it up for the others to see. "The axe was buried in the man's chest with a single blow."

Tolen studied the image for a few seconds. He had seen the results of brutal deaths before, but never using a halberd. The gash to the man's chest was enormous and bloody. He noticed that Diaz glimpsed at the picture and quickly looked away.

Bar's expression belied her relative inexperience with gruesome

22

cases. At times like these, with her bobbed blonde hair and long bangs, she looked as young as she was. Sheila Shaw also blanched slightly and shifted in her seat. The 61-year-old director of the Smithsonian Institution—with her proper demeanor and sensible blouse, skirt, and shoes—had just passed beyond her comfort zone.

"There were no witnesses," Vakind said, returning the photograph to the folder and running a thumb over his firm chin. "Authorities did find a partial fingerprint at the scene, but it matched over 11,000 people in the Interpol database. Of that number, only four are currently in Spain. Two are dead, one is in prison, and one was at the other end of the country with a solid alibi. There are no other leads."

"Does the Cathedral have a security system? Cameras?" Tolen asked.

"Yes," Diaz responded, "a security system, but no video cameras. The Cámara Santa was broken into in 1977, and an alarm system was installed at that time. Unfortunately, it has not been upgraded since, and as you can imagine, has become antiquated. That is why a night guard is on site. The system was easily disarmed by the intruder or intruders before entering the Cathedral and Cámara Santa."

Vakind added, "Three days later, on September 2nd, an American archaeologist, Phillip Cherrigan, was found dead in his motel room in Palmar Sur, Costa Rica. He had been decapitated with what appeared to be a sword, although the murder weapon was not found." Vakind eyed the folder as if he were about to show them the image of the headless man, then must have decided against it.

The color had still not fully returned to Dr. Shaw's face as she spoke. "Are we to assume the two crimes—the murder and theft of the Sudarium in Spain and the murder in Costa Rica—are related?"

"They *are* related," Vakind replied.

Diaz chimed in. "In both cases, the manner of death mirrored the martyrdom of one of Jesus' Apostles." He paused, and Tolen sensed a pained hesitance. Diaz visibly swallowed and continued. "The security guard was killed with a halberd in the manner of the Apostle Matthew; your American archaeologist was beheaded with a sword like the Apostle James."

"*That's* your connection?" Bar blurted out incredulously.

Tolen gave her a furtive look. One thing he had stressed to her before was that when Director Vakind conducted a briefing, all bases had been covered beforehand. There was obviously something more to connect the two crimes. Bar shrank as she received Tolen's nonverbal message.

Vakind eyed Bar and continued with a modicum of sarcasm. "In fact, there *is* more, Analyst Bar. After the second murder, the Spanish press received a communiqué from a group that called themselves the 'True Sons of Light.' The group claimed responsibility for both murders and the theft of the Sudarium. The press had a field day with it, printing the letter in every major newspaper in the country. The 'True Sons of Light" claimed as their charter to..." he picked up a piece of paper from the folder and read from it, " '*Dispel the fraud upon humanity that Jesus ever existed as an historical figure.*' They vowed to continue to acquire these '*hoax*' relics mankind has collected, such as the Sudarium. Thus," his eyes turned back to the paper, " '*humanity will be rid of this deception.*' They also vowed to '*stop those who propagate the lie with false evidence,*' " he looked up, then back down at the paper, "threatening to do so by '*executing them in the same manner in which the Apostles were silenced.*' "

He looked up gravely at those assembled before continuing. "An added dilemma was that Spanish authorities had chosen to suppress the news of the initial theft and murder, hoping to solve the case quickly and return the Sudarium to the Cámara Santa before anyone knew it was missing. Only the police and the church canons knew the truth. As you heard Inspector Diaz say, the Sudarium is a treasured Spanish relic. News of its disappearance would be taken very hard by the Spanish people and Christians everywhere."

"Its significance to our country *cannot* be overstated," Diaz cut in; his eyes fiery and his words filled with resounding passion. He paused, glancing up toward the ceiling and then back to the people seated around the table. His next words softened in reverence. "It is a treasure that the people of Spain hold dear—an earthly connection to our Holy Savior, Jesus Christ."

"By the time the 'True Sons of Light' released the communiqué to the press, the United States was involved," Vakind continued. "We urged the Spanish government to rebuke the claim of the Sudarium's theft. Since the Sudarium is only removed and displayed to the public three times a year, we felt there was time to locate the culprits, whoever the 'True Sons of Light' are, and return the Sudarium before the next showing. The Spanish agreed, and have publicly denounced the claim in the communiqué, insisting that the Sudarium is safe in storage within the Cámara Santa." Vakind paused. "We've also warned several governments, including Italy, where the Shroud of Turin is maintained, that the CIA has received information about the possibility of thefts of artifacts related to Jesus Christ."

Diaz looked down. "The problem is the guard's…Javier's… death." When he looked back up, his eyes had turned glossy.

Tolen understood in an instant: Javier was someone close to Diaz. Bar and Dr. Shaw must have realized this as well. For a few seconds, the room remained quiet as they all waited for Diaz to continue.

"The guard who was murdered—he was my brother, Javier Diaz. Certain members of the Spanish press have learned Javier worked in security at the Cathedral of San Salvador and that he is no longer employed there. Despite the government's denial that a theft of the Sudarium ever occurred, some have become suspicious because of Javier's…um…disappearance. Some are even claiming he was involved, which they say explains why no one can find him now." The muscles in the Spaniard's neck went taut. His teeth clenched as his voice escalated, and he practically spat the next words. "Some say Javier is a member of this 'True Sons of Light.' So until the press knows the truth, my brother cannot receive a proper Christian burial in the family mausoleum!" Slamming a fist on the table, he closed his eyes and exhaled in an attempt to calm himself.

No one spoke.

Dr. Shaw looked to Director Vakind, finally breaking the silence. "No disrespect to Inspector Diaz or the Spanish government, but why did the U.S. become involved? Why did we advise them to deny the claim by the 'True Sons of Light' that the Sudarium had been stolen?'"

"Because," Tolen began, having read the hidden message in Vakind's words, "there is U.S. involvement in the crime."

"Correct," Vakind confirmed. "Another partial fingerprint found at the Costa Rica murder site had too few pattern points to make more than a generalized identification, but when Spanish authorities analyzed the hard copy of the communiqué, they were able to lift a single, clear print. It was unmistakable. The match also tied the partial prints from both crime scenes: the Cámara Santa in Oviedo, Spain and Palmar Sur in Costa Rica."

"*Sí*...yes," Diaz said with a thinly veiled smirk. "We know *exactly* who did it."

Vakind nodded reluctantly. He looked Tolen squarely in the eyes. "The man we're looking for is Boyd Ramsey."

A hush fell over the room. Bar's expression was nothing short of utter surprise. While Tolen remained stoic, he understood her astonishment.

Vakind turned, looking to Dr. Shaw as he explained for her benefit, "Boyd Ramsey was a CIA analyst. The man is in his sixties and retired last year. Last I heard, he was living in the Smoky Mountains just outside Gatlinburg, Tennessee, but no one in the States has seen him in months. We were able to track him to Spain earlier in the summer, but he disappeared there.

"Somehow, information has leaked in Spain about Ramsey and his CIA background. Rumors are now swirling that the 'True Sons of Light' is a cover group for a U.S.–backed plan to steal the Sudarium, and some are claiming the theft has already occurred. This information has recently flooded the Internet in Spain, spawning wild conspiracy theories. A groundswell of backlash is growing. If, by the next display date, the Sudarium is confirmed to be missing, it will fuel tremendous outrage toward the U.S. Several European radical religious sects have already promised severe retaliation against U.S. citizens at home and abroad. As you can see, the situation has escalated into an international issue which could turn extremely deadly."

"To complicate matters," Diaz interjected, "the Sudarium is to be displayed on September 14th for the start of the Feast of the

Cross. That is the day the canons of San Salvador are to remove the Sudarium and use it to bless thousands of people in an elaborate and hallowed ceremony. That gives us less than four days."

"I assume all efforts to find Ramsey thus far have been ineffective?" Tolen remarked.

"Ineffective? That's an understatement," chided Diaz with a harrumph.

"When we started, we had two weeks. The CIA committed a full complement of agents to the search for Ramsey, but we've reached a dead end, and time is running out," Vakind said.

"Apart from Boyd Ramsey, have we found out anything about this group, the 'True Sons of Light'?" Bar asked.

"Oddly, no; only that they may have derived their name from a Jewish sect which existed in Israel around the time of Christ called the 'Sons of Light.' " Vakind looked back to Tolen. "You've been called in because of your skills and your working relationship with Boyd Ramsey. Given that there are less than four days until the start of the Feast of the Cross, I'm dedicating Analyst Bar to be your eyes and ears here on the ground in DC. She will have access to every database and resource necessary to assist you. Also, the Spanish government has been gracious enough to loan us the services of Inspector Diaz. Tolen, I need you to team with Diaz and find Boyd and the Sudarium before this turns into a bloody international incident."

Diaz spoke slowly, looking in turn at everyone in the room. His anger from earlier had subsided, but his struggle to remain calm was apparent. "Your government has assured Spain the Sudarium will be returned in time. Upon your advice, we perpetuated the lie that it is safe, discrediting the communiqué received by the press. If the Sudarium is not returned, the U.S. will feel the wrath of terrorism from religious radicals, and the Spanish government will experience the outcry of its own people. I cannot emphasize how critical it is that the killers are brought to justice and the Sudarium returned before Friday morning at 9 a.m. when the Cathedral of San Salvador opens its doors to the thousands of worshippers who will be in attendance."

Diaz's words hung in the still room.

"What was archaeologist Phillip Cherrigan working on in Costa Rica when he was killed? Surely not searching for a relic tied to Jesus Christ in Central America?" Tolen asked.

Vakind responded. "Cherrigan was a biblical archaeologist, and he had teamed with a British archaeologist, Dr. Jade Mollur. They were doing some sort of work on the Dead Sea Scrolls, I believe. I don't have the details. At the time Cherrigan was killed, Mollur was in the United States. Subsequently, after attending Cherrigan's funeral in New Jersey several days ago, an attempt was made on Mollur's life when she was driven off the road. She only suffered minor abrasions."

"Do you think it's related?" Sheila Shaw asked. "I didn't realize vehicular homicide was an Apostle's death."

"At the CIA's request, and for her own protection, she's been detained by local police in Morristown, New Jersey. Tolen, you and Diaz are to pick her up, question her, and return with her to Costa Rica this evening to examine the crime scene. It's the best we have to go on right now. Oh, and one more thing to consider: as I mentioned, the 'True Sons of Light' may have gotten their name from the ancient Jewish sect 'Sons of Light.' The 'Sons of Light' are also known as the Essenes, a monastic community which included scribes—"

Tolen finished the thought, "—who lived on the shores of the Dead Sea. The Essenes are credited by most scholars as having written the Dead Sea Scrolls, and if Phillip Cherrigan and Jade Mollur were conducting research on those scrolls, Dr. Mollur is the obvious starting point."

CHAPTER 4

September 10. Monday – 4:01 p.m. Washington, DC

Samuel Tolen and Inspector Pascal Diaz rode in a chauffeur-driven car which Vakind had arranged to drive them to Ronald Reagan National Airport. They were booked on the next flight to Newark, New Jersey.

After the debriefing, Tolen had learned in a sidebar conversation with Vakind that former Director of Operations, Carlton Tannacay, had been relieved of duty. His insistence that the Spanish keep the theft of the Sudarium quiet, which implied CIA guilt, had proven to be career suicide.

Tolen also found out from Vakind that Diaz had requested to act alone in the U.S. but had been denied, so his pairing with Tolen was not to his liking. At the same time, Tolen found it odd that Vakind had consented at all to allow Diaz to participate in the investigation given his personal relationship to one of the victims. No doubt the CIA had been coerced by the Spanish government, or more likely succumbed to internal bureaucratic pressure, to include Diaz. Either way, it was Tolen's problem now, and it was not productive to dwell on decisions he could not influence. Tolen wanted to ensure Ramsey got a fair trial. He feared Diaz might be too trigger-happy given the opportunity for revenge. He would rein Diaz in if the need arose. It would not be the first time he had worked with a challenging partner.

Tolen considered Diaz's situation. He felt for the Spaniard, losing his brother so suddenly and tragically. Family members can never be replaced. Tolen knew this all too well. The scars of his own mother's sudden passing when he was young remained even to this day.

Riding in the car, there had been few words between Tolen and Diaz. Diaz was brooding, his discord visible in his perpetual scowl. Halfway to the airport, and shielded from the driver by a Plexiglas curtain, the inspector broke the silence. "So this Tiffany Bar is your resource? She seems young and inexperienced. I am not sure your government understands the magnitude of the situation. Frankly, Tiffany Bar sounds like the stage name of a stripper."

"Analyst Bar has done many things, but that's one job which doesn't appear on her resume," Tolen responded nonchalantly. He was not about to be played.

"So you have worked with her in the past? Before she graduated from grammar school?"

Tolen responded sedately. "To set your mind at ease, Inspector, Tiffany Bar graduated *summa cum laude* with a dual bachelor's and master's degree at 17. She earned a doctorate from Princeton in forensic research and analysis before her 20th birthday. She and I have worked together on several assignments in the past, and I assure you that whatever maturity she might lack is more than offset by her ability to research and analyze data."

"She looks like a lost child."

"Only two people have achieved perfect scores on the CIA Analyst entrance exam, a test where a 100% was once thought to be impossible to obtain. One is the man we're after, Boyd Ramsey, considered the premier CIA analyst. The other was Tiffany Bar."

Diaz looked unimpressed. "That's comforting. She has the same qualifications as the man heading a terrorist organization."

"We are fortunate to have her assistance in our endeavor."

Diaz's entire demeanor changed, and he looked incensed. "Endeavor? My brother was murdered by a ruthless killer: *your* Boyd Ramsey. The sacred cloth bearing Jesus' blood was stolen by atheist radicals. We are on a holy mission to return the Sudarium to its place among the people of Spain and bring the culprits to justice, and you refer to it as an *endeavor*?"

"I worked with Ramsey for ten years. As far as I'm concerned, his involvement is undetermined at this point."

"Undetermined? What is *undetermined* when Boyd Ramsey's fingerprints are found at both crime scenes and on the letter sent to the press?"

"I know the man personally. It's not in his character to murder."

"Señor, men are often persuaded to new vices when properly motivated. I believe you should stand back and look at the situation objectively. Though I may be driven by my brother's death to catch those responsible, I am still an inspector and will observe the facts rationally and impartially. It would serve you to do likewise."

Indeed, Diaz was right. Men could change. Tolen had seen it countless times in this profession. Yet he simply could not fathom what might cause Boyd Ramsey to affiliate himself with a radical, anti-Christian sect. The man had no qualms about other people's beliefs or religion.

"Now you want me to feel comforted that the American CIA is involved with finding one of their own?" Diaz mused. "Aren't you the ones who employed a man for a decade who was sending American secrets to one of your enemies?"

It was true. The CIA had been plagued in the last two decades with acts which had brought worldwide embarrassment. The agency's assistance in locating and confirming Osama bin Laden's hiding place at the compound in Pakistan had been one of the few feathers in their cap of late. Tolen considered raising this point, then opted to change the subject instead. If they were going to work together, he wanted to keep the lines of communication open. He chose a topic he knew Diaz would welcome. "Tell me more about the Sudarium and its history. I could stand a refresher from the perspective of someone at its source."

There was a sudden gleam in Diaz's eye. Then he set his face to a thoughtful yet almost beatic pose as he proudly recited the history of the Sudarium from memory. "Certainly, as I said in our meeting, the Sudarium is the holy cloth which was wrapped around the head of Jesus Christ just after the crucifixion while He was still on the cross. The Bible mentions it in John, Chapter 20, Verses 6 and 7:"

Then Simon Peter, who was behind him, arrived and went into the tomb. He saw the strips of linen lying there, as well as the burial cloth that had been around

*Jesus' head. The cloth was folded up by itself, separate
from the linen.*

"You can see where John pointed out specifically that there
were two cloths: the Sudarium and the larger linen that wrapped
the body, which some say is a reference to the Shroud of Turin.
Interestingly, unlike the Turin cloth, whose recorded history begins
in the Middle Ages, the Sudarium can be traced back to 614 AD
when Persia attacked Jerusalem. To avoid destruction by the
invading forces, it was first moved to Alexandria, then across
Africa. It eventually made its way to Spain by way of the masses
fleeing the Persians. It was carried in the Arca Santa. The chest
and relics within were given to Leandro, Bishop of Seville, and
then it was moved to Toledo until 718 before being sent further
north to escape destruction by the invading Muslims. For a time,
it was kept in a grotto ten kilometers from Oviedo. Alfonso II had
a chapel erected, the Cámara Santa, to house the Arca Santa. This
building was later incorporated into the Cathedral of San Salvador.

"In 1075, the Arca Santa was officially opened before King
Alfonso VI. A manifest was made of the relics contained within,
including the Sudarium. It has been kept in the Cámara Santa
in Oviedo ever since and, as you know, is only brought out and
displayed three times a year: Good Friday, the Feast of the Cross
on 14 September, and its octave on 21 September."

"In the briefing, you mentioned the blood type on the Sudarium
matches the Shroud of Turin: AB positive," Tolen said.

"Si, a rare type that only three percent of the world's population
has, but there are other similarities between the two cloths as well.
Three species of pollen specific to the region around Jerusalem
are on both the Sudarium and on the Shroud. Also, the Sudarium
contains traces of pollen from Israel, Africa, and Spain, confirming
its documented history of flight from invading armies that took it
from Jerusalem through Northern Africa and eventually to Oviedo.

"Tests have confirmed that the man whose face was covered
by the Sudarium had a beard, moustache, and long hair tied up at
the nape of the neck. These are the same findings as the Shroud,
although most people of Jewish descent at the time had those
features, so it is not an unusual finding. In addition, the stains on

the Sudarium show a series of wounds produced in life by some sharp objects, such as, say, from a crown of thorns. These, too, match the Shroud."

Tolen could not resist playing devil's advocate, but he did so delicately. "I understand Carbon-14 dating places the Sudarium's origination in the 7th century."

"True," Diaz said firmly, surveying Tolen. To Tolen, the Spaniard seemed to welcome the question, which could only mean he had a convincing rebuttal. "About thirty years ago, an Italian Professor, Pierluigi Baima Bollone, conducted the carbon dating, but even he was unable to vouch for the validity. He is quoted as saying, '*the result is not easy to interpret due to the well-known difficulties of dating textiles and to the conditions under which the sample was kept when it was taken in 1979 until it came to us in 1983.*' At a conference on the Sudarium in the 1990s, participants agreed, stating that '*textiles left alone in normal atmospheric conditions are prone to becoming highly contaminated.*'"

"Are *all* inspectors in Spain this well versed on religious relics?" Tolen asked.

"You can attribute some of my newfound knowledge of the Sudarium to my long flight to the U.S. I had plenty of time to read and needed to focus my mind somewhere other than Javier's death for awhile." Diaz paused and cocked his head sideways; his eyebrows pitched in concern. "Your use of the term 'religious relic' is quite troublesome. You say it as if you are referring to any class of artifact in history: a wheel from a 3rd–century Roman chariot, an amulet from an Egyptian tomb, a Chinese terracotta warrior statue." He leaned toward Tolen, speaking slowly. "The Sudarium is *the* cloth which touched Jesus' face when He died for our sins and commended His soul into the Lord's hands. It is not a mere artifact; it is our connection to the Savior of Mankind. To refer to it as anything less is blasphemy."

There was a momentary silence before Tolen responded. "Point taken."

It must not have been the response Diaz sought. He wheeled in his seat, obviously intent on pushing the conversation further. He raised a finger as if to make a resounding point. Just then, Tolen's cell phone beeped. He fished it from his inside coat pocket and answered, forcing Diaz to retract his hand from the air and turn back in his seat to sulk.

"Yes, Ms. Bar?" Tolen answered and listened intently.

"I see. Okay, nice work. Please let the director know, as we discussed."

He hung up and turned to Diaz.

"A lead?" Diaz asked.

The news was troubling. Tolen was reluctant to share the information with Diaz, but that would sour their already rocky new partnership. They had less than four days to find the Sudarium and return it to Oviedo, Spain. Any chance of being successful was going to take their mutual cooperation. Fracturing Diaz's trust was not an option.

"Boyd Ramsey had a short relationship with a woman in San Francisco eight years ago and fathered a child. The boy was unknown to the Agency. He confided in me and, to my knowledge, I was the only one who knew about his son, Nolan. I asked Analyst Bar to check on Nolan, hoping that maybe Boyd had made recent contact." Tolen exhaled. "The boy and his mother were killed a year and a half ago by a drunk driver in an automobile accident."

Diaz slowly nodded his head, a grim grin forming upon his face. "It seems we have a man who blames God for his son's death, and thus, we have a motive."

The problem is, Ramsey never had faith to begin with, Tolen thought.

CHAPTER 5

September 10. Monday – 7:38 p.m. Morristown, New Jersey

Upon landing at Newark International Airport, Tolen and Diaz took a taxi to Morristown. Traffic was steady, but they had missed rush hour and reached the outskirts of town a respectable forty minutes later. The driver turned off Interstate 287 onto South Street where low brownstone buildings and newer office complexes were sprinkled on either side of the road. It was a typical small New Jersey township consisting of mostly vacant buildings, a result of a decade's worth of economic downturn.

They passed a downtrodden grocery/liquor store, where several people were milling about outside, and turned into the parking lot of the Morristown police station. The light-faced, two-story contemporary structure seemed severely out of place among the nearby aged and weathered buildings. They exited the cab, and Tolen instructed the driver to wait for them.

Inside, the cool flow of air conditioning was a welcome relief to the late summer humidity. Tolen flashed his credentials to the desk sergeant, a middle-aged man with deep dimples in his cheeks and blond crewcut hair. They had obviously been expected, as the officer slid a clipboard with a prisoner release form before Tolen. "I've never been so happy to see a female detainee leave this station house. That one in there is a real piece of work. Don't get cut on her words," the sergeant warned sarcastically.

Diaz raised an eyebrow and gave Tolen a vexing stare. Tolen signed the paper, and the sergeant wordlessly waved Tolen and Diaz toward a secured door to the side. There was an electronic buzz, and the door clicked open.

Inside, they were met by a portly male officer who seemed uncertain if he should greet them with a smile or a solemn expression. It was a clear indication that the local authorities also knew Tolen was CIA. It was a reaction he had seen before.

"You're here for Dr. Jade Mollur?" the man asked, casting his eyes from Tolen to Diaz. He continued to vacillate between a grin and a frown unable to decide where to stop.

"I'm Samuel Tolen," Tolen said, extending his hand in an attempt to put the man at ease. "And this is Inspector Pascal Diaz from Spain."

The man shook their proffered hands. The officer finally landed on a grin. "Pleasure to make your acquaintance. I'm Tom Rennsol. We don't get many feds this way. You think someone's trying to kill this Dr. Mollur?"

"It's a distinct probability," Tolen responded. "Did Dr. Mollur arrive with any personal effects we need to collect?"

Rennsol nodded. "Yeah, a laptop, clothes, and some manila folders with papers in a PC case. They'll be waiting for you at Sarge's desk as you leave." Rennsol stood in place as if expecting to field another question.

Tolen was anxious to secure Dr. Mollur and be on their way. They had a long flight ahead of them to Costa Rica. "May we see the prisoner?" he prodded, his tone firm yet personable.

"Certainly, certainly," Rennsol said stirring. He turned and waved them through another secured door with a porthole window to a series of holding cells and then followed behind. Once inside the corridor, they heard a succession of faint clicks. An unexpected fragrance filled the air.

"This smells much better than our Spanish jails," Diaz said to Tolen.

"And most of ours," Tolen added.

The first cell on the left held a shoddily dressed man asleep on the low rack. The next cell was empty. They approached the third, and last, cell.

Tolen had conjured up an image of Dr. Jade Mollur as a frumpy, scholarly woman in her fifties. Instead, an attractive woman with short black hair stood behind the bars glaring at them with hazel eyes. Her left hand was cocked on her hip; her right hand turned sideways drumming her fingernails incessantly on one of the iron bars: the source of the clicks. She looked no more than thirty-five years old, medium height, with a smart figure, wearing black dress pants and a black, long–sleeved blouse. She had obviously not changed clothes since Dr. Phillip Cherrigan's funeral. The woman eyed Tolen and Diaz with an uncompromising glare. She spoke with an edge to her decidedly British accent. "Are you with the British consulate?" The finger drumming stopped as she waited on their response with steely eyes.

Rennsol had halted at the door, watching the interaction. Tolen ignored the question, instead speaking to Rennsol in an easy voice. "We have transportation waiting."

"Right, one second," Rennsol said, roused back to action. He momentarily fumbled with the keys, found the right one, sprung the lock and pulled the cell door open. Dr. Jade Mollur remained in the cell, eyeing the two men. She reiterated her question in a callous tone; each word enunciated slowly. "Are…you with…the British…consulate?"

Diaz stepped forward, extending his hand. "Madam, would you please come with us? We're in a rush," he said curtly.

She arched her eyebrows and looked at him incredulously. "You're in a rush? You're in a rush?!" she fumed. "I've been in this cell for two days, detained without cause, after someone ran *me* off the road! For TWO DAYS! And now *you're* in a rush! Excuse the bloody hell out of me if I don't take your hand and dance away with you!"

Diaz dropped his hand with a disgruntled exhale and turned away. "English women," he jeered under his breath.

Dr. Mollur looked to Tolen. She stepped out of the cell to within inches from his face. Tolen did not budge.

"Who are you?" she asked.

Tolen spoke casually as he looked her straight in the eyes, unblinking. "I'm Agent Samuel Tolen with the CIA. The man you just annoyed is Spanish Inspector Pascal Diaz," he said, pointing to Diaz. Diaz acknowledged her with a dismissive wave and turned away.

Tolen had expected her frustration. She had, in fact, been detained at the jail without so much as an explanation after the attempt on her life. It would not be easy dealing with her, since they were under strict orders not to divulge the murder of Pascal's brother, Javier, or the theft of the Sudarium. At best, they would share partial truths, focusing on the threat to her life.

"The sodding CIA and a brash Spanish inspector. Isn't this my lucky day?" she said. "Will you please explain what is going on?" She remained within inches of Tolen's face.

"I'll be happy to," he said, holding his ground and speaking in a low voice, "but for your own protection, we must be going. Time is of the essence."

"I'm not taking one step forward until you answer my questions," she snarled. She lowered her voice, causing her words to seem even more venomous. "Why in the Queen's name does the American government send one of their secret agents for me? Why was I held against my will? *I* was the bloody victim here. Do you know what happened to me?"

"Yes, we do," Tolen said in an even tone.

"Then why was I held prisoner? And why are you and this…," she pointed to Diaz with a disgusted smirk, "man…here to get me out? Where are you taking me?"

Tolen answered, "Your questions, while valid, are not pertinent at this time."

Dr. Jade Mollur's face turned a unique shade of red. She huffed, took several steps backward into the jail cell, and pulled the door closed. It locked with a *clink*. "Until you answer my questions, I'm not going anywhere," she said with a sarcastic smile.

Officer Rennsol had been standing to the side quietly watching the show. Tolen motioned for him to unlock the cell door again. Mollur tightened her hands into angry fists at her side and then retreated to the lower bunk bed and sat down, continuing to face the cell door.

"Diaz," Tolen said, motioning the man over. He leaned in and whispered as the inspector neared. "Please gather Dr. Mollur's things and wait for me in the cab. Tell the driver I'll be right out."

"Gladly," Diaz said, giving the woman one more scathing look. Rennsol accompanied Diaz back through the secured door.

"This is regretful, Dr. Mollur," Tolen said, entering the jail cell. He approached the bunk bed quickly, grabbed one of her wrists, and lifted her to a standing position before she could object. Her eyes grew wide in disbelief at what the man was doing.

"I am not going with—!" she shouted, before Tolen cut her words off with his next move.

Tolen withdrew his Springfield .45. He turned it around and handed the butt end to her. She took it even as bewilderment spread over her face. "What....what are you doing?"

He spoke quickly. "You're going to need this. It holds seven rounds and one in the chamber. I anticipate the first attack will come shortly after you leave the station. They're inflicting painful deaths in the same manner as Christ's Apostles were martyred. Your partner Cherrigan was beheaded with a sword like James. We're aware of another man who was killed with a halberd, similar to Matthew. Of course that still leaves crucifixion with head down, scourging on an X–shaped cross, beating, flaying, lancing, burning, and stoning. I wish you the best," Tolen said sincerely. He turned and departed, leaving the cell door open. He strolled back up the austere corridor toward the secure door.

"Wait!" he heard her voice call from behind him. Mollur had already caught up to him. She was holding the gun butt between two fingers, allowing it to dangle. "I don't want this. I don't like guns." Her tone was reserved. He took the pistol and deposited it inside his coat. She looked at him for a long moment then sighed. "Oh, bloody hell! Okay, let's go, but can you at least tell me where you are taking me?"

"Back to Palmar Sur, Costa Rica," he said. Tolen turned and waved at Rennsol through a porthole window, and the door buzzed open.

"Do I at least get to know why someone killed Phillip, and why they're trying to kill me?"

"That's what we're here to find out." Tolen stepped aside, allowing Dr. Mollur to pass first. She stared hard at him, and then proceeded through the open security door.

Tolen followed behind her, passing through a pleasant trail of the woman's alluring scent.

CHAPTER 6

September 10. Monday – 9:02 p.m. Newark International Airport, New Jersey

They had flown into Newark International Airport on a commercial flight, but the remainder of their journey would be in more comfortable and private accommodations. Vakind arranged for a CIA-owned jet to take Tolen, Diaz, and Mollur to Costa Rica and any points beyond. The pilot was the unflappable Reba Zee, whom Tolen knew very well from numerous past assignments.

On the drive to the airport, Tolen convinced Jade—she had asked to be called by her first name—that the taxi was not the place to address her questions. She remained quiet the rest of the ride, staring out the window.

They arrived at the Terminal C unloading zone on the upper deck. The area was brilliantly lit, still bustling with activity despite the late hour. The taxi driver successfully wove through a throng of double-parked cars, vans, buses, and pedestrians and came to a halt. As the threesome stepped onto the sidewalk amid a sea of travelers, skycaps, and stacked luggage, Tolen's cell phone rang. He threaded his way to a sidewall for privacy.

"Tolen," he answered.

"Vakind asked me to call you." Bar continued on rapidly without waiting for a reply. "On August 24th, a medical laboratory technician in Roanoke, Aaron Conin, was found murdered on the street in Vinton, Virginia, where he lived. Several weeks prior to his death, he'd received a call from Boyd Ramsey. We're unsure what link the two might have had, as there's no indication they

41

had ever met or talked before. Since the crime was deemed a random mugging on the street, his apartment was never processed by a forensic team. Vakind has asked local police to go over the apartment with a fine-toothed comb. He thought you might want to take a detour there before heading to Costa Rica. I'll send the address to your phone. Oh, and tell Reba Zee I said hey!"

"Got it. Thank you."

He returned to the others, who were waiting silently to the side of the pneumatic entry doors leading to the concourse. Tolen looked to Diaz. "We have to make a stop before continuing on to Costa Rica. There's a new development. I'll explain when we're on the plane."

Diaz gave Tolen a quizzical look but nodded his understanding.

Jade stared annoyingly at the two men with her arms folded. She had her PC bag slung over one shoulder. It looked heavy. "You owe me answers, Mr. Tolen."

"As soon as we're on board. You have my word. Can I carry your bag for you?"

She rolled her eyes, and exhaled in frustration. "No, but there is one thing you can do for me. I was told by the local Costa Rican authorities that all of Phillip's belongings were temporarily confiscated as part of the crime scene. Is there any way you can find out if his PC and his notes were found in his hotel room?"

Tolen did not hesitate to pull out his cell phone. He spoke to Bar, and she agreed to have an answer within several hours.

Fifteen minutes later, they were at the south tarmac strolling through the dark where several private jets were parked. It was a muggy evening, but a slight wind at their back cooled them as they walked. Ahead, a Learjet 85 was stationary on the taxiway, its running lights glowing. A burly woman with a shock of gray hair wearing a bombardier flight jacket was standing beside the stairwell leading to the jet's cabin. She wore a whimsical smile that broadened as they approached.

"Tolen, good to see ya," the woman said in a thick southern drawl.

"Reba Zee," Tolen acknowledged, shaking her hand. "Reba, I'd like for you to meet Spanish police inspector Pascal Diaz and archaeologist Dr. Jade Mollur."

"Pleasure to meetcha," she said, nodding her head cordially in turn as she pumped each hand. "So I understand we're headin' south…and I mean the *deep* south."

"Yes, but there's a small change in plans. We have to make a detour first, to Roanoke."

"Well, that'll be a much shorter haul. We should get there round about an hour or so. Climb aboard and get comfy while I reset the flight plan. We'll be streakin' in no time."

"How's Frank doing?" Tolen asked with a smile.

Reba Zee laughed. "As talkative as ever."

The three passengers boarded the plane and moved to the front quadrant of seats. The well-lit cabin was spacious and luxurious and smelled of fine leather. It had four seats at the front: two sets of two, facing each other, and four more in the same arrangement aft. Avionics was just beyond a closed and secured door. To the left of the cockpit door was a lavatory. A fully stocked galley took up the rear of the cabin. Reba disappeared inside the cockpit, closing the door behind her.

Diaz turned to Tolen. "What country is your pilot from? I don't quite understand the dialect."

"Texas," Tolen responded with an almost-perceptible grin.

Jade went to the lavatory carrying her bag. When she returned several minutes later, she was clad in a white tank top with light brown hiking shorts and tennis shoes.

Diaz looked at her appraisingly. Even Tolen had to admit she had a striking figure, with her long, toned legs, firm torso, and shapely shoulders. Her short, dark hair accentuated her high cheek bones and hazel eyes.

Jade stared at Tolen as she took her seat. "I'd appreciate some answers now." Her tone had softened, but there was no less determination in her words.

Tolen and Diaz had agreed on the context of information they would share with Dr. Mollur long before arriving at the Morristown jail. They would offer facts she could confirm, yet stop short of acknowledging the Sudarium's disappearance. The communiqué from the "True Sons of Light" had hit the Internet and been widely read. It was possible Jade had already heard the claim, along with the Spanish government's denial of the theft. If pressed, they would throw in a benign fact to give the illusion that she was being brought into their confidence. The deceit was not favored by Tolen, but in this case, it was necessary.

"Not long ago, a fanatical group calling themselves the 'True Sons of Light' sent a letter to the Spanish press denouncing the historical existence of Jesus of Nazareth. Their charter was twofold: stop anyone from searching for physical evidence that might substantiate the claim of His existence, and steal any historical relics that claimed direct association with Him. Their threat mentioned that they had already killed two archaeologists in the same manner as Apostles."

"That's what you meant back at the prison," she said, her eyes locked on him.

To her side, Diaz added, "The first man murdered was an archaeologist in Israel." It was a lie. "He was killed with a halberd."

Jade's voice turned sullen as she continued his thought. "And the second was Phillip: beheaded with a sword," her words trailed off with a shiver as she looked down. It was the first sign of pain she had shown. She lifted her eyes after a long moment. "What about the Sudarium?"

"I see you've heard the news," Tolen acknowledged. "That part of the letter was false. It's still unclear why the group made the claim that it had been stolen. My guess is they were trying to create an upheaval with the Spanish citizens. As radical groups are prone to do, they attempted to create turmoil with blatant lies."

Jade pointed to Diaz but kept her eyes directed to Tolen. "Then why is a Spanish Inspector here if the Sudarium of Oviedo is safe and sound?" The distrust in her voice was thick.

Diaz responded, "I'm part of an international task force working with the CIA, Italian AISI, and French DGSE, among other international agencies."

"He's in the States assisting in the search for an American who we believe is leading the 'True Sons of Light,'" Tolen added.

"And you think this man killed Phillip Cherrigan and then tried to kill me?"

"The attempt on your life is curious in that it doesn't match with the Apostle-style executions. Then again, they may have been trying to disable your vehicle and take you somewhere where they could finish the job in another manner fitting their self-prescribed forms of murder."

Tolen turned to address Diaz. "We're stopping in Virginia because Boyd Ramsey had contacted a medical lab technician in Vinton, Virginia, who was subsequently found dead on the street several weeks ago. We need to know if there's a connection between this death and the others and also see if there are any clues which could help us find Ramsey."

"Seems like a thin lead," Diaz remarked.

"Given the lack of information we have to go on, we must follow every possibility," Tolen countered.

"Are you aware of the origin of this fanatical group's name?" Jade chimed in.

"Yes," Tolen began, " 'True Sons of Light' appears to be a derivative of the 'Sons of Light,' one of the names given to the people who penned the Dead Sea Scrolls."

"Did you know that Phillip and I were working on a find related to the Dead Sea Scrolls; specifically the Copper Scroll?"

"Yes, but not the details."

Jade sharpened her eyes in thought, "Odd coincidence."

"I agree," Diaz said.

Tolen folded his hands in his lap. "Tell me about your relationship with Dr. Phillip Cherrigan."

Jade leaned back, stiffened slightly in her seat, then relaxed her shoulders. "Purely professional. He was a biblical archaeologist who contacted me last year. I'd had some experience with cryptic ciphers, and he was on the verge of cracking a code embedded within the Copper Scroll text." Her speech faltered as her eyes rimmed with tears. "I...I still can't believe he's gone."

Tolen read her body language: her pronounced reaction the moment he mentioned Dr. Cherrigan, her defensive posture, and now her withered features.

"Why were you two working in Costa Rica? It's halfway around the world from the Holy Lands."

She seemed hesitant to talk. She bit her bottom lip, and looked from Tolen to Diaz and back again to Tolen. She inhaled deeply then spoke in a reserved voice, "We found a coded message within the Copper Scroll which led us there."

"Led you to Central America?" Diaz snorted and waved a hand, rejecting such a ludicrous notion.

Jade ignored Diaz and continued. "Have you ever heard of the Stone Spheres of Costa Rica?"

"Yes," Tolen nodded. He suddenly understood. "That's why you and Cherrigan were at Palmar Sur?"

Jade nodded.

"What are these spheres?" Diaz asked, looking down at a magazine he had just picked up from a side slot. He was trying to appear disinterested, but his voice betrayed his renewed curiosity.

Jade responded, "In the Diquis Delta region of Southern Costa Rica, there are more than 300 carved spherical stones ranging in size from a softball to several meters in diameter. Their origin and purpose are an enigma; lost in history."

"And what could these stones possibly have to do with the Copper Scroll?" Diaz asked, looking up.

"The text we deciphered in the Copper Scroll helped solve the age-old mystery of the origin of the Costa Rican spheres: they were replicas of the stone that sealed Jesus' tomb and which, according to the Bible, was later found pushed aside on the third day after His crucifixion. The creation of countless numbers of these spheres was a way to pay homage to the resurrection. Equally astonishing, the text also mentions one of the stones as a starting point."

"A starting point for what?" Tolen asked, fixing her with his azure eyes. His interest was also firmly aroused now.

"From the cipher, we discovered that Joseph of Arimathea authored the Copper Scroll. Yet more remarkable is that we found a cryptic clue to Joseph of Arimathea's final resting-place." Jade recited from memory:

> *I will be entombed far across the waters where I have helped to instill Christianity. Once I told the native people of Christ, they took it upon themselves to create countless numbers of perfectly round*

46

stones, as a sign of reverence to the one stone that
covered Jesus' tomb after the crucifixion. These
hewn stones are spread in and around their village.
The stone sphere with the creature of anonymity will
lead to my tomb.

Tolen remained silent as he digested this information. Costa Rica? Even he had his doubts.

"You think *the* Joseph of Arimathea's body is in Central America?" Diaz scoffed. "The very man who went to Pontius Pilate and asked for permission to take Jesus' body after the crucifixion to prepare it, then placed the body in his own family tomb?"

"Let me be clear," Jade responded. "I'm aware that the original family tomb where Jesus was placed was in Israel. After He was said to have been resurrected, Joseph of Arimathea's family never used that tomb. What we found indicates he built a second tomb for himself in or near Costa Rica."

"That's ridiculous," Diaz muttered.

Jade ignored him and went on. "We were in the process of looking for the stone sphere which would direct us to the tomb's location when Phillip was murdered."

The cockpit door opened, and Reba Zee sprang forth. "Let's saddle up. We're going top side. Time to ride the wind," she said with a gregarious smile. Reba Zee was a top-flight pilot who loved to display her exuberance. Tolen had learned long ago to appreciate the woman's talent, even if she sometimes required a translator to be understood.

Diaz and Jade stared at the woman dumbfounded.

Reba Zee returned to the cockpit and closed the door. Moments later, the jet engines revved, and the plane nudged forward before breaking into a steady taxi. Once they were airborne, the lights from New York City sparkled in the distance, illuminating the horizon to the east as the cabin lights were doused and the interior fell into murky darkness.

"Texas *is* in the United States, correct?" Diaz asked.

Tolen nodded.

CHAPTER 7

September 10. Monday – 11:58 p.m. Vinton, Virginia

It was a cloudless night and a pale moon hovered on the horizon against the backdrop of a star-filled sky. The streets were quiet.

Police transportation had been arranged from the Roanoke Airport to the crime scene. A uniformed officer had been waiting for them when the jet landed.

The squad car pulled to a stop at Maple and Union Street, and Tolen, Diaz, and Jade exited the vehicle. The streetlight cast a limpid glow over a bald man with a crinkled face and fair skin who approached them. He was dressed in slacks, a white dress shirt, and a sports coat. He wore what looked like a permanent scowl, and Tolen figured he must be a plain-clothes detective who was not enamored with pulling a long, late shift.

"Agent Tolen, Inspector Diaz, I'm Detective Maurice Shuski of the Roanoke PD," he did not bother to offer a handshake. His voice was gritty. He glanced warily at Jade.

Tolen read his thoughts. "This is Dr. Jade Mollur. She's assisting us."

Shuski regarded her for a moment before continuing. "My captain told me to give you the red carpet treatment. Come on, and I'll show you the crime scene. It's two-and-a-half weeks old, but I thought you might want to see where the man's body was found." He paused, staring at Tolen. "I thought the CIA had no domestic police authority?"

"Our investigation has international ramifications," Tolen responded as they began walking down the alley. Diaz and Jade

48

trailed closely behind them. "Had Aaron Conin lived in Vinton for long?"

"A couple years. He worked in Roanoke at a medical laboratory and lived there until two years ago when he moved to the outskirts here. Vinton is practically a suburb of Roanoke."

"How was he killed?" Diaz asked.

"Strangled, no prints."

"The crime has been deemed a random mugging?" Tolen asked, as they reached a dumpster at the far end of the dark alley. A foul smell rose up to greet them. Jade covered her nose and gagged.

"It's impossible to say if it was random, but his watch and wallet were taken," Shuski pointed at the dumpster. "His body was found in there with the trash. He'd been dead at least 24 hours before the trash collectors found him."

"So death occurred here in the alley?" Tolen asked.

"There's nothing to make us think otherwise," Shuski responded defensively, wiping the skin atop his head. He cocked his head hard at Tolen. His tone hardened. "What exactly are you looking for? You think this was a premeditated killing? The forensics guys covered this alley like a blanket. Are you suggesting we missed something?"

"Not at all. I believe you and your team have handled this crime scene very well."

"Then why did your director call my captain to get me out of bed to process the victim's apartment sixteen days after we found the body?"

"Aaron Conin had been in contact with a man who is wanted for questioning in a case involving several overseas murders."

"I see," Shuski said, wiping a bead of sweat from his cheek. "So you think this wasn't just a mugging?"

Tolen did not respond. He peered back down the alley where they had just been. It struck him as odd that anyone would come down this dead-end alley, unless of course they were throwing away or picking up trash. "Was anything unusual found with the body?"

"His keys to his apartment, car, office, oh, and Conin's cat skulking around the outside of the dumpster. One of the officers felt bad for the animal and adopted it. As I said, there was nothing to suggest this was anything more than a brutal mugging."

"Do muggers in Virginia often strangle people?" Diaz asked. His tone was flavored with cynicism.

Shuski took exception, turning to Diaz. His response was terse. "I'm running this investigation." He glared back at Tolen. "You want to tell me what's going on?"

Tolen could have easily pushed his authority, but decided instead to play on the detective's moral compass. "The man we're looking for is a former government operative." It was a half lie: Ramsey was CIA but never an operative. "It's imperative we discover his whereabouts as soon as possible. Lives are in imminent danger." That part was the truth, for all they knew.

Shuski looked suspiciously from Tolen to Diaz and even to Jade, who seemed distracted, shuffling in place.

"Lives, huh?" Shuski finally said with an audible exhale. "What do you need from me?" he said resignedly.

"I understand the forensic team is processing Aaron Conin's fourth-floor apartment as we speak. May we see it?"

"C'mon," Shuski said, motioning with his hand. "It's a couple blocks over."

Shuski led the way. Tolen fell slightly behind.

Jade and Diaz pulled beside Tolen. Jade spoke in a low voice, "Seems like a mugging to me," she hesitated, "but you're not convinced, are you?"

Tolen spoke so Shuski would not hear, "Have you ever heard of someone living on the fourth floor of a building who allowed their cat outside?"

"You think he was killed at his apartment and moved here," Diaz interjected softly, "and that's how the cat got out?"

"Or someone broke into his apartment after killing him, but that doesn't seem likely since his keys weren't taken. Either way, the perpetrator didn't want investigators led back to it."

They continued down the still street where only an occasional passing car disrupted the silence. The air was warm, but there was a gentle breeze pushing against them as they left the narrow alley.

Tolen's cell phone chirped, and he recognized the number. He slowed, motioning the others to go ahead so he could talk in private.

"Tolen," he answered.

It was Morris Vakind. "Are you on site at Aaron Conin's murder scene?"

"Yes, we arrived a few minutes ago. I believe this was more than a simple mugging," he paused, speaking softer, "Morris, you don't think Boyd Ramsey did this, do you? We both knew the man. He was not a fanatic. Even with his son's death, I don't believe it would have made him into a killer."

"The evidence is stacked against him, although it does appear a little too convenient. By the way, how did you know about his son? Even the agency didn't have that information."

"He had confided in me," Tolen paused again, then changed the subject. "Morris, Ramsey is an agnostic, but he has nothing against other people's religious beliefs."

"Nevertheless, continue to target Ramsey as the primary suspect. I have a call with Spanish authorities at 1:45 a.m. Give me an update before 1:00." The phone went silent with a click.

Tolen hung up. He caught up with the rest of the group, and they entered the apartment building. Shuski advised them that the elevator had been inoperable for some time, and they would be forced to climb the rickety stairs. The air was heavy with the smell of lacquer as they made their way up. They reached the apartment at the far end of the fourth floor minutes later. It was cordoned off low across the open doorway with the signature yellow crime-scene tape. Shuski stepped over it followed by the other three. They stopped inside where the entry hallway opened to the living room.

There were four forensic technicians decked in white coats and plastic gloves ambling about. One of the technicians turned to Shuski upon seeing the intruders. He appeared to be in charge.

"Shuski, we're working here," he said in an annoyed tone. His nametag read 'Fulton McCray.' It seemed Mr. McCray had also been awakened this evening for extra duty and was also in a sour mood.

"McCray, this is Samuel Tolen with the CIA. This investigation may fall under their jurisdiction," Shuski said.

"May?" McCray responded.

Tolen stepped forward. "Mr. McCray, we need to determine if

Aaron Conin's death is linked to a man we're after."

"Well, I can tell you we've been here for over an hour now and, so far, have found nothing out of the ordinary."

"Do you mind if we look around?"

"Knock yourself out. You know the protocol," McCray said, handing them three sets of gloves. Tolen took two, returned one set to McCray and pulled two gloves from his inner coat pocket. He handed the other two sets to Diaz and Jade, respectively. Jade looked at him in confusion. She leaned in and whispered, "I know nothing about forensic work....and I really have to use the bathroom."

Tolen turned to Shuski. "Bathroom?"

"In there." Shuski pointed.

Tolen asked again, "For personal use?"

"First floor, near the broken elevators."

Jade did not wait. She scurried out of the apartment and vanished down the hallway.

Tolen and Diaz donned their plastic gloves. Tolen looked over to where two technicians were dusting the long coffee table for fingerprints. He moved before an open doorway. "I'll check this bedroom," he said to Diaz. "It looks like Conin's. You check the guest room." Tolen pointed to a door down a brief hallway off the other side of the living room. Diaz nodded, and moved in that direction.

Tolen entered the bedroom and was met with the subtle aroma of lilac. The bed was unmade. The nightstand and dresser held small lamps, some decorative pieces of art and a few scattered Post-it Notes. He read each one. Reminders of to-do items: pick up dry cleaning, change oil in car, pay bills; nothing out of the ordinary. He opened the closet door. Clothes were hung up, shoes on the floor, sweaters folded on a top shelf; again, nothing unusual.

Tolen retreated from the closet to the living room. McCray was busying himself dusting for fingerprints at the kitchen counter. Detective Shuski was nowhere to be seen. Tolen had smelled cigarette smoke on the man's coat. He was probably outside satisfying his addiction.

Tolen heard a subtle mechanical whirl and spotted the source:

a contraption in the corner of the living room. It was low and square, and his curiosity drew him to it. Only after he came closer did he realize it was a high-tech litter pan with a plastic doorway and a connecting receptacle to sift through the litter and filter out the excrement periodically; more proof the cat was an indoor pet.

Tolen turned toward McCray. "Mr. McCray, have you found any prints besides Conin's?"

"Not unless you count the cat. There are feline pawprints everywhere; more than Conin's fingerprints."

Tolen returned to the master bedroom. He moved to the adjoining bathroom. The doorknob caught his eye, and he bent down to examine it.

"Find anything interesting?" Jade called as she walked up from behind.

"Maybe," Tolen said. He had not heard her enter the room. "The keyhole has what appears to be scrape marks, as if someone was trying to unlock it forcefully."

"If Conin's the only one who lived here, why would he lock the bathroom door?"

Tolen gave her a knowing look with one eyebrow raised as if to say, "Exactly."

She answered her own question, suddenly recognizing Tolen's reasoning, "Be...cause...he was on the inside and someone was trying to get at him?"

Tolen stepped into the small bathroom. Jade stood in the doorway observing him.

Everything was in perfect order: the toothbrush was secure within a plastic travel case, a folded washcloth on the edge of the sink, a stick of deodorant, dental floss, Vaseline, and an electric shaver spaced apart with precision. This was a problem, Tolen realized. The arrangement of everything was too precise.

"What is it? What do you see?" Jade asked.

"Let's get Diaz and be on our way. It's a long flight to Costa Rica."

CHAPTER 8

September 11. Tuesday – 1:24 a.m. Roanoke, Virginia

At the Roanoke Regional Airport, the tarmac was dark. The outside air had cooled considerably. Commercial airline traffic had ceased hours ago. There were no other private jets in sight, leaving the Learjet 85 as the lone aircraft on the taxiway. Jade, Tolen, and Diaz sat comfortably aboard the private jet waiting for departure. Jade looked out the window. A light rain had begun falling several minutes before, misting the glass and blurring the outside world. An ethereal glow of lights escaped from the terminal windows in the distance.

Over an intercom, Reba Zee advised them they would take off within minutes.

"You think Conin's murder was premeditated?" Jade asked Tolen.

"Yes, I believe the killer trapped him in the bathroom and then killed him. The toiletry items were probably in disarray after the struggle, but the murderer arranged them back in place too precisely. Conin's body was then moved to the alley to stage a mugging."

Diaz looked confused. "This doesn't appear to have anything to do with our... mission. Boyd Ramsey made one call to this lab technician. For all we know, he might have misdialed the number. There is no other evidence linking him to Boyd Ramsey."

Tolen's cell phone rang, and he answered. "Yes, Ms. Bar? I see," he said after a moment of silence. "Thank you." Tolen hung up.

Tolen looked to Jade. "Dr. Cherrigan's PC and other personal files were missing from the crime scene. Are you sure they were in his motel room?"

She felt her spirits sink. "Absolutely." Then a terrible thought struck her. "We can't go to Costa Rica!" she blurted out.

"Why not?" Diaz asked.

"Because whoever killed Dr. Cherrigan and stole his notes now knows where to look for the clue which will lead to Joseph of Arimathea's tomb…and that clue is here, in the United States."

"I thought you said these, these…" Diaz made a circle in the air, swirling his finger theatrically, "…Costa Rican stone spheres hold the clue?"

"They do. Or should I say, one does," Jade said, reaching to the side and sliding a laptop PC from her bag. She propped it in her lap and booted it up. "Remember what I said about the deciphered text: *The stone sphere with the creature of anonymity will lead to my tomb?* Phillip…I mean…Dr. Cherrigan and I didn't know what 'creature of anonymity' meant—I still don't—but we searched every stone we knew to exist in Costa Rica for an image or etching of a creature on it. It was a daunting task, given the 300 or so spheres in and around Palmar Sur and the numerous ones dispersed throughout the country."

The engines roared to life, and the plane taxied slowly toward the runway. Jade felt pressure to make her case, so she pushed on. She spun the PC toward them so that they could see the screen. It was a map of Costa Rica with plotted red points, primarily grouped at Palmar Sur, although some were quite a distance away. "Ultimately, we were disappointed. None of the stones contained a picture of a creature."

"What were you expecting to learn from this stone if you had found it?" Tolen asked.

"That's just it. I won't know until I find it. I assume it will be directions, or possibly a map, to Joseph of Arimathea's tomb," she said, turning the screen back toward her.

"In Costa Rica?" Diaz asked.

Jade nodded.

The plane turned and came to a halt. A quick glance out the

window confirmed they were in position on the runway for takeoff. It would only be a minute or so before Reba Zee gunned the engine and they went airborne southward toward Costa Rica. She needed to convince them quickly.

"Look," Jade began, "Joseph of Arimathea was a very wealthy man; possibly one of the richest men of his time. He made his fortune as a metals dealer. Many scholars have theorized he traveled to South and Central America as part of his trade business."

"You're talking about sailing across the ocean 1,400 years before the first Europeans discovered the New World," Diaz exclaimed in amazement.

The engines revved up again, and there was a jerk as the brakes released. The plane began rolling down the runway, tires bounding over the rough surface as it picked up speed. Out of sight in the cockpit, Reba Zee flipped a switch that doused the cabin lighting, and the three passengers were mired in darkness, save for the weak light coming in through the windows and the glow of Jade's computer screen.

"An early cross-oceanic expedition is not inconceivable," Tolen cut in.

Even as the plane rumbled ahead, Jade felt welcome relief that Tolen was siding with her. She offered him a half smile before she realized she had done so.

Tolen continued. "There is evidence to point toward ancient cross-oceanic travels. In Munich, in 1992, researchers began a project to investigate seven 3,000-year-old Egyptian mummies. A toxicologist discovered the presence of nicotine and cocaine in all seven mummies. Before Columbus, these plants had not been found anywhere in the world outside of the Americas, suggesting there had been trade trips as early as 1500 BCE."

Jade was surprised that Tolen was familiar with these findings.

The cabin tilted, and Jade felt her stomach lurch as the plane left the ground soaring upward. The craft continued to climb sharply. The rumble of the engines threatened to drown out their conversation.

Tolen seemed unfazed by the gut-knotting takeoff.

Diaz chose not to challenge Tolen's facts. "You still haven't answered the question as to why you want us to stay in the U.S. You've already said the stone spheres and the tomb are in Central America."

"There are only two Costa Rican spheres we haven't examined, and they're both in the United States on display as ornamental pieces. One is in the museum of the National Geographic Society in Washington, DC. The other is in a courtyard near the Peabody Museum of Archaeology and Ethnography at Harvard University in Cambridge, Massachusetts. I had just flown to the U.S. to check these two stones when Dr. Cherrigan was murdered in Costa Rica. Then I was on my way to the airport after his funeral to go examine the stone in Washington when I was driven off the road and nearly killed.

"Now that the killers, these 'True Sons of Light,' have Dr. Cherrigan's notes, they'll surely go after the stone. Once they discover that the last two spheres are in the United States and get to the correct one, Joseph of Arimathea's tomb, an archaeological treasure, may be lost to these renegades," Jade pleaded. She unexpectedly felt a surge of emotions which threatened to bring tears. She valiantly fought them off.

Tolen spoke in his normal nonplussed cadence. "I don't see the relevance. Proof of Joseph of Arimathea's existence does not prove the physical existence of Jesus Christ. It's not a threat to the 'True Sons of Light.' There is no reason to think they will abandon their mantra to take time for an archaeological quest which does not satisfy their directive. While I appreciate the magnitude of the discovery, first and foremost, we need to find Boyd Ramsey. We will proceed to Costa Rica as planned."

Diaz nodded in agreement, obviously content with Tolen's declaration.

It was not what Jade wanted to hear.

The plane leveled off and reduced airspeed. The noise in the cabin likewise diminished. With each passing minute, they were moving further and further away from where she desperately needed to go.

Jade looked at the bright PC screen still displaying the plotted points in Costa Rica. She had withheld the full message from the

Copper Scroll, wary of sharing the information with them. With the theft of Phillip's notes, she was now forced into a position she had hoped to avoid.

Jade turned to Tolen. The agent was staring out the side window. Diaz had propped his head on the seat rest and closed his eyes.

"Okay, there's more," Jade said in resignation, breaking the silence. She dragged the back of her hand over her forehead, temporarily pushing aside her short dark bangs.

Tolen slowly turned toward her. Diaz brought his head forward and opened his eyes.

"Joseph of Arimathea's tomb wasn't the only thing mentioned in the coded message."

Tolen coaxed her to continue with a subtle nod.

Jade looked down at the PC keyboard and opened a Word document. "Here's the translation Dr. Cherrigan and I discovered in the Copper Scroll." She read aloud:

> *I will be entombed far across the waters where I have helped to instill Christianity. Once I told the native people of Christ, they took it upon themselves to create countless numbers of perfectly round stones, as a sign of reverence to the one stone that covered Jesus' tomb after the crucifixion. These hewn stones are spread in and around their village. The stone sphere with the creature of anonymity will lead to my tomb.*

Jade exhaled, looking up. "What I didn't tell you is that there was more," she looked back at the text and continued reading:

> *The stone sphere with the creature of anonymity will lead to my tomb...and will start you on your journey of enlightenment. From my tomb, follow the path to the message on the wall. In turn, the message on the wall will lead the righteous man to the earthly objects of Jesus Christ. Only the man who has patience, is meager, and holds faith will arrive safely.*

"Dr. Cherrigan and I believe the *earthly objects of Jesus Christ* to be a fabled cache of Jesus' possessions: personal belongings, robes, sashes, sandals, and quite probably objects mentioned in the Bible. The right stone sphere will not only lead us to Joseph of Arimathea's tomb but ultimately to a trove of artifacts which can be directly tied to Jesus of Nazareth. The value of such a collection would be incalculable, not to mention the single greatest archaeological discovery of all time."

"And the ultimate target for the 'True Sons of Light,' " Tolen said. His blue eyes radiated briefly as moonlight cut in through the window on the left side of the fuselage. He opened the armrest of his chair and picked up a telephone handset. Jade watched him push a single button and speak, "Reba Zee, change in plans. We're not leaving the country quite yet."

CHAPTER 9

September 11. Tuesday – 1:42 a.m. McLean, Virginia

Morris Vakind strolled down the tiled corridor, passing scores of people engaged in conversation. Every conference room he passed was in use with the doors closed. Somewhere out of sight, he could hear printers at work and the whirring of surveillance monitors. While most governmental facilities in the Washington, DC area had long since gone dormant, the Langley headquarters building was a beehive of activity. The CIA never stopped working.

Vakind reached the end of the hallway and veered into a small conference room, closing the door behind him. As usual, the tiny enclosure was chilly. He walked to the podium and punched a series of buttons on the control panel. A flat panel screen promptly slid from its recessed groove in the ceiling, and the static CIA symbol displayed onscreen. He took a seat at the short walnut table and glanced at his watch. It was 7:45 a.m. in Madrid, Spain.

This was not a meeting to which he was looking forward.

Suddenly, the screen came to life. It was segmented into two panes. The right portion remained as it had been, showing the CIA symbol, although now only half of it was visible. On the left appeared a live head-and-shoulder shot of the President of the United States, Gretchen Fane. Her black hair, with its signature gray streaks, was pinned up. There was a general weariness in her gaze. Her deep, dark eyes indicated another long day. Vakind realized that he probably exhibited the same signs of fatigue.

"Good evening, Madam President," Vakind addressed her, "or more appropriately, good morning."

"Director Vakind," she acknowledged. "I'm bringing the Spanish officials on now. Presidente del Gobierno, Luis Jose Tezman will be in attendance."

President Fane's Spanish counterpart; although he was known as the prime minister in most worldwide media, in the constitutional monarchy of Spain, his official title was president of the government.

The heat was about to be turned up even higher. Vakind gathered his thoughts.

The right half of the screen flickered and then burst to life. In the center of the picture was President Tezman. Two men sat on either side of the Spanish president. One had a mustache and the other was bald and clean shaven. All three men were dressed in dark suits and light-colored ties. None of them were smiling. In fact, they wore a collective scowl.

Thirty-one minutes later the audio/video feed from Madrid cut off, and half of the screen displayed the partial CIA logo. President Fane remained on the other half. It had been a brutal meeting with the Spanish president reiterating his demand that the Sudarium be returned before the start of the Feast of the Cross in 73 hours.

"Jesus Christ, Vakind," President Fane started in now that they were the only ones left on the video conference. "I know it's water under the bridge, but why did Tannacay ever promise to find the Sudarium by this Friday? Not only has Boyd Ramsey disappeared, but no one's ever heard of the 'True Sons of Light'."

It was a rhetorical question. Tannacay was the former Director of Operations who had convinced the Spanish government to deny that the Sudarium had been stolen after the communiqué from the 'True Sons of Light' hit the press. He was trying to cover up that an ex-CIA agent was responsible. From there, the situation had snowballed. Somehow, additional information reached the press— an unconfirmed leak—that a CIA agent was involved. Again, the U.S. convinced the Spanish officials to deny it, but by that time, religious fanatical groups had become suspicious of a cover-up. Sentiment toward the U.S. was already low in Europe, so the fuse to the powder keg was lit. If the Sudarium was proven to be missing on September 14th, all hell was going to break loose, and the target would be any and all U.S. citizens in whatever locations the terrorists could reach them. The whole sordid affair had taken on a life of its own. Tannacay had immediately been relieved of his position. Vakind had assumed the acting role of DO, controlling a staff of more than 1,000 clandestine service operations officers. If he thought his job was hard before, the difficulty had just multiplied exponentially.

"Madam President," Vakind spoke, "Samuel Tolen is now assisting in the matter."

There was a pregnant pause. "You pulled him off leave?"

"I didn't see that we had a choice."

President Fane stared at Vakind for a long moment. "Given the circumstances, you made the right decision." Another pause ensued. "Director Vakind, I have no choice but to warn U.S. citizens abroad by this Thursday, September 13th, if the Sudarium has not been found. I'll have a press release prepared which will say America has received terrorist threats, and we're going to DHS security threat level red for citizens traveling overseas. We'll have to put our overseas embassies and military bases on highest alert. Every consulate must be told of this situation."

"Madam President, the actions will be noticed. You'll be tipping off the fanatical groups that we are, indeed, responsible for the Sudarium's theft if you do so. We'll be admitting guilt."

"We'll blame the terror alert on some anti-American faction based in North Africa. It'll have nothing to do with Spain or other European countries."

"You realize it won't matter, right? It will be seen exactly for what it is: preparation against attacks when the Sudarium is confirmed to be missing a day later."

"At this point, Director Vakind, I don't give a damn. We owe it to our citizens. They will be warned," she said resoundingly.

"Understood," Vakind relented.

The transmission went dead.

Morris Vakind leaned back in the chair, locking his fingers behind his head. He stared at the ceiling, contemplating the ramifications. The room was still. Only the low hum of white noise filled the audible void. He agreed with the president's decision.

The protection of American citizens was a top priority. On the flip side, in doing so, it had effectively cut the time to search for the Sudarium and return it to Spain by a day.

Tolen had been integral in the 2010 on-site surveillance which had identified Osama bin Laden's compound in Pakistan. Vakind had the utmost confidence in him, as did President Fane, especially after the ordeal in Sri Lanka a month ago. Compared to those missions, the odds of successfully recovering the Sudarium were miniscule, and the timing for Tolen and Diaz, which had already been impossibly tight, had just been squeezed even further.

CHAPTER 10

September 11. Tuesday – 2:26 a.m. Flying over New York State

"Once on the ground, we'll head directly to Cambridge. Analyst Bar and a CIA operative, Agent Lattimer, are on their way to the Washington, DC, site to check the stone sphere there," Tolen said after returning from the cockpit. He took a seat beside Jade. Diaz sat across from them. Outside, the engines rumbled, propelling the jet through the dark night.

Jade felt a continuing rush of optimism. The fact they might actually find information which would lead to Joseph of Arimathea's tomb brought a feeling of anticipation, yet she tried hard to temper her excitement. She kept reminding herself it was probable the *creature of anonymity* was not an overt image. If, after checking these last two stone spheres they came up empty, it meant one of two things. Either they had been unable to locate all of the spheres, which was a distinct possibility given how they had been spread throughout Costa Rica over the centuries, or it meant she would have to start examining them all over again. Either way, after the CIA agents checked the sphere in DC, and they examined the Harvard stone, she would have her answer.

Another potential roadblock was that, even if they found the directions to the tomb, they had no way of knowing if such directions would still be relevant today. Ancient texts frequently mention landmarks which are unrecognizable today or no longer exist.

Yet, if they did find the stone—and the directions—the possibility existed they would not only find the tomb of Joseph of Arimathea, but they would reach the end treasure as well: *the earthly objects of Jesus Christ.*

The thought of such a wondrous discovery brought a mild shiver. Suddenly, a sneeze overcame Jade before she barely had time to cover her mouth.

"God bless you," Diaz said.

"Thank you," Jade said with a nod.

Tolen spoke, "It's interesting that the origin of the word *bless* is from the English word *bledsian,* which means 'to consecrate with blood.' In essence, when you say 'God bless you' to someone, the literal meaning is, 'God bathe you in blood.' "

Diaz stared at Tolen with a raised eyebrow and a disgusted frown.

Jade found herself suppressing a laugh at Diaz's expression.

Tolen flicked an overhead cabin light on, turning toward Jade. "Isn't it true Jesus is only mentioned in two pieces of literary work in the first century?"

"I'm not the biblical archaeologist. That was Dr. Cherrigan. But yes, according to what I've read, Jesus of Nazareth is referenced in the Bible, of course, and also by the Jewish historian Flavius Josephus."

Tolen nodded. "It's interesting that Josephus wasn't born until 37 AD. In a single paragraph, he mentions Jesus' crucifixion and resurrection, thus confirming his divinity. Oddly, no writer before the 4th century makes reference to Josephus' text."

"And what does that mean?" Diaz said in an irritated tone, inclining his head.

Tolen continued. "It's interesting if you consider Flavius Josephus was an orthodox Jew, yet he strongly upholds the Christian ideology with this one paragraph. Strange that Josephus would make such a brief mention of a figure who was considered so prominent."

Diaz's face colored. "Are you not a Christian?"

"We're not here to discuss my beliefs, Inspector Diaz. I'm simply mentioning the facts."

Diaz stared at Tolen incredulously. "These so-called facts... you don't believe Jesus existed?"

"I only mentioned the evidence as it has been cited."

"You're asserting that Flavius Josephus, the historian, made up the information about Jesus? Is that what historians in America do? Make up history?" Diaz asked with rising agitation.

"Actually, I think Josephus was an intelligent man who penned only factual information," Tolen responded in an even tone. Jade was intrigued at how he remained calm in the face of Diaz's growing anger, but even she was unclear what point Tolen was trying to make.

Diaz shook his head in confusion. "Then, Señor," he half smiled, "you have just contradicted yourself. If he only wrote the truth, and he mentioned Jesus in his writings, then there is your evidence that Jesus existed!"

"I agree with you."

Tolen's response surprised both Diaz and Jade. Diaz gave a confused smile. Jade watched as Tolen offered her a furtive gaze. At that moment, she realized the other shoe was about to fall.

Tolen went on. "The fact is, the first person known to have quoted Josephus' text related to Jesus was Bishop Eusebius about the year 340 AD. The hyperbolic language in this single paragraph—such as the use of the word 'divine' and 'foretold'— was incongruent with the Jewish historian's style of writing. This has led some scholars to conclude that Flavius Josephus' tome had been altered, possibly by Bishop Eusebius, and the reference to Jesus was integrated hundreds of years *after* the original text was written."

Diaz's face twitched in bewilderment.

Jade's own religious beliefs aside, she found amusement in watching Diaz squirm. Once again, she was impressed by Samuel Tolen's breadth of knowledge.

"It doesn't matter," Diaz snorted. "The Bible holds the truth. Jesus Christ was the Messiah."

"I'm not arguing the authenticity of the Bible. This is just educated speculation," Tolen responded. "Discounting Flavius Josephus' account, the only place Jesus is ever mentioned in all of history is in the New Testament. There is no other historical record of his existence."

Diaz elected not to respond and the interior of the plane went quiet except for the steady drone of the engines. The Spaniard grabbed a small pillow to the side, turned his back, and settled into it against the seat. Jade could hear his breathing and knew the discussion had angered him terribly. Diaz's faith was obviously his guiding force, and she had no quarrel with that. She might resent his brusque mannerisms, but all people are entitled to their beliefs.

Diaz, she had figured out. Samuel Tolen, however, was a complete mystery. The American was the complete opposite of the Spaniard. Where Diaz had a fiery temper, Tolen kept his under complete control. Where Diaz took his beliefs on faith, Tolen appeared to open his mind to possibilities. He seemed to teeter between faith and tangible facts, as if balancing on the precipice between the two, unsure which way to fall. There was no denying he was intelligent and well read. That much was apparent when he had, yet again, exhibited his knowledge of history. His comments regarding the Jewish historian Flavius Josephus and the possibility of tampering with the man's work centuries later had surprised her. It suggested Tolen not only knew the esoteric arguments surrounding the historical Christ figure, but that he had studied the facts in detail. She sensed that, in everything he did, Tolen had a profound need for absolute understanding and, in turn, absolute truth.

Indeed, Samuel Tolen intrigued her with his insightful analysis and his logical disposition. He was a man of few, but effective words. She felt incredibly safe in his presence, and it had nothing to do with the pistol he had shown her at the jail. She sensed that before he resorted to physical violence, he leveraged his intellect. She just wished he had come clean about whatever was going on. She was sure she was only getting part of the truth.

A short time later, the plane lazily pitched forward in descent. Jade looked down to see the darkness give way to the ubiquitous glow of white. Even at this early hour, the lights of Boston saturated the landscape.

Two minutes passed, and the cabin suddenly began to rattle. It turned out to be a harbinger of things to come, as moments later the entire plane shook violently like a toy in the grasp of a child throwing a temper tantrum. Jade felt her body whipped to one side, before she was violently jerked straight up. If not for the seatbelt restraint, she would have slammed into the ceiling. She bit her tongue as she settled harshly into her seat, her teeth slamming together with aching force. The plane continued listing hard from side to side, jostling the threesome with great force.

Reba Zee's voice broke through the cabin speaker. "A little turbulence, folks! We're gonna ride it out!"

Jade could taste the warm flow of blood. Her tongue ached, and her gums were on fire. She tried to steady herself by grabbing the armrests of the chair, only to have her grip broken, leaving her hands clutching at air with each tumultuous lunge of the fuselage.

In the frenzy, she looked across at Diaz, who was staring her straight in the eyes. With considerable difficulty, he raised a hand to his chest and crossed himself. Then he closed his eyes and relaxed.

Seconds later the cabin dipped abruptly and settled. As quickly as it started, the plane steadied into an easy descent. Tolen seemed unconcerned as he straightened out his shirt and his coat.

The otherwise excitable Spaniard also appeared unbothered by what had just happened. At no time had he shown any fear of death, and was now quite calm; a bastion of tranquility. If tragedy had come, it appeared Pascal Diaz was ready to accept it.

In many ways, she envied such staunch beliefs, which led to a twinge of remorse on her part. Buried within the recesses of her soul, an ember of hope yearned for days gone by when her own convictions were just as passionate, back to a time when archaeological evidence was secondary to blind faith.

CHAPTER 11

September 11. Tuesday – 3:01 a.m. Cambridge, Massachusetts

Tolen, Diaz, and Jade stepped from the Learjet stairs onto the gray tarmac under a crystalline sky. The temperature was warm but not stifling.

Tolen's cell phone rang. He dug it from his coat pocket and answered as they walked toward a gate.

"Tolen, it's Bar. I'm standing outside the National Geographic Museum on M Street with agent Lattimer. We just came from inside the Explorers' Hall. Museum officials weren't exactly thrilled about getting out of bed this early. I've thoroughly examined the Costa Rican stone on display. I didn't find a thing."

Tolen thought for a moment. "Is it on a stand?"

"A short pedestal, yes, and I know where you're going. The part of the pedestal which cradles the base of the sphere is made of a clear material. I got on the ground and examined the underside from the bottom up. Zilch, nada, nothing. No pictures, designs, or writing. This isn't the stone you're looking for."

"Okay, Bar. I'll be in touch."

"Call me at the office. I'm going back there to get a cat nap, but I'll have the phone near my ear in case you need anything."

****

Jade watched Tolen hang up. "Anything?"

"There was nothing on the stone sphere at the National Geographic Museum in Washington. My colleague examined it thoroughly."

"Then we're down to one," Diaz said.

Jade felt a strange blend of exhilaration and fear. It would either be a home run or a strike out when they examined this last stone.

Ahead, at the open gate, a man stood by a two-door, black sedan wearing a dark polo shirt, dress shorts, and deck shoes. "Agent Tolen," he called out, offering his hand as they approached. "I'm from the university, Jason Weedly." Tolen had arranged for an escort to the campus to save time and clear any hurdles for them to examine the stone. The young man before them was clean cut with perfect teeth. He appeared to be a student, only older, probably pursuing post-graduate studies.

The American equivalent of an Oxford man, Jade thought.

Weedly herded them into the vehicle and took the wheel. He was silent for most of the thirty-minute ride through the dark and lifeless streets, until they approached the Harvard University campus. Once they reached Kirkland Street, Weedly turned north between a structure on the left—the Busch Building—and the William James Building on the right. "This is Divinity Avenue," he said. "The Peabody Museum is just ahead."

Divinity Avenue. The coincidence of the street name was not lost on the passengers. Jade half smiled to both Diaz beside her, and to Tolen riding in the front seat next to Weedly. Each returned her look as if to say, *What else would the street that might lead to a cache of Jesus' personal belongings be called?"*

They passed by a large, sprawling structure on the left: Fairchild Biochemical Laboratory, and then Yenching Library on the right. Just beyond the library stood the Semitic Museum adjacent to a quiet side street.

"Here we are," Weedly said.

They stopped before a multi-story red brick building on the left. A prominent sign announced they had arrived at the **Peabody Museum of Archaeology and Ethnography**.

Weedly explained as a tour guide would: "This museum, founded in 1866, is one of the oldest anthropological museums in the world. It connects to a perpendicular structure at the back—a natural history and zoology museum—that, in turn, connects to a structure running parallel to The Peabody. The sphere is on display in the courtyard formed by the U-shape of these joined buildings."

Weedly shut the engine off, removed the keys and unlocked his door. He was about to get out when Tolen stopped him. "Please wait here for us."

The young man seemed a bit confused but complied. "You'll have to circle around the Tozzer Library, which walls most of the courtyard from Divinity Avenue. The stone is nestled near the crux of the Peabody and the library."

"Thank you, Mr. Weedly. We won't be long."

The three exited the car. Tolen surveyed the red-brick Victorian edifice before them, then turned in a full circle eyeing the street, adjacent buildings, and manicured landscape beyond. For the first time, Jade noticed Tolen was wary, as if he expected an ambush. Come to think of it, he had duped her marvelously with the story at the jail that her life was in imminent danger, but neither Tolen nor Diaz had shown the least bit of concern regarding an attack the entire night. Until now, that is.

A shiver ran up Jade's spine.

Tolen proceeded slowly along the lamppost-lit brick sidewalk, shifting his head from side to side. Diaz and Jade followed close behind. Diaz, too, seemed to be moving cautiously. The smell of fresh-cut grass rose to meet them, stirred by a mild swirl of a breeze. An industrial air-conditioning unit hummed loudly somewhere out of sight. In every direction, the campus was void of life except for light shining from upper-story windows of buildings on either side of Divinity Avenue.

"You guys are making me nervous," Jade whispered.

Neither man responded. Instead, the threesome continued past the Tozzer Library as Weedly had advised. At the end of the building, Tolen led them into the courtyard and down a wide swath of pavement lined with thick overhanging trees. Tolen slowed even further as they proceeded through the shadows of the courtyard. Jade felt her pulse notch up. If someone wanted to ambush them, this would be a prime place. She noticed Tolen was now moving more cat-like than human, practically slinking through the gray darkness with stealthy precision. She had been unaware until that moment Diaz had fallen into step behind her so that the three were in single file as they moved deeper into the closed courtyard.

Ahead, the thick tree cover cleared. A pallid glow of moonlight penetrated a stone-paved glade, through which they passed. Further on, the trees once again enveloped the walk, and they plunged back into shadows. As they approached the end of the library, a small creature scampered up a nearby tree, causing Jade to jump.

"Bugger," she mumbled. She paused to catch her breath with a hand to her chest then quickly started forward again, knowing Diaz was likely to barrel into her if she remained stationary.

The trees once again fell away, and the sidewalk was dressed in muted moonlight. Tolen stopped at a circular section of brick pavement near the Peabody Museum building. A large, bulbous object loomed in the darkness. Chest high and perfectly round, the sphere was seated upon a hexagonal base of stone at least a foot thick, held in place by three solid stone braces atop the ornamental base.

"This…this thing is big," Diaz exclaimed.

Jade nodded as she explained, "The Costa Rican spheres were first discovered in the 1940s by workers clearing land for banana plantations by the United Fruit Company. Primarily, the spheres are found in and around the small village of Palmar Sur. It is believed they were initially created in the 1st century, but no one knows for sure. This one was a gift from the United Fruit Company to the Harvard museum following the 1964 World's Fair in New York." Jade eyed the massive stone. "It weighs about 600 lbs."

Tolen removed an object from inside his coat pocket. There was a click and a stab of light hit the ground. Tolen raised the flashlight beam to the pedestal.

MONUMENTAL STONE SPHERE
PRE-COLUMBIAN PERIOD
DIQUIS DELTA, COSTA RICA

"You're on, Dr. Mollur," he said, taking a step to the side to allow her room to pass. He offered his flashlight, but she turned it down, pulling a penlight from her pocket.

"This will go much faster if we all search," Jade said.

Tolen nodded, and he and Diaz went behind the stone. Jade began her examination opposite them, moving the light extremely slowly over the hewn surface.

Diaz's words floated to her from the other side of the stone sphere. "Surely an image on a rock displayed here for almost fifty years would have been noticed before now."

"*The creature of anonymity,*" Jade reminded him, maintaining her focus. She was not going to get drawn into his pessimism. She eyed the stone intently, slowly passing the thin beam over the convex surface, occasionally pausing to investigate tool marks from the sphere's original carving untold centuries before.

She started at the top and worked her way down. It was a laborious process, and several times her mind fooled her, incorrectly matrixing images of animals from the various marks. Upon closer examination, they proved each time to be nothing more than obscure scrapes across the stone's surface.

Halfway down, Jade felt her spirits begin to wane. Then she had an even more disconcerting thought: what if *the creature of anonymity* was an image embedded inside the stone? At a minimum, the reexamination of the hundreds of spheres with stone-penetrating radar equipment would take months, possibly years, and would cost thousands of dollars she did not have. It might take a long time, if ever, to raise the money needed through donations or grants.

As they worked, she noticed that Tolen occasionally glanced sideways at her then took in the surrounding area, scanning the dark shadows under the copse of trees which filled the courtyard. He was obviously still on alert, and it made her skin tingle, causing a whirlwind of emotions to knot up inside her.

With only one-quarter of the stone left to search, her hope was rapidly slipping away. The excitement which had kept her exhaustion at bay was evaporating. The thought of having to begin the search in Costa Rica all over again without Phillip was almost unbearable.

Jade was now kneeling, leaning on the stone pedestal for support, as fatigue was settling in. The red-brick pavement bit into her bare knees as she craned her head sideways to examine the underside of the stone. The moonlight did not reach here, and she slowed her examination even more, hoping upon hope for some image which would stand out in this last section of stone surface as she contorted underneath it.

"I've seen that on the back of some of your American vehicles."

She had been so entrenched in her thoughts that Diaz's voice startled her. She had practically forgotten that Tolen and Diaz were searching the other side of the stone. They had barely made a sound.

"What?" she said, as a charge of exhilaration returned. She scurried to her feet and went around to the other side of the stone.

Tolen and Diaz both faced her as Tolen said, "Long before Christianity, the symbol of a certain creature was known as 'the Great Mother.' It was linked to fertility, birth, feminine sexuality, and the natural force of women, and was acknowledged by the Celts as well as many pagan cultures throughout northern Europe."

Jade stared at him curiously, wondering where he was going with this.

"Around the 1st century, the creature was adopted by early Christians. There were probably several reasons for this. For one, Jesus' ministry is strongly associated with it, and two, it was considered an innocuous symbol persecutors would not link to Christians. When a Christian met someone new, they would draw a single arc in the sand. If the other person completed the drawing with a second, inverse arc overlapping the first one, it was known they, too, were Christian."

Tolen turned toward the stone and shined the flashlight on the surface at the midpoint. It was slightly darkened from the surrounding surface. He held up a bottle of water for Jade to see. "We wet it to get the etching to show up better."

Excitedly, Jade squatted and moved closer to the stone. Tolen poured some more water on the surface and two pronounced lines approximately two inches long appeared: arcs joined at one end and overlapping at the other end.

"Of course!" she exclaimed. "Ixthus! The Christian Fish! That's what it meant by *The creature of anonymity.*' It helped protect the identity of Christians!" She held her gaze on the image. The lines were unmistakable, but it was no wonder the image had never been noticed. Not only was it faint, but it was so obscure that it was unrecognizable unless you were specifically looking for it. She briefly considered the depths of Samuel Tolen's knowledge on the subject, but there was no time for that now. She pushed away from the stone and stood. It suddenly dawned on her she had no idea what to do next.

"So we have the correct stone. Now what?" Diaz spoke her thoughts for her.

Jade scratched her cheek in thought. The thrill of the discovery slowly gave way to reality. Two arcing lines did not make a treasure map, nor did they lead to any further clues.

"We take a look inside," Tolen broke the silence. He knelt down and shined the flashlight on the image, running a finger in a circle on the surface around the fish, tracing a razor thin, almost invisible indention six inches in diameter.

Jade realized the significance. The stone had been plugged.

CHAPTER 12

September 11. Tuesday – 3:48 a.m. Cambridge, Massachusetts

Pascal Diaz looked at his watch. He was growing anxious with this fanciful treasure hunt. "We have less than 72 hours to find the Sudarium, and you want to open up this stone?"

Jade, who was propped on the pedestal, turned a shadowed face toward Diaz. "Sudarium?"

Mierda, Diaz swore silently to himself.

"We'll discuss it later," Tolen reassured her. "For now, we must proceed expediently."

Jade shot a suspicious gaze from Diaz to Tolen before turning back to the stone. "Do either of you have a pocket knife?"

Diaz removed one from his trouser pocket and handed it to Jade. "It is an heirloom from my grandfather in Tolédo. Please do not break it."

Jade took the knife, opened it, and wedged the tip of the blade into the narrow crevice while Tolen held light to the area.

A sharp crack behind caused all three to turn. Diaz quickly pulled his HK USP Compact 9mm and had it leveled into the darkness of the tree cover beyond. He looked to Tolen, who brandished his pistol in the same manner. Tolen shined his flashlight over the grounds where the light was all but sucked up in the darkness. After several seconds of silence, both men holstered their weapons. Diaz realized the sound had probably been a tree branch breaking under the weight of some small creature.

"Please continue," Tolen said, urging Jade on.

The Brit went back to work on the stone, slowly working the

tip of the blade along the cutout. Within minutes, she had whittled a reasonably deep crevice following the circular outline. Then she used the tip of the blade to try to pry the stone plug out. Diaz winced as he watched the blade tip bend almost to the breaking point without any movement of the stone.

"It won't come out," she said, discouraged. "It may not be a plug, after all."

"I doubt you can apply the leverage needed with that blade," Tolen remarked.

Suddenly, the roar of an engine split the night. At the far end near the library building where they had entered the courtyard, a set of headlights lanced into the darkness. A vehicle raced through the web of tree trunks, the engine whining and tires squealing as they transitioned from hard ground to pavement. The vehicle turned, targeting them in its headlights.

It was barreling straight toward them.

Tolen grabbed Jade's arm, and slung her away into a patch of nearby low ground ferns. Tolen and Diaz drew their weapons. Tolen dropped into a shooter's position on one knee, but Diaz remained upright, uncertain if he should move out of the car's path or hold his ground. He took a nervous step to the side, and then steadied himself. Tolen did not budge.

The car lunged forward, negotiating between the trees. The churn of the engine grew louder. The headlights were nearly blinding as Diaz tried to shield his eyes with one hand while continuing to aim with the other. Finally, he could wait no longer and fired several shots in succession. Instead of slowing, the car increased speed, the engine raging. The white lights blocked out everything. Diaz sent several more shots to a spot just above the right headlight hoping to get lucky and hit the unseen driver. The vehicle closed quickly. Diaz felt a wave of nausea.

Tolen had yet to fire a shot.

"Shoot, damn you!" Diaz barked at Tolen.

There was a single deafening pop. The headlights veered slightly, and Diaz dove to the side, landing hard on the brick pavement. A torturous groan of iron followed. The right front of the car slammed into the stone sphere, knocking it from its perch, sending it ambling slowly toward the side of the Peabody Museum Building…and Jade. She frantically rolled away, barely out of its path. After a dozen feet, the sphere struck the wall with a thud. The car came to a violent halt as the undercarriage caught on the now-empty stone pedestal. The air suddenly filled with the smell of gas and oil. The headlight beams knifed ahead, lighting the stone sphere where it had come to rest against the dented wall. The motor raced, sputtered, and died. Everything went quiet.

Diaz rose to his feet breathing heavily. He had no idea what had happened to Tolen until he saw the CIA agent quickly approach the vehicle, open the passenger door and lean in with his gun aimed inside. Tolen stood upright and looked over the car at Diaz. "He's dead."

Jade was still on the ground. The 600-pound stone sphere had missed crushing her by inches. She pushed herself up, too dazed to bother brushing off the grass and twigs which stuck to her hair and clothing. One knee was cut and bleeding. In the spotlight, she cast a long, lean shadow on the stone and the building wall behind her.

Diaz and Jade joined Tolen at the vehicle. Diaz went to the driver's side and reached in, pushing the body off the steering wheel and removing the dead man's wallet. He could now see the man was older, sixty or maybe even seventy years old. A bullet had entered his forehead. "Is this Boyd Ramsey?" he asked Tolen.

Tolen shook his head. "No."

Jade walked away, holding a hand before her mouth as if she might be sick.

Diaz turned his attention back to the body. He read the man's identity, "California driver's license, Richard Mox, from Santa Barbara." He looked up at Tolen. "Do you know this man?"

"No, but I'll have Tiffany Bar check him out."

Diaz looked over the vehicle with increasing familiarity. "Isn't this our car?"

Tolen nodded. "Which begs the question: what happened to Jason Weedly?"

"Look at this!" Jade exclaimed.

Diaz looked up. Jade was standing next to the stone sphere, framed by the headlights soaking the wall. "The plug fell out!" She excitedly pointed to the dark circular hole near the top of the sphere.

Diaz and Tolen approached. Tolen shined his flashlight inside the cavity for everyone to see. It was cylindrical, approximately eight inches deep with smooth walls and a flat base. There was nothing inside.

"This has been a waste of time," Diaz commented.

"Obviously not or that man wouldn't have tried to kill us," Tolen said with a thoughtful look.

Tolen dipped his head and scanned the ground. His eyes traced a path back toward the car. Jade trailed behind.

"You think something fell out of the stone sphere?" she asked.

He did not respond.

Diaz followed Tolen and Jade as they walked back toward the vehicle. They moved off the pavement into the low fern hedge, where Jade had been thrown by Tolen. The headlight beams created a mosaic of patchy visibility through the low foliage.

"There!" Jade pointed to a recessed area hidden from the light. At first, Diaz saw nothing. Tolen and Jade squatted, and Diaz followed. Sure enough, there was a small heap of light-colored objects in the vegetation. Jade carefully lifted one and examined it. Tolen shined his flashlight on the tiny pile.

"They're rock fragments; what's left of the plug," Jade said, turning the piece over in her hand, eyeing it meticulously.

Tolen lifted a piece from the ground. He nodded his concurrence. He nudged aside another fragment.

Jade stared at the small rock in Tolen's hand, then carefully picked through the jagged pieces on the ground.

Diaz noticed a line of blood stretched from her knee to her ankle. Even with the distraction, he found himself briefly admiring the form of her bare leg.

After a few moments, Jade drew in a sharp breath. Her hand was frozen in mid-air over the tiny pile. Then she slowly lowered it, and pushed aside one of the larger rocks. Underneath it was a long, thin, tan object. To Diaz, it resembled a dirty cigarette.

Jade lifted the object delicately. Diaz saw her fingers tremble. He had no idea what she had found, but it must be significant.

"Is that rolled parchment?" Tolen asked, focusing the flashlight on it.

Jade looked to both men, and nodded absently as if in utter disbelief. She wiped her forehead with the back of her hand.

"What does it mean?" Diaz asked.

Jade looked to Tolen, who nodded his head reassuringly as if to say, *go ahead and unroll it.*

Jade twirled the tiny roll slowly in her fingers until a loose flap appeared. She tenderly tugged on the edge of paper and began to unwind it, stretching it the entire six inches in length. It had writing that was unfamiliar to Diaz.

"Oh brilliant!" Jade exclaimed. "It's ancient Hebrew. This was most likely penned by Joseph of Arimathea!"

"Can you read it?" Tolen asked.

"Yes," Jade responded breathlessly. She swallowed and read it aloud slowly:

> *Search for the three stone jars. They will be found when you look for what was offered on the first day. The first jar is at my tomb. Travel from the south. My tomb is through the three-sided rock doorway at the sea.*

CHAPTER 13

September 11. Tuesday – 4:39 a.m. Cambridge, Massachusetts

Tolen, Jade, and Diaz returned to the plane at Taylor Hughes Airport by taxi. They had been unable to locate the young driver, Jason Weedly. It appeared that Richard Mox had killed him and stashed the body in order to steal the vehicle.

Tolen had an uneasy feeling regarding Mox's actions. Frankly, it made no sense. It had been a weak attack, a desperate plan to try to kill them. Nothing on the man or in the vehicle suggested affiliation with the "True Sons of Light." The fact that Mox worked alone was equally puzzling.

Tolen talked briefly to Bar on the cab ride back from Harvard. He asked her to check on the dead driver and to engage the local Cambridge police regarding the incident, the corpse in the university courtyard, and the missing young man. There was no time for them to get caught up in a police investigation, and Bar would justify Tolen and company leaving the crime scene due to a domestic terrorism threat identified by the CIA. They could do so without giving specific details, and it would appease the local authorities.

Jade had remained contemplative, studying the small parchment during the cab ride. Now, on board the plane, she laid it gently on a side stand, took a napkin doused with water and rubbed the blood from her leg. As she did, she looked hard at Tolen.

He knew the question was coming. Diaz had spilled the secret.

"What about the Sudarium? It's been stolen, hasn't it?"

"Yes," Tolen admitted. He had decided telling Jade the truth would not jeopardize their mission. In fact, it might enhance their efforts. He could deal with the repercussions from Vakind. "It has to be returned to the Cathedral of San Salvador in Oviedo, Spain, before 9:00 a.m. this Friday for the start of the Feast of the Cross. If not, all hell's going to break loose."

Jade nodded. She did not appear angry. In fact, her expression was pained, as if she were hurt at not being included in the circle of information. "This is *exactly* why we must reach the treasure of Jesus' artifacts before this radical group does."

"Why? We have the only clue: the parchment. Surely, the location of your treasure is secure now," Diaz said.

Tolen smiled.

Jade cocked her head. "What?"

"By finding this first clue, we've elevated our stature," Tolen began. "We're not only the group's target, we're now their number one priority. We will continue the search and allow the 'True Sons of Light' to come for us. This is how we'll find Boyd Ramsey."

"That's a comforting thought," Jade said. "Who is Boyd Ramsey?"

"He's the CIA analyst I mentioned before," Tolen took a few minutes to explain, including the murder of Diaz's brother, Javier, at the Cathedral of San Salvador.

Shortly after takeoff, Tolen's cell phone dinged and he answered.

"Well, your Mr. Mox was a very unremarkable man," Bar started immediately upon hearing Tolen's voice. "Seventy-two-year-old widower, retired from the public sector in archaeology six years ago, working for the State of California. No criminal arrests, but he had run up some gambling debts and was headed for bankruptcy. You may find it interesting that in 1986, before he worked for California, Mox participated in the excavation of a first-century fishing boat at the northwestern shore of the Sea of Galilee in Israel. The boat is considered to be the same type Jesus and his disciples used."

"I recall the discovery," Tolen remarked. "Anything else?"

"We have a team going through Mox's house, but nothing so far. I'll keep digging to see what I can uncover. Oh by the way, police and university officials weren't thrilled with what you did to the campus courtyard, not to mention the damage to the stone sphere, building wall, and the corpse you left behind. They did find Jason Weedly alive, though. He was tied up and gagged in some nearby bushes. Did you find what you were looking for there?"

"Yes, please advise Director Vakind we're on our way to Costa Rica."

Tolen concluded the call and shared the information with Diaz and Jade.

"What was the *discovery* Bar mentioned to you?" Jade asked.

"Mox was part of an archaeological excavation of an early-Christian-era fishing boat in the Sea of Galilee in the 80s. Curiously, though, there's nothing in his background to suggest terrorist activity. In fact, the man appeared quite grounded," Tolen paused momentarily. "Let's focus on the Hebrew writing." He motioned toward the parchment.

Jade lifted it carefully and held it in her lap as Diaz looked on.

Tolen removed a laptop from underneath his seat where it had been secured. Two were kept on board at all times. The second was in the cockpit with Reba Zee.

He pulled up a text document program and had Jade translate the Hebrew once again so he could document it in English. He typed as she read it:

> *Search for the three stone jars. They will be found when you look for what was offered on the first day. The first jar is at my tomb. Travel from the south. My tomb is through the three-sided rock doorway at the sea.*

"Quite a riddle," Diaz remarked.

"What are your thoughts?" Tolen looked to Jade.

"Well," she exhaled, "the first line of text seems straightforward. We have to find three stone receptacles. I have no idea what '*look for what was offered on the first day*' means. It's too vague."

"Interesting that the message specifies *three stone jars*," Tolen said. "The number three is often used in reference to Jesus: he preached three years, on the third day he arose from the dead, Peter denied him three times, three men were executed on the cross—Jesus and the two thieves—he was thirty-three at the time of his crucifixion, three entities in the Trinity: Father, Son, and

Holy Ghost."

Jade stared at Tolen curiously. "Is biblical ideology a hobby? You seem to have more than just a passing knowledge on the subject."

Tolen responded with a mere smile. "The next three lines reference the location of Joseph of Arimathea's tomb. '*The first jar is at my tomb. Travel from the south. My tomb is through the three-sided rock doorway at the sea.*' "

"It's vague," Diaz said.

" '*Travel from the south,*' suggests south is the point of origin and implies the tomb is to the north. Keep in mind the stone sphere was originally in or near Palmar Sur, Costa Rica, so it's somewhere north of there."

"Well, now, that narrows it down," Diaz said, arching his eyebrows to emphasize his sarcasm.

"Not really," Tolen conceded, "but the final line does: '*My tomb is through the three-sided rock doorway at the sea.*' Coincidentally, it's another reference to the number three."

"You know what is meant by a *three-sided rock doorway?*" Jade asked, leaning forward. There was a sparkle in her eye that had been there since they first found the tiny roll of parchment.

"No, but *at the sea* implies the shoreline." He brought up an Internet search engine and conducted a search using the terms, "three-sided," "rock," "doorway," "Costa Rica." While it returned thousands of hits, nothing appeared to be a landmark at the coastline. He tried again using 'three-sided,' 'opening,' 'Caribbean Sea,' 'Costa Rica.' He tried a third, fourth, fifth, and sixth time using a combination of the terms. Still nothing promising returned.

Tolen sat back and shrugged. "Nothing from word searches. I'll go to satellite imagery and use Palmar Sur as a starting point and move north up the coastline of Costa Rica to search for something which fits the description."

"CIA technology?" Diaz asked.

"Google Earth."

Tolen accessed the Internet using a Comsat connection. He launched Google Earth and zoomed in on Palmar Sur. Then he shifted on a horizontal plane to the east where Costa Rica met the

Caribbean Sea. He would begin his search there. His hope was that this three-sided rock doorway was the entrance to a cave and was notable enough to have been photographed. He looked across the aisle at the weary faces. "Why don't you two get some sleep? I'll wake you if I find anything."

Each nodded, grabbed a pillow, and closed their eyes. Tolen flipped an overhead switch, and the cabin went dark. Within minutes, Diaz was snoring. Jade continued to shift in her seat with her eyes closed as if unable to get comfortable. Tolen suspected the excitement of the archaeological hunt was making it difficult for her to relax.

Tolen spent the next 25 minutes examining amateur pictures that people had posted online of scenes along the eastern seaboard of Costa Rica. He continued his search up the shoreline until he came to Nicaragua. His vision began to blur as he reached Honduras, and he took a moment to look away from the laptop to give his eyes a rest.

He looked across at Jade. Her smooth skin and delicate facial features were accentuated in the radiant moonlight streaming in through the windows. She finally appeared to be resting peacefully. Still clad in her white tank top and khaki hiking shorts, she had curled her firm legs up on the seat and was in a tuck position with her head on the pillow, propped on her knees. Even in the shadows, there was no denying her femininity. Stunning looks and a mind; a rare and tricky combination, Tolen thought.

To her side, Diaz was snoring like a bear.

He was teamed with quite a pair: a beautiful English archaeologist and a revenge-minded Spanish police inspector. He could not remember working with a more odd combination of partners.

Just then, the image of his father lying dormant in the hospital bed in Jacksonville popped into his head. It came suddenly and without warning, as if someone had used a remote to change the channel of his thoughts. With absolute clarity, he could see the man's dark, withered face, and his sunken eye sockets draped with rubbery eyelids. His emaciated arms stretched down at his side. He envisioned the white sheet permanently pulled to the top of his chest, rising and falling with his slow, shallow breathing as the machine hissed and pumped on the wall behind.

Tolen shook the thought away and looked at his watch: 5:56 a.m. local time, 11:56 a.m. in Spain; 69 hours before the Sudarium was to go on display in Oviedo. He rubbed his eyes, fending off fatigue; it was time to get back to work.

Tolen had exhausted the eastern seaboard of Central America, at least the range he considered to be within reason, and now moved to the western shoreline. He was feeling far less optimistic about finding a *"three-sided rock doorway at the sea"* on the Pacific side, since he assumed the cross-oceanic journey Joseph of Arimathea made to reach the area would have been via the Caribbean Sea. Nevertheless, Tolen resumed his search, diligently examining every posted picture along the western coast, north of Palmar Sur.

He followed the coastline almost to Nicaragua to a peninsula jutting out at the northwest end of Costa Rica when he pulled up a picture titled, "Formacion Descartes Santa Elena." He studied the image for only a few seconds.

Minutes later, both Jade and Diaz were wiping sleep from their eyes as Tolen explained what he found. " 'Formacion Descartes Santa Elena' is a natural recess in the coastal land wall. It's framed in a triangular outcropping of rock with the apex reaching about 20 feet high and leaning slightly to the right." He turned the laptop around to show them the image on the screen: a *"three-sided rock doorway at the sea."*

A sleepy smile blossomed on Jade's lips. Diaz seemed unaffected.

"How do we get to it?" Jade asked.

"The entire coastline in that area is mountainous, and where the land meets the water, there's a sheer cliff face. It's only accessible by water. I've already contacted Bar and asked her to secure us a boat from a nearby fishing village. It'll be an eleven-mile boat ride."

"If this is a known land formation, why hasn't the tomb already been found?" Diaz asked.

"We won't know the answer to that question until we get there. We'll land in Costa Rica by 1 p.m. Until then, we better all get some rest."

In truth, Tolen realized with some consternation that Diaz's question was valid. The tomb might have already been found in antiquity and plundered. The more troubling possibility, though, was that the tomb was never there.

The certainty was they would know before nightfall.

****

At 8:40 a.m. Eastern Time, Tolen unbuckled his seat belt and rose from his chair. Jade and Diaz were both fast asleep in the dark cabin. He looked out the nearest window. The droning engines were pushing the plane through the morning skies far above the silky surface of the Atlantic Ocean. Tolen quietly walked to the rear and grabbed two bottles and three shot glasses from the galley bar. He carried them back up the aisle to the cockpit door. He knocked lightly and entered. Reba Zee turned in her seat. She was flying by autopilot and had been reading. Upon seeing Tolen, she silently laid her book to the side.

She had been expecting him.

Without a word, he handed her one of the shot glasses. Then he popped the cork on the non-alcoholic champagne and filled her tiny glass. He filled the other two shot glasses from the contents of the second bottle: a 25-year-old Chivas Regal Scotch. He held onto one glass and placed the other one on a side stand.

"Who's that one for?" Reba Zee asked.

"Frank."

Reba Zee gave an appreciative nod.

By odd coincidence, this was their fourth time working together on the infamous anniversary, and this would be their fourth time sharing a traditional moment of remembrance.

"How's my girl, Tiffany, doing?" Reba Zee asked, passing the minutes until it was time.

Tolen grinned. "She's coming along. I forgot to mention earlier, she said to tell you hello."

"I haven't seen the child in over a month. I hope to get to DC soon and stop in for a visit."

Tiffany Bar had formed an unusual relationship with the elder pilot, bordering on a mother/daughter kinship. Bar's mother and father had divorced when she was eight years old. Her mother had turned to alcohol, and their relationship had been strained ever since. Reba Zee had lost her husband, Frank, to a terrorist attack when his plane exploded just after takeoff from Belfast two years ago. Yet Reba Zee swore that she spoke to Frank every day. After Tolen introduced the two last year, Reba Zee had taken Bar under her wing. They had even vacationed together in Mexico. The stout, gray-haired pilot with the brusque mannerisms who spoke English with a pronounced Texas drawl, and the diminutive, blonde-haired girl who spoke Spanish better than the inhabitants of Cancun made quite the pair.

Tolen checked his watch: 8:45. He waited patiently for the next minute to tick off. Once 8:46 arrived, he hoisted his shot glass into the air, as did Reba Zee.

"To those who have fallen…," Reba Zee said, a tear threatening to fall from her eye.

"We will never forget," Tolen finished solemnly.

They both gulped down their respective shots, and on the exact minute of the anniversary when the first airliner was flown into the North Tower of the World Trade Center, Samuel Tolen and Reba Zee commemorated all the people in the world whose lives had been lost as a result of terrorist activity, including Frank.

For a long moment, Reba Zee stared at the third, full shot glass sitting stoically to the side. "Okay, back to business," she finally said, forcing a grin.

Tolen rose and was about to return to the cabin when he paused. "Would you like to take a break? I can take the wheel for a few hours."

"Are you kidding?" Reba Zee said with a smirk. "No one who's sipped alcohol is touchin' my baby."

CHAPTER 14

September 11. Tuesday – 2:04 p.m. Northwest coast of Costa Rica

Tolen had to keep the speed down as the vessel pushed west through the waves, rising and falling with each comber. The salt in the breeze was strong, and, in a way, invigorating. The sky was clear and bright. To starboard, the shoreline of Costa Rica fell away and blended seamlessly into the Nicaraguan coast in the distance. Ahead, the dark blue horizon stretched out to infinity. Yet it was the port side Jade was watching with building anticipation, as they paralleled the barrier of gray, mountainous walls which abutted the sea and reached to lofty cliffs overhead.

If she had not been so anxious about their quest, Jade might have felt more sympathy toward the inspector. It had taken Pascal Diaz all of five minutes riding aboard the 25-foot boat to turn green from seasickness as they pitched and swayed in the choppy waters of the Pacific Ocean. The Spaniard had quickly disappeared below deck where he now lay on a mattress in a small cabin, hugging a pillow. Diaz's attitude was vexing at times, but no one deserved to suffer as he was at that very moment.

Jade held onto the rail beside Tolen on the upper wheelhouse deck as he guided the boat. He occasionally lifted his sunglasses to glance at a handheld GPS display on his iPhone to mark their position. His mastery of the vessel was apparent. He was very much at ease as a captain.

This truly was a man of many talents.

As they rode in silence, the boat tossed to and fro. She found herself involuntarily stealing glances at Tolen's form. He stood erect, dressed in long dark pants, wearing a dark sports jacket over a white tee shirt. When the jacket opened with each brush of wind, it revealed a muscular chest, a well-defined mid-section, and a holstered pistol. With smooth cheekbones set against a firm jaw, he exuded confidence, without appearing arrogant. Samuel Tolen had an undeniably regal appeal.

Although in desperate need of a shower, Jade had at least managed to secure five hours of sleep, which was miraculous, considering the adrenaline rush that had swarmed her when Tolen had shown them the picture of the land formation. It matched the clue so precisely she was certain they would find Joseph of Arimathea's tomb inside the cave, and it might be the first step to finding archaeological evidence which would confirm Christ's existence. Tolen and Diaz, on the other hand, had remained reserved. As monumental as the discovery would be, their priority was focused on capturing Boyd Ramsey and recovering the Sudarium. They viewed their efforts as a trap; a means to get to the 'True Sons of Light.' Yet, even knowing the possible danger, she could not suppress the exhilaration she was feeling, and despite the warm sunlight drenching her skin, she tingled with excitement. It had been a long search for the stone sphere referenced in the decoded Copper Scroll text. Her only regret was Phillip could not be here to experience the moment with her.

The water continued to churn, frothy and alive, dipping the bow of the slow-moving vessel into a trough just before the next wave lifted it up again. It had been like this since leaving the dock where they had rented the boat, and there was no indication it would calm any time soon. Jade was certain Diaz would not come topside until he was forced to debark. Even she began to wish for calmer water as the boat gyrated in the turbulent seas.

Through sunglasses, Tolen intently assessed the agitated surface, slowing as they crested each wave, then gunning the motors as they climbed from each gully. The stiff wind kept the temperature moderate.

Jade spoke above the drumming of the twin Mercury motors. "How long have you been with the CIA?"

He remained focused ahead. "I joined the agency immediately

after college, much to my father's disapproval."

"Not a fan of bureaucracy?"

"He was a pacifist. He never saw the need for such a governmental agency."

His responses seemed measured. Jade noticed that he referred to his father in the past tense, and was void of any emotion as he spoke, although it was hard to tell behind shielded eyes. Her intuition told her he was covering pain.

"You said that all hell will break loose if the Sudarium is not returned by 9:00 a.m. Friday. What did you mean?"

"There will be considerable, and deadly, backlash toward U.S. citizens if it's discovered missing. The Spanish government, at the urging of the U.S., covered up the theft with the hope of finding it before then."

"The U.S. is trying to cover their arse because this Ramsey fellow is ex-CIA?"

"Correct, although it's not in his character to lead a radical sect; especially one intent on killing archaeologists and stealing relics that are thought to be tied to Jesus of Nazareth. Ramsey is agnostic, but he saw religion as a personal choice no one else had the right to criticize."

The conversation lagged for a few seconds. "What about you?" Jade said, trying to brush her black bangs out of her eyes to no avail, as the wind whipped her hair constantly.

Tolen turned toward her and removed his sunglasses revealing his enchanting blue eyes. "Come again?"

"What about you? What's your take on religion?"

"Like Ramsey, I believe it's an inherently personal decision. Belief is a choice, not an obligation, as any organized religion would have you think."

"Do you believe Jesus was crucified on the cross and died for our sins?"

Tolen paused before responding. "It was the French philosopher, Voltaire, who said, '*If God did not exist, it would be necessary to invent him.*'"

Jade looked at him, unsure of how to respond.

He took the invitation to continue. "I believe there is a clear delineation between fact and belief. A belief shouldn't directly conflict with a fact; otherwise, you're wearing blinders, ignoring all reality."

"Then how do you distinguish between the two?"

Tolen turned back toward the bow as he steered. "What I know for a fact is that the Bible claims to be a record of truth, and in support of its claims, long forgotten places and cities mentioned within its text have been discovered. In several cases, the existence of historical figures has been confirmed, such as King Herod, whose tomb was discovered in 2007. The reality, though, is there is no documented historical support for the existence of Jesus."

Jade felt mild frustration in his circular logic. "You don't believe Jesus ever walked the Earth? You realize that eleven of the twelve Apostles preached His word and died as martyrs? Doesn't this offer more than just a compelling argument for His existence? Would they really subject themselves to heinous deaths if Jesus hadn't existed, and they didn't believe in His teachings?"

"Is there any historical proof, beyond what's in the Bible, that any of the twelve Apostles existed?"

Jade was momentarily speechless, but then managed a surprised, "Well, no; no hard archaeological evidence."

"Don't misinterpret what I'm saying. I'm not making a judgment. You found a code in the Copper Scroll which supports the existence and travels of Joseph of Arimathea and references objects belonging to Jesus. All of it is intriguing, but we must keep an open mind. It may have simply been instigated by someone perpetuating a story."

"A deception? From the first century?"

Tolen did not respond. Instead, he returned the sunglasses to his eyes and concentrated on the tumultuous waves meeting them head on. A fishing boat was anchored several hundred yards on the right. Seagulls looped above it, squawking as they looked down on the half-dozen occupants who were dragging in a seine net. It appeared to be a lucrative catch as they worked fast to pull the fish into the boat.

She felt a swell of rejection. "So you're in Diaz's corner? You think the deciphered text—the clue from the stone sphere—it's all an elaborate hoax?"

Tolen's words remained calm. "Fact versus belief. We'll know soon enough."

Jade stared at Tolen, unsure what to say. She wanted to argue the point. She refused to accept that the search she and Phillip had undertaken was based on a 2,000-year-old ploy. The thought was extremely unsettling.

Tolen stood at the helm, busy guiding the boat. He had stated his position then abandoned the discussion and left her struggling for answers. His points were salient, yet bloody well disturbing, as was his laconic speech and stoic veneer, she thought.

"Do you mind telling me what religion you are?" Her words had more of an edge than she planned.

"I was raised Methodist." There was a slight pause as he again turned to look at Jade, removing his sunglasses. "And you? Where do you attend now?"

The comeback question caught her off guard. "I…um…I was raised a member of the Anglican Church, like most British citizens, although I have to admit, I haven't attended church in a few years…17 to be precise.

"I'm curious," she continued, hoping to avoid further confrontation. "You seem to have significant knowledge of global history. Is that some sort of CIA prerequisite?"

For the first time that afternoon, Tolen smiled. "No, I have a master's degree in world history to go along with a PhD in criminology."

"You have a doctorate and don't use the title in your name?"

"I always found it a bit pretentious to ask people to call me Dr. Tolen. Dr. Tolen is my father."

"A family lineage of PhDs," Jade said. "You're quite an educated man to be a secret agent."

"Secret agent. Now that's an antiquated term. The official title is 'clandestine service operations officer.' "

"You just made that up," she said in a whimsical tone.

"Not at all, although it no longer fits in my case, especially given my current assignment supporting the Smithsonian Institution. These days, I'm more of an international liaison."

There was a slight twinkle in his eye. She suspected his work with the Smithsonian better suited his intellectual side. "How did you come by such a plum assignment? Surely you don't get to choose the position that makes you the happiest? You are working for the government. They have rules against happy employees." Playfulness had seeped into her voice, and she felt at ease again. It was in complete contrast to how she had felt only minutes before when they were discussing religion and faith, and it was a welcome change.

Tolen smiled and looked down. "Some people are just lucky, I guess."

She wanted to press him again about how he had acquired his early-Christian-era knowledge, but she was reticent about falling back into another uncomfortable discussion. "Did you specialize in any certain time period or culture? Every world historian I've ever met had a favorite topic."

"As a matter of fact, I've always been very fascinated with Egyptian history—the pyramids, the sphinx, the historical cities, monuments, funerary temples, mummification techniques, and so on. Ancient Egyptians left an indelible mark on history unlike any other past civilization. I believe we have only scratched the surface of the discoveries yet to be made there."

"Phillip also had a fondness for Egypt," Jade replied. Her thoughts drifted back to the last time she saw him alive. He was waving goodbye from the airport terminal as she boarded the flight to the States. She could see him staring at her through the window. He had his usual intellectual grin which she found so remarkably attractive.

She realized their conversation had gone silent, and she discarded the image, searching for something to say. "Prior to our teaming up to decode the message and search for the stone sphere in Costa Rica, Dr. Cherrigan had been involved with an excavation not far from the Giza Plateau. A section of floor in the basement of a hotel had collapsed, revealing an underground tunnel. Unfortunately the passageway ended after a short distance and no artifacts were found."

"I recall reading about it."

Again there was a lull, but it was soon broken by Tolen's voice carrying over the sound of the engine and churning ocean. "There it is."

"There what is?" she said. His words had been so placid, the meaning had been lost on her. Then she saw the direction Tolen was pointing and turned to the south.

There, shadowed in the gray stone facing, was the triangular doorway of Formacion Descartes Santa Elena.

****

After a visit that morning to his sister Cecily at the German prison, Haufmer Langstrafenanstalt, Nicklaus Kappel had returned on Simon Anat's private jet to the estate in Switzerland. Ever since his boss had become a recluse due to his condition, it was one of the few perks: nearly unquestioned use of the man's private plane.

Kappel was surprised to see two of Anat's contemporaries—the obnoxious old Englishman, Walter Ganhaden, and the Brazilian, Shauna Veers, a woman whose face was so tight from cosmetic surgeries that her smile looked painted on—departing from the estate just as he arrived. As usual, his employer offered no explanation for their visit, and he did not bother to ask. During his tenure working for the billionaire, Anat had shared some of his most private thoughts with his personal assistant, yet the man also held some closely guarded secrets (like what lay behind the steel door on the second floor). Kappel's role was to listen, respond when asked, and never ask too many questions.

Kappel spent the rest of the afternoon and early evening catching up on his duties, which went unattended in his absence. As was usually the case these days, his employer seemed indifferent about where Kappel had gone with his jet or what he had been doing that morning.

Now, as evening fell, in the privacy of his office, Kappel checked to see if anyone had responded to his email. There was only one reply: Gordon Nunnery. Kappel vaguely recalled him from the gathering last year. He reached down and removed a thick folder from the bottom drawer. He thumbed through it until he came to Nunnery's file where he looked at the man's picture and dossier.

This is not a very imposing man, he thought. Then he smiled. Yet he's enough of a threat to keep things moving ahead on target.

CHAPTER 15

September 11. Tuesday – 3:01 p.m. Northwest Coast of Costa Rica

The ocean nestled against the sheer gray façade which towered above them, creating a deepwater shoreline. Fortunately, the base of the Formacion Descartes Santa Elena was just a step above the ocean surface, and, therefore, they would not have to scale the stone wall to enter.

Tolen brought the boat to within 150 feet of the land formation before cutting the engines. He purposely kept the vessel at a distance in case anyone came by. He wanted it to appear they were trying to conceal their activity, when in reality he welcomed any of the 'True Sons of Light' who wished to engage them.

After they weighed anchor, it took the efforts of both Tolen and Jade to get Diaz topside. The tough, roguish inspector was a mess; a puddle of queasy discomfort. They helped him into the small dinghy behind the boat. Diaz slumped in his seat and grabbed his head. "Please, God, make it stop," he said through deep, labored breaths. He looked up at Tolen, who was prepping the outboard motor to pull the cord. "At first I thought I was going to die," Diaz said, then formed his mouth as if to belch, yet nothing came out. His face was an unnatural shade of green. "Now I fear I'm going to live."

Jade looked at Tolen. A mild grin brushed across her face. "Maybe you should take his gun away from him."

"He'll be fine once we get to firm ground."

Tolen could sympathize with Diaz. He had become seasick, or motion sick as it is also called, as a child, the first time his father took him on the water. To this day, he recalled the horrid feeling of headache, nausea, and dizziness.

Tolen removed his jacket. Out of the corner of his eye, he saw Jade do a nearly imperceptible double-take when she noticed the linear scar on his right forearm. She refrained from asking the obvious question. Instead, she helped him load the tools—pickaxes, flashlights, rope, electric lanterns—into the dinghy. Then they took their seats. Tolen sat aft and cranked the small outboard motor. Diaz was in the middle, head down in his hands. Jade was on the bow, staring appreciatively at the formation in the slate wall.

Once the motor started, Tolen grabbed the tiller and aimed the small craft for the wall. The brisk wind and steady current forced Tolen to tack ahead, aiming to a point at the wall before the formation in order to offset the forces of nature.

Ahead, the triangular opening grew larger. The discovery of Joseph of Arimathea's tomb, if made, would be monumental. Not in his wildest dreams would he have foreseen the find of a biblical site in South America. The thought of it still seemed improbable.

The sunlight angled in from the west, lancing a shadow across the recessed opening and darkening the inside. In fact, there was no way to tell how deep the cave extended, because it faced due north, so the sunlight never reached very far inside.

Tolen had found no information to suggest anyone had ever ventured into the cavity. It was apparently relevant enough to have been named, yet not distinctive enough to be worthy of closer investigation—or at least no one had documented their findings. This was probably due to its inaccessibility.

Tolen looked to either side and behind. There were no boats visible on the horizon, only whitecaps dotting the vast blue terrain to the north. A cloudless sky stretched overhead. In the slower-moving craft, the sun's warmth intensified as the cool wind became shielded by the cliff facing. The air remained saturated with salt and sea. The rumbling motor propelled them forward despite the current's best effort to draw them backward.

"This is crazy," Diaz muttered, his face still in his hands. "No one traveled here from the Holy Lands across the ocean two thousand years ago."

"Actually," Tolen began, "in 1970, Thor Heyerdahl, a world-renowned explorer and archaeologist from Norway, sailed a twelve-meter papyrus boat from the old Phoenician port of Safi, Morocco to Barbados. His journey crossed the widest part of the Atlantic, some 3,200-plus miles. Heyerdahl proved that modern science has long underestimated early seafaring technology."

Jade gave him a subtle smile, apparently impressed once again with his knowledge.

Diaz offered no response other than to continue to bemoan his discomfort.

Nearing to within fifty feet of Formacion Descartes Santa Elena, Tolen cut the motor speed to half. Just then, the boat abruptly stopped, jerked forward, and stopped again. Tolen killed the engine.

Diaz lifted his head weakly. "What's....the matter?" he asked in a throaty voice.

Jade looked at Tolen with palpable concern.

Tolen lifted the motor by tugging on the powerhead and tilting the prop out of the water. The skeg, the extended piece that guards the prop, had impacted something under water. With the lower half of the motor now raised, he could see the twisted metal at the end. "There's a rock bed, or possibly a seamount just below the surface adjoined to the underwater base of the wall. We struck it."

"A subduction zone?" Jade asked.

"There's no way to know. We don't have a depth finder. It means we can't take the boat all the way in. Even if we kept the motor up and paddled, it's not worth the risk of slicing the bottom of the craft on a jutting piece of underwater structure. We'll have to swim the rest of the way. The tide is low, but rising. I'll pull the long lead rope to the formation, and we'll tie the boat up there so it doesn't drift away."

Jade looked down at the water. Diaz had plugged his face in his hands again.

Tolen opened a rear compartment and tossed a 25-pound anchor out from the stern. Then he tied it off on one of the cleats.

"How can we swim over there and carry the tools?" Jade asked, still eyeing the water. She seemed anxious.

Tolen removed three life jackets from underneath his seat.

He tossed one to each person. He grabbed the two pickaxes and, one at a time, launched them across the water into the Formacion Descartes Santa Elena where they landed with a clang and were lost from sight. He took the extra coil of rope and draped it over Diaz's shoulder and neck like a bandolero wearing a gun belt. The man hardly seemed to notice in his sickly state.

Tolen removed a large plastic bag from his pants pocket and proceeded to place the flashlights, electric lanterns, and his Springfield pistol inside. He motioned for Diaz's weapon, and the man groggily complied. Then Tolen closed the bag off, making sure it sealed shut, and tied it to the end of the bow rope. "Diaz, if you can get that coil of rope over, I'll get the rest as I take the bow rope. I'll go first, followed by you, then Jade. As I stretch out the bow rope, you can both use it as a guide. Hopefully, we'll avoid any jagged rock protrusions if we go slowly. Everyone take your time, and keep your shoes and clothes on," he said, happening to look at Jade.

"Did you think I was going to strip starkers before you two?" she asked, arching her eyebrows.

"Let's go," Tolen shrugged as he grabbed the plastic bag and lead rope. He slipped over the gunwale into the water.

Diaz pushed himself up and plopped over the side of the boat. Jade was last, entering the water tentatively. Next to the boat, the threesome stood upon a forest of jagged rocks four feet below the surface.

Even with the weight of the flashlights and lanterns, the plastic bag, with its pocket of air, remained buoyant. Tolen kept a firm grip on it as he started trudging forward. Diaz followed behind, and Jade fell in line after the two men.

With any luck, the stone protrusions at their feet would remain at the current depth and not impede their progress. As Tolen proceeded further ahead of them, the lead rope stretched out, and Diaz and Jade grabbed it as they went. Not surprisingly, the water was warm as the waves sloshed against Tolen's chest, slowing his progress.

Halfway to the opening, the pointed rocks below became increasingly deeper. The tips also sharpened. Without shoes, their feet would have been cut to shreds. Tolen was forced to swim, gliding into the teeth of the swells. In turn, Diaz and Jade also went horizontal, paddling across the surface. Tolen maintained a firm grip on the lead rope and plastic bag as he swam vigorously, knowing he only had to cover another fifteen feet. He was a strong swimmer, and even fully clothed, he cut through the swells. Within seconds, he reached a flat, underwater stone ledge which angled slightly upward into the shadows of the wall crevice. He climbed onto the dry stone, turned, and helped Diaz up, and then Jade. Tolen noticed a chalky smell as the threesome took a moment to remove their life jackets and allow their clothes to drain water. Tolen tied the end of the line around a fortuitous rock formation with a curved stone that created a small circle, perfect for his needs. Then he proceeded to open the plastic bag and disperse the flashlights and lanterns. He handed Diaz his pistol and returned his own weapon to his wet holster under his left arm. Each switched their flashlight on.

Reaching the Formacion Descartes Santa Elena was easier than he had expected. Yet when he looked into the cave where the lights cut through the shadows, Tolen knew the real challenge was just beginning.

There was a three-foot-high, uneven rectangular opening in the back left corner of the recess. It was irregular enough to be the work of nature, but precise enough to be manmade. Tolen made his way over to it, knelt down, and shined his flashlight inside. "There's another cave." He crabbed through, and Diaz and Jade followed.

This second cave was clearly natural with its seven-foot scabrous ceiling. It was also completely empty. A dozen feet in, it ended at a wall of craggy black-and-gray stone. There were no other outlets.

They were at a dead end.

CHAPTER 16

September 11. Tuesday – 3:33 p.m. Northwest Coast of Costa Rica

"There's nothing here," Diaz remarked. Jade noticed his voice sounded nearly human again. The stable footing had cured his seasickness almost immediately.

As Tolen surveyed the walls and floor, Jade detected a faint burnt smell.

"Someone has been here," Tolen said as he moved to the rear left corner of the cave floor and kicked at a low, dark pile of soot. Dust stirred into the air. "Ashes. Probably from a campfire. No telling how long it's been here."

Jade shot him a discouraged look.

"It doesn't mean someone found the tomb. May have simply been someone seeking shelter," Tolen tried to reassure her.

She appreciated his attempt to mollify her, but she was not convinced. She desperately wanted this to have been Joseph's tomb.

Jade turned and felt the rock edge along the lower rectangular entrance they had passed through. "This opening is manmade. See? There are tool marks," her voice gained back some enthusiasm.

"What does it matter?" Diaz said. "There's nothing here."

Jade strolled to the left wall and began to examine it. Tolen flicked on one of the electric lanterns, throwing suffused light about the room.

"The cave appears natural," Tolen remarked.

"I would agree," Jade said, sliding the tips of her fingers along the smooth surface. Tolen and Diaz came to her side.

Diaz remained disinterested. "We got soaking wet for nothing,

102

and now I get to ride back in that boat while my stomach turns in knots again. It's time to leave this treasure hunt and talk to the authorities about Dr. Phillip Cherrigan's death. Time is running out."

Jade spun around. "We're not going *anywhere* until I've had a chance to examine this room." Her words were clipped, her tone annoyed.

Diaz offered a single grunt and took a seat on the stone floor. "You do what you have to do. Then we're leaving."

Jade's eyes shot daggers at the man. She started to turn away in disgust then wheeled back on Diaz. "Do you realize the discovery of artifacts which could validate Jesus' existence would be earth-shattering?"

"One does not need physical evidence to know that Jesus existed and was the Son of God," Diaz responded calmly.

"That's the point, Diaz," Jade said. "You don't require tangible evidence, since your beliefs hinge on your faith; but a cache of Jesus' possessions, incontrovertibly tied to the man, would be proof to others who may not have the level of faith you possess."

Diaz's brow furrowed. "You speak of this cache as if we don't already have objects from His past, when, in fact, we do. The Sudarium, the Shroud of Turin...those linens once touched the body of the Savior." Irritation had crept back into his voice.

"Even you must realize, Diaz, there's no way to prove the authenticity of either relic indisputably," Jade added. "These, too, must be categorized as items of faith."

Diaz looked incensed. "So you think the Sudarium is a fake?"

Jade tightened visibly. "I never said that." *Stay calm.* "My understanding is there's no positive proof to claim it even existed in the first century."

"It's mentioned in the Bible!" Diaz fumed, his rising agitation evident.

Tolen responded calmly. "If archaeologists could find tangible evidence, those who doubt Jesus' historical existence would be forced to accept the truth. The find would be monumental for both historians and biblical pundits."

To Jade, Tolen seemed introspective as he spoke this time.

"There's also the possibility that the earthly objects of Jesus may be referring to his remains," Jade said. She was thinking as an archaeologist, but even as the words left her lips, she realized it was a mistake to bring up the point in Diaz's presence.

"His...what?" Diaz screwed his face. "There *are* no earthly remains of Jesus Christ! Have you not read the biblical account of the resurrection?! I will listen to no more of this blasphemy!"

Jade gave up on Diaz. She continued to guide her fingers over the wall, keeping the flashlight in her other hand to provide focused light.

Tolen spoke, "What are you hoping to find, Jade?"

"Another symbol like we found on the Harvard sphere, perhaps," She turned to Tolen, her hazel eyes pleading as she lowered her voice. "This has to be the place. The description matches the clue so perfectly. There's got to be something we're missing."

Tolen joined Jade at the rock face, and the two meticulously inspected the left wall. It took about twenty minutes to examine every square inch, but they found nothing unusual—no images or symbols. It was merely a flat wall of stone. Jade turned and drifted to the wall behind them.

Tolen looked at the wall where Jade now stood, then at the back wall. Diaz was seated in the middle of the room watching them. He had unshouldered the rope, taken his shirt off, and was wringing the seawater out of it.

"Let's examine this one next," Tolen said, motioning to the rear wall.

Jade followed his recommendation.

The two began studying the wall judiciously. It appeared to be the same as the other three walls. Tolen stepped back and studied it momentarily.

By now, Diaz had also come over to see as he struggled to get his wet shirt back on.

Without a word, Tolen left the room through the low rectangular opening and returned seconds later with a pickaxe. He used the point to tap on the left wall, then the right. Jade heard the distinct thuds. These were solid stone walls.

He moved beside Jade and Diaz and tapped on various places

104

along the entire back wall. Each time he rapped on the stone surface, he heard a distinctive tinny sound, unique from the other walls.

Jade's eyes lit. "It's hollow," she said, nearly breathless. "This is a false wall!"

Diaz remained nonplussed.

Jade turned to Tolen. "How did you know?"

"It's the only wall precisely perpendicular to the floor." He aimed his flashlight to the right. "That wall is slightly leaning in; the other two leaning away. Those walls are what you'd expect in a natural formation, but this wall is perfectly vertical. It may be manmade."

"Diaz, please go get the other pickaxe and give me a hand."

Diaz left the room. Tolen began to chip away at the wall. It gave way easily. Whatever the wall's composition, it was not solid stone.

By the time Diaz returned, Tolen had forged a tiny opening through the six-inch-thick wall. The instant he broke through, Jade signaled for him to halt. She crowded against the wall and aimed the flashlight through the opening. She placed her hand to her forehead as she felt her face flush. She could hardly believe the sight before her. Her next words came out excitedly, "There's a large chamber beyond this wall. I believe it's the tomb!"

She could barely contain herself as she stared back in awe through the opening. The rush of excitement caused her to shake. Before she knew it, Tolen had placed an arm around her for support as he moved beside her, glimpsing inside using his own flashlight.

Even Diaz seemed stunned by the visage beyond. "It's unbelievable," he said, his mouth gaping open.

Jade turned to Tolen. As if the fog suddenly cleared from her mind, Jade looked down at Tolen's arm and awkwardly pulled away from his grasp. "I'm…I'm fine," she stuttered. She looked at Diaz, who was still transfixed before the opening. "Do you believe me now?" she called to him.

Diaz said nothing. He silently picked up the axe and went to work on the wall. Tolen joined him.

It was only a matter of minutes before they created an opening large enough for them to pass through. There was no hesitancy from Jade, who promptly went first, her flashlight stabbing into the dark hole where she disappeared. Diaz followed, and Tolen passed through last, each carrying a lantern and a flashlight. Diaz once again had the coil of rope hoisted upon his shoulder.

Even by flashlight, Jade could tell the place was enormous. As soon as they turned their electric lanterns on, she gasped. The cavernous chamber was immense, like the interior of a massive cathedral. The circular walls curved upward, creating a lofty dome overhead. The room seemed to self-illuminate, the result of bright, bold images which adorned the ceiling: colorful pictures in hues of every color, orchestrated together in an elaborate fresco depicting men and angels, prophets and beggars, kings and servants, soldiers and priests.

All three stood in place, marveling at the sight.

"This is extraordinary!" Jade said in awe, her British accent heightened by her excitement.

****

Tolen felt a chill race over his body. It was either from his still-damp clothes or the undeniable excitement he now felt. The dust became strong in his nostrils, and he could taste the flavor of ancient stone with each inhale. The chalky aroma was not pure; it blended with something else he could not distinguish.

Around the chamber at ground level were niches carved into the walls every dozen feet or so. Each niche had a waist-high ledge containing a stone-carved cross. No two crosses were the same; each varied in height and width. Equally as remarkable, a large pond dominated the majority of the room. The base had apparently been carved out to form a subterranean pocket filled with fresh water. Where they stood, a narrow walkway ran the perimeter of the entire room, encircling the pond.

There was absolute silence as they took in the grandeur of this monstrous cavity and the spectacle of its features and intricate artwork. It was unlike anything Samuel Tolen had ever seen. He felt a mild touch of reverence.

Tolen turned to look at the niche behind when he heard Jade

audibly inhale a second time. He spun around to see what had caught her attention. Diaz was already staring out at the water.

"My God," Jade said, "look." She pointed to the center of the large pond.

Tolen spotted a miniscule round island slightly elevated from the surface of the pond; a gray dimple in the middle of the watery landscape. It appeared as a hump, made of smooth stone and no more than nine feet in circumference.

This was not what had caused Jade's reaction, however. It was the large circular boulder sitting in the middle of the island that had made her gasp.

"It's another stone sphere!" she exclaimed.

CHAPTER 17

September 11. Tuesday – 4:19 p.m. Northwest Coast of Costa Rica

It all felt so surreal to Jade. It was the archaeological discovery of a lifetime; of a hundred lifetimes.

Without much thought, she sank to the stone floor and began taking off her wet tennis shoes.

"What are you doing?" Diaz asked.

"That stone over there is our next clue," she said, tugging off one shoe. "Look around. The tomb's not in here, but it must be nearby. That sphere will tell us where it is. The first jar is probably inside it, like the roll of parchment was inside the stone sphere at Harvard."

Tolen stepped to the edge of the walkway and looked down at the water with a flashlight beam cutting through the surface. "I'd advise against swimming, Jade." He bent down, placed a finger in the water, and raised it to his lips.

"You can advise all you want. Nothing's going to stop me from getting over to that tiny island and examining that stone."

Tolen pointed down. "It's saltwater. I didn't recognize the scent before. It was masked by other smells."

"Salt...fresh...doesn't matter," Jade said, ripping off her second shoe and rising.

Tolen continued. "The water is very deep. It's not a gradual drop off like a beach. The flashlight beam doesn't reach the bottom."

"I know how to swim," she said, making her way beside him.

She started to squat in preparation for lowering herself into the water when Tolen grabbed her firmly by the underarm and kept her standing.

"What the bloody hell are—!" she cut herself off. Where Tolen had aimed the beam into the water, a large, dark, torpedo-like shape flashed by underneath the surface. She involuntarily gulped so hard her throat burned.

"What in God's name was that?" Diaz barked.

She saw another black form move past. This time it had a wide, thick, perpendicular appendage at the front of a body of considerable girth and length. Surprisingly, it turned and was lost from view underneath where they stood on the perimeter walkway.

"What we're standing on is not solid," Tolen said. "It's a ledge over water and runs in a circle along the wall of this room. Somewhere below, probably underneath the ledge, this pond leads out to the ocean. This ocean water was already in this cave before Joseph of Arimathea carved this room. It's a natural body of water."

Jade continued to stare into the water. Ghostly large figures moved by more frequently now. Each had the trademark feature jutting out to either side of its head. "Hammerhead sharks," she finally realized with a sigh.

"Not good," Diaz added.

"Hammerheads rarely attack humans, but as I said before, I would advise against going in the water with them."

Jade felt a sting of defeat.

Unexpectedly, Diaz pulled his pistol and aimed it at the water.

"Please don't," Tolen commanded firmly. "That will complicate any chance we have of making it to that stone. If you fill the water with blood, even shark's blood, you'll create a feeding frenzy that will exacerbate the situation."

Diaz eyed Tolen with disdain. It was obvious to Jade the inspector did not like being told what to do. For a moment, they remained locked in a stare.

"Let's reconnoiter the cavern to see if there are other options," Tolen finally said breaking the silence.

Diaz grimaced momentarily then begrudgingly re-holstered his weapon.

Jade watched Tolen as he used his flashlight to examine the walls and ceiling. Something in the distance caught his interest.

"There's a cone extending down from the ceiling. It appears to be directly over the small island."

Jade raised her flashlight beam above the island. Sure enough, nine or ten feet up, the cave dipped to a point like a large stalactite. "Manmade?"

"Not sure. Leave one of the lanterns here, and we'll take the other two." Tolen began walking counterclockwise, following the stone pavement along the wall. Jade fell into formation behind Tolen and Diaz, eyeing the water nervously and remaining as close to the wall as possible.

They passed one niche after another. Jade longed to stop and examine each of them, but that would have to wait for another time. Each unique cross was carved out of natural rock polished to a smooth shine and was adjoined to the solid stone altar. Some had squared sides, some had rounded edges. The craftsmanship of these ornate crosses was unsurpassed. By her reckoning, in order to complete the several dozen in the room, plus the idyllic frescoes upon the domed ceiling, it would have taken either many years or many artists working on them simultaneously, or both. Joseph of Arimathea's stories of Jesus must have had a dramatic effect on the locals to garner the amount of skilled artistic labor needed to create this magnificent place.

She looked across the water at the large stone mounted upon the island as they followed Tolen. It seemed perfectly round, and much larger than the Harvard courtyard stone. Jade now wondered if this sphere on the tiny island might have been the first stone sphere carved; the parent of all the rest the Costa Rican villagers created over the last two millennia.

Then an even more astounding thought struck her: *Could this be the original stone which once covered Jesus' tomb?*

The thought was mind-boggling, and she shook it off just as Tolen came to an abrupt stop. They were about a third of the way around the circular cavern. The craggy entryway was still visible across the water where they had left the first lantern.

Tolen faced one of the niches. He looked at Jade. "Why do you think the stone sphere was placed in the center of the room where it's inaccessible?"

"It may be a test. We're not supposed to be able to get to it easily."

"Very unlikely," Diaz retorted. "You think someone wanted to test *our* fortitude 2,000 years after constructing this place?"

"Not necessarily us, but *someone*," Jade responded. "Why leave clues and riddles? Joseph of Arimathea wanted someone who was righteous and diligent to follow the path he had laid out."

"Look," Tolen pointed to the niche at their side.

It was not that different from the others they had passed, although the cross was the smallest one yet. Jade knelt down to examine it closely, drawing her flashlight to illuminate the small cross and the concave wall behind. There were tiny dark splotches near the four ends of the cross, and more dark stains scattered on the wall at the rear.

Jade looked over her shoulder at the men quizzically. "Blood?"

Diaz squatted, nudging beside her. He seemed just as intrigued as she was. "What could it mean?"

"This is the starting point," Tolen said.

Jade rose, not understanding the message Tolen was trying to convey.

Tolen spoke, "If you're trying to reach a destination, there are always three possible choices: ground level, which, in our case means swimming through shark-infested waters; underground, which is obviously not an option; or, lastly, above ground."

Tolen guided the beam up the gray wall immediately above the niche. Jade followed the light. She spotted a small groove of cutout stone with a solid piece the thickness of a broom handle embedded within. She had no idea what she was seeing until Tolen roamed the light upward, and continued to trace a path to the ceiling and out over the water. The procession of carved handholds continued every several feet, blending into the fresco overhead, and finally stopping at the point of the inverted cone which stretched downward toward the tiny center island.

It was a way to get to the stone sphere.

CHAPTER 18

September 11. Tuesday – 4:41 p.m. Northwest Coast of Costa Rica

Jade appraised the line of handholds cut into the stone. It was a test, she thought, not only of spiritual belief, but of strength.

Tolen wasted no time. He pocketed his flashlight and stepped onto the niche altar, avoiding the small cross. The first handhold was at the top of the six-foot-high niche. He gained a grip and hoisted himself up using only his arms. His muscles tightened like a twist of iron, and he pulled himself upward and grabbed the next handhold with his free hand. Once again, Jade noticed the lengthy scar on Tolen's right forearm and wondered what had been the cause.

Although she kept in shape, Jade knew this was going to be difficult. She had been a gymnast in college, but that had been more years ago than she cared to consider. She tried mentally to block out the fact they would be moving over water where sharks awaited any slip.

"Jade, you go next," Tolen said, after lifting high enough to lock a foot in the lowest handhold.

Jade jumped up on the small altar and grabbed the first handhold. She was straining to support her weight while she reached to grab the next one. Tolen snagged her hand and pulled her up. It had been unasked-for assistance, and she did not appreciate the assumption she needed help. She looked up and started to object, but then saw the earnest gaze in Tolen's eyes. It was not one of pity, but of caring. Once Jade secured her grip, Tolen turned and continued to climb. Jade followed, but at a slower pace. Soon Diaz was also scaling the wall, muttering and complaining.

Once she got her feet in the holds, the climb became much easier. The light from below elongated her silhouette, casting an eerie shadow on the wall above. She moved slowly, ensuring each grip before she released the other hand. The walls were cold and reeked of dust, and the only sound in the massive chamber was the heavy breathing and grunting as the threesome climbed.

Tolen quickly arrived at the curvature of the domed ceiling. "This is where it gets tough," he called back down.

Jade paused and looked down. Diaz was laboring to catch up. She wondered if the man was up for the challenge.

Below, the lanterns kept the cavern lit, but the surface of the water remained dark. Jade saw black shapes patrolling the depths, indistinguishable forms swishing past as if waiting for their opportunity to feast. They occasionally created large eddies where their hulking bodies meandered close to the surface. Jade felt her breath catch at the sight. She paused and looked away from the water, staring at the wall inches from her face. She had to remain calm and fight the panic that was on the verge of setting in. Jade took a deep breath, exhaled, and looked up at Tolen.

Tolen swung out to one of the handholds at the curvature and was now dangling precariously. Jade watched him stretch to the next higher handhold. He moved slowly. The handholds here were closer together, accommodating the strenuous climb. When Tolen was four handholds away, Jade followed.

She was not prepared for the pain which enveloped her arms and shoulders as she strained to secure her grip to each new, higher hold as the ceiling curved up. It was a grueling endeavor, and she forced the thought of both the pain and the sharks from her mind. Beads of sweat broke out on her arms, face, and neck, and she prayed her hands would not become slippery. Her muscles ached, and her body twisted back and forth as she slowly proceeded. On and on she went, pulling herself up and over, following in Tolen's path. Behind, she could hear Diaz struggle as he breathed mightily.

As she went, she was vaguely aware of the marvelous artwork on the ceiling. She was too preoccupied to pay it much attention, yet she knew it was truly masterful. Even after all this time, the faint smell of paint oils was still detectable, commingling with the aged stone.

Ahead, she saw Tolen moving lithely, swinging from side to side as he pirouetted in mid-air from one handhold to the next. She followed after him steadily, trying to ignore the intense burning of her arms. When she had secured her very next hold, she ventured a look back at Diaz. The man was closer than she had expected; his face red from the effort. Sweat was pouring from his brow, and he grimaced as he went. "This is *not* where I imagined myself: hovering above hammerhead sharks!" He shouted cynically.

Suddenly, a harsh pop sounded. Jade was so startled she nearly lost her grip. She struggled to secure two hands on a single handhold as the echo bounced from the far side of the massive cave. She looked down toward the direction of the sound. Near the entrance was a man clad in dark pants and a light shirt holding something. There was a flash of light and another resounding pop. Jade felt something whiz by her face. Rock fragments scattered above her head, ricocheting into her cheek.

The man was shooting at them!

"What the hell?!" Diaz yelled from behind.

Jade looked to Tolen in desperation. Her mind was reeling, and she was seconds away from losing her grip on the handholds. Everything was happening so quickly. She watched Tolen reach to his holster and withdraw his pistol as he held on with one hand. He swiveled his body in the air and fired a shot at the man.

In the distance, the man seemed surprised and dropped to his knees. He lifted the rifle and fired again. This time the shot struck the ceiling near Tolen. The CIA agent had drawn the gunfire away from Jade. Tolen fired two times in succession, but he was unable to steady his body, and the shots missed. One struck the water near the ledge where the man now knelt. The man returned fire, and in a horrifying instant, Jade watched Tolen wince, let go of his grip and freefall to the water some 35 feet below. He landed with a loud splash.

Jade could barely comprehend what had just happened. "Tolen!" she screamed.

"*Mierda!*" Diaz screeched from behind her. A second later, she heard another large splash.

She looked down to see Diaz break the surface as gargantuan shadows hovered around him.

Tolen was nowhere in sight.

A chill swept up her spine and filled her very being. She was the last one hanging and was completely vulnerable. Jade did not have the nerve to look back at the shooter. She knew what was coming. Her arms were cramping, and she could barely hang on. She felt a wave of nausea as she braced for the inevitable.

The sharp crack of gunshot was immediately followed by a burning sensation on her forearm. The sight of the blood pooling on her skin, more than the pain, caused her to jerk and release the stone handle with both hands. The fall happened so fast there was no time for her to think. The next thing she knew, she was under water with saltwater burning her nostrils.

In a moment of morbid fear, she opened her eyes. Amidst rising air bubbles, she saw devilish looking creatures swimming nearby, so close she could have reached out and touched them. Their wide snouts cut through the water like long, flat razorblades, leading thick torsos and arcing tailfins. Beyond, more of the dark, cloudy shapes moved aimlessly. There were too many to count. She screamed inwardly in terror, struggling to keep her mouth closed and hold her breath.

She now saw the dark tendril of fluid spinning into the water from her stinging arm. The bullet had grazed her, and she was bleeding into the water. She froze in horror.

Then a primal urge took over. Her lungs burned for air. Instinctively, Jade clawed and raked her way to the surface. A long, slimy object slid against her, and she thought her heart would burst from her chest. She continued to push upward, bursting through the surface, gasping harsh lungfuls of air.

Jade tread water as large hammerheads swirled by her, brushing her legs as she kicked. Each time they made contact, she yelled, expecting to feel teeth ripping at her flesh. Her breathing became uncontrollable, and she felt as if she were going to hyperventilate.

Then it happened.

The strike came at her shoulders. She was yanked backward

with force. She loosed a bloodcurdling scream. In a panic she fought to break the hold, yelling and slapping the water around her.

"Stop! Stop!" she heard the familiar voice call from behind her. "Jade, stop fighting me!"

It took a moment for her to realize it was Diaz. He was trying to pull her away from the mass of hammerheads converging upon her.

She was only vaguely aware that the lantern near the cave entrance had been extinguished. The man with the rifle was no longer visible in the dim light.

"We have to get to the island!" Diaz yelled. A series of pops struck the water around them. One narrowly missed Diaz.

The man on shore was still firing from the concealing darkness. Jade heard a bullet sizzle by her ear as a sense of impending doom enveloped her.

"Swim...now!" Diaz commanded.

Jade did not have time to think. She merely turned, spotted the island 20 feet away, and began stroking toward it. Even with her aching arms and the laceration from the bullet wound, she pushed on. The mammoth body of a hammerhead bumped against her, sending her into a frenzied churn through the water. With each stroke, she prayed the sharks would not attack.

When her feet struck solid stone, she realized she had reached a ramping plateau which led up to the tiny stone surface of the island, but her progress was impeded before she could clear the water. The smooth, slanted sides of the island's underwater surface made it impossible to scale. For the moment, she would have to remain in the shallow water. Diaz threw the wet coil of rope ahead onto the dry stone and directed her to the backside of the island where they could take partial cover behind the large stone sphere. Bullets continued to whiz past intermittently, striking the water nearby.

Jade was uneasy about still being submerged in the water, but in reality, she knew it was too shallow for the hulking hammerheads to reach them here. At least for the moment, they were safe from the sharks and out of the shooter's line of fire, but it would not be long until the attacker moved around the room's circular ledge to get a clear shot. They could avoid him for a while by shifting around the stone, but for how long?

"Mierda! I lost my gun in the fall," Diaz cursed.

Diaz pushed his wet hair back over his forehead. His features softened into a look of uncertainty. Jade recognized the expression for what it was: pessimism regarding their chances of survival. It shook her to the core.

"Do you have any other weapons?" she asked.

"I only have this," he said, reaching to his ankle under his pant leg. He withdrew a knife from a scabbard.

A knife was no defense against a man with a rifle 70 feet away. As bullets continued to strike the water nearby, an equally disheartening thought struck her.

Samuel Tolen was dead.

CHAPTER 19

September 11. Tuesday – 5:14 p.m. Northwest Coast of Costa Rica

Gordon Nunnery was not a killer by nature. He had been spurred on by mankind's deepest, darkest desire. He had made the choice, carried it through, and was now engaged in a gunfight. Fortunately for him, he had a far better vantage point than the two hiding in the water behind the large, round rock on the backside of the blip of an island.

He repositioned his Browning Semi-Automatic Grade VI Blued rifle and tried to sight the targets. He had never been much of a hunter, and, although light and compact, the weapon felt awkward. The site was off, but he only found that out when he fired the first few shots as his targets hung from the cave ceiling.

Still, he had hit the lead man and dropped him into the water. Nunnery had wondered if he could kill a human being when it came time. Strangely, he felt unaffected.

The end justifies the means, he thought.

The middle-aged man continued to monitor the stone, firing now and then. He was waiting for a head to poke out from the side so he could get a clean shot. He had been caught off guard when the black man suspended by one hand had returned fire, but the couple now hiding behind the large round stone seemed to be unarmed.

Nunnery sat on the stone floor, his legs drawn close to his chest at the water's edge. He rested his elbows on his knees to support the rifle and steady his aim. Nunnery considered repositioning by moving around the perimeter walkway, but the couple would be expecting it, and they could easily avoid him by swiveling around the island, thus keeping the stone between their two positions. In this manner, they could continually evade him. Sure, he might get off a shot or two, but he had no desire to move, at least not yet. He felt comfortable here in the shadows after dousing the lantern. Once the tide crept up, they would be forced to make a move. He would simply wait them out.

He drew back from the rifle sight and scanned the still water. To the right, a lantern was lit on the walkway, illuminating the lavish, decorative paintings on the domed ceiling which reflected off the mirrored surface of the water. What a remarkable sight it was with its vibrant colors and artistry. This large chamber looked and smelled ancient. Surely this was a priceless discovery in its own right. He wondered how the three had ever found this place.

Just then, Nunnery caught a fleeting shadow out of the corner of his eye. He wheeled around, with his rifle at the ready. The formless figure came at him in an instant. Nunnery had no time to react. He inadvertently squeezed the trigger, firing a hapless shot into the stone wall. Then he felt a hard impact to his skull that he never saw coming. His vision blurred, and he was aware of the weapon being pulled from his hands after the fact. He let it slip from his grasp as easily as if he were offering it away.

Nunnery reeled against the stone wall. His vision cleared enough for him to make out the black man standing to the side. Water was dripping from his clothes. Surprisingly, the man was unarmed. Nunnery lurched toward him with his hands outstretched, but the man was lightning quick and defended himself by dodging to the side so that Nunnery completely missed and fell hard, his head impacting the stone surface near the edge of the ledge. Disoriented, he staggered to his feet, nearly toppling into the water. His head throbbed as if a freight train was tunneling through it. The black man stood quietly nearby, unmoving.

The world flickered and spun, then slowly settled into a static scene as he caught his balance. A gash on his forehead sent a warm flow of blood down his face, burning into his right eye. Nunnery knew he was defeated. He slowly raised his hands in a gesture of surrender.

There was a *tink*, and then something struck his leg. Startled, he shuffled backward, but the stone floor evaporated below his foot. He teetered and then plunged, staring upward at the maze of colors on the ceiling mural, as he struck the water. The colors danced, and the images faded in and out until they were swallowed up through his watery visage. Gordon Nunnery felt a tremendous grip of pain to his head just before his world fell into dark oblivion.

****

Surprised, Tolen looked to the stone floor at the object that had come to rest after striking the shooter's leg. It was a long knife with a serrated blade. He turned and saw Pascal Diaz kneeling beside the stone island, half submerged. Tolen quickly moved to the edge and looked into the water. There was a commotion of activity several feet below the surface; the signature attack pattern of several large sharks wracking their heads back and forth. The man had gone under and disappeared into a carnal feeding frenzy.

The last thing Tolen had wanted was the attacker to be killed. They needed to question the man.

"Are you okay?!" Jade yelled, appearing beside Diaz.

Tolen was furious. They had just lost their only lead to the 'True Sons of Light' and to Boyd Ramsey. "Why did you throw a knife?!"

Diaz appeared baffled. "I…thought," he hesitated, "you were fighting with him. The darkness makes it difficult to see what was happening. Is he dead?"

"Sharks got him," Tolen said. He noticed a coat on the ground near the wall. He knelt down and grabbed it, trying to temper his anger. Inside, he found a wallet containing a Saskatchewan driver's license with the name Gordon Nunnery. First an American had attacked them at Harvard, and now a Canadian had attacked them in Costa Rica. Tolen fanned through the rest of the man's wallet. The only thing he found of interest was a receipt in German from a dry cleaner in Switzerland. Nothing suggested affiliation with a radical group.

Tolen rose and moved to the side where the rifle lay. He kicked a shell casing out of the way, picked the weapon up, and examined it from the stock to the end of the barrel. He checked the load: .22

caliber bullets.

It made no sense.

"I'll be back," Tolen said. He took the weapon and stepped through the aperture in the wall leading into the smaller cave. He slid underneath the low opening into the second, outer cave. He was anxious to know if anyone else had accompanied Mr. Nunnery. If so, they were most likely waiting in a boat nearby. When Tolen reached the entrance to Formacion Descartes Santa Elena, though, he saw their dinghy bounding on the choppy water nearby and their larger vessel beyond. No other vessels were in sight.

Tolen noticed a second rope tied off at the small rock formation where their dinghy was tethered. The rope was taut and pulled hard to the right, running along the stone to the side of the Formacion Descartes Santa Elena. He leaned out, following it with his eyes. A jet ski was nuzzled into the stone wall, scraping against the rock facing with each swell. The man had come by himself.

Tolen returned to the cathedral cave after tossing the rifle into the ocean water.

"Everything okay?" Diaz called.

"I'm coming over."

Tolen had swum through the mix of hammerheads after feigning being shot and falling into the water. His knowledge of their aggressiveness, or lack thereof, toward humans had not been mistaken, and he passed through them without incident to the far side of the cave. By pressing into the wall and moving slowly, he had kept to the shadows and come up behind Gordon Nunnery so that he could take him alive.

The end result, though, was not what he had hoped for.

The subsequent shark attack on Nunnery had surprised Tolen. Something had contributed to their newfound aggressiveness. Now, looking into the black water, he saw there were considerably more bodies lurking below the surface than before, and their frenetic activity had increased. No longer were the large creatures moving lackadaisically; now they were slicing through the water, darting this way and that. Tolen caught an unwanted sight: the tail fin of a bull shark cutting across the top of the water…and then a second one. The smell of blood had brought more ferocious creatures into the mix. Bull sharks, noted for their unpredictable and aggressive behavior, are thought to have killed more humans than any other shark, including great whites. With the introduction of these man-eaters, the situation had indeed worsened and sealed Gordon Nunnery's fate.

In order to rejoin Jade and Diaz, Tolen would have to make his way to the small island as they originally started: via the ceiling handholds.

Several minutes later, Tolen had traversed the wall and dome via the handhold path. The task got particularly tough when he arrived at the downward cone over the tiny island. He used the handholds to back down to the point and then drop the nine feet to the hard surface where he adeptly landed on his feet beside the large stone sphere. Using the rope Diaz had tossed on the dry surface, he pulled Jade and Diaz off the slippery, sloping sides and onto the island.

Tolen noticed Jade applying pressure to her forearm. "Are you okay?"

She nodded, "It's a flesh wound...not deep. I've almost got the bleeding stopped."

Tolen ripped off a strip of cloth from the bottom of his shirt and tied it around the wound as a makeshift tourniquet.

He turned to Diaz. "Because of you, our only lead to the 'True Sons of Light' is dead," Tolen said, staring the man squarely in the eyes. He was still irritated at Diaz's carelessness at throwing a knife and causing Nunnery to slip into the water.

"I thought your life was in danger. Don't bother thanking me," Diaz swelled visibly with anger as he stepped toward Tolen, crowding in until they were nearly thumping chests.

Jade wedged between the two with her hands. "Enough testosterone." She turned to Tolen. "Don't blame him. I thought I saw a glint of metal as well. We thought he had a handgun. The light was dim, and I agreed with Diaz that he should throw the knife and try to distract him."

The two men slowly separated, although they never broke eye contact.

"Who was he?" Diaz asked in an annoyed tone, rubbing a finger at the side of his nose.

"His name was Gordon Nunnery. Apparently, he was another recruit of the 'True Sons of Light.' He showed up exactly as we had hoped, but his timing was less than optimal."

Tolen noticed Jade was already busy looking over the stone sphere. He turned away from Diaz and addressed her, "Is this one of the stone spheres from the Palmar Sur area?"

"It's definitely manmade. I can see the chisel marks. My guess is *yes*."

"Find any writing?" Diaz asked. "Maybe it has a cavity like that stone in the States."

"We'll know soon enough." She continued to examine the stone intently using her water-resistant flashlight. Tolen and Diaz joined in, and all three studied the stone's exterior for some time before Jade stepped back and exhaled in disappointment. "I don't get it. Where is the clue? Where is Joseph of Arimathea's tomb?"

Tolen considered the stone. One curious aspect of it was that it sat in what appeared to be a circular depression. This meant several feet of the stone lay in a recess, which made the underside impossible to examine. The reason it had been placed in the depression was obvious. The architects of this place had done so to hold the sphere in place.

Jade stepped beside Tolen, warily looking to the surface of the water only a few feet away. The smell of the saltwater was particularly strong. A dorsal fin split the surface nearby, turned sharply, and disappeared. "We need to check the underside. It's all that's left," she said.

Tolen nodded. "Diaz, give me a hand. Let's nudge this stone out of its mount. As soon as we do, we'll have to get to the other side to stop it from rolling off this slope."

Diaz joined Tolen to one side of the stone. Jade stood to the side. The two men placed their hands upon the curved surface and pushed in unison.

The sphere didn't budge.

"Again," Tolen said.

Both men heaved, and there was a slight give at the base as it rocked momentarily then settled back in place.

"One more time," Tolen commanded.

"It's too heavy," Diaz said.

"Again," Tolen said calmly. He closed his eyes, focusing his store of strength. "On the count of three." Tolen counted off, and they pushed hard. Unexpectedly, Jade slipped between them and helped with a healthy shove to the stone. It was just enough extra force to cause the sphere to teeter and then break free from the depression, but before either man could regain his balance and move to the front side, the stone rolled off the small slope and into the water. They watched with chagrin as it continued rolling lazily down the side of the underwater mount, sinking deeper and deeper into the water until the top disappeared below the surface. It sent a wake rolling across the surface where it reached the perimeter ledge.

"Bloody hell! We'll never see it now!" Jade yelled as the last air bubbles popped on the surface where it had submerged. A shark fin broke the water and cruised nearby. The desperation in Jade's face caused her cheeks to flush.

While Jade and Diaz stared out at the water in disappointment, Tolen turned to where the stone had rested. He moved to the recess at the center of the small island. He stopped and looked down. *Of course*. He turned back to the others. "The stone wasn't the clue."

Jade and Diaz turned at the same time. Jade asked, "What do you mean?"

Where the sphere had been locked in place, the depression appeared bottomless. The massive stone had plugged a hole two-and-one-half feet in diameter. Tolen looked into the dark opening. Then he looked at Jade with a slight smile. "The stone was the doorway. There are stairs leading down."

CHAPTER 20

September 11. Tuesday – 5:44 p.m. Northwest Coast of Costa Rica

With flashlight in hand, Jade lowered herself through the circular hole. There was a small stone platform four feet below the opening. One at a time, they dropped down to it. Tolen opted to go last, searching the shadows of the cave for movement to ensure they were alone. Just before he lowered himself, he happened to look at the water in relation to the small island. What was once an area nine feet across had compressed to roughly seven feet in diameter. The island had shrunk. Also, he noticed the circular hole was polished at the edges and beveled inward. A sticky substance, like sap, rimmed the edges.

Suddenly, the design of the tiny island with the stone sphere made sense.

He lowered himself through the hole. The steps were braced by the stone wall on the right. The left side of the staircase was open, and their flashlights revealed a small manmade room to that side with perfectly carved stone walls.

Once on the platform, they proceeded down the steps in single file, stooping to avoid hitting their heads on the ceiling until they were low enough to stand erect. A malodorous aroma thickened as they descended.

Only after they had reached the bottom of the sixteen-step staircase and looked about the enclosure with their flashlights did they discover a corridor leading from the room. Before going any further, Tolen looked at his watch with concern.

"What is the matter?" Diaz asked.

"The tide is rising. The stone sphere sealed this opening for two millennia, and now that we've uncorked the chamber, it will soon flood with seawater once the incoming tide rises over the island. There is no way to stop it. My best estimate is we have thirty minutes. If we stay down here any longer, we'll drown in the incoming tidewater."

"Then let's get going," Jade urged. "We have a tunnel to explore."

Diaz was less than enthusiastic and stared at his watch. Before he could object, Jade began moving away.

With their flashlights stabbing the darkness, Tolen and Diaz followed her down the narrow tunnel leading away from the entry room. The corridor was tight with a seven-foot ceiling. The passageway had been carved from the rock and the walls and ceiling were perfectly symmetrical. Tolen reached out and touched the surface of the side wall and found it coarse. There had been no attempt to smooth the walls here.

Tolen was amazed at the architectural prowess of whoever had designed this place. If the water above was naturally resident in the cave as they suspected, then how were the builders able to orchestrate this complex? The tides would have made it impossible. He realized his original assumption was incorrect. The only way to build this underground facility was to do so prior to water ever being allowed inside the cathedral cavern. He theorized the entire area was most likely constructed from a preexisting mount in the deep floor of the cave whose base was well below sea level. From the top, which was now the tiny humped island, the builders had most likely burrowed straight down, carving out the corridors and rooms. They could then have cut an opening in the side of the cathedral room somewhere near the base which allowed the seawater, and the sharks, inside. He marveled at the ingenuity and wondered if this had been Joseph of Arimathea's creation or whether he was the benefactor of some native Costa Ricans' ability. It was an answer he would probably never know.

The tunnel went on for some way. They reached an intersection where a perpendicular corridor cut across their path. Jade looked to Tolen silently as if to ask his opinion on which way to go. When he offered no suggestion, she turned right and led them down another straight hallway similar to the first. It was much shorter, and they soon reached a dead end. They retraced their steps, reached the intersection, and continued across. Again, they arrived at a wall which marked the end of the tunnel. They returned to the intersection, and continued up the original corridor.

Other than the manmade entry room with its stairs, and the corridors, they had seen nothing of archaeological significance: no artifacts, carvings, decorative nuances, or artwork; nothing to suggest these austere passageways held anything more than open space heavy with dust and stale air.

Tolen watched as Jade trained the flashlight beam ahead. Her pace had quickened. He could sense her anticipation. Truthfully, he had been experiencing the same swell of sanguinity, yet the farther they went, the less confident he became. It brought to mind the Egyptian Pharaohs and the preponderance of tomb raiders who had plundered and wrecked the lavish, treasure-filled crypts in the Valley of the Kings. It was hard to dismiss the possibility that, even if Joseph's tomb had once been here, it had been robbed in antiquity. Chances were, they were hundreds, if not thousands, of years too late. It was a grim thought.

Ahead, Jade's light struck a solid milky-white wall, darkened in green patches where lichen grew. They had reached the end of the corridor. Her body language said it all: shoulders slumped, gait slowed. By the time they neared it, Tolen thought she might collapse in frustration and disappointment. He felt a similar dampening of his spirits.

A fascinating if not odd irregularity in the corner of the wall became visible as they approached. On the left side, a squared area had been cut inward where the side wall would have normally joined with the rear wall. Tolen noticed a similar gaping groove on the right side in the wall. Both notches ran from floor to ceiling. There appeared to be enough room to squeeze inside between the rear wall and the side walls.

Jade turned to Tolen with renewed optimism. Diaz seemed restless.

"Pick a side," Tolen encouraged.

Pausing only for a second to decide, Jade wedged herself in the slot on the left and momentarily pushed her head beyond the end of the wall and out of sight. She drew back with an elated smile. "We can get through. The corridor continues on the other side of this wall."

She led them through. What they had thought was an end wall had turned out to be a simple partition. The corridor ran on in a straight line. Jade angled her light from the stone floor and into the distance. To her dismay, the corridor reached a doorway ahead which opened into a dark room.

Jade hurriedly led the small group forward, walking faster now. Tolen felt his own anticipation building again. Diaz lagged behind, mumbling his discord, harping about the lack of time left.

Jade pressed on, breaking into a trot. The corridor spilled into a spacious room with a pitched ceiling which slanted upward and away. The expansive area was as large as a small house with a floor of polished stone. One wall had a low stone bench carved into it. Other than that, the side walls were bare. The back wall contained an exquisite fresco of a lush, tropical landscape covering the entire surface. Tolen could make out the focal point of the painting: an oasis set atop a sandy hill accentuated with bright, dazzling colors which seemed wet from fresh paint, as if the artwork had been recently completed. The room was immaculately preserved.

"Oh my god," Jade exclaimed. "Look at that stone. Do you know what that is?"

It took a moment for Tolen to realize where Jade was focused. At the base of the fresco, just right of the center of the wall, was a circular stone, the size and shape of a semi-truck tire. It was pressed flush against the wall. He had originally overlooked it, since it was camouflaged against the artwork, blending into the desert scene.

"What is it?" Diaz asked.

"It's a Jewish rolling stone," she said in awe, unblinking. Jade was too mesmerized to offer any further explanation.

Diaz turned to Tolen with an unspoken plea for clarification.

"It's a disk-shaped stone that sealed Jewish tombs, carved from rock during the Second Temple period in Israel. The practice ended in the first century," Tolen said. "Although most tombs to date have been found with square blocking stones, four burial caves in and around Jerusalem have been found with these round stones."

"Is this the type of stone that sealed the tomb of Jesus?" Diaz asked. His voice took on a sudden air of respect.

"There's considerable difference of opinion among biblical scholars. The Bible mentions a very large stone which took two or three men to move. In contrast, a single man could move a typical rolling stone. Consider Jade's deciphered text that the Costa Rican spheres were created to pay homage to the stone that covered Jesus' tomb. It therefore stands to reason the stone sealing Jesus' tomb was completely round and considerably larger."

Jade strolled forward, keeping her light fixed upon the stone. Tolen could almost see her mind poring over the possibilities. *The only reason to have a rolling stone slotted against the wall was to cover a low opening leading to a tomb: Joseph of Arimathea's tomb.*

Tolen and Diaz joined Jade at the stone. Together the threesome easily rolled it to the side. Sure enough, a circular hole penetrated the thick wall behind. A puff of stale air wafted out. Jade ignored it as she dropped down and quickly scurried through on her hands and knees, aiming her flashlight ahead.

As Tolen lowered and prepared to enter, they heard Jade's muffled voice.

"Don't come in," she said. "It's a small tunnel that dead ends. There's...something ahead." There was a pause. "Oh my God!"

"Are you okay?" Tolen called out. He could see the heels of her shoes ahead. She was moving awkwardly, wobbling from side to side, backing up. "I've found it!"

Seconds later, she trundled out, backing clear from the opening. She tugged at a square stone box which slid onto the smooth floor. Jade sat on the ground, breathing heavily, staring at the box. Sweat had beaded on her cheeks. "It's his!" she intoned breathily. "See the inscription?" Jade pointed to the side of the box.

Tolen recognized the writing as Hebrew.

"Joseph of Arimathea," Jade read it aloud. "My God, we did it!"

"It's his ossuary," Tolen said with understanding. Together he and Jade lifted the stone lid while Diaz looked on. The moment it was opened, a fetid smell rushed out. Diaz shined his flashlight inside.

Recognizing the contents, Diaz quickly crossed himself several times. "Madre de Dios," he said softly in reverence.

Inside was a heap of blotchy brown bones; human bones of every ilk and shape. In one corner lay an intact skull with its empty, shadowed eye sockets staring at them.

"This is incredible," Jade uttered breathlessly.

Tolen turned to Diaz. "It was an ancient Jewish custom to collect the bones of a corpse after it had lain on a stone bench for one year. Most likely, that stone bench," Tolen said, pointing to the side wall where the low fixture had been cut. "The bones were then placed inside a box such as this, called an ossuary."

Diaz gazed at the bones in the box and crossed himself yet again. "I know what an ossuary is, but this is unholy. We should not be disturbing this man's remains."

Jade looked at Tolen. He could read her eyes. As overwhelming as this find was, her unvoiced question loomed: *where was the stone jar that the clue from the Harvard sphere had referenced?*

Tolen reached in the box and gently shuffled the bones around, searching to see if a small jar might be resting underneath. The bones were dry and splintered—a metacarpal here, an ulna there, a cracked tibia next to a broken femur. Pieces were piled deep. As he moved the brittle bones aside, he could not help feeling a sense of wonderment that he was touching the remains of Joseph of Arimathea.

It was not textbook archaeological protocol, and he knew it, but the tide was rising, and they were running out of time. He hesitated, then lifted the skull from the box and examined it closely.

I'm looking into the face of Joseph of Arimathea, he thought.

Diaz backed away as if the skull were about to come to life and release a demonic force upon them. Tolen turned it toward Jade. Her expression was impossible to read. It was somewhere between archaeological exuberance and hallowed reverence. Tolen carefully placed the skull back inside the ossuary.

Diaz was pacing to the side. He was obviously uncomfortable with their situation.

"There's nothing here," Tolen finally said. He looked at his

130

watch. "We don't have long before this place begins to flood."

"Then where is the stone jar? It's got to be here somewhere." There was desperation in Jade's voice. They returned the lid to the ossuary and she rose, moving about the room. The only sound was Jade's light footfalls as she stalked about like a lioness in distress. For a second, she stared at the wall-sized fresco then lowered her eyes in deep thought.

Suddenly, Tolen heard a faint, almost indistinguishable noise. It was constant, and both Jade and Diaz lifted their heads when they also heard it. It was coming from outside the room, somewhere up the corridor. He withdrew his pistol and silently motioned for each to turn off their flashlights. Pressing against the wall to the side of the doorway, Tolen spun and quickly shined his flashlight up the corridor, gun aimed at the light's beam. Diaz had taken position behind him.

The corridor was empty. Tolen could see the partition wall they had circumvented. A gurgling sound was now audible. He lowered the beam and looked to the corridor floor where water was snaking lazily past either side of the partition wall and running toward them in lines like fingers stretching out.

The tide had already breached the tiny island above and water was entering the underground caverns.

CHAPTER 21

September 11. Tuesday – 6:10 p.m. Northwest Coast of Costa Rica

Diaz cringed at the advancing flow of water. "I thought you said we had more time?"

Tolen checked his watch. "I overestimated."

Jade stood to the side listening to the men exchanging words. Then, as if she had not heard their conversation, she resumed her scrutiny of the colorful wall.

"Jade, I know this is disappointing, but we have to leave now," Tolen urged, walking to her and gently grabbing her uninjured arm.

She shrugged away from him with determination. "Not until we have the next clue. It's here. I know it is."

Tolen sensed her frustration. She refused to look either man in the eye, and her slack posture indicated she had doubts about her own claim.

"Jade!" Diaz shouted. "Do you want us all to drown down here?"

She ignored him.

Tolen stood beside her, gazing at the painting. Deep down, he was also reluctant to abandon their only opportunity to continue the search. He thought for a moment. "We're not using logic. The directions were in the parchment clue, remember?"

"The clue…," Jade repeated with a slight lift of tone.

Tolen quoted it from memory. "It said, '*Search for the three stone jars. They will be found when you look for what was offered on the first day.*' "

"We don't know what that means, remember?" Diaz said, his

face contorted in frustration.

Tolen pondered the sentence. "Consider Joseph's time. What would have been offered on the first day?"

"On the first day of what?" Diaz asked.

Jade's face went blank.

Diaz walked away in a huff. "You're going to seal our doom if we don't get out of here, and I, for one, am leaving," he said as he headed toward the doorway. He hesitated at the entrance, though, and looked back at the others, waiting.

"The end game," Tolen said with sudden realization.

Jade gave him a quizzical stare.

"Jesus' cache is the end game. The niches in the cathedral cave above, each holding a tiny replica of the crucifixion cross; and consider how the corridors of this underground complex intersect. That's why there was a perpendicular tunnel even though it led to nowhere. It wasn't functional; it was cut to form a cross: another way to pay homage. True, this is the tomb that held Joseph of Arimathea's remains, but everything is decidedly focused on Jesus Christ," Tolen said. "Therefore, it stands to reason the clue is referencing the *first day of Jesus' life*."

A knowing look blossomed across Jade's face. "The Three Wise Men; the gifts the Magi brought to the baby Jesus in Bethlehem!"

Diaz re-engaged from the doorway. "You mean gold, frankincense, and myrrh? But none of those is in this room."

"Exactly," Jade looked to the artwork. She was now brimming with optimism. "Gold, frankincense, and myrrh are somewhere in the picture. We've got to find them quickly."

Jade and Tolen moved close to the wall, examining the fresco. Diaz lingered near the opening to the room.

It stood to reason the *gifts* would be embedded within the focal point of the scene: the oasis. "Look for anything resembling three containers the Wise Men could have used to hold the gifts," Tolen said.

The gurgle of water became louder. Tolen looked back at the doorway to see a tiny stream enter the room. It was running along the smooth floor and building speed as it flared out toward them.

Jade and Diaz had seen it as well.

"Keep looking," Jade urged.

It occurred to Tolen that the gifts might not be grouped together on the wall. They might be separated. Then a more probable scenario struck him: the gifts may be in their natural state. Apparently, the same notion had occurred to Jade.

"Isn't this a resin-producing tree?" Jade asked.

Diaz was staring down with concern at the water that now blanketed the entire cave floor.

"Frankincense and myrrh are, indeed, derived from the resin of certain trees," Tolen explained calmly as he eyed the tree Jade pointed to on the right of the oasis. It was a squat tree, more like a large bush shaped like an umbrella, with a twisting trunk and dozens of tiny, paired thin leaves on wiry limbs. "Yes, that's a *boswellia sacra*. The extract creates frankincense."

He looked at Jade. Water was filling the room quickly and had already reached their ankles.

"Break through the wall," she said with a pained expression. To do so, they were sacrificing astounding historical artwork, but the reality was, the seawater was going to envelop the area within minutes anyway and destroy everything down here.

Tolen wasted no time. He sloshed through the rising water and reached the closed ossuary. It was another decision he regretted having to make, but the situation forced him. The water had already crested the top of the box as he reached down and removed the stone lid. Water poured into the box, saturating the bones. They lifted to the surface and began to float around like some gruesome skeletal soup. Tolen carried the square stone lid back to the painting and slammed it into the wall at the exact spot of the *boswellia sacra* tree. A piece of the stone lid chipped off, flying back into Tolen's face, dangerously close to his right eye. The wall appeared undamaged.

The water continued to rise. Tolen squinted to protect his eyes and made numerous strikes into the wall without success. Their unspoken assumption had been that they would find an empty cavity behind the image of the tree, which would hold another stone jar and, in turn, another clue to their quest. After a series of thumps to the wall, though, it became obvious they were wrong.

It was solid stone.

"This is insane," Diaz said. "Let's go!"

"No, wait!" Jade shouted, moving along the picture, pointing to the far side of the oasis. "Isn't that another resin tree?"

Tolen was just about to side with Diaz when he looked to where Jade was directing their attention. The tree was much larger, with four large trunks leaning away from each other which lifted to a swell of high canvassing limbs. "It's a *commiphora gileadensis*. Myrrh is derived from it." He felt a renewed sense of hope. Without being asked, he moved over to the wall, lifted the stone lid and bashed the area at the tree's trunk. It gave easily. Fragments of stone crumbled inward.

"There's a cavity!" Jade shouted euphorically.

Tolen continued to strike away at the image of the tree with controlled force. When enough of the wall had given way, he dropped the stone lid into the water. He used his hands to break the rest of the fragile surface away, creating an opening approximately eighteen inches wide. Jade shined her flashlight inside the cavity where a small, capped stone jar sat on a ledge. Surprisingly, it was Diaz who reached inside and grabbed it. The moment he pulled the jar out, he handed it to Jade. Jade fetched a small plastic bag from her pocket and delicately wrapped the jar inside, then she sealed the bag to make it water tight.

Diaz shined his flashlight about the room. The water was closing in on their waists. The bones of Joseph of Arimathea floated around them in ghostly eddies.

"It seems we have just killed ourselves for a stone jar," Diaz said glumly.

Tolen could not disagree.

CHAPTER 22

September 11. Tuesday – 6:19 p.m. Northwest Coast of Costa Rica

By the time they made their way back to the tunnel, the seawater was almost up to Jade's chest. Leaving the tomb chamber had been exceedingly difficult; a combination of walking and swimming upstream. She shivered in the rush of water as she was the first to reach the slot at the edge of the partition wall. The smell of salt saturated the cool, underground air. She had lost her flashlight moments before when it slipped from her hands and fell into the water, swept back toward the crypt in the surging current.

Even as they fought to escape the flooding underground chamber, she had two disconcerting thoughts. The first was whether the jar they had just risked their lives for was empty. They did not have enough time to confirm the contents. Second, she wondered if there might have been other jars hidden in the room which they had missed and left behind. The Harvard sphere text had mentioned three jars. Ultimately, these might be moot points. Jade knew the odds were now stacked against them, and the room was sure to be lost forever once it flooded with seawater. She hated to admit it, but Diaz was right. It had taken them too long to find the jar. Now, the corridor was filling fast. It would only be a matter of minutes before the entire underground structure would become one with the ocean.

The threesome squeezed by the partition wall, struggling against the surging water to pass, then proceeded up the corridor. Diaz and Tolen used their lights as a guide to pierce the dark cavern and the rippling surface ahead. Jade found it easier to swim, yet she also realized the current drove her back if she did not stop on occasion and secure her footing.

The going was exhausting and nerve-wracking. The corridor was swelling with water. Progress slowed and became increasingly strenuous. Soon, the water would be over Jade's head, and she could barely contain her rising fear. Somewhere in the distance, there was a steady pounding.

They passed the intersecting corridor, and she found she could no longer stand and reach the cave floor. As she tried on tippy toes, water washed over her face, and she coughed out a mouthful. Swimming was her only option now, but when she tried to make headway against the pummeling water, she found herself drifting back into one of the men. At that instant the tunnel became darker. Another flashlight had been lost. Someone grabbed her firmly from behind and thrust her forward, lifting her so that her head remained above water. She felt two strong hands clutching her around the waist as they moved against the current. A single strand of light cut the corridor ahead, revealing their proximity to the entry room. Jade felt helpless. She was at the complete mercy of whoever was supporting her.

The smell of brine strengthened in the decreasing layer of air. A constant sound like muted static grew ever louder.

Jade shivered uncontrollably.

When they reached the channel where the rushing water from the entry room fed the main corridor, the current was maniacal. It was like the mouth of an ocean funneling the incoming tide into a small river. The compression into the smaller channel created an ungodly onslaught of water. She could feel the man struggling to move them forward, and their progress became agonizingly slow. There was nothing Jade could do to help. Even elevated, water was now gushing over her face, and she choked on mouthfuls of saltwater that burned her nose and throat.

They kept inching ahead through the narrow manmade corridor, attempting to enter the room with the stair steps leading to the ceiling opening. With herculean effort, the man holding her maintained his ground and slowly nudged them forward. She heard him groan and spit water and thought she recognized Tolen's voice.

By now, she knew the water must be close to eclipsing his head.

Jade was bearing the brunt of the surging force. The monstrous impact felt like it was about to crush her chest. She breathed in sharp gasps, taking in equal amounts of air and water, then hacked and gasped, desperate to clear her lungs. She felt the man teeter, and Jade said a silent prayer. If he lost his balance now, the rushing water would send them back down the corridor into the partition wall where they would be pinned. Even if they could fight their way back—which she doubted they could—there was no time. The entire underground area would reach capacity within minutes.

Jade reached forward, grabbed the corner edge of the wall, and pulled with every ounce of energy she had left. It was just enough to stabilize the pair, allowing the man to right himself. He must have gained solid footing and, with considerable effort, pushed them beyond the intake of water. Her grip broke away from the wall, and she felt the slice of the stone edge across her bandaged arm. They pivoted around the corner and braced against a side wall inside the room. Jade choked out the saltwater and turned to the side, laboring to breathe. She could not hide her astonishment as she looked into the haggard, soggy face of her savior, Inspector Pascal Diaz. Tolen was on the other side of the Spaniard.

"Y..you?" she stammered.

Diaz was too tired to respond as he paddled in place.

Slowly, they swam farther and farther away from the opening where the current was much less severe. A hissing, bubbling noise in the room was nearly deafening.

Jade watched Tolen as he held the flashlight out of the water with one hand while treading water with the other. The beam of light licked the room, strayed upward, and targeted the ceiling opening where they had entered the underground cave. Water was pouring through the hole, cascading downward as a solid mass, as if the entire Pacific Ocean was trying to invade the caverns. The beam of light sparkled off the torrent, and Jade felt her insides turn to putty. She could see the watermark creeping up the wall. There was less than four feet of airspace left in the room, and it was being squeezed out fast.

She looked back down the corridor. Through the dim light, the seawater had plugged the passageway, rising well above it. It was as if the connecting corridor had never existed.

"We can't get through that downpour of water!" she said in a disheartened voice.

Tolen swam over to the steps, which were now submerged. The platform below the circular opening, which they had dropped upon when they had entered the room, was all but obscured by the gushing blast of water. Reaching the steps and gaining footing, he tried to force his way through the downward flow. Jade watched as Tolen disappeared into the massive waterfall, then as his dark figure was thrust back into the pooled water away from the deluge. Tolen swam back to where Jade and Diaz were nested against the wall, paddling to remain afloat.

Jade's body ached, her muscles were approaching exhaustion. She had no idea how long they had been swimming, but it was long enough that her legs were beginning to cramp, and she forced herself to fight through the pain.

"We're trapped," Diaz said. "We can't get through that incoming water."

Jade awaited Tolen's response. The man seemed to have nine lives, and she hoped against all hope he had a plan to save them now. Less than three feet of air remained. The cave ceiling approached like a vise ready to wring out their last breath.

"You're right," Tolen finally admitted.

His vanquished response brought the morbid reality home. "Oh God," Jade murmured. The beam of light Tolen kept trained upon the waterfall began to cloud through her tears. She could not believe she was about to die.

Tolen spoke again over the rushing sound of water. "Follow me."

Jade looked to Diaz in confusion. Wordlessly, they did as they were told. Tolen swam, leading them to the steps where the threesome found footing near the top, just to the side of the blasting waterfall amid a spray of water. The ceiling was now less than two feet away.

"We have to wait," Tolen said loudly over the sound of the water.

"Wait for what?" Diaz barked.

"Once this room fills, the flow will stop and pressure will equalize."

Jade understood the simplicity in Tolen's words. *Of course! They can't fight through the falling water, but they can leave the cave once the seawater is no longer flowing into it.* She lifted her hand to brush her dribbling bangs from her eyes.

Tolen gave her a solemn look.

"What?" she asked. Then she noticed he was staring at her forearm. She turned it toward her, realizing for the first time the makeshift bandage was gone. The gunshot flesh wound had been gashed. She remembered scraping it against the edge of the stone wall when she and Diaz pulled themselves into this room. Blood was flowing freely. Oddly, she now felt its sting.

The sharks, she thought in horror.

Their heads were now brushing the ceiling as they were forced to swim above the steps to remain above water.

"There's no time to bandage it," Tolen said. He handed Diaz the flashlight, and the Spaniard took it without question.

Jade swallowed hard. "You and Diaz have to go." She reached in her pocket and pulled out the watertight bag with the jar. Her head was spinning, and her words felt surreal, as if they were coming from someone else. "Here, take this. They're going to be...be after me."

"No," Tolen pushed the bag back to Jade, "secure that jar."

Jade had no strength to argue. The water had approached to within inches of the ceiling, and they had to turn their heads upward to keep breathing.

"But—" Jade inhaled a mouthful of water which cut off her words. She expelled it forcefully and fought for another breath of air in the compacted space. Her ears were now under water, and Tolen's words muffled. The flashlight beam was glowing upward from under the moving surface.

"Take one last breath of air and hold it when I say," Tolen directed. Then he moved in front of Diaz, and Diaz slid next to Jade.

Jade had never experienced such formidable terror. Even if they made it safely out of here, the sharks waiting above would be a much crueler fate. She felt like drowning herself, but a little voice told her to trust Samuel Tolen.

"Now," she barely heard Tolen's muted words through the water.

Jade drew in air until she felt like her expanding lungs would rupture, then she held it. She faded below the surface, and opened her eyes. The saltwater burned, but it was imperative that she be able to see what was going on once they swam up from the room.

The light was suddenly gone, and they were cast in blackness. She reached out and grabbed Tolen's shirt. For several long seconds, the man did not move. Her air was running out, and she again considered taking matters into her own hands by ending her life with a big gulp of seawater.

Tolen finally shifted, dragging her forward as she held on. She could feel the slight rush of water as they reached the opening where a pall of light shown through. He passed through the hole and she followed. They immediately broke the surface. Tolen swung to the side, and hoisted Jade from the opening and onto the stone island where they stood in knee-deep water. Diaz emerged beside them. Jade gasped the semi-fresh air, momentarily thankful they had escaped, but as she rubbed the saltwater from her eyes, she took in the horrid truth.

All around them, the sharks were cutting through the water in a frenzy. The surface boiled with activity. For the time, the submerged island afforded them protection. The large sharks were unable to breech the shallow water, but their curiosity was obviously piqued as they glided by only a few feet away.

"Anybody see the rope?" Tolen shouted.

They had left the coil of rope on the tiny stone island once they rolled the stone sphere away. Now, it was nowhere in sight.

"It's washed away," Diaz lamented.

The threesome looked up at the cone pointing down at them. The tip was nine feet above the stone island, but the first handhold was three feet beyond that.

"We can't reach it without the rope," Tolen said.

The water churned a short distance away as the nose of a bull shark broke the surface, its mouth parted slightly, revealing too many ghastly teeth to count. Jade cringed at the sight as the wake rolled against her knee, causing her to shake.

Tolen spoke authoritatively. "We've got to swim."

"Are you crazy?" Diaz said.

"There's no other way off."

The thought made Jade numb. "We'll be devoured alive."

Tolen stepped up to Jade. "We need to stop that bleeding. The material of your shirt is better suited. May I?"

Jade was too frightened to respond. She nodded weakly, staring at the menacing creatures darting through the water around them. Tolen stood before her and ripped off a band of material at the bottom leaving her midriff bare. As he did, his hand brushed against her stomach. His touch brought a sensation of comfort; of life. He then proceeded to wrap her arm tightly until she winced in pain. "We need the bleeding to stop completely. Once we get safely to the perimeter ledge, I'll loosen it. We've got to go fast before your arm becomes numb."

Tolen turned, looking from Diaz to Jade. "We'll form a triad in the water, keeping our backs to each other. If they attack, we want to see them coming. They're looking for an easy meal, and we're not going to give it to them. They're sensitive at their gills, nose, and eyes. If one comes close, strike at those places. Let's go."

Without hesitation, Tolen walked off the ledge. Diaz followed, and Jade forced herself to move quickly in order to catch up with the men. A shark swirled by Tolen but made no attempt to challenge him. Diaz backed into Tolen, and Jade huddled against their two backs as the threesome slid off the underwater ramp.

"Let's move," Tolen said as he led them outward.

A second later, Jade felt the smooth stone footing disappear, and the water grew colder as she submerged up to her neck. The three swam in place momentarily, concentrating to maintain their positions, backs touching as they faced outward. The dim light made it difficult to keep track of the creatures in the murky water, which set her nerves on edge. The configuration of bodies also meant they were constantly touching each other as they swam. The first few times she felt Diaz's arm skim against her side or Tolen's leg kick into hers, she mistook them for a shark and her heart nearly stopped.

"Move slowly," Tolen instructed.

Like a three-sided creature, the tiny cluster of humanity stirred themselves through the water upon Tolen's directions, with the agent on point. Diaz and Jade were primarily facing backward. The progress was agonizingly slow as they kept their eyes vigilantly on the roiling water around them. The sharks seemed curious but so far had not displayed any aggression.

Jade could feel the tight tourniquet biting into her forearm. The sense of feeling was quickly evaporating from her hand as she paddled, sticking to Tolen and Diaz like a magnet. Tolen kept them moving to ensure they remained in a tight pack. She noticed the sharks seemed to give them a wide berth, at least from her vantage point at the rear, and Jade felt minimally encouraged.

The fishy-smelling brine in the air remained thick. The only sound was their gasping breaths and the occasional surface disruption from the sharks patrolling around them. Jade's muscles protested vehemently to the perpetual strain of remaining afloat.

Briefly turning her head to the side, Jade estimated they were more than halfway to the wall. Just as her hopes of survival were rising, a large figure rose up and broke the surface a dozen feet away, its black eye turning toward Jade. She felt a jolt of panic. She forced herself to swim using minimal movement, praying not to draw the creature's attention. The shark remained on the surface, pivoted right, then spun left with a furious swish of its tail.

In the next instant, it ripped through the water toward Jade, head cocked to the side, jaws breaking the surface with protracted razor-sharp teeth.

Survival was instinctual. She targeted the lone black eye which was visible. With a shriek, she reached out her hand and drove a finger into the beast's eye just as its jaws were about to clamp down on her torso. The creature broke off the attack as if it had been struck by lightning. It made a pronounced turn, erratically sideswiping Jade, sending a wave washing over her head. Reflexively, she flung back into the two men, nudging all three of them several feet through the water. Completely unnerved, she struggled for air on the verge of hyperventilating.

"*Mierda santa!*" Diaz exclaimed, his voice laced with horror at what he had just witnessed.

"What happened?" Tolen shouted from behind.

Jade's mouth had gone dry. She was in mortal fear the creature would attack again at any moment. She strained her vocal chords until she could force the words to come out. "I was attacked… I'm…okay!"

"We're almost there, Jade. Hold on," Tolen urged. He moved them faster now, and Jade concentrated on staying with the pack, eyeing the water, mouthing prayer after prayer she would make it out alive and the menacing creature would not return.

The surface of the water continued to boil with the ominous activity several feet away. Her pulse was racing so fast she feared a heart attack was imminent. She had to fight the urge to turn and swim as fast as she could to shore.

"We're at the ledge," Tolen said after what seemed like forever. Before Jade could react, she felt a hand spin her around. It was Tolen. Both men pushed her up, and she scurried onto the ledge. The tide was still rising, but the water had only just reached the elevated flat stone surface. In unison, Tolen and Diaz raised themselves up to it and cleared the water.

"Thank God," Diaz said, bending over with his hands on his knees, breathing hard.

Jade moved to the wall, turned, and leaned against it, exhausted.

Tolen untied Jade's tourniquet and dropped it at their feet. She rubbed the spot, trying to work the soreness out as her arm tingled with pinpricks and feeling returned. She felt the cool air in the cavern on her mid-section where her skin was now exposed.

For a moment, all three stood gazing at the shark-infested lagoon as water ran off their clothes.

The tiny island in the middle no longer existed. There was no evidence it ever had.

CHAPTER 23

September 11. Tuesday – 7:26 p.m. Northwest Coast of Costa Rica

The wind had died down, yet the ocean surface remained a choppy blue. The sun was setting at their back. Tolen guided the boat back toward the docks along the northern shore of Costa Rica.

Gordon Nunnery's jet ski had come in handy. Tolen used it to ferry Jade, then Diaz, back to the dinghy to avoid any more shark encounters.

Diaz was sequestered below deck, a self-imposed confinement after succumbing to another bout of seasickness. After what they had been through—being shot at, nearly drowning, and swimming through a school of sharks—it seemed nonsensical that it was the pitching of the boat in rough seas that once again incapacitated the Spanish law officer.

Standing beside Tolen at the helm, Jade removed the small jar from the plastic bag. For the first time, they would be able to examine the five-inch-long relic in detail. The bulbous cap was fashioned into a tiny human head. The base of the jar was in the shape of a drinking glass. It flared out at the top where the cap was seated. The face on the head had curly short hair, a beard and mustache, but was not familiar to either Jade or Tolen.

"Do you think it's *him*?" Jade had asked.

"Joseph of Arimathea?"

"Yes."

"Everything else Joseph has left for us has to do with Jesus."

Jade stared at the small bust atop the jar with fascination. "It's staggering to consider we could be looking into the face of Jesus.

145

This in itself may be a priceless relic," she remarked.

"Shall we see what's inside?" Tolen asked.

Jade stared down at it in her fingers. She chewed briefly on her bottom lip, making no effort to open it.

"What's the matter?"

She looked up at him with trepidation. "What if it's empty? What if we almost died for nothing except to placate my crazy obsession?"

"And what if this jar contains information that will lead you to the single greatest archaeological discovery in mankind's history?"

Jade looked down. "I'm sickened that the tomb of Joseph of Arimathea was destroyed. If we left any clues behind, our efforts will turn out to be for naught."

"You're holding exactly what we needed to find," Tolen said reassuringly.

She looked down at the small container again. Jade drew a lingering breath and released it. Taking the jar in her left hand, she gently grabbed the small bust and pulled. For a moment, it stuck. Then it slowly worked loose. The cap separated from the main body of the jar with a scrape. With some hesitancy, she looked inside.

Tolen watched her intently.

Jade dipped two fingers into the opening, tilted the jar, and very carefully pulled out a tiny parchment roll. A wide smile sprouted upon her face and her eyes twinkled. "This is spectacular!"

He could see the exhilaration in her eyes, and it became infectious.

She looked back down at the roll, then again inside the jar. "There's something else inside." She handed Tolen the roll, then she tipped the jar and a tiny cloth bag spilled into her hand. It was bound with a thin string. Jade lowered it below the level of the boat console to fend off the wind. She gently untied the bag, spread the collar, and they looked inside.

Tolen recognized the natural, crushed material. "It's myrrh."

Her expression turned to awe. "Do you think this is the myrrh Jesus received as a baby?"

For several long seconds the two stared at the myrrh in silence. Then a stiff, swirling breeze threatened to blow the substance into the ocean and Jade retied it, placing the tiny cloth bag back inside the jar. She returned the stone jar and lid to the larger plastic bag, wound it in rags to protect it from breaking, and deposited it in a storage compartment in the center console.

Jade paused and took a deep breath, seemingly to calm herself. Tolen couldn't blame her. His own sense of wonderment had ballooned.

"May I?" she finally asked, motioning to the object in Tolen's hand. He handed her the miniscule roll, and she delicately unwound the ancient paper. She looked up. "It's Hebrew again," she said, her eyes alive with the revelation this was the next clue. She translated aloud:

> Travel from the west. The path to the 64th goes through the petra in banishment. There you will find the second jar.

"Once again, not exactly an easy message to decipher," Jade remarked.

Tolen momentarily digested the sentences. "*Petra* is Greek for 'stone.' "

"Petra is also an ancient site in the Jordanian governorate of Ma'an. It's an area with extensive biblical significance," Jade added. "The Bible mentions it as the place where Moses struck his staff on a rock and water sprang forth. It's also where Moses' brother, Aaron, is said to be buried on Mount Hor, known today as Jabal Haroun. The rock-carved, red city of Petra is concealed behind rugged mountains and is difficult to reach, and even if this is what the clue is referring to, we have no way to know where to start looking." A look of disappointment streaked over Jade's face but vanished as her gaze narrowed and sharpened. "You still haven't told me how you know so much about the history related to Jesus of Nazareth. In the underground caverns, you knew the exact name of the trees from which frankincense and myrrh are extracted. That's not exactly common knowledge."

Tolen chose to focus ahead and not look Jade in the eyes. "As I mentioned before, I have a degree in world history. At one time, you might say I was a student of being a student. I retain most of what I read."

"I see."

He knew she didn't. "*Travel from the west. The path to the 64th goes through the petra in banishment. There you will find the second jar,*" he repeated the translation hoping to return their focus to the clue. "Any idea what is meant by 'the 64th'?"

Jade shook her head.

"What about the term 'banishment'?"

Again, Jade shook her head.

Tolen pulled his cell phone from the storage compartment, careful not to disturb the stone jar. "Excuse me a moment."

Jade nodded, still staring at the tiny parchment.

"Bar, I need some information," Tolen said once he heard her pick up. "Tell me what you can find on a man named Gordon Nunnery."

"Another guy who tried to kill you?" She asked whimsically. "Let me guess. Mr. Nunnery is no longer with us."

"He had a Saskatchewan driver's license," Tolen pulled the identification from his pocket and read the numbers on the license to her.

There was a moment of silence before Bar spoke. "Gordon Nunnery. Fifty-eight-year-old Canadian by birth, born in Quebec. Physicist involved with particle research. Also a proponent of the String Theory. His most recent stint was four years working at TRIUMF in Vancouver. TRIUMF is one of the world's leading subatomic physics laboratories, in case you didn't know. Divorced with two grown sons. Clean record. No arrests; a few parking citations. Definitely not a bad guy. Well, except for trying to kill you."

Nunnery was similar to the man who had attacked them at Harvard: Richard Mox. Neither man fit the profile of a member of an anti-religious sect such as the "True Sons of Light."

"I found a receipt in his wallet to a dry-cleaning business in Switzerland. I'll text the information. It's in German. See what you can find out, okay?"

"How do you know it's a dry cleaner if it's written in Germ—" she cut herself off. "That's one of the eight languages you know, isn't it? I used to think I was worldly because I knew Spanish," she chuckled.

"Yes, but you've mastered Spanish for every local dialect in Mexico, South America, and Spain. Don't sell yourself short, Bar," he paused. "Did you uncover any dirt on Mox?"

"We found nothing at his house in California to implicate him as a member of an overly zealous group, and nothing to tie him to Boyd Ramsey," Bar paused briefly. "Tolen, you know we have less than 56 hours to locate the Sudarium, right? Vakind's getting chewed out every few hours now by Spanish officials and every hour by the president. I know the director gives you autonomy, but have you got anything to go on?"

Tolen did not respond to her question. Instead, he said, "I'll be in touch, Ms. Bar." He hung up, considering her question. Time *was* running out, and the leads had been few. He had hoped to encounter more of the "True Sons of Light" so that they might lead him to Ramsey or the Sudarium or both. So far, though, they had struck out. Their only choice now was to follow through on this maddeningly slow hunt and hope more people affiliated with the "True Sons of Light" came after them. His gut told him they would. Unless they could decode this last clue, however, their chase would come to a screeching halt.

Tolen considered the circumstances of both attacks on them. They had been feeble attempts, and in each case, the men had acted alone. Their weapons of choice had been most unusual. Mox had tried to run them over with a car. Nunnery had fired at them with a .22-calibre hunting rifle; not exactly a killer's weapon. The rifle was more effective in hunting small game. The fact that one was an ex-archaeologist and the other a physicist was equally baffling, as was Gordon Nunnery's ability to find them inside the cathedral cave when Tolen was sure they had not been followed.

One other aspect was even more troubling: neither of the attempts appeared to emulate apostle-style deaths. Why had the radical group suddenly altered their *modus operandi*?

CHAPTER 24

September 11. Tuesday – 9:28 p.m. Murciélago, Costa Rica

Tolen, Jade, and Diaz sat at a small round table in a motel room in Murciélago eating dinner. Reba Zee had the plane parked at an airport three miles away. Tolen had put her on alert to be ready to take off at a moment's notice.

Unfortunately, they were still baffled by the stone jar text. And with the weight of the ticking clock bearing down on them, Diaz became more agitated and obstinate. While Jade did not state it aloud, she had conceded to herself the possibility that they might never solve the obscure message on the tiny roll of parchment.

Jade took several bites of gallo pinto, dabbed a piece of rice from her lips, and stood. She began to pace the room. "64…64…64," she repeated to herself, as she toyed with her newly bandaged forearm.

"What of 64?" Diaz said, keeping his face down to the plate as he ate.

"It says, '*The path to the 64th goes through the petra in banishment.*'" She sat down on the bed, flipped her laptop open and began typing frantically. She searched for the file she and Dr. Cherrigan had worked on. It contained an imaged copy of the Copper Scroll and the English translation. When she found it, she clicked it open. "That's it!" she exulted.

She looked at Tolen. He put his fork down, walked over to the bed, and sat down beside her. Diaz continued to shovel food into his mouth.

"Unlike the rest of the Dead Sea Scrolls," she continued, "which were written on parchment or papyrus in the 2nd century

BCE, experts say the Copper Scroll dates between 50 and 100 AD. This places it squarely in the lifetime of Joseph of Arimathea, which makes sense if you consider he was a metals dealer with ready access and familiarity to copper. Also, the style of writing on the Copper Scroll is unusual. It's similar to Mishnaic Hebrew, with an unusual orthography; quite different than the other Dead Sea Scrolls' texts. Actually, about the only similarity of the Copper Scroll to the Dead Sea Scrolls is that they were found in the same area, in caves in the cliffs overlooking the Dead Sea in Israel. It's the only reason they're linked at all.

"The Copper Scroll also has other characteristics which make it unique. While the rest of the Dead Sea Scrolls contain most of the books of the Old Testament and other non-biblical text such as community rules, the Copper Scroll is a listing of sixty-three underground hiding places said to contain hordes of gold, silver, and aromatics. Although people have searched the deserts of Israel, not a single one of the 63 treasures have been found. Curiously, the sixty-fourth, and last, description is said to lead to a more detailed duplicate of the Copper Scroll. The scroll's last line gives the location and begins as follows: '*In a dry well that is at the north of Kohlit…*' Unfortunately, no one knows the location of Kohlit.

"Another unique facet of the Copper Scroll is that scholars don't know what every word in the text means. This vagueness, combined with the high probability that the landmarks mentioned in the text no longer exist, is the primary reason most people believe the treasures will never be located. Some scholars believe the Copper Scroll is a work of fiction, since there's never been agreement on who authored it or who supposedly hid the treasures."

Diaz spoke with a mouth half filled with food, "So this roll you found in the jar is referring to the sixty-fourth, and last, item listed in the Copper Scroll? How does that help you determine the location of the next jar?" He raised his wineglass and took a healthy gulp of Sangria. "We're wasting time." Diaz waved his hand dismissively then stabbed his fork at the meat.

"You believe that the clue we found is leading to the duplicate of the Copper Scroll," Tolen nodded his understanding.

"Possibly," Jade stood again and walked the room. She reached

GARY WILLIAMS AND VICKY KNERLY

one wall, turned, reached the next wall, and stopped. "Could it be?" she said to herself, in a whisper. She went to the keyboard and brought up the image of the Copper Scroll. "Even though Cherrigan and I were able to break a code embedded within the Copper Scroll, which started our pursuit of the stone sphere, we were never able to solve one riddle. In the scroll, following a handful of listed locations of treasure are groupings of two to three Greek letters. They have been well documented and studied. To date, their meaning is a complete mystery. The letters do not form any words. More intriguing is why they are written in Greek when the rest of the scroll is in Hebrew. Behind the sixty-fourth listing, there are three Greek letters. See, here they are," Jade pointed to the screen.

"Eta, Sigma, Iota," Tolen read them aloud. "You're right. It doesn't spell a Greek word."

"No, but I had a chance to examine the actual Copper Scroll on display at the Archaeological Museum in Amman, Jordan. I believe there is a fourth Greek letter which preceded the other three. It's very faint. Remember that the letters had to be chiseled into the Copper Scroll, and it appears this one was done so lightly it's almost imperceptible. I believe it's the Greek letter *Nu*. When you add Nu before Eta, Sigma, and Iota you *do* get the Greek word: νησι. Translated, it means *isle*."

Jade returned to the laptop keyboard, pecking in a search on a web browser. "I'm typing in the words 'petra' and 'banishment' from the tiny parchment roll, combined with the words, 'Isle' and 'Greek'." As she did, the assembled words rang vaguely familiar.

Jade hit enter to run the search. Jade skimmed the search results and could barely withhold her excitement. She flapped her hands excitedly and was almost bouncing where she sat.

Tolen's eyebrows elevated slightly as he looked at her. He spoke before she could get the words out. "The Apostle John. He was the only Apostle not to be executed. He died of old age."

"John wrote Revelation when Jesus returned and spoke to him in a cave," Diaz added, wiping his mouth with a napkin and leaning back in his chair. "What about him?"

"The clue is referring to John!" Jade exclaimed.

"John wrote the Book of Revelation while he was on the Greek Isle of Patmos where he had been *banished*," Tolen added.

"And guess what, gentlemen?" Jade began, still focusing on the laptop screen. There was a slight tremble in her voice. "I know what *Petra* is referring to." She paused for a moment to compose herself. She looked up, her face beaming, her hazel eyes swimming. "Tolen, as you said, *petra* is Greek for rock. Well, there's a famous petra on the Isle of Patmos. It's called Kalikatsou. It's a massive natural rock formation perched at the head of a barren mudflat at Grikos Bay at the southern end of the island. Because of its peculiar shape, it's tied to numerous myths. More importantly, throughout recorded history, it has been a refuge for many hermits, one being the Apostle John when he was exiled on Patmos where he wrote the Book of Revelation!" She paused. "Gentlemen, '*The path to the sixty-fourth goes through the petra in banishment*' is referring to Kalikatsou on the Greek Isle of Patmos!"

CHAPTER 25

September 12. Wednesday – 4:47 a.m. Dietikon, Switzerland

So far, so good, Nicklaus Kappel thought as he sat at his desk in the dark study. The only light in the room came from his computer screen and bathed his face in a blue wash. The Bai Hao Yin Zhen tea had just kicked in, and he felt the first caffeine rush of the new day. The warm air passing through the ductwork above created a subtle, tranquil hum.

With any luck, in a few more days he could catch up on his sleep. For now, there was work to be done.

He ran a hand over his head feeling a slight tingle. The chase was proving to be interesting. While he was banking on the existence of the cache, common sense told him it was a long shot. Now he was forced to reconsider.

Kappel, dressed in shorts and a tank top, stood and walked to the window, silently moving across the wooden floor in bare feet. The curtains were closed, and he pulled them open with a quick tug of the drawstring. He looked out the double-paned window down onto the well-lit grounds where the pristine gardens spread out below, buffered by a rise which flattened before reaching the iron fence somewhere beyond in the blackness. Already, the colder weather was starting to take its toll. Soon, the snowfall would blanket the rolling landscape for months and the opulent plants and fragrant rose bushes would die, only to be dug up and replaced again next spring. Life and death, over and over: how many times had he witnessed it now? Twelve? Thirteen years? Whatever the answer, it was too many.

He found himself unconsciously rubbing his hands together, then one hand massaging the top of the other where circular welts rose permanently. Painful memories returned, and in turn brought the hatred and bitterness that regularly festered within him these days. It was getting harder and harder to continue in his role, yet he knew his time was limited. It would serve him well to remain in his station a few more days. Besides, there were worse circumstances in which a person could find himself: jail, for example, like his sister, Cecily.

He stared out the window at the lavish grounds and, for the hundredth time, vowed to free Cecily very soon.

He returned to his chair before the computer monitor and clicked on the icon for his email application. It opened smartly with a chime to reveal one unread message in his inbox.

"Ah ha," Kappel said upon seeing the sender's name. He opened the communication and read it. Then he pulled a printout from the desk drawer and laid it to the side of his keyboard. One at a time, he typed each recipient on the list an individual email containing an identical message:

> Those on the trail of the cache are going to the
> Greek Isle of Patmos. You will find them at the
> petra at Petra Beach. Same prize awaits the victor
> as long as you play by the rules.

Thirty minutes later he keyed in the final name from the list and sent the last email. Kappel locked his fingers from both hands, turned them out, and cracked his knuckles. The hideous rings on his hand momentarily faced him. Then he closed the email application. Kappel pushed his chair from the desk, rose, and again walked to the window. Outside, it was still dark in the distance, but below the grounds remained brilliantly lit by a multitude of incandescent lamps perched along the knoll. He felt a vile hatred rankling his soul. He willed himself to remain patient. He could make it. He had to make it. Then he would see Cecily again and get her out of that hellish nightmare. His dear, sweet Cecily; the only woman he had ever known.

Together, they would leave Europe forever.

CHAPTER 26

September 11. Tuesday – 11:00 p.m. Murciélago, Costa Rica

The stone jar with its tiny roll containing the Hebrew text and the small bag of myrrh was secured in a compartment in the plane's cabin. They departed Costa Rica with 16 hours of flying time ahead of them. Traveling east, they were going to lose another eight hours, which meant they would reach the Isle of Patmos sometime after 11 p.m. Wednesday night; a loss of one full day. It had taken Tolen considerable effort to convince Diaz that it was their best course of action. The members of the "True Sons of Light" would consider them even more a liability now and undoubtedly were preparing another attack. They desperately needed to capture one of the cult members alive. The incident at Formacion Descartes Santa Elena had nearly been disastrous. Tolen realized that even he had been so swept up in the thrill of discovering Joseph of Arimathea's tomb that he had let his guard down.

While his rationale to Diaz seemed prudent, he wondered if his personal desire to find the cache of Jesus' possessions was overruling his efforts to locate the Sudarium. He had convinced himself the Sudarium had never left Europe, which meant, sooner or later, they were going to have to make the trip overseas. Still, he harbored secret doubts about the course of action he was endorsing. He felt the ultimate truth tugging at him, and he could not deny the grip it had.

Two hours into the flight, Tolen excused himself.

"I'm going to check on Reba Zee and offer her some company," he said, unbuckling his seat belt. Tolen rose and reached the cockpit door. He knocked four times, entered, and closed the door behind him.

"Well, hey there, Tolen!" Reba Zee said spinning her head to greet him. "What brings you to my neck of the woods?"

"We have a long flight ahead of us. Just checking in to see how you're doing."

"You know I make these types of trips all the time. Piece of cake," she said with a short snort. Then she watched Tolen as he sat in the chair beside her, and a smile spread across her face. "I know you. You wanted privacy from those two."

"I need to speak with Vakind."

"Funny you mentioned him. He called just before you walked in. He's on channel eight waiting to talk to you."

Tolen picked up the receiver and punched the number. "Vakind?"

"Tolen, I'm here with Sheila Shaw and Tiffany Bar. I have to answer to both the Spanish president and President Fane again in several hours. Ms. Zee tells me you're en route to Europe. What's the latest?"

"We still have no hard leads on Boyd Ramsey. We're pursuing a historical artifact which constitutes a prime target for the 'True Sons of Light,' thereby making ourselves a target. We were attacked in Costa Rica. Like Boston, it was a single assailant, but he died before we could extract any information," Tolen paused. "Morris, nothing about this feels right. Neither assailant was a trained killer or had past affiliations with religious sects or fundamental terrorist groups. Richard Mox was 72 years old; not the age of a typical fanatic."

"I saw their bios, and I agree," Vakind acknowledged. "I've asked Bar to search for any links between Richard Mox, Gordon Nunnery, Boyd Ramsey, and Aaron Conin, the laboratory technician in Vinton, Virginia. Other than the one cell phone call, we still can't tie Ramsey to Conin. Bar has also been in contact with Canadian law enforcement regarding a search of Gordon Nunnery's house."

Bar added, "Just like Mox's house, Nunnery's was clean, although one thing unusual turned up: a cigar found in an ashtray on his desk."

"Why is that unusual?" Tolen heard Sheila Shaw ask.

"According to friends, family, and his ex-employer TRIUMF, the man wasn't known to be a smoker; not even in recreational situations."

"Closet smoker?" Sheila offered.

"If so, he has one expensive closet," Bar replied. "The cigar we found was a Gurkha Black Dragon. It wasn't the discounted version released in 2007. This was one of the 2006 originals. The blend included extremely old and rare tobaccos collected from all corners of the world. At $1,150 per cigar, it's the most expensive cigar ever made, and get this: they were only sold by the 100-count box. That's a tidy sum of $115,000 per box. Only five hand-carved, camel-bone boxes were ever produced. I've contacted the company in Honduras that makes them and have requested a customer list. So far, they're not cooperating, but we're trying to apply pressure."

"The Honduras government generally supports U.S. initiatives and is considered an ally," Vakind added. "We'll get the list."

"Only one of these cigars was found at Nunnery's place?" Tolen asked.

"Yes," Bar responded.

"Which seems to indicate it wasn't his," Vakind commented. "Our initial assumption was that he must have had a visitor who left it behind."

"The problem is," Bar continued, "when we performed iodine fuming, the only prints we found on the cigar were Nunnery's. Oh, and that Swiss dry-cleaning receipt you found in his wallet appears to be from a trip last year to Europe. I'm still digging to try to find his reason for going there. It doesn't appear to have been for any company business. Flight records show he was only in Switzerland a day before returning to the States. He has no friends or family there either."

"Did you find out why he no longer worked at TRIUMF?" Tolen asked, hoping for some association between his motive and his prior employer.

Vakind answered, "His employment was terminated six months ago. He began running unsanctioned particle physics experiments. He did so under the guise of a project he was working on, but once it was discovered he was using TRIUMF resources for tests outside his project's parameters, he was summarily dismissed."

"What kind of experiments was he conducting?" Tolen asked.

"No one's really sure," Bar replied. "Even as he was being let go, he never divulged what his unsanctioned tests were. As I told you before, he was a proponent of String Theory, or, as it's commonly called, the theory of everything."

"Which is what?" Tolen heard Vakind ask.

Tolen answered for her. "It's a theorized manner of describing the known fundamental forces and matter in a complete system. Tiffany, are you suggesting he was trying to prove String Theory with those unauthorized experiments?"

"Purely speculation on my part, but get this: his boss told me he had an unusual hobby: paranormal investigation."

"You mean like what they do on those television shows where they go to houses and try to capture evidence of apparitions? Ghost hunting?" Shaw asked in a tone that implied incredulity.

"Yes."

A particle physicist who believes in ghosts. That's an unlikely combination, Tolen thought. He switched subjects. "Bar, please find out which of Boyd Ramsey's fingers left prints at the murder scenes in Oviedo, Spain, and Palmar Sur, Costa Rica, as well as on the communiqué to the Spanish press."

"What are you looking for?" Vakind asked.

"Just a hunch. Morris, do the Spanish authorities have any leads on how the information of Boyd Ramsey's fingerprints leaked to the press after the communiqué was received?"

"None they've shared."

"Bar," Tolen continued, "I'd like the police report on Dr. Jade Mollur's accident when her car was run off the road in New Jersey."

"I'll forward it to your phone as soon as the call's over."

It was Vakind's turn to speak. "Do you have reservations about Dr. Mollur?"

"Morris, I had to tell her about the Sudarium's theft. The situation warranted it. She understands it's confidential, and since she's in my company, there's no danger she'll tell anyone else."

Tolen heard Vakind exhale. He knew the director was not thrilled with the news.

"I'll trust your judgment, Tolen. You've earned that much."

"Ms. Bar, I'd like you to make a trip to the Roanoke Laboratory where Aaron Conin worked," Tolen said. "Find out what you can about him from his boss and search his PC."

"Will do."

"Tolen," Vakind's voice slowed, "we've received a report that a fanatical religious group called the Flagellants, based in Italy but with members representing many European, South American, and yes, even North American countries, has planned an attack on the United States the moment the Sudarium is confirmed missing. While we've been unable to confirm any background regarding the 'True Sons of Light,' we know for a fact the Flagellants existed in history."

"They were a medieval religious sect, if I recall," Tolen said.

"Correct," Bar replied. "Their devotional practice included public disciplinary beatings. They started in northern Italy and gained a large following during the 14th century when the Black Plague ravaged Europe. They've existed in one form or another since then. Our intel tells us their popularity and membership experienced a huge upturn at the new millennium, and they're quite capable of—and in fact welcome—violence as a means to prove their religious point."

"Too bad we can't place the two opposing radical groups—the 'True Sons of Light' and the Flagellants—in a locked room and let them fight it out," Shaw remarked.

"We have strong reason to believe the Flagellants will carry out their threat," Vakind continued. There was a slight hesitation, and Tolen sensed the acting director had more unfavorable news. His next words were measured. "President Fane has decided to make an announcement on Thursday morning, 24 hours in advance of the start of the Feast of the Cross, to warn U.S. citizens at home and abroad of a possible terrorist attack. She's going to blame some paramilitary radical group in North Africa."

"Why a day before the Sudarium will be displayed?" Tolen asked in surprise. "We'll be tipping our hand. We might as well admit that the U.S. is, in fact, responsible for stealing the Sudarium. There's a high probability it will prompt the Flagellants to strike earlier than planned."

"I made the same argument, but the president is sympathetic to the risks of Americans everywhere, as she should be. It's a calculated gamble. I do have an idea which may help circumvent a premature attack, but it's going to take some political finagling."

Tolen had great respect for President Fane. In her shoes, he would do the same thing. "Morris, I need every minute I can get. Can you try and convince President Fane to delay issuing the terror alert until 12 hours before the Sudarium goes on display Friday morning?"

"It's difficult to ask the President of the United States to change her stance without a valid and urgent reason."

"I can't wrap my mind around it yet, but we're missing something. Ask her to do it for me. I will take full responsibility."

For a moment, the line went quiet. "I'll see what I can do," Vakind finally replied.

"Thanks, I'll be in touch."

As Tolen hung up, he turned to Reba Zee. "Reba, after we're asleep tonight, sweep the interior of the plane, please. I want to know if we have any electronic passengers."

"Aye aye, captain."

CHAPTER 27

September 12. Wednesday – 10:20 a.m. Roanoke, Virginia

Tiffany Bar arrived at Herking Medical Laboratory by taxi after landing at Roanoke Regional Airport. The morning air was cool; the temperature threatening to usher in autumn ahead of schedule. The scent of a nearby sugar maple tree drifted to her. Traffic was steady, but pedestrians were few.

The free-standing building on Rorer Avenue was considerably smaller than she anticipated. The light-colored brick facade was set off by dark-blue awnings over two windows in the front. She approached the flat structure, attempting to peer through the heavily tinted front glass doors with no luck.

Bar proceeded inside carrying a folder and her purse. She was met by a young, attractive blond male receptionist. Actually, he was too perfect: perfect clothes, teeth, fingernails, and eyebrows. He offered a contrived smile as she approached the front desk. No one else was in sight.

"Ah, yes, you must be Emily Carson here for the paternity test. Please be seated. A technician will be with you shortly."

Bar reached into her purse. She stared hard at the man, flipping a long blonde strand of bang behind one ear, as she held out her credentials for him to read. "Analyst Tiffany Bar, Central Intelligence Agency, here to see Dr. Felix Willside."

"Oh…oh," he stammered. "I'm so sorry, Ms. Bar. Please, come with me. I'm Kyle Jenkins. Dr. Willside is expecting you."

He led her through a door and into a stark, white hallway where their shoes clicked across the linoleum. She was greeted by a septic smell mixed with the aroma of floor wax. They passed a closed door, then a second, before arriving at an open office. The nameplate on the outer wall read, Dr. Felix D. Willside.

"Ms. Bar is here to see you," Jenkins announced.

A large man with short gray hair and wire-rimmed glasses looked up from a PC screen where he sat at a small desk in a tight office. He had a broad face with eyes set too close together. He also had the biggest ears Bar had ever seen; bent over and aimed at her like two satellite dishes.

He stood, towering above her. She took his proffered, meaty hand and shook it. "I'm Dr. Willside. I'm the head of the laboratory," he said in a meek voice which seemed incongruent with his hulking frame.

"Pleasure," Bar replied, craning up at the man.

"Shall we?" he motioned with his hand. "I'll show you Aaron Conin's workspace. It's really a shame to lose a man so young, and in such a vile fashion." His voice was so soft, Bar strained to hear him over the white noise being piped into the building.

He lumbered forward, and Bar fell in step behind him as he turned right down the hallway. His lengthy gait propelled him quickly to the end of the corridor where a doorway led to a large room. Bar had to double-step to keep up. They entered the laboratory where a woman was huddled over a microscope. There were work counters running the entire perimeter of the room and another vast island counter with an assortment of data screens, CBC tube rockers, culture stations, and other instruments gobbling up the counter space.

"This is Mira Nichols. She worked with Mr. Conin on blood and genetic testing."

Mira looked up from the microscope with a faint scowl as if bothered by the intrusion. Seeing her boss, she quickly feigned a smile. The African-American woman was in her mid-thirties, pudgy, with long, wiry hair tied in a dark bun. She lacked any makeup.

Mira walked over to them and extended her hand to Bar.

"I'm Tiffany Bar," she said, shaking the woman's hand.

"Mira, Ms. Bar is an analyst with the CIA," Willside said.

"They're looking into Aaron's death."

Mira's eyes turned inquisitive. "I thought it was a mugging? Why would the CIA be involved?"

"Yes, it was a mugging," Bar responded, "but Mr. Conin may have been in contact with someone else we're looking for, which gives the case international implications."

"Mira, please show Ms. Bar where Aaron worked and the PC he used. I'll be in my office if you have any questions for me." Willside turned back to Bar with a courteous nod. He pivoted smartly and headed toward the hallway.

"Dr. Willside, before you go…" Bar withdrew a sheet of paper from the folder in her hand, examined it, and handed it to Dr. Willside. "Please check the names on this list. I need to know if any of these people have ever conducted business here, either as a vendor or client."

"Certainly," the large man said mildly. "I won't have this information by the time you leave, though. It may take a few hours."

Bar handed the man her card. "Please call me as soon as you've had a chance to vet the list."

Dr. Willside nodded his understanding, turned, and disappeared up the hallway carrying the paper and Bar's card.

Bar spun back to Mira Nichols. "If I may ask you just a few general questions," she began. "How long did you know Aaron Conin?"

Mira rubbed the side of her neck as if working out some stiffness. "Years. Almost four, I think. Conin was a loner and wasn't close to me or anyone else here at Herking. I suspect he'd gotten bored with his job. Not to talk bad about the man, but he had a very lax attitude in the months leading up to his death."

Bar tilted her head slightly. She sensed some form of animosity. "So in your opinion, Mr. Conin wasn't a good employee?"

"I'm not his boss. It's not my place to comment about his job performance."

Strange, I thought you just did, Bar thought.

Mira continued slowly, as if she wanted to give an appearance of reluctance. "I do believe he may not have *always* had the

164

company's best interest at heart."

"How so?"

"Let's just say the man's morals might have been skewed. I can't prove it, but to me, it seemed there were times he was performing work which had nothing to do with samples coming in through the *official* process," Mira's tone had turned conspiratorial.

"You're suggesting that he ran unauthorized lab tests on the side?"

"I think Aaron knew people who paid well for test results. That's all I'm saying. Again, I have no proof, but he was very protective of certain test data. What I can say for sure is that there are more saved documents on his PC than are entered in the LIS."

Bar was familiar with LIS, or Lab Information System. It was a type of software which tracked and stored information generated by medical laboratory processes by interfacing with instruments and equipment associated with workflows. "I thought LIS prevented unauthorized tests by auditing the equipment to ensure records matched the number of processes run?"

Mira chuckled with a smirk. "In theory, that's the intent. It's a highly configurable program. As technicians, we learn ways around it."

Tiffany noticed a tray of bar-coded plastic bags to the side, each containing a form and one or more Vacutainer tubes of blood. "You primarily analyze blood samples in this lab, correct?"

"That's right, but we also extract DNA from hair, fingernails, saliva, and bone; just about anything organic from the human body."

"Where is his PC?"

"It's in the corner. We don't have dedicated workstations and PCs, but Aaron tended to gravitate to that one, so it was informally known as his." She led Bar toward the corner. To the side, Bar saw a centrifuge, a faucet perched over a deep sink, and an automated analyzer. Mira stopped at an isolated workstation with a PC. There was a thin lap drawer beneath it, partially open.

"I'll have to confiscate this PC."

Mira shrugged. "You'll have to discuss that with Dr. Willside."

Bar looked at the PC and the rest of the scant surface of the desktop. None of the usual types of personalization could be found in the work area: pictures, written quotes, mementos. "Has this area been…cleaned…since Conin's death?"

"No one's touched it." Mira paused. "I don't mean to be rude, but I have a boatload of work. We have yet to replace Conin, and I've been pulling twelve-hour days. Can I escort you back to Dr. Willside's office?"

"No bother. Please, resume what you were doing. I want to look through the lap drawer."

Mira's expression was a cross between confusion and downright ridicule. "I looked in that drawer the other day searching for a report. You're not going to find anything of interest there." Mira turned and walked back to the inbox tray.

Bar swallowed, quelling her annoyance with the woman. She took a seat on the desk chair and slowly opened the lap drawer. She found a few objects inside: two pens, one pencil, a ruler, a bottle of hand sanitizer, a small tissue packet, and a notebook pad that appeared unused.

Bar picked up the pad of paper and thumbed through the pages. Her first assumption had been accurate. It was unused. She withdrew the small packet of tissues, examined it, and returned it to the drawer. She looked at the clear liquid inside the small bottle of hand sanitizer. There was nothing unusual here, but then again, she had no idea what she was looking for. The mere fact Tolen had asked her to come here implied he thought it might be beneficial, and Tolen was seldom wrong.

Reaching her hand inside the drawer, Bar felt around the underside of the desk. She retracted her hand, closed the drawer, and stood from the chair. Out of the corner of her eye, she was aware of Mira Nichols watching her.

Bar slid the chair aside and squatted before the desk. She examined the underside of the drawer and saw nothing out of the ordinary. Then she slid her hand to the back where the metal curved upward and out of sight. She started on the left side and felt her way blindly along the cold surface to the right.

Suddenly, she touched a small, cool cylindrical object. It was restrained by some sort of tape. Bar quickly rolled to the ground, crooking her neck to see what it was. In the dark underside of the drawer, she saw a piece of duct tape holding a vial. She gently pried the duct tape loose and pulled the vial away. It appeared empty.

When she rose, Mira was standing over her.

"Did you...find something?"

Bar startled, but she did not respond. She scrutinized the vial closely now in the light. It still appeared empty.

Then she saw it—saw them—resting at the bottom of the tube.

CHAPTER 28

September 12. Wednesday – 6:42 p.m. Keene, California

Forty-two-year-old Nelson Whitacre arrived at the condemned church and drove around to the rear, parking on the dilapidated, cracked pavement in a line of cars, trucks, and SUVs. He stepped from his SUV, turned to face the cross at the apex of the building and said a quick prayer.

The air outside was comfortable. As usual for this time of year in the valley, there was almost no humidity, but the mosquitoes from the nearby woods were out in force. He slapped at his face, squashing one of the pesky insects into his cheek, then wiped the blood away.

Whitacre turned and headed toward the fellowship hall: a large, white standalone building behind the parking lot. Paint was peeling off the clapboard structure, and the rain gutter on the side had broken free and fallen to the ground. Behind, the Tehachapi Mountain range loomed in the distance.

He knew the others were waiting for him inside. His time for salvation had come. His wife's recent death had been the final straw.

It had only been a year ago when he and Shelly had joined the Flagellants. Members of the group had approached them where they attended church at Mount Sinai Baptist in Los Angeles. Somehow, they knew of the couple's frustration and disillusionment with organized religion, and, ultimately, he and Shelly had converted. America had become a godless country, and they welcomed the opportunity to support a Christian group that was willing to take action in order to keep humanity in God's good graces. With the changing times and advancing technological forms of communication such as the Internet, smart phones, and social networks, humans had lost touch with God. This was true everywhere, but it was especially so in the United States of America where the country had fallen into an irreparable state of disrespect to the Power to which they owed everything. Prayer had been banned from schools long ago, and atheism was running rampant. The separation of church and state was not only atrocious, it was heretical. Their former church had preached passive tolerance, and it had outraged the Whitacres. Those people sought to forgive the sins of others, but the Whitacres knew the truth. There are times when godly vengeance is not an option, but a heavenly obligation. No change comes about without sacrificial action.

After Shelly's death from pneumonia, Whitacre had questioned God's decision to take his wife, but the Flagellants were there to explain. Now he realized his path had been set in stone. He understood the natural order of things with renewed clarity. God had imposed His will. As a righteous man, he would never question the Higher Power again.

Whitacre rapped on the locked door, and it opened moments later. The Italian, whose name he still did not know, wordlessly escorted him in. The man was tall and lanky, standing easily at 6'9" with a high forehead and pale skin. He was clad in a dark suit and tie. Whitacre thought of him as a pensive undertaker who was leading them to the Promised Land.

A circle of chairs had been arranged in the middle of the large room. There were exactly twenty-one. He was the last to arrive and took the only empty seat beside Leon Smith, the 58-year-old retired fireman. Smith had also lost his wife six years ago to leukemia. He was suffering from arthritis, which caused the ex-fireman to hunch over, even as he sat in his seat.

Whitacre briefly looked at the others seated in the room. They came from different backgrounds and nationalities, yet they had been brought together by one common purpose: they were 21 who would change America.

The dark-haired Italian moved into the center of the circle. The room remained absolutely quiet as he slowly spun, eyeing each of them with a thoughtful nod. Then he spoke with a commanding voice. "For too long, mankind has been perverted by scientists, philosophers, physicists, and the like. One does not need to undertake a quest to know the truth. The Bible is the key. The misguided people of today have forgotten that every question is answered within its hallowed pages."

He paused and the room remained quiet. Forty-two eyes continued to be fixed on the Italian.

"Governments kowtow to the atheists and agnostics, so quick to appease these dissenters. Why must they be allowed a voice? Why must governments entertain their rhetoric when they dismiss the Almighty's word?

"I'll tell you why. Men of the devil have gained power. The American CIA is leading the charge. The venerable Sudarium, specifically mentioned in the Good Book, has been taken by this infernal organization." The Italian's eyes glazed, his forehead reddened, his voice rose in a crescendo. "The heathens must be taught a lesson! God's gift to man, the physical shroud which touched our Holy Savior's face, is in the hands of godless people! By His word, there will be punishment for this action!"

His voice suddenly honeyed and his words came slower. "We are of one people. We are His people. We have been tasked with serving the Lord when all others would stand by and do nothing against the tyranny of the devil's apostles. The CIA has launched an attack on the truth: the one truth that is not to be questioned. We will not let this transgression against humanity go without retribution. As God smites the sinners, we too shall use His hand to bring about the change which is necessary!"

The Italian looked around the circle studying each man's and woman's face. "You have come here voluntarily, each of your own accord. The Kingdom of Heaven awaits your arrival where you will pay eternal homage to the Lord, and by His grace, you will fulfill your duties here on earth. Remember, you are the 21 destined, the 21 blessed. The wrath of God will be felt to the far corners of the planet when you are done."

The Italian motioned for them to rise. In unison, the 21 people stood and bowed their heads. He spoke in a hallowed whisper.

"Father, into your hands I commit my spirit."

"It is finished," the 21 replied as one. Leon Smith's voice boomed the loudest from Nelson Whitacre's side.

They raised their heads, opened their eyes.

"We will reconvene back here at 6 p.m. tomorrow evening. Take care of your affairs, and celebrate your last hours on God's earth. Know that your soul will soon be in heaven and your deeds in His name will live on for eternity. We will wait for confirmation, then strike with vengeance when the time comes. God bless you all."

Whitacre looked up and smiled. He could feel God's power. It penetrated his very being. He felt more alive than he had in his entire life. The truth would be known.

In the corner of the fellowship hall there was a closed door. Whitacre knew the contents within that room held his destiny. As the result of the Sudarium's theft, death was about to reign down on American sinners. The spilled blood would be squarely on the hands of the CIA. Afterward, the American people would revolt. They would have no choice. Change was coming, and the government, which had become so politically correct, would once again embrace God. It was all there before them. Those who chose to side with the devil would no longer be in control. It would be a most glorious time.

No longer would Whitacre sit idly by and be an observer. He would become one of God's soldiers, armed to carry the fight.

In less than two days, Nelson Whitacre knew that he would once again be united with Shelly.

CHAPTER 29

September 12. Wednesday – 10:42 p.m. Flying over the Mediterranean Sea

They were in the sixteenth hour of the flight when Reba Zee came over the intercom to advise them they would be landing within 45 minutes.

Jade felt refreshed, renewed, despite the nagging flesh wound on her arm from the gunshot. She had caught up on sleep, and once again she felt the thrill of the hunt. She was eager to land on the Isle of Patmos and search the Petra, even though, as she kept reminding herself, it was a stone landmark the height of a three-story building. She deduced the next jar would be somewhere inside it, yet she had no idea where to look once they got there. Still, the thought of continuing the search was tantalizing.

To her side, Tolen was resting peacefully. She had heard him working on his laptop throughout the flight as she had drifted in and out of sleep. He had only dozed off within the last hour. It seemed he could subsist on minimal sleep.

Jade stared at Diaz across the aisle. He was looking at a *TIME* magazine. Like Jade, he had slept for a considerable time, snoring like an angry bull, but now he was wide awake. He perused the magazine, flipping to the next page after only a brief moment, pausing, then onto the next page. He spoke English very well, but she wondered how accomplished he was at reading the language.

Diaz looked up at Jade as if sensing her thoughts. He maintained a bland facade. "I only look at it for the pictures," he said with a touch of droll wit.

172

Jade found herself smiling involuntarily. Diaz did not seem to have much of a sense of humor, so his sardonic comment took her by surprise.

Diaz kept his eyes locked on Jade. He closed the magazine and lowered it to his lap. "What is in this for you?" he asked with his gravelly accent.

The question surprised her. "Pardon me?"

"What is in it for you?" His words had turned crisp and coarse, as if he harbored some malice.

"You mean finding the cache of Jesus' artifacts?"

Diaz nodded slowly.

He was baiting her, and she knew it. She rehearsed her response in her mind for a few seconds before speaking. "Well, I am an archaeologist, Diaz, and finding artifacts related to Jesus of Nazareth is the kind of monumental discovery that anyone who has ever worked in this field dreams of making."

"Fame and glory. That's it?" he asked, leaning forward in his seat with a vexing gaze. His discontent was obvious.

Before he had a chance to continue, she went on. "It would also substantiate the historical existence of Jesus Christ to non-believers. Can you imagine the religious singularity that it would bring about? No longer would people argue whether Jesus, the man, ever walked the earth. It would be a unifying truth."

Diaz relaxed back in his chair as his face softened slightly. It was obvious her explanation had been palatable to him, and he had no rebuttal. He looked out the cabin window.

"Diaz," Jade spoke softly, "two things: first, thank you for helping me in the underground tomb. I would have never made it without you. And second, I never offered my condolences for the loss of your brother, Javier."

"Javier," he repeated amidst a long exhale. "I've been going so fast, I've hardly had time to think about him. He was a good man, a good brother." His entire demeanor suddenly turned melancholy. "I am going to miss him dearly. He was my last surviving family member." He turned to Jade. "Thank you. You also have my deepest sympathy regarding your partner's death."

She was pleasantly surprised by his sincerity and warmth, yet the thought of Phillip's death was still too painful to dwell upon. She chose to focus the conversation back to Diaz's brother. "Did Javier have a wife? Children?"

"Unlike me," Diaz said, rubbing his stubbly face, "he had once been married. It only lasted a short time. There were no children." He paused. "At his wedding, I was his best man. We were very close." Diaz made a raucous snort which took Jade a moment to recognize as a laugh. "I remember writing a message on the bottom of his shoes so that when they knelt to take their vows, the whole congregation could read it."

Jade smiled. "What did you write?"

Diaz grinned and replied, "It said, 'I am' on his left shoe, and on his right shoe 'a virgin.'"

"You're kidding," Jade laughed heartily.

"No, we played jokes like this all the time with each other," Diaz looked down at nothing in particular. "Now he has been taken from this earth far too soon. I no longer have him to talk to."

The conversation had turned maudlin once again. Jade felt for Diaz. His pain was deep.

"My only consolation is in knowing he is with our Lord and Savior, Jesus Christ." He crossed himself. With that, he turned back to his magazine.

With Jesus, Jade thought. She once believed in the same ideology. Based on their recent discoveries, it appeared Jesus was a real historical figure, but there seemed to be no way to prove His divinity. The stories had most likely been embellished, propagated by organized religion in the hundreds and hundreds of years following His death. While she believed in Jesus, the man, these days she struggled with the blind leap of faith to Christ the Savior, as she had done when she was younger. Her studies had revealed to her that the Emperor Constantine and the Council of Nicaea had determined the divinity of Jesus Christ in approximately 325 AD. It seemed odd that it took a consensus of religious leaders to arrive at this conclusion. Jade was well aware as an archaeologist that when men document history, some tampering with the truth and slanting of facts always took place, either to appease themselves or market the concepts to the rest of the world. There were no such things as unbiased historical records. She wanted to believe Jesus Christ was divine—the Son of God—but logically, she had trouble reconciling such dogma.

The nose of the plane dipped, and the craft angled downward. They were on their approach to the airport on the Isle of Patmos. The sky outside was pitch dark. The only noise at the moment was the drone of the engines.

Tolen remained still, in a sound sleep by her side.

CHAPTER 30

September 12. Wednesday – 11:58 p.m. Isle of Patmos, Greece

Bahadur Aslan pressed his wet back uncomfortably against the jagged wall of Kalikatsou. He had been positioned here for nearly four hours now, ever since darkness had fallen over Petra Beach. His sixty-six-year-old body was stiff and fatigued. Earlier in the day, he and his partner, Mecnun, had been able to monitor activity on the Petra from comfortable chairs along the beach as they blended in with the European tourists. Once darkness had fallen, they had taken positions on either side of the massive rock at the tip of the short peninsula overlooking the bay. The thunderstorm an hour ago had drenched them. To add to their irritation, minutes ago a mild wind had arisen, chilling them to the bone.

Shaking, Bahadur wrapped his soggy, sour-smelling coat around himself with one hand while he used his other hand to prop the stock of the rifle on the stone ground.

He looked up. The moon was masked by a collage of translucent clouds, yet the penetrating light soaked the beach across the way. The dark swells of rocky earth behind lifted quietly on the horizon as a ghostly backdrop. The smell of salt filled the air. Waves tumbled gracefully onto the sandy beach, barely audible from where he stood. Otherwise, there was silence as the dark bay tossed lazily with gentle swells.

Few tourists had ventured out; only stragglers who stayed on the beach until dusk and then had made their way inland to hotels, restaurants, and other destinations. Since nightfall, Bahadur had only observed one couple strolling in the dark, and they had

176

scampered off into the dunes behind the beach, probably for a clandestine session of lovemaking.

Thus, the waiting continued.

Bahadur heard faint voices riding in on the wind. Nervously, he squatted and grabbed the binoculars from a rock ledge to his side. He was cloaked in darkness, shielded from the moonlight by the towering side of the Petra, but still he rose slowly. He did not want to risk any sudden movement that might reveal him in the shadows. He brought the binoculars to his eyes and surveyed the beach. There they were: a man and a woman, walking barefoot along the shore at the edge of the waterline. The woman, wearing shorts and a tight tee shirt, had short hair and an alluring figure. The man holding her hand was larger, bulky but not overweight, wearing a jacket and pants rolled up to his knees. No doubt, this was another couple on vacation looking to screw under the Greek moonlight, Bahadur thought with an inward shrug. Such things were outside his experience any more.

The salty breeze brought another unwelcome chill.

Bahadur kept watch as the couple continued up the beach toward him. Their words, although indistinguishable, became louder and carried a lively, flirtatious tone. The woman laughed, and their banter filled the air. The man gave her a playful shove, and the woman nearly toppled over in the surf. Her laughter ceased, and she rejoined the man, taking his hand into hers.

The closer the couple approached, the more uncomfortable Bahadur became with their presence. Bahadur considered sneaking around to the far side of the Petra to alert Mecnun, but he refrained. That would be ridiculous. They were obviously no threat. He would simply monitor the man and woman until they were clear of the area.

The couple paused, turning toward each other in what Bahadur was sure was a lovers' gaze. They hesitated, then slowly hugged, but something was wrong. Their embrace looked awkward, contrived.

After a brief moment, the couple broke away and resumed walking toward the Petra, never once looking toward the colossal fixture. Something was not right. In the dark, Bahadur quietly hoisted his rifle. Raising it to eye level, he sighted the woman's chest in the crosshairs of the scope. Even with the cool winds, his fingers were wet from perspiration as he touched the trigger. He had never shot another human being. The notion of murder was difficult enough, but killing people who were most likely in the wrong place at the wrong time was hard to justify. He tried to steel himself, protracting the argument in his head. They were behaving too suspiciously. He convinced himself that this was not just an innocent couple out for a stroll on the beach.

He struggled to maintain his aim and stop his shaking.

The couple was now within 50 feet. He would allow them only a few more steps before sealing their fate. He would shoot the woman first then deal with the man. He prayed their faces remained dark and cloaked. He did not want to see their expressions.

He silently willed them to stop. They never did. He pivoted slightly and used the side of the stone wall as a brace to steady the weapon. Bahadur aligned the crosshairs at the center of the woman's torso, took a deep breath and held it, then gently squeezed the trig—

With startling force, the rifle launched from Bahadur's hands with a whizzing sound. Dazed, he heard the distant sound of a male voice yelling, "Get down!" His hand ached. Bahadur looked down at it in the dim light and saw the dark fluid gushing from a ragged hole where his palm should have been. The sight of torn veins and exposed meat turned his stomach to mush. It had to be a bad dream. He continued to stare blankly at his wounded hand, wondering why he did not feel anything. He wheeled around, delirious, confused as to what to do next. A severe cramp struck his right leg, causing him to buckle. He grabbed at it and collapsed to the hard stone.

Only after someone had lifted him up and put their arm around him did his thoughts coalesce around the fact he had been shot... twice. He looked at his mangled hand, then at his leg where blood was spilling out onto his pants through a dark, wet hole in the fabric.

"I've got you, Bahadur. I've got you," the man whispered. "Quiet now so we can get away. Rafet is waiting."

Even in his fog, he recognized the man's voice. Mecnun pushed him along, circling the Petra to the back side against the bay.

****

Tolen broke into a full gallop toward the Petra from the white sand dunes where he had been positioned. His first shot had dislodged the rifle, and the second shot had disabled the man. As he suspected, the second man stationed at the Petra had come to the first man's aid, and they were now circling behind the monstrous outcropping for cover. In doing so, they were trapping themselves. Between him and Diaz, they could flank their position and force the men to surrender. It was imperative they capture the two alive.

Tolen neared the massive stone. It was as wide at the base as a house and as tall as an aged oak tree. Diaz was waiting for Tolen in the shadows with the Beretta 9mm Tolen had provided as a replacement for his lost firearm in Costa Rica. He had just put his shoes back on. As planned, Jade had hidden somewhere off the beach once the shooting had started. Tolen feared Diaz and Jade would have trouble pulling off the 'couple in love,' and he was right. He had been forced to take the shot much earlier than he preferred. Luckily, he had still found his mark both times.

Tolen silently gestured for Diaz to circle the Petra to the right. Tolen went left. They would corner the two assailants at the backside of the stone where it abutted the bay. With one injured, there was no danger of them swimming away. If Tolen's suspicion was correct—that these were also novices and not trained mercenaries—apprehending the two men should be relatively easy.

Tolen eased around the stone, slowly circumventing its rocky side. The moon was shining on the bay, and the farther he went, the lighter it became. Halfway around, he heard a rumbling sound. The smell of the saltwater suddenly blended with the aroma of diesel exhaust. Instinctively, Tolen abandoned all efforts to approach stealthily and rushed around the stone. He arrived at the back and was met by Diaz approaching from the other direction. The two men heard the strain of the diesel engine accelerate and watched the dark form of a fishing boat race away from the Petra, parting the water, leaving the bay for the open sea. The assailants had gotten away via a water escape, something neither Tolen nor Diaz had anticipated, taking with them any chance of closing in on Ramsey and the Sudarium.

Diaz threw his hands up in disgust. "Maldígalo todo!"

Tolen felt immense frustration. He was off his game. He should have anticipated the move.

Looking out over the bay at the vessel fading away into the darkness, he could hear his father's words: *You can stand there defeated, or deal with those elements within your control and move on. Which makes more sense?* Tolen gathered himself and turned to Diaz, who was still pacing on a small stone ledge. "Let's see what we can find."

CHAPTER 31

September 13. Thursday – 12:06 a.m. Isle of Patmos, Greece

"Any chance they'll return?" Jade asked apprehensively after Diaz returned with a coil of rope they had hidden near the beach.

"Extremely doubtful," Tolen responded.

Jade peered upward at the gargantuan mound of stone before them. It was as if the natural formation had sprouted from the sea. Like a giant lump of unmolded clay, it was pockmarked with massive indentations and jutting stone fingers casting eerie shadows on the grassy knoll below. "Wow, I knew this thing was big, but I had no idea the true size of it. It could take hours, even days, to examine the visible surface area, and that's *if* we can even reach it at all." Something caught her eye in the darkness, running up the side of the stone. "Are those...steps?"

"They're hewn from the rock," Tolen began. "I read they were carved long ago, possibly during the early Christian era, by hermits who took refuge here, including the Apostle John."

"Let's get on with it," Diaz said, extracting a flashlight from his coat. He aimed the light to lead them to the base of the irregular stairs as he turned toward Jade. "Once again, we have no idea what we're looking for, right?"

"I think it's a safe assumption to say we need to find a tiny image of either gold or frankincense since we located myrrh at the Costa Rican tomb," Jade responded.

Tolen, who had been carrying the rope, hoisted the coil and handed the rifle to Diaz. "Here, you carry this," he said.

Diaz looped the harness over his shoulder and pitched the

weapon on his back. He began to ascend the stone steps. Jade followed on Diaz's heels. Tolen went last. They each carried a flashlight.

It was a precarious climb, especially in the dark with nothing to hold onto. They could only brace against the rock wall to the side as they went. The steps were fashioned from the rough stone, cut at different widths and lengths and were unevenly spaced. With a slight breeze swirling around the massive formation, Jade felt a twinge of vertigo as they climbed. The tang of briny air was constant.

She trained the light down, taking one step at a time, ensuring she had firm footing. At each step, she paused, raised the flashlight and examined the stone wall to the side, running her fingers over the craggy surface.

Jade felt a certain mystical aura surrounding this place. She was most likely traveling the same ancient staircase the Apostle John had once climbed. A mild shiver passed through her.

Of necessity, their pace was slow, deliberate, and purposeful. Jade and Diaz scanned the walls silently as they climbed. Tolen followed behind. Curiously, Jade noticed he was giving the stone façade only a cursory check.

Jade surmised that if they could find the appropriate image—which equated to finding a needle in a haystack—it was going to lead inside the Petra. She only hoped the clue was accessible and not on an obscure side of the Petra, which would require they somehow rappel down the massive rock formation. The thought of dangling by a rope in the dark brought a rise of anxiety. Based on the monumental effort which must have gone into creating the cathedral cave and the underground tunnels in Costa Rica, she doubted Joseph would have purposely sought the less arduous method. If there was one thing Dr. Jade Mollur had already learned about Joseph of Arimathea, it was that he did things on a grand scale with considerable forethought and planning.

"Did the Apostle John write the Book of Revelation on this rock?" Diaz called back.

"Not according to legend," Tolen responded upward. "The Cave of the Apocalypse is northwest of here in the center of the island. John was said to live there between 95 and 97 AD. According to the Bible, that small cave is where John heard the voice of God, and the image of Jesus appeared before him. From these encounters, he wrote the Book of Revelation."

"Yet," Jade added, "it's thought John also spent time on this Petra. It may have been a place of meditation or spiritual renewal."

Spiritual renewal: the phrase sounded somewhat self-serving to Jade. For a moment, she considered how far they had already come on this quest. As resourceful as Dr. Phillip Cherrigan had been, she knew that she and Phillip would never have achieved the same degree of success in finding the stone jar in Central America and now, hopefully, the next stone jar here, all while averting death. While he was a brilliant academician, Phillip was not in the best physical shape. In more ways than she cared to admit, without Tolen's and Diaz's assistance, she certainly would not have made it this far.

They continued their slow trek upward. Three more steps and Jade ventured another look back. Instead of inspecting the wall, Tolen was now using his light to trace a line on both sides of the stair steps and farther out on the rocky wall. She wondered if he was really hoping to see a tiny carved image from such a distance.

Farther and farther they climbed until they were within sight of the summit.

Jade frowned. Again she looked at Tolen, who had his flashlight beam moving away from them on a horizontal line across the ragged stone wall.

"There," he said. "See that flat shelf along the wall?"

"You see an image?" Jade asked.

Diaz had also turned to look downward toward Tolen's flashlight beam.

"No," Tolen paused. He looked out over the moonlit bay reflectively. "We think the clue from the jar from Joseph of Arimathea's tomb ties to the 64th listing in the Copper Scroll, right?"

Jade nodded.

"What does line 64 say?"

Jade thought for a moment. "I don't recall it verbatim. It

mentioned that the duplicate scroll with the detailed inventory of the other 63 treasures, including a more exact description of all the locations, would be found in a dry well at Kohlit."

"Correct. The operative words being 'dry well.' " With that, Tolen repositioned the coil of rope on his shoulder and, to Jade's surprise, stepped out onto the thin ledge. He flattened himself against the wall and inched ahead. One misstep and he would tumble off the stone lip and plummet two and a half stories to the outcropping of rock at the base. Jade involuntarily held her breath as Tolen slid slowly away.

"Where are you going?" she yelled.

Tolen stopped and turned toward her as much as he could on the ledge. "In addition to the carved steps, hermits long ago cut a cistern out of this rock."

The meaning instantly registered with Jade. "The cistern *is* a well!"

The shadowy figure of Tolen proceeded along the five-inch-thick ledge. Surprisingly, he had turned his flashlight off, proceeding by the glow of the moon. Without thinking of the implications, Jade found herself instinctively following him. Once on the narrow ledge, she froze. She closed her eyes and fought to control the panic. *Move slowly*, she willed herself, reopening her eyes. With a measured slide of her foot, she inched her way to the side then drew her other foot alongside. All the while, she pressed into the rough stone, trying to get a hold with her free hand while the other hand awkwardly gripped the flashlight. Jade reminded herself she had been an athlete; a gymnast capable of tumbling, flipping, and landing on a four-inch beam. *Move slowly and precisely*, she told herself again.

In similar fashion, she saw Diaz follow her. When he looked at her, she felt a kindred spirit. His stiff expression and vaulted brow suggested he was not enamored with crossing the narrow ledge either, yet both of them pressed on, following after Tolen, who moved unerringly with balanced precision.

After a nerve-wracking dozen feet of creeping along the brink of stone, a burst of wind caused Jade to pause, fearful she might lose her balance. She steadied herself, waiting for the stiff breeze to calm. The Mediterranean night air had warmed with the passing of the storm, and she felt perspiration gather on her forehead.

The light ahead drew her attention. Tolen had come to a stop and switched his flashlight back on. Thankfully, he was standing on a much thicker section of ledge that dipped inward into a wide crevice.

"Just a few more feet," Tolen urged Jade, holding out his hand for hers. When she finally grabbed Samuel Tolen's hand and felt his warm, firm grip, she knew that even if she had lost her balance, he would not have let her fall. Moments later, Diaz joined them on the small plateau. He stepped beside them with a sigh of relief and a face full of sweat.

Jade looked at the dark crevice and turned her flashlight on. The beam licked the stone ahead, splitting the walls to either side, and landed in a small alcove which came to a point. A natural stone roof pressed down over it. Only then did she notice that the small plateau they stood upon angled slightly downward, channeling into the alcove where a circular recess of undetermined depth had been cut in the stone floor.

Its design was apparent. The cistern had been engineered long ago so that when rainwater fell on the plateau, it funneled into the alcove, which was shaped like a wedge, and was captured in the deep hole. The stone roof prevented the water from evaporating in the direct sunlight: exceedingly functional and genius in its simplicity.

They entered the small alcove. Jade led the way. The stone surface was slick, and she moved carefully. All three had their flashlights on and, as if acting like a single mind, the three beams sought the depths of the circular recess when they arrived at the edge. The strong stench of stagnant water rose to greet them as they stood over the opening.

"It's deep, and it stinks," Diaz said, shucking off the rifle and laying it to the side.

Jade looked for the bottom of the well. Her light reflected off water at least a dozen feet down. The shaft was forged three feet in diameter and bored symmetrically from top to bottom.

"I'm going in," Jade said. "Can you lower me by the rope?"

Tolen took the rope off his shoulder and unwound it. With a series of quick ties, he made a harness which he fitted over Jade's torso and secured underneath her arms. Then, with a flashlight in her hand, Tolen and Diaz lowered Jade.

Not normally prone to claustrophobia, she felt an intense sense of confinement as she slipped below the plateau into the stone tunnel. The rope was painful, burning her underarms as it supported her. She tried to leverage her feet against the mottled wall to offset her weight but found that doing so impeded her descent. She decided to suspend her full weight against the rope and bear the pain in order to reach the bottom faster.

There was no way to know the depth of the pool at the base. When she finally reached it, she tentatively stretched a foot to the surface and found the water was only an inch and a half deep.

"I'm at the bottom! Give me some slack!" she yelled upward. Two dark faces stared down at her. "There's hardly any water here."

Diaz had been right about one thing. The smell was horrific. She removed the harness and turned in a circle, sloshing the water. She inspected the walls. The sides were rough and sharp, and she took care as she ran her fingers over the surface.

After exhausting her examination of the wall, she shined the flashlight at her feet and knelt. Quarters were cramped, and she maintained her balance only with great effort. She placed her hand below the surface of the water and touched the stone bottom. The thin layer of water was warmer than she had expected. She found the base to be smooth and curved at the edges where it met the walls, forming a shallow bowl. The only aberration was in the dead center: a set of concentric circles, a small one just inside a larger one, interlocking with a second, similar set of concentric circles. She was struck with a rush of excitement.

"I've found something! There's an image at the base, and I think it's supposed to be gold rings!"

CHAPTER 32

September 13. Thursday – 12:31 a.m. Isle of Patmos, Greece

It suddenly occurred to Jade they had nothing to use to break through the base. As if reading her mind, Tolen called down, "We're lowering a hammer on the rope."

She rose and shined the flashlight up to see the hammer secured in a knot coming slowly toward her, swinging from side to side. When it was in reach, she grabbed it, untying it from the rope. She started to ask where the hammer had come from, but she was sure she already knew the answer. Tolen was prepared for any situation.

Jade took the hammer by the handle and knelt back down. With her target as the exact center of the small base, it was difficult for her to get an angle from which to strike it. She scrunched against the wall, moving her feet out of the way, but then found herself nearly toppling into the other side. Next, she tried to straddle the center but found that to be awkward as well. No matter what angle she took in the compact area, she could not strike with enough force to do any damage. To complicate matters, every time she smacked the base, a spray of water shot into her eyes and onto her clothes.

"Jade, any progress?" Tolen's voice rang down from above.

"No, it's too bloody cramped in here to break through. I can't get a good swing," she said in disgust, wiping the pungent water from her face. "*Yuck.*"

There was a moment of silence before she heard, "I'm going to lower another tool down."

"Little good it'll probably do me," Jade muttered to herself.

Moments later, the rope came down again dangling an object.

Jade had trouble making out the odd shape through the scant light. When it neared, and she recognized what it was, she crinkled her face in confusion. She untied the knot and held the object away from her like a venomous snake. "What am I supposed to do with a gun?"

"Shoot at the floor," Diaz said in his gritty voice.

"I've never shot a gun in my life," Jade said, eyeing the weapon with consternation.

"I'll walk you through it," Tolen's mellifluous voice called down. Unlike Diaz, his tone had a way of putting her at ease.

She drew a deep inhale of the rotten-smelling air, and then exhaled, looking down at the watery base. She had come this far and was not about to give up now.

"Okay," she relented, "tell me what to do."

"There's a safety lever on the side. Slide it off."

Jade found it and complied. "Got it."

"Get in a stance with your feet as far away from the target area as possible without jeopardizing your balance. Aim the gun and squeeze the trigger gently but firmly to fire a round. Once you break through, you should be able to enlarge the opening with the hammer."

Why does this feel like a bad idea? Jade thought.

Nevertheless, she spread her feet apart. With one hand, she kept the flashlight directed down. With the other hand, she pointed the barrel of the pistol toward the rings. She had no idea how to aim the weapon accurately, so she squatted to within a foot of the surface of the water to ensure she hit the target. Anxious to get it over with, she closed her eyes tight, took a deep breath, and pulled the trigger.

****

A deafening blast resonated up the stone shaft. Tolen heard a crunch, a crackle, and the pitter-patter of stone falling away. The glow from Jade's flashlight vanished in the darkness.

"Jade?!" Tolen called down into the inky blackness. He aimed his flashlight into the deep cavity and saw the base was still intact, yet Jade was nowhere in sight.

"What happened to her?" Diaz asked, scurrying around the edge, using his flashlight to search out the shaft. "She's gone!"

"So is the water," Tolen remarked. He rose, turned, and spotted the rifle nearby on the ground. He quickly retrieved it and tied an end of the rope to the mid-section of the rifle. He lobbed the balance of the rope down the tunnel. Tolen laid the rifle across the middle of the hole. It extended beyond the opening by several inches on either side. He climbed in the hole, avoiding the rifle and holding the rope as he went. The rifle shifted slightly on the lip with his weight. "Stay here until I find out what happened."

He lowered himself on the rope, hand over hand. His muscles strained under his own weight. With the flashlight in his pocket, the darkness was pervasive until Diaz caught him in his beam from above. Even so, Tolen was unable to get a clear view of what lay below. He gave up trying, instead focusing his energy and attention on reaching the bottom of the well as quickly as possible.

"Jade?" Tolen called out again as he went.

No response.

He looked up to see the dark head of Diaz looming above.

"Is she there?" Diaz yelled down.

"Give me a minute," Tolen replied, clutching the rope and lowering himself the rest of the way. He suddenly felt solid stone at his feet, but instead of the base being horizontal, the surface was angled downward. He paused, found footing against the edges of the wall, and was able to hold the rope with one hand and remove the flashlight with his other hand.

When he turned the light on and shined it down, he was shocked by what he saw. The rest of the rope evaporated somewhere out of sight. The stone base was mostly gone. Only a lip around the edge where he had gained footing was still in place. Below that, a smooth wormhole tunnel corkscrewed out of sight. What had appeared as the well's bottom from above was an optical illusion. In reality, it was the descending, curved walls of a continuing tunnel.

"Diaz," he called upward, "when Jade shot the floor, it broke the entire base, and she must have collapsed through it. The tunnel continues down as a spiraling shaft. Unless it's exceedingly long, we should have enough rope to make it down, and also have a way out. Come on down. Just be careful not to dislodge the rifle above."

There were indistinguishable utterances. Then he heard Diaz above breathing heavily as he started down the rope.

"Jade!" Tolen yelled down the winding tunnel, cupping his hand to the side of his mouth.

He paused to listen. The only sound was Diaz working his way down the rope, panting from overhead.

Tolen was not going to wait. Jade was most likely incapacitated. He turned the flashlight off and deposited it into his pocket. Once again, he was mired in darkness. Tolen stepped down into the curved shaft while holding onto the rope. He moved into it backward, walking his hands down the rope as his feet, then his legs, made contact with the walls. Tolen was pleased to discover the walls were polished stone. Sliding down them would be the equivalent of going down a playground slide. Depending on if and where it emptied out, Jade might have survived. Then again, if the cave drained out into a deep recess…He didn't want to think about it.

Tolen wormed his way down feet first on his stomach, using the rope to assist him. The angle of the corkscrewed walls was such that he was almost ready to let go of the rope completely and skirt his way down by keeping his hands and feet spread and in contact with the sides to brake as he slid. With the sleek walls, though, he was unsure if he could maintain the required pressure to avert a freefall, so he continued his blind descent as quickly as he could, using the rope as a guide. After several winding turns, he felt the rope jostle in his hands, pulling taut from above. This signaled that Diaz had reached the base and was following him down the twisting shaft.

Tolen lost track of the number of revolutions as the corkscrew shaft wound into the bowels of the Petra. He grew increasingly concerned that the rope, which was seventy-five-feet long, would run out before he reached the end.

When his feet no longer felt hard stone, he stopped. He had reached the end of the tunnel, and the end of the rope. A sweet musk rose to meet him. Tolen drew his knees to his chest and turned on his back, compacting his body. This allowed him to withdraw his flashlight from his pocket, while holding onto the rope with his other hand. He stretched his legs back out and shined the flashlight over his body to see where the spiraling shaft had ended.

The light failed to find a wall. Confused, Tolen directed the beam down and was thankful to see a brown, wrinkled floor three feet below. Jade was nowhere in sight, yet his visage was obscured by the angle. He pushed his way out of the tunnel and carefully stood upright.

Jade was crumpled at the base of the wall. He had nearly stepped on her.

Anxiously, he knelt down beside her and touched her wrist. Thankfully, he felt a strong pulse.

"Jade?" he said, laying a hand on her back. Her face was pressed to the rumpled floor, which Tolen realized was a bed of sticks and dried leaves. She roused, sat up in a daze, and brushed the natural debris from the side of her cheek.

"Are you okay?"

"Yeah, yeah. I remember...falling," she stammered, pushing her dark bangs out of her eyes. "Where are we?"

"At the end of a secondary tunnel, deep inside the Petra. It appears we're in another cavern," he said, helping her to her feet. Leaves and twigs clung to her clothes and her bare skin. She took a moment to brush them off.

"The floor is covered in dried debris which cushioned your fall and may have saved your life."

"Tolen, did you find Jade?" Diaz's voice echoed down through the wormhole.

"Yes, she's safe." Tolen reached down and found his pistol among the branches. He latched the safety back on and reholstered it.

A few seconds later, Diaz popped out of the hole, turning his body awkwardly to reach the floor, nearly falling.

"What is this place?" Jade mused, turning her flashlight about the round room.

"Hell," Diaz scoffed, rising beside her.

The circular room was rather small. It had a domed ceiling

191

adorned with a mosaic of vibrant colors, artwork as impressive as the cathedral cave in Costa Rica. A dozen carved pilasters ran up the walls, equally spaced around the room. Thankfully, there was no water to contend with here. Beyond that, the chamber was reminiscent of the Costa Rican cave, except on a smaller scale, and with pilasters instead of the niche altars.

Jade shined her flashlight on the nearest pilaster and drew in a sharp breath. "Look at the faces."

The pilaster was a mass of distraught and tortured expressions formed with such precision that Tolen could see rivulets of sweat running down some of the cheeks. Fused faces were elongated, twisted in agony. It was as if they had all just experienced some cataclysmic torment which was so horrifying, so painful, they had lost their minds.

"That's disturbing," Diaz remarked.

Tolen turned his flashlight to the floor and began walking. The dry twigs and branches snapped crisply with the weight of each step, and he got the distinct impression he was moving across thick padding. He stopped and tried to locate the true floor. Even after kicking close to six inches of debris aside, all Tolen found were more layers of thin, brittle sticks and dried, rotting leaves. There was no telling how much natural debris coated the austere cave floor. Oddly, the smell of decaying wood and rot remained tinged with an unusual musky fragrance.

Three beams of light lanced about the cavern. Except for the debris lining the floor and the pilasters nestled against the walls, the room was empty. Tolen spotted a fissure in the far side of the room which sliced up to the ceiling. A gap of at least two feet led into total darkness.

"There," he called to the others, focusing his light on it.

The threesome approached the vertical crevice. It was jagged and crusty; lichen caked at the edges. Jade shined her flashlight inside, where a long, dark corridor stretched into the distance. Unlike the underground chamber in Costa Rica, this hallway had a warren of doorways carved on both sides; at least ten, maybe more. The ground coating of dried twigs, leaves, and small limbs continued into the passageway.

"We must be under the Petra. This corridor might even extend under the bay," Jade remarked. She slid through the crevice first, followed by Diaz, then Tolen. The ground continued to crunch sharply beneath their feet as they walked. Ahead, the openings to either side were staggered. The first one they came to was on the left and cut perfectly through four inches of stone. It was approximately the size and shape of a house doorway.

Jade turned her light into the room. They were met with a surprising sight.

The stone floor was clear and visible, and at least a foot below where they stood in the passageway. There was a narrow threshold across the entrance that reached up twelve inches and prevented the branches and twigs in the corridor from spilling into the room. The small enclosure was void, save for a six-foot-long, white, rectangular stone box that was perched low on a gray, stone pedestal in the center of the room. It was fitted on top with a lid which overhung by no more than an inch on all sides.

"What is that?" Diaz asked.

"I...I think it's a coffin," Jade said.

Tolen thought the same thing, yet he was having a hard time processing who might warrant such a secretive and exclusive tomb, unless, perhaps...

They stepped down carefully into the room and walked up to the long stone box. There were no writings or markings on the top. Jade examined the barren sides. "There's no indication *who* or *what* is inside." She touched the surface. "It's coarse. I think it's made of limestone."

Tolen looked at Diaz. The unspoken message was received. Diaz went to one end, Tolen to the other. They grabbed the thick stone lid and slowly slid it to the side. It scraped like fingernails on a chalkboard. They stopped after only a few seconds to peer into a six-inch gap where Jade held the flashlight in place. The two men crowded beside her. The smell that reached them was harsh.

Sure enough, they saw disarticulated human remains inside, replete with a skull lolled to the side, facing them. Tolen could tell by the pronounced, angular bone structure and narrow hips that it was a male.

Diaz leaned back and crossed himself. "Why do we keep disturbing the dead?"

"Any idea who this is?" Tolen asked Jade, disregarding Diaz's comment.

"Not a clue," she turned her eyes to him as she spoke. She held his gaze for a moment, but said nothing more.

"Let's pull the lid back further," Tolen said, anxious to know more about the man in the stone box.

"Why?" Diaz contested. "We're looking for a jar, no?"

Surprising Diaz, Jade nudged the man aside and gripped the end of the heavy lid. Together, she and Tolen slid it further, angling one end off the stone box so they would have unimpeded access to the upper section of the remains where they could view the head and chest.

Tolen leaned in. Although the skeleton was disjointed—the tendons and ligaments having decayed long ago—the bones had settled in place approximately where they had been during life. This meant the vertebrae, including the bones of the neck, lay in a nearly perfect line, but at the base of the skull, at least four vertebrae were missing.

"Help me push it back," Tolen said.

This time, it was Jade who objected. "Already?"

"Come on," was all Tolen said in response.

Diaz seemed relieved to cover the remains. It only took a few seconds to slide the stone lid back in place.

Tolen quickly led the other two back to the doorway and left the room, stepping up to the passageway and producing the familiar crack of branches and twigs. With his flashlight beam knifing the darkness ahead, Tolen found the next doorway on the right. As he had expected, it led into a room identical to the first enclosure: same tall threshold of stone, which held the branches and debris out of the room, same barren floor, another unmarked stone coffin. Again, there were the skeletal remains of a man inside. This time, examination showed the man's frontal skull bone had been caved in, cracked numerous times. Again, Tolen made no comment. He knew he was frustrating both Jade and Diaz, but he had to be sure.

The third, fourth, and fifth rooms revealed identical situations.

The enclosures and coffins were carbon copies. The only difference in each room was the male remains and their condition.

CHAPTER 33

September 13. Thursday – 12:56 a.m. Isle of Patmos, Greece

Jade had had enough. "Stop, Tolen. No more until you explain what's going on."

To both Jade's and Diaz's mounting frustration, Tolen did not answer. Instead he stepped up into the crunchy corridor and shined his flashlight to one side of the long passageway and then the other, pausing on each doorway ahead.

"What are you searching for?" Diaz asked.

"One more, then I promise I'll explain," Tolen said, looking Jade squarely in the eyes. Unexpectedly, she saw a profound reverence there. She nodded her agreement almost involuntarily.

"We're wasting time, Tolen," Diaz growled. "We should be looking for the second jar."

"How do you know the jar isn't in one of the coffins?" Jade rebutted.

Diaz said nothing.

Tolen led them into the sixth room. When Diaz and Tolen moved the coffin lid aside, again they saw the remains of a man. Tolen leaned in with the flashlight and looked over the bones, eventually gliding the length of the stone coffin to examine the remains. At one point, he fanned his hand over the skeleton, causing a puff of dust to arise.

Jade could tell Tolen knew something. Even in the dim light, the knowledge brought a reflective gaze to the man's blue eyes.

She momentarily allowed the facts to stack up in her mind: a dozen or so rooms, each with a coffin containing the skeletal remains of a man, each seemed to have suffered varied afflictions... and then it struck her: of course!

Tolen must have seen the recognition in her eyes. He nodded in agreement. "I believe we've found the bodies of the Apostles."

Jade looked at the skeleton in the coffin and then up at Tolen.

"How can you be sure?" Diaz asked.

"There are twelve rooms; catacombs, if you will. And although we haven't examined all of them, we have looked at half. The types of wounds inflicted on the six bodies—or should I say, five—are consistent with the manner in which the Apostles are thought to have died. Only one Apostle's death is specifically cited in the Bible. The death of James, son of Zebedee, is recorded in Acts 12:2. The Bible states he was, 'put to death with the sword.' The common belief now is that he was beheaded. The first skeleton was missing vertebrae, which is the result of being decapitated."

The words struck a morbid chord with Jade. The memory of Dr. Phillip Cherrigan's brutal death by decapitation brought a lingering ache.

Tolen continued. "The rest of the Apostles' deaths are speculation based on church tradition and, in fact, vary widely."

"The second body we examined had the skull crushed in; a style of death linked to several of the Apostles. One, the other Apostle named James, was said to have been thrown from a temple steeple and survived, only to be beaten to death with a club. The third, fourth, and fifth crypts also have injuries consistent with Apostles' deaths."

Diaz's face tightened. "You said five of the bodies had wounds indicative of the Apostles. What about the sixth one?"

"This body," Tolen said, pointing downward. He directed the light to the lumbar vertebral section of the spinal bones, which lay in a perfect line at the base of the stone box.

Tolen looked to Jade. "Notice anything different about these bones compared to the other five bodies we looked at?"

Jade was struggling to understand what Tolen wanted her to see. None of the bones were missing as far as she could tell.

"Everything's in place," she said with a confused expression.

"Look again."

Jade re-examined the remains. Suddenly, she understood. Rather than what might be missing, he wanted her to notice the *condition* of the lumbar bones.

"This man had osteoporosis!" she blurted out. "It's degenerative. The loss of bone substance is substantial. By the severity, I'd say he lived a very long life."

Tolen nodded. "There are no other visible injuries. I believe this is the Apostle John, the only Apostle to die of old age. Someone, most likely Joseph of Arimathea, took great care to assemble the twelve Apostles post-mortem here in these catacombs where they could be protected without reprisal from authorities who may have opposed Jesus' teachings."

Diaz shook his head to the side as if he were choking on the information. "You're saying this is the Apostle John…and the other eleven Apostles who served Jesus Christ? It can't be. I know for a fact Peter is entombed in the crypts underneath the Vatican."

"There is no incontrovertible historical evidence to suggest Peter was *ever* in Rome," Tolen said. "Also, there are supposedly tombs for other Apostles: John in Turkey; Thomas in India; James, son of Zebedee, in your home country of Spain. In each case, there is no conclusive archaeological evidence to confirm the bodies are there. Consider St. Philip Martyrium of Hierapolis, Turkey. He is claimed to be buried in the center of the building. Despite extensive efforts to find it, no grave has ever been discovered."

The three stood motionless gazing down at the remains of the man.

This is the Apostle John! Jade thought. *All twelve apostles are here!* She could barely absorb the discovery. Of all the things they had come across in the last 48 hours, this was the most titillating and mind-boggling.

"Let's keep looking," Tolen's words drew Jade back to reality. He led them out of the room, stepping back up to the crinkling corridor of branches. Their flashlights danced over the gray walls and, as they came to each entryway, they momentarily peered inside the musty-smelling rooms. As expected, they found elevated stone coffins in the last six rooms identical to the previous rooms. Then the procession of rooms cut into the stone corridor ended.

As Tolen had said, there were exactly twelve: *twelve rooms for twelve apostles.*

The hallway continued into the distance. As lengthy as the underground corridor had been in Costa Rica, this passageway was even longer, with no end in sight. They moved cautiously, walking on the branches that littered the floor. Jade wondered for the umpteenth time why it was here. Equally as puzzling was why none of the debris from the hallway was inside the twelve rooms of the Apostles where low restraints had been fashioned at the entryways to hold it out.

The musky smell Jade had first noticed in the circular room was still prevalent. Jade's light skirted off the walls, probing ahead, yet could not reach the passageway's end. "This is a long tunnel. Maybe we should go back and check the other six coffins to make sure the stone jar is not in one of them?"

Tolen merely responded, "I don't think it'll be with any of the bodies."

They proceeded through the darkness, pressing farther and farther up the corridor. The ground debris was ever-present and crunched and cracked loudly with each step. They finally arrived at an intersection. A second corridor cut perpendicular to the main one, shooting off to the right and left. It, too, was flooded with a layer of the same detritus.

"This is also laid out as a cruciform," Diaz remarked, referring to the similarity to the Costa Rica catacomb.

Jade extended her arm, shining her flashlight ahead up the main shaft. The beam struck a distant wall. "It's a dead end. We need to search this intersecting corridor. Which way?"

Tolen pointed, indicating the tunnel to the left.

Jade took the lead. After a short distance, they reached a curve where the passageway leisurely banked right until it completed a ninety-degree angle. They were now paralleling the main passageway.

"So much for the cruciform shape," Jade said.

In the distance, her light found a doorway. "Look!" she said excitedly, tromping ahead on the thick padding. She found herself jogging, her flashlight beam swaying across the floor and walls as she went. She could hear Tolen and Diaz crunching quickly behind her, keeping pace. There had been a flash of light, a reflection of some sort coming from inside the opening which had caught her attention. She dashed ahead and reached the opening, breathing heavily. Jade quickly guided her light about the interior of a room approximately the size of a master bedroom. Natural debris also covered the ground in this room, but it was otherwise empty. The ceiling was somewhere high overhead, lost in the murky darkness.

Just as Tolen and Diaz joined her, their collective attention was immediately drawn to the back wall. A large flat area of yellowish hue shimmered back at them. It was approximately four feet tall and seven feet wide, shaped in a perfect rectangle. Jade rushed toward it, her heart pounding.

She reached her hand out. Even as her fingers met the cold surface, she struggled to believe it. It was a thin sheet of lustrous metal, like a giant placard, embedded into the wall. Hebrew writing was etched into it, scribed in typical right to left fashion. Sentences were composed in a series of columns covering almost the entire surface area.

She turned to Tolen and Diaz standing nearby, her mouth agape. "It's the duplicate of the Copper Scroll! The one mentioned in line sixty-four. Except this time...it's been etched on a sheet of gold!"

CHAPTER 34

September 13. Thursday – 1:18 a.m. Isle of Patmos, Greece

Jade was so enthralled with the glimmering display that she failed to notice Diaz until he was standing in the left corner. His flashlight beam fell on a small object propped on a tiny shelf. He lifted it and turned back to Jade and Tolen, presenting the jar with a smile. "The wall is nice, but I believe this is what we came after."

Jade nodded. She was pleased they had found the stone jar, but at the moment, she continued to focus on the columns of text. "This is...not...right...," she said in a confused voice as she slowly translated it in her mind.

"What do you mean?" Tolen asked.

Jade turned toward him. "This is supposed to be a duplicate of the Copper Scroll, but it's... not. Yet...it is."

"Time to leave. We have what we came for," Diaz said.

"Wait. No, not yet," she said, still eyeing the Hebrew text. "I'm...struggling to understand." Her voice drifted off as she continued to scrutinize the writing.

"There is no reason to *understand*," Diaz said tersely. He opened the lid with the minute carving of a man's head and revealed the tiny roll. "We have the jar with the next clue, now let's go. This place is a crypt for the Apostles, and we should not be here."

"Wait!" Jade yelled. Her voice echoed beyond the room down the corridor. "I need to read this," she said, giving Diaz a cold stare.

Tolen seemed oblivious to their querulous exchange of words.

Jade suddenly felt something solid land on her shoulder, and slink down her right arm. She screamed, shaking her arm frantically.

The object fell to the stick-covered floor. All three shined their flashlight down but saw nothing beyond the natural debris. Acting as one mind, they swung their flashlights up to the ceiling to look for the source of whatever had landed on Jade.

A dozen feet above, a sloped overhang started at the back wall and angled down toward the center of the room. There appeared to be a gutter where more small sticks, branches, and leaves were clustered. The ceiling above it was substantially higher and ashen.

"It was just a stick that fell on me," Jade said. She turned her attention back to the curious text. Out of the corner of her eye, she noticed Tolen continued to examine the strange section of overhanging roof.

"*Let's go*," Diaz demanded, this time more urgently, as he slipped the jar inside his jacket.

Jade turned to him with steely eyes. "I only need a few minutes to translate this. Then, and only then, will we leave," she growled back. Jade once again turned to the wall.

Tolen was still looking to the ceiling.

Jade watched as Diaz abruptly stepped to one end of the gold scroll and took out his pocket knife. "You want to read this? Then we'll take it with us." He wedged the knife underneath the edge of the gold plating and began to pry it away from the wall.

Jade heard a scraping noise emanate from above. Tolen was still staring upward. There were several thumps as something fell from the ceiling and struck the matting of sticks. Jade shined her flashlight down to see two light-colored stones that had settled on the ground. Tolen reached down and picked one up.

Diaz paused briefly then returned to working the blade in between the wall and the edge of the gold scroll.

Another object struck the floor, cracking a branch with a brief flash.

"What the bloody hell *is* that?" Jade asked.

Tolen's eyes revealed a sudden understanding. "It's flint. Diaz, please stop what you're doing."

Diaz had already jabbed the tip of the blade behind the gold scroll yet again and had pried the thin sheet slightly away from the wall. "See? I can get this off, and we'll take it with us."

His words had no sooner died than a barrage of flint began falling from the high roof. The three were forced to retreat flush against the wall with the scroll. Flint rocks rained down after skipping across the partial ledge above. Sparks ignited, bursting and falling in a cascade of flickering light. With utter horror, Jade realized the angled ledge with the sticks and twigs was being set ablaze as the flint fell from high above and ignited the fertile debris. Fire now dripped onto the dry, stick-covered floor.

In an instant, the floor erupted in flames.

They had no choice. They ran ahead, scampering over the burning area before it completely blocked their way. They spilled out into the corridor. The back of Diaz's jacket caught fire, and Tolen patted it quickly using his own shirt over his hands to extinguish the flame.

Jade looked back into the room and saw it was being swallowed in vaulting yellow flames. Smoke was already pouring out into the passageway. It had taken mere seconds for the falling flint to spark the dry, brittle debris, catch fire, and completely destroy the room.

"It's a trap!" Tolen yelled as the fire crackled harshly. "That scroll was never supposed to be removed from the wall!"

Jade stared at Diaz sternly.

"How was I to know?!" he said, spreading his empty hands apart in appeasement and shrugging his shoulders defensively.

The heat pushed from the room and pressed against them. Jade looked to the ground and was aghast to see the floor from the room streaking outward on fire, coming toward them at a frenetic pace. Not only was the room a deadly snare, it was now horribly obvious, with the corridors filled with highly flammable tinder, the entire complex was part of the elaborate trap.

"Move!" Tolen ordered. He led them back down the corridor at a run. Jade followed, nearly stumbling on the jagged sticks. Diaz passed her, reaching back as he did to assist. When they reached the curved portion of the corridor, Jade stole a look back. The fire was racing toward them like a carnivore pursuing its prey. Oddly, it was running along the wall in a perfect line following the right side of the corridor. Her heart raced, and Jade turned forward, not wanting to see, feeling as if she was being chased by some primitive creature.

Tolen shouted to them as they ran. "That sweet smell I noticed earlier is some kind of accelerant. It's probably underneath the branches. We've got to get out of here. This whole place will be consumed in fire in a matter of minutes."

"What about the rooms with the coffins? They have no debris. We can go into one of them to avoid the fire," Diaz offered.

"We'll die of smoke inhalation," Tolen said flatly.

They reached the intersection where the tunnel offshoot met the main corridor. Jade could feel the flames licking at their heels. She looked back briefly. "It's following a pattern, staying to the right side," Jade stated in a loud voice. There was no response from either Tolen or Diaz.

The threesome dashed ahead, snapping sticks as they went. One by one, they raced past the crypt rooms where the Apostles were housed, laboring to run on the pad of natural detritus. They soon passed through the fissure and found themselves in the main room where the corkscrew tunnel had originally brought them. Jade turned. The fire shot inside the circular room and darted along the right wall. As it streaked around the perimeter, the main cavern floor, in turn, also caught fire, and smoke began billowing toward the ceiling. Tolen led them toward the wall on the far side where the spiraling tunnel exited upward. The end of the dangling rope was barely visible inside the wormhole, but before they could reach it, the fire had wrapped around the room and blocked their escape. The flames grew intense, snaking upward into the curved tunnel. Tolen took a step forward as if he might try and barge through the fire. Jade put a restraining hand on his arm. "No!" she shouted, as they watched the rope catch fire and the blaze escalate. The heat intensified exponentially.

Their only avenue of escape was gone.

Smoke quickly clogged the enclosure, and all three began to cough. Jade turned to see the chain of fire continue to encircle the room. It would seal their fate within seconds. She felt a flush of panic. Tolen grabbed her hand and bolted back toward the crevice where they re-entered the corridor. Diaz trailed close behind. An instant later, the circular cave was completely engulfed in fire.

A short distance into the corridor, Jade turned back. The heat rapped her in the face with an almost physical force. Amid the blaze, the carved faces on the pilasters behind resembled a macabre scene of sinners being eradicated within a fiery pit. Diaz's haunting comment earlier about hell seemed eerily prophetic now. As she watched, the smoldering trail of flame emerged from the circular room and streamed along on the unburned side of the corridor toward them, attacking in a straight line. It was absolutely relentless. Jade was sure its aggression was driven by some demonic intelligence.

Tolen pulled Jade along the passageway, gliding over the branches and staying to the side of the tunnel which had yet to catch fire. It was odd to see one side of the passageway burning ahead, while the other half remained unlit. Whoever had planned this had done a remarkably demented job of ensuring the victims would be corralled by the fire and allowed only certain avenues of escape. The purpose for it, though, was not clear.

The smoke was hovering at chest level in the tunnel, restricting their view. Jade coughed and hacked as Tolen pulled her along. The heavy-footed Diaz was close behind. The fire to their side flicked at them with gnarled fingers, crackling and popping loudly, trying to snatch them as they raced past. Jade felt the heat lapping at her skin, and an acrid smell filled her lungs.

She had no idea where Tolen was leading them, and she wondered if it really mattered. There had only been one point of ingress and egress, and that was now blocked. They were trapped. Their bodies would be consumed by fire within minutes. The thought of burning alive terrified her.

"We've got to go in one of these rooms!" Diaz barked.

Against Diaz's protests, Tolen pushed the group up the corridor. Even in her panicky state, Jade knew taking refuge in one of the Apostles' crypts would mean certain death. Smoke in the rooms on the other side of the corridor was growing thicker by the second. As soon as the fire arrowed back up the tunnel and ignited the full breadth of flammable debris, all twelve rooms would be consumed in smoke.

They had to keep moving and try to outrun the pursuing fire.

Sheer desperation kept Jade going, even though her pragmatic side told her they were only forestalling the inevitable.

Tolen suddenly made a drastic change in direction, cutting hard to his right where there was no fire. For a moment, Jade thought that he had relented to Diaz and entered one of the crypt rooms, but there was no stone coffin here, only a corridor. They navigated a curve to the left that straightened. Only then did she realize where they were. At the juncture of the main corridor where they had originally turned left, eventually discovering the room with the gold scroll, Tolen had now turned down the opposite corridor to the right. It was the only passageway they had not investigated.

The inferno had yet to reach this tunnel, although there was no doubt in Jade's mind the flames zipping up the main corridor would soon change that. This passageway, too, was laden with dried sticks and branches. The fuel would send the raging fire chasing after them. Although the tunnel was stuffy with smoke, at the moment it seemed less coarse, and Jade's coughing abated somewhat. "Where are we going?" she managed to choke out.

"Away from the fire," Tolen responded.

"And into certain death," Diaz added morosely. The man was chugging behind with deep, raspy gasps.

Ahead, the smoke thinned further, and Tolen's flashlight cut into a dead-end room similar to the Gold Scroll room but with two differences: there was no scroll mounted into the wall, and the ceiling was a mere seven feet high. They had no sooner entered the room when the scorching line of fire arrived at the doorway. Jade turned when she heard the sound of the conflagration chewing up the branches. The flames rose up in the corridor, licking six feet into the air. Her chest tightened into an agonizing knot. They were moments away from being burned to death.

At some point—Jade was not sure when—Tolen had released her hand. She now found herself cowering into Diaz's chest. She could feel the man's pounding heartbeat. Smoke poured into the small room, and both she and Diaz began to cough harshly as dark ash drifted down on them. Somewhere behind, she was faintly aware of Tolen crowded against the back wall. Jade watched as a line of fire entered the room, zipping around the walls from both sides, destined to meet at exactly where Tolen stood. Her eyes burned, and tears blurred her vision.

Jade heard Tolen yell over the sizzling and popping of the flames. "Down!"

Jade felt a weight land hard upon her and Diaz, sending them both to the debris-covered floor. In the next instant, a deafening blast sent rock fragments raining down upon them. Before she could comprehend what was happening, a noise like a freight train bearing down on her was followed by a surge of water which pummeled her into something solid. There was intense pain, and her scalp tingled. Almost as quickly, it passed.

Jade's world faded to black.

CHAPTER 35

September 13. Thursday – 3:06 a.m. Isle of Patmos, Greece

Jade woke up in bed on top of the covers. A ceiling fan spun slowly overhead, and there was a hint of vanilla in the air. Other than the electric hum of the fan's rotors, the room was silent. Her back hurt, and she had trouble remembering where she was or how she had gotten here. Nothing made sense. She brushed her short bangs off her forehead and found them slightly wet.

Jade sat up. *What happened?* She searched her memory, dropping her head into her hands and closing her eyes. Then it all came back to her in a rush. Tolen, Diaz, and she had been searching underground, somewhere below the Petra in the catacombs of the Apostles, when Diaz triggered an ancient trap. The place caught fire, and she remembered fleeing into a room where they were trapped. There was an explosion, and she recalled a painful impact.

That was all she could remember. *How had she gotten here?*

She looked around. A decorative lamp on a bureau across the way provided generous light. The room had a single bed and a large window with bright orange curtains. The clock on the nightstand read 3:09. Was that a.m. or p.m.?

Her PC bag was atop a small round table, along with some papers and a small stone jar.

The jar! She suddenly remembered.

The front door opened, and Tolen entered carrying two cups of coffee. Startled, Jade sprang to a sitting position on the side of the bed, anchoring her bare feet on the floor. She was surprised to find herself in a fluffy white terrycloth bathrobe. She gapped it open at the collar, looked straight down, and was shocked to see nothing but skin underneath the material. She quickly drew the robe closed up to her neck, feeling her face color with embarrassment.

"What happened? Why am I dressed like...*this*?" she said.

"We blasted our way out of the underground tunnels," Tolen said, taking a seat next to Jade on the bed. "Are you feeling okay?" His words were soothing, compassionate.

"Blasted our way out? How?"

"I used a limited explosive charge I brought from the plane. It did the trick," Tolen said, locking her in his azure blue gaze. She could smell a tinge of his cologne, and it settled on her with calming assurance.

"James Bond of the Americas," Jade said playfully. Her tone came out much more lightly than she had planned. Then again, why the hell not, she thought. It appeared once again Samuel Tolen had saved her life...and Diaz's, too, for that matter.

Jade noticed Tolen was dressed in different clothes. He had on a long-sleeved, tan button-up shirt with perfect creases, dark dress slacks, and dress shoes.

Jade reached a hand around and rubbed a sore spot on her lower back.

"Are you in pain?" Tolen asked.

"A bit. Feels like I bruised a muscle," she nodded, biting her bottom lip. For the first time, she did not try to hide her vulnerability from Tolen.

Tolen rose, went to the bureau, and returned to the bed with a plastic prescription bottle. He handed her an unmarked pill. "Here," he said, placing the pill in her hand and handing her a glass of water from the nightstand. "It's a mild muscle relaxer."

She swallowed it with a sip of water and returned the glass to the nightstand. She noticed the bandage on her arm had been changed and a fresh one applied. The wound was expertly dressed with a brown patch held in place with white medical tape.

"I hope you don't mind," Tolen began, "but I changed your bandage."

For some reason, she felt her cheeks blush. "Um...where are we?"

"In a hotel not far from Grikos Beach and the Petra. Reba Zee made arrangements while we were exploring."

"How exactly did you know where to set the explosive to get us out?" she said, crossing a leg. The robe crept up to her thigh. She pulled it down slowly to cover her knee.

"All along I thought there had to be another passage into the tunnels. Physics dictated that the Apostles' stone coffins couldn't have fit down the spiraling wormhole at the cistern. They had to have been placed inside via a different path.

"When we retreated to the room at the end of the last arm of the tunnel, I found another image etched into the stone: two gold rings, like you discovered at the base of the cistern. I reasoned it was an alternative opening…or had been at one time. This meant that the wall had been resealed and was probably substantially thinner. As it turns out, the cave room was under water, abutting to the bay. After the charge detonated and created a hole in the wall, ocean water burst inside. Diaz and I got you out, but only after you were thrown into the stone wall and knocked unconscious. We pulled you to the surface and brought you back here. Amazingly, from outside, it appeared nothing unusual had happened to the Petra, and, in fact, it hadn't. Everything had been below ground. There's no evidence of the labyrinth or the fire, which was put out by the influx of seawater." Tolen paused.

Jade wanted to ask who had changed her out of her wet clothes and placed her in a robe, but she refrained. Then she considered a far greater implication: the Gold Scroll had been lost. The fabulous tombs of the Apostles were destroyed. "It's all gone."

"It was an elaborate trap," Tolen said, "but the tombs may still be intact. Remember, the branches were intentionally kept out of the rooms with the coffins. Now we know why."

Jade thought for a moment, considering the design of the underground structure. "The place was absolutely fascinating. Did you notice the pattern of the tunnels? At first we thought it was a cruciform, but the intersecting tunnel had passageways which curved and ran parallel to the far end of the main tunnel. It formed the shape of a trident."

"Which begs the question, why would Joseph of Arimathea

have engineered such a design?" Tolen remarked.

"That's exactly my point. I don't think he did," Jade said. She stood, ensuring the robe stayed tightly around her, retying the drawstring. She began to pace, feeling energized by her sudden revelation. She also sensed Tolen's eyes fixed on her.

She sat back on the bed and turned toward him, unconsciously laying a hand on his leg. "What do you get when you combine a trident with the country of Greece?"

Jade looked into Tolen's eyes. She could feel warmth and kindness, and the depths of his intellect. She became conscious of her hand touching his leg, and she slowly withdrew it.

Understanding suddenly flashed over Tolen's face. "The Greek god, Poseidon. Greco-Roman mythology dates back to long before the Christian era. Are you suggesting the cave structure predates Joseph of Arimathea?"

"Yes. Consider the pilasters with the hundreds of carved faces. Remember how their expressions were twisted in agony? Frankly, there was nothing Christian about them. It's far more indicative of early Greek artwork.

"My guess is that those caves and corridors were constructed by the Greeks in the shape of the trident long before the time of Joseph and the Apostles of Jesus, probably to pay homage to Poseidon. Somehow, Joseph knew of this place and decided it would make a good location to house the bodies of the Apostles and the copy of the Gold Scroll, although the twelve rooms holding the remains of the Apostles were surely not part of the original Greek design. Most likely, they were cut during Joseph's day. The booby trap is a bit of a mystery, though." Jade settled into a thoughtful expression.

Tolen interrupted her reverie. "I believe it's a continuing test. Remember, Joseph's tomb in Costa Rica was also rigged. Once we rolled the stone off the mound and the tide rose, it was inevitable that the underground rooms would fill with ocean water, yet it gave us a chance to get to the jar and get out. Jade, what was the last line in the original text you decoded?"

She thought for a moment. "It said, '*Only the man who has patience, is meager, and holds faith will arrive safely.*' "

Tolen repeated, "*patience, meager, and faith.* I think each of the destinations in the journey requires us to apply one of these rules. In Costa Rica, '*patience*' referred to dealing with the tidal water.

"With the caves underneath the Petra, '*meager*' implied not taking the valuable gold the scroll was etched upon.

"In both situations, the traps weren't designed to stop us from reaching our goal, but to make it so we had to be judicious and heed the instructions. We were required to go in, get what we needed, and get out, nothing more. In Costa Rica, we simply took too long, and the tide rose before we put the clue together that we needed to be looking for one of the Three Wise Men's gift. Here at the Petra, we went against the edict."

Diaz and his pocketknife. "And now that fantastic place is lost," Jade said, discouraged.

"Jade," Tolen began, looking intently at her, "what did you see on the Gold Scroll? You kept saying something was wrong with it. You said it was a duplicate of the Copper Scroll then you commented it wasn't. What did you mean?"

Jade had completely forgotten about the text. She had read it moments before the room had been set ablaze, and they were running for their lives. She had had no chance to digest the information completely or share what she had interpreted with the others in the ensuing turmoil. "It...it was remarkable. Instead of having more detailed directions which would lead to the location of the 63 treasures listed in the Copper Scroll, the gold scroll implied that the 63 treasures don't exist. They're a ruse. Yet it emphatically states the 'shrine of the earthly objects of Jesus Christ' does exist!"

Tolen stood up and walked to the drawn curtain at the window, deep in thought. He pulled back one side, looked out, and turned back to Jade. "That's exactly what I read as well."

"You can translate ancient Hebrew?" she asked in amazement.

"I'm not fluent, but I understand it on a rudimentary level."

Then, suddenly struck with the need for truth, Jade transfixed an inquisitive gaze at Tolen. "Level with me. You have much more than a passing fancy on Christian-era history, specifically as it relates to Jesus. You've tactfully avoided responding to my question about your depth of knowledge on several occasions."

He offered a small smile that hinted at sadness. He rose from the bed and turned away without a word.

"I've seen that look in your eyes. Something is troubling you," Jade lowered her voice, "something you can't seem to accept."

He did not respond.

"How did you get that scar on your forearm?"

Tolen slowly turned toward her. He regarded her for a moment as he approached, seemingly weighing his options. Then his words flowed with characteristic calmness. "Last month, I was on assignment in Sri Lanka. A family member of a high-ranking U.S. official happened to be there at the same time. The CIA is not responsible for this family member's safety, but I uncovered information regarding an assassination attempt. I thwarted it, was electrocuted, and received this scar in the process."

Jade swallowed. "By definition, the term 'electrocuted' implies you *died*."

"I was pronounced clinically dead after eight minutes. Three minutes after that, eleven minutes after the event, I revived in the ambulance. Doctors had no explanation, and I suffered no brain damage."

"That qualifies as a miracle in my book," Jade said unblinking.

Tolen looked away, down, then back at Jade. A look of mystification washed over his face. His features stiffened. "I'm sure you've read about near-death experiences where people report a feeling of warmth and contentment. They see a calming white light which beckons them. Some have seen loved ones who've long been dead. By and large, these accounts are consistent."

Jade suddenly felt closed in, as if the air around them had tightened into a thick knot. She assumed Tolen's near-death experience differed, and she was not sure if she wanted to hear it. Yet she had to ask. "Is that what you experienced?"

He looked her squarely in the eyes, and his voice never wavered. "No, I saw, felt, and heard absolutely nothing…no inner peace, nothing. It was as if I was in limbo, where I floated in darkness."

Jade understood. "That's why you're so interested. You want an answer regarding an afterlife."

"Religions give us explanations which, by their very nature, cannot be conveniently challenged. People believe without a shred of proof because the very essence of religion is belief based on faith. It's no wonder church parishioners are often referred to as "the flock." They are dissuaded from thinking for themselves, in applying logic, questioning facts. Churches shun the intellect and covet unquestioning followers. Religion is the one time in life when people don't want you to be rational."

"Surely you must know most doctors consider those near-death experiences physiological, not metaphysical. They're simply subconscious-driven illusions."

"Which makes it harder for me to reconcile. If it were merely physiological, there would be no deviation from one person to the next. I should have undergone the same experience as everyone else." He paused as he exhaled, still deep in thought. "My father is lying in a coma in Florida. He was in an automobile accident. He had executed a living will. Last week, I visited him on six consecutive days, each day intent on turning the paperwork over to the hospital administrators. I never did. I cannot bring myself to end his life, especially given the uncertainty of what I experienced."

Now Jade fully understood. His accumulated acumen regarding Jesus, the Apostles, and the Christian era was not out of concern about his own mortality, but his father's.

Tolen inclined his head slightly. "Do you realize the only reason Christians believe in life after death is because of the story of Jesus' resurrection? Yet throughout history, there have been dozens of mythical figures: Horus in Egypt, Attis in Greece, Krishna in India, Mithra in Persia, to name just a few, who are all said to have virtually the same traits of birth and death as Jesus. Each was born of a virgin mother on December 25th and resurrected on the third day after death. The story of the sun god, Horus, can be found in Egyptian hieroglyphs 1,500 years before the Christian era began. There are hundreds of similarities in the textual story between Jesus and Horus. Most scholars now agree Horus is the basis for the Jesus figure in the Bible. In addition to the virgin birth, Horus is said to have performed miracles and was crucified. It's plain to see that early Christians plagiarized Egyptian and other cultures and traditions as the foundation for the New Testament, just as the writers of the Old Testament embellished upon the Epic of Gilgamesh to come up with such stories as Noah's ark. Even discrediting the persistent rumor that Jesus may have fathered a child, all the facts suggest there *never was a man named Jesus of Nazareth.* He is nothing more than a hybrid; a long line of legendary figures adapted from other cultural myths."

Jade looked at him incredulously. "Tolen, are you not influenced by what we've discovered, what we've seen? The ancient Hebrew clues, the cathedral-like cave in Costa Rica with the incredible frescoes, the underground cave system here on Patmos; I can tell you it's caused me to contemplate things in a different light. Have you considered that the stone rooms and corridors under the Petra may have been the cave where the Apostle John saw the vision of Jesus and received the inspiration to write Revelation? It was said John heard God's word from such a fissure in the cave wall. If you recall, the main room with the faces on the pilasters where the corkscrew tunnel emptied had a gaping crevice which led out to the passageway. It fits the description perfectly."

Tolen nodded. "Yes, it does, but consider the sickly sweet smell we surmised was some form of accelerant under the bedding of branches and twigs on the floor. I believe when that underground cavern and passageway were first carved out by the Greeks long before the Christian era—as you so astutely surmised—the floor was already holding some natural fluid, possibly crude oil, which had seeped up from the earth. If the Apostle John were down there for more than an hour, the concentrated fumes would have made him lightheaded, causing him to hallucinate. Combine his impaired state and the early Greek artwork on the pilaster with the faces of men contorted in agony, and, in his delusional state, he might have easily gotten the idea for the horrific story of Revelation."

Jade countered, "But we found Joseph of Arimathea. We found the twelve Apostles. Isn't the evidence more compelling than ever?"

"Jade, we found the remains of men mentioned in the Bible. We have not found concrete evidence of Jesus Christ, and despite the fact mankind has been collecting artifacts related to Christ for two thousand years, none of them hold up under scrutiny. I have to say, in that regard, the 'True Sons of Light' are right. Quite probably, mankind *is* perpetuating a lie. Consider that Jesus was said to be nailed to the cross by three, maybe four, nails. Yet there are 30 'holy nails' in storage across Europe which are revered as holy objects. There are also enough wood chips from the *true cross* spread across the European continent to build an entire city block of houses. Also, neither the Shroud of Turin nor the Sudarium of Oviedo can be carbon dated to the 1st century. Most recently was the discovery of the 70 lead codices which referred to Jesus found in a cave in Jordan. They were thought to have dated to the 1st century until it became clear from the multiple dialects that, in all probability, they had been forged within the past fifty years. The physical evidence just doesn't pan out. Your own Stephen Hawking put it best when he said the notion of an afterlife is wishful thinking for those afraid of death."

There was a knock on the door, and Tolen answered. It was Diaz. He was carrying a cup of coffee, and he plopped down at the table. Diaz was in casual attire, sporting long pants, a baggy collared pullover, and a corduroy jacket. "Feeling better?" he asked, looking at Jade.

She nodded. She saw no reason to continue the conversation with Tolen, especially in front of Diaz. Instead, she looked to the table where Diaz was now leaning back, taking another sip of coffee. "Have you looked at the roll?"

Tolen strolled to the table and lifted the jar delicately. "No, we were waiting for you to wake up." He gently removed the cap—another small bust of a man—removed the tiny rolled parchment with two fingers, and handed it to Jade. He then tilted the jar, and several pieces of yellowish fragments fell into his palm. As expected, it was gold. He returned them to the jar and recapped it, placing the jar back on the table. He looked at it for a moment curiously.

"What's the matter?" Diaz asked.

"Although this jar appears to be the same size as the Costa Rica jar, it feels considerably heavier," Tolen said, "and not just because the contents differ. I believe the jar is thicker. Interesting."

Jade paid little attention to his remark. She was concentrating on the tiny roll in her hands. The paper felt brittle and aged. Here was another piece of forgotten history, she mused. Similar to the others, the tightly wound parchment bore the same brown discoloration. She held it for a long moment without moving. According to the message inside the stone sphere they recovered from the Harvard courtyard, this was the second of three stone jars. After this one, they had one more to find. Sitting in a hotel room on a Greek island with an America CIA operative and a Spanish police inspector about to continue on a 2,000-year-old treasure hunt seemed more surreal than real. She briefly closed her eyes and then reopened them to make sure she was awake.

Tolen retook a seat beside her. Again, his cologne wafted into her nostrils. The invigorating scent merged with Jade's rising anticipation of reading the clue.

They were actually doing this. They were well on their way to making the most remarkable discovery in the history of mankind. The thought of it caused a tingle to rush up her spine. She fought to discard the shiver without the men noticing.

She unrolled the small parchment, taking considerable care not to tear the material. Again, there was Hebrew text. She read it aloud:

Of the Father, Son, and Holy Ghost, only the Son is charged with holding the contents on high where the ancients knew no god but themselves in the desert. Travel from the north. As David faced the lion, you will face the lion incarnate. Aim at the one on the left, and dig at his right foot. There you will gain entry to the Holiest of Highs. The third jar marks the end of your journey, but all three will be needed.

The clue was vague and certainly more convoluted than the last one. Her mounting hope turned into complete confusion. She looked to Tolen, hoping he might regale her with knowledge of what the text meant.

His expression was bland. It was clear he was just as baffled as she was.

She looked to Diaz who could only offer a shrug.

The only consolation was the last line. It was specific. In essence, it said, *find the third jar and you're there.*

If only they knew where *there* was.

CHAPTER 36

September 13. Thursday – 3:41 a.m. Isle of Patmos, Greece

Time was running out. They had just over 30 hours to return the Sudarium to the Cathedral of San Salvador in Oviedo, Spain.

Tolen lay in bed fully clothed with the lights off in a room next to Jade's. Diaz was in the next room over from her. They were exhausted and had agreed to get a couple of hours rest before continuing.

Tolen's body was wracked with sore muscles and bruises. Fatigue had set in. Since their next move was unclear, though, he fought against sleep, trying to figure out how they should proceed.

He had continued to dwell on the blown opportunity with the two assailants at the Petra, berating himself for having been so unprepared not to consider an escape via the bay. He had obviously not been thinking clearly. To have any chance of success, he had to galvanize his focus on the matters at hand.

His cell phone rang.

"Tolen," he answered, retrieving it from the nightstand, feeling an ache in his tricep.

"Hey, did I wake you?"

"Not at all, Ms. Bar," he said, sitting up on the side of the bed in the dark.

"I visited the Roanoke Laboratory where Aaron Conin worked. I confiscated his PC and searched his desk. I found a small capped vial taped under his drawer containing several fibers. They were barely visible to the human eye. I had it analyzed and just got the results minutes ago. The chemical content and makeup are

219

identical to threads examined several years ago from the Sudarium. Unfortunately, I couldn't find any data related to it on Conin's PC. Either he never had a chance to conduct the tests, or he thoroughly erased all the records. I have the techies trying to recover all deleted files now."

"Bar, when was Conin murdered?" Tolen asked as he absorbed the information Bar had fed him.

"August 24th."

Tolen allowed Bar's words to sink in.

"Oh, crap!" Bar said. "How did Aaron Conin have access to the Sudarium before it was stolen on August 30th?"

"Exactly," Tolen said. "It doesn't make sense."

"Also," Bar continued, "remember the receipt you found on Gordon Nunnery from the cleaner in Switzerland? It was dated December 9th. Well, last year, on that same day, your attackers—archaeologists Richard Mox and physicist Gordon Nunnery—flew into Zurich International Airport; and get this: Boyd Ramsey also flew in that same day, but I can't trace where any of them went after they arrived in Switzerland. None were booked into a hotel, hostel, or any place else I could find."

"Did you look outside the city at surrounding towns?"

Bar chuckled. "I checked the entire country of Switzerland. They weren't registered anywhere. For one night, they fell off the grid. The next day, all three men flew out to their respective home countries."

"What about Aaron Conin? Was he in Switzerland?"

"No, and beyond the fact he had fibers from the Sudarium and Ramsey made a phone call to him, I still don't know his relationship to anyone involved."

"Speaking of Boyd Ramsey," Bar continued, "you asked about his fingerprints at the Oviedo and Costa Rica crime scenes and on the communiqué sent to the Spanish press. Strangely, the print in all three cases—the partials and the full print—are from Ramsey's ring finger on his left hand. Do you think they were planted?"

"I'd rather not speculate."

"Vakind was able to convince President Fane to hold off escalating the terror alert until 12 hours before the Sudarium is to go on display. That gives you...18 hours to find the Sudarium and return it to Oviedo for the start of the Feast of the Cross."

Tolen released a silent sigh. Diaz had been right. They had spent too much time on a treasure hunt which had diverted Tolen from his primary objective: securing the Sudarium. With 18 hours until the first potential strike against U.S. citizens, Tolen still had no idea where Boyd Ramsey or the Sudarium were. Time was now his enemy, and given the fact that thread samples from the Sudarium were found in Conin's lab, his assumption that the holy relic had never left Europe now appeared wrong. Again he scolded himself for getting so far off track.

"But the best is yet to come," Bar continued. "The Honduran company, Gurkha, provided the names of the people who purchased the Black Dragon cigars like the one found partially smoked in Richard Mox's house. Of the five boxes, two were purchased by one man: billionaire Simon Anat. Perhaps not un-coincidentally, Mr. Anat lives in—"

"—Dietikon, Switzerland." Tolen finished her thought. "He is a Hungarian shipping magnate; the fourth richest man in the world with net worth hovering around $29 billion."

Bar continued the thought. "Exactly. Simon Anat used to be quite a public figure but has become a recluse within the last two years. He's stopped conducting interviews, attending benefits, or participating in any philanthropic activities. No one's gotten a photograph of him in over a year and a half."

There was no hesitation from Tolen. "Bar, please contact Reba Zee and have her prepare for takeoff. I'll be leaving for Zurich, Switzerland immediately. Let her know I'll be at the tarmac in 20 minutes."

"I've already taken the liberty of contacting Reba Zee. The plane is fueled and waiting to go."

Tolen hung up his phone. He sat on the edge of the bed still in the dark. The room was quiet except for the droning of the air conditioner. Light was shining through the bottom of his door from the hallway. A momentary shadow passed, and then the light returned.

****

As tired as Jade was, her sore back was interfering with her sleep. The muscle relaxer Tolen had prescribed had taken the edge off the pain, but she still felt a dull throb. She faded in and out of sleep, nudged awake every so often by a stab of discomfort. After a short while, she gave up trying. Instead, she focused on the clue from the last jar. She had already read it so many times she had it memorized:

> Of the Father, Son, and Holy Ghost, only the Son is charged with holding the contents on high where the ancients knew no god but themselves in the desert. Travel from the north. As David faced the lion, you will face the lion incarnate. Aim at the one on the left and dig at his right foot. There you will gain entry to the Holiest of Highs. The third jar marks the end of your journey, but all three will be needed.

Jade rolled over on her back, feeling a sting. She stared up at the dark ceiling.

The three had discussed the text for some time. Their mutual conclusion was the cache of Jesus' objects would be found somewhere in Israel. The reference to "desert" made the task of deciphering the clue even more daunting. Sixty percent of the country was desert: the Negev Desert alone covered 55 percent of the land mass of Israel, or roughly 4,700 square miles, and the Negev's landscape is not inviting, consisting of a mix of rocky mountains, plateaus, and deep craters punctuated with dry riverbeds.

The reference to "*lion*" was intriguing. She recalled Dr. Cherrigan once discussing the use of the term in the Bible where lions are mentioned repeatedly; the most notable being the story of Daniel in the lions' den. Lions were also frequently used as an allegory to represent strength, celestial good, and celestial truth.

Also intriguing was the clue which mentioned all three jars would be needed. The jar they found in Costa Rica containing myrrh was secure aboard the plane in the cabin locker. She wondered if there might have been something else about the jar they missed.

What was it Tolen had said: the second jar felt heavier than the first, as if made thicker.

Jade heard a *tink* that startled her. It had come from the door. She turned her head to the side. There was another faint *tink* sound. She was just about to call out and ask who was there when she heard a click, and the door popped open enough to allow a sliver of light to come in from the hallway.

Jade closed her eyes and pretended to be asleep, but her pulse was suddenly racing. She considered screaming. If the intruder had a gun, she would be dead before Tolen or Diaz arrived. Instead, she lay motionless, her heartbeat screaming in her ears. She dared a look through slitted eyes. The door pushed open, sending the hallway light into the room, backlighting the figure. The dark form moved silently inside the room, closing the door behind. The only light now was a thin line of white seeping in from under the door. The figure paused, as if appraising the dark room.

Jade's mind spun in dizzying circles. She tried to think how she could defend herself like this: lying down without a weapon. She was completely vulnerable. She tried to remain calm and think of options, but nothing came to her. Restraining her breathing caused her nearly to hyperventilate.

The shadowy figure moved to the table and seemed to be feeling around in the dark.

Jade involuntarily held her breath. Once she realized what she was doing, it was too late. There was no way to exhale without being heard in the still room. She held her breath knowing each second she retained air, she would eventually be forced to release it with an even greater push and, no doubt, be heard. Her lungs began to ache.

At the table, the figure had lifted something and was examining it in the dim light.

The burning in her lungs grew intense.

The figure placed the object down and slowly moved to the bureau. In the scant light, Jade stole a peek and thought she saw the person holding a handgun. Her lungs now screamed for air.

Just when Jade had exhausted her air and knew she could hold it no longer, the door of her room burst open. A figure rushed inside, catching the intruder's face in the beam of a flashlight. The two ran at each other and collided, tumbling into the wall. There was a high-pitched scream and a torrent of knocks. Jade expelled the air and scurried to her feet, nearly knocking down the nightstand lamp as she frantically sought the switch to turn it on.

In an instant, the room was lit. The commotion against the wall had died down. Samuel Tolen held onto a woman from behind as he raised her to her feet. The woman's long, black disheveled hair fell across her angular face as she struggled to break free. She was of average height and build, with pale-colored skin, clad in dark coveralls like a car mechanic. Tolen's grasp was firm and after a moment, the woman gave up trying to escape.

Tolen moved her to the table, kicked a chair out, and plopped the intruder down in the seat. "Sit," he ordered firmly, his tone acrimonious. He took a position between her and the doorway, after he locked it from the inside.

The woman spoke in a foreign language. Jade was sure it was French.

"Laissez moi partir. J'ai rien fait de mal."

Surprisingly to Jade, Tolen responded in the same language. "Pour commencer, pourquoi ne pas parler de cette effraction?"

"Si vous me laissez pas partir, je vais crier."

Tolen responded, "J'ai pas le temps de jouer. Parlez anglais maintenant, ou je vous coupe les doigts l'un après l'autre."

"Alright, alright," she suddenly said in English with a strong accent.

Jade was glad to hear the conversation switch to a language she understood.

"Who are you?" Tolen asked.

She looked at him with a smirk. "You can't figure that out?"

Jade came off the bed. She was wearing a long tee shirt which fell to mid-thigh. Her fear was gone. She approached the woman with a sudden rise of anger. "Who the bloody hell are you, and why are you in my room?"

The French woman gave Jade a surly look but said nothing.

Tolen reached into his pocket and pulled out a compact knife. He flicked a switch and the blade sprang out, stout and serrated.

Without hesitation, he stepped forward and clamped the woman's left hand down on the table. He quickly brought the knife down, and Jade involuntarily cringed.

"No, no wait!" the woman shouted. "I'm after what you're after...the proof."

Tolen paused. He lifted the blade to her eye level. "Who are you?"

She hesitated. Then, with a defeated grimace she said, "My name is Claudia Denoit."

"Are you with the 'True Sons of Light'?" Tolen asked.

"Quoi? I have no idea what you're talking about," she replied, never breaking eye contact with Tolen.

Tolen released her hand and moved back between Denoit and the door. "Is anyone else with you?"

She shook her head, no.

"What *proof* are you after?" Jade said, glaring down at the woman.

"The same proof you are!" the woman snarled.

"To destroy it?" Tolen asked. His voice was calm but firm.

The French woman gave a throaty laugh. "No, Monsieur." Her eyes settled on Tolen. Her expression went rigid. "To the contrary."

Tolen pressed within inches of her face. Jade took an awkward step back to allow him room. "Simon Anat sent you."

There was a pregnant pause. "I do not know of this man." She shifted, looked over Tolen's shoulder at nothing, then brought her gaze down to the table.

Simon Anat? Jade thought.

Tolen rose smartly with a certain primal urgency Jade had not previously witnessed. She half expected him to begin cutting off Denoit's fingers. Instead, he pulled a pistol from inside his jacket and handed it to Jade, flipping the safety off.

"Shoot her in the kneecap if she moves a muscle. I'll be right back." Jade was speechless. There was no point in arguing. Tolen had already turned and walked out the door, closing it behind him.

Jade looked at the woman. She pivoted around to the door, keeping the gun leveled at Denoit the entire time.

****

Tolen stepped out into the hallway and headed quickly to his room. He had cord and a gag in his bag he could use to bind Denoit. Finally, they had someone who could give them answers. Once he had said the name of Simon Anat, her body language and eye movement indicated he had struck a chord.

His cell phone rang just as he stepped into his room. It was Director Vakind.

"Tolen, what's your status?"

As he dug through his bag to fish out the cord, Tolen explained that they had just apprehended a suspect. He promised to call Vakind shortly with more information. He hung up just as he pulled out a gag, when suddenly there was a tremendous *slam* and trampling from the hallway.

Tolen dashed out into the hallway and saw Jade's door open. Jade staggered out, holding her chest, trying to catch her breath. Tolen looked into the room. It was empty.

Claudia Denoit was gone.

"She rushed me...slammed me into the door," Jade wheezed. "The gun's on the floor in the room."

Diaz stepped from his room, gun drawn. He was barely dressed, and looked half asleep. "What's going on?" He rubbed his eyes, slinging a shirt on.

"Diaz, take the stairs at that end," Tolen pointed down the hallway toward one end. "Look for a Caucasian Frenchwoman with long dark hair and average body type wearing black coveralls. I'll take the other stairs."

Diaz wordlessly turned and the two men raced in opposite directions. Tolen sailed down the stairs, taking two steps at a time. When he reached the lobby four floors down, it was empty. The front desk was unmanned. Moments later, Diaz joined him. He simply shook his head.

CHAPTER 37

September 13. Thursday – 4:14 a.m. Isle of Patmos, Greece

Tolen reconvened with Diaz and Jade back in Jade's room where she handed Tolen his weapon. "I'm...I'm sorry," she said. "She rushed at me so fast, I didn't know what to do."

Tolen was angry with Jade, but he checked his emotions. He had only planned to be out of the room a few seconds. The phone call from Vakind had delayed him. The comment for Jade to shoot Denoit in the kneecap was to scare Denoit into staying put. It had failed.

Tolen told Diaz about the intruder, who she was, and how she had escaped. Then he looked at his watch. "We have just over 29 hours before the Feast of the Cross begins." *And 17 hours before President Fane tips the fundamentalist group off by elevating the terrorist alert*, he thought to himself. "I'm flying out, but will be back in the afternoon. I need you two to stay here. Diaz, you can expect another attack. I'm certain of it." He said it with conviction, even though there was really no certainty to it. "Try to take them alive."

Diaz's face grew intense, and he started to object. Tolen walked away before the inspector could spew the first word. Tolen went to his room, grabbed his bag, and returned to the hallway. Diaz was waiting for him there.

"And exactly where are you going?" Diaz pressed.

"I'm following a thin lead. With time running out, we need to leverage our manpower. You and Jade stay here, effectively to remain as targets for the 'True Sons of Light.' I'm going to

Germany. The CIA received intel that Boyd Ramsey may be there." It was another lie. "I will be in touch."

"You want us to stay here with a bullseye on our chests?" Diaz asked.

"Guard Jade," Tolen ordered.

Tolen left with Diaz still objecting and threatening to call his superiors.

Fifteen minutes later, Tolen arrived on the tarmac several miles inland from the hotel. The early morning air was comfortable with only a slight breeze. The sweet smell of gardenia and bougainvillea perfumed the air. The pre-dawn skies were clear.

Tolen was content to be working on his own at the moment. While Diaz was quite capable, he was often narrow-minded and resistant, and he slowed Tolen down. Jade had also become a distraction. He found himself drawn to her inquisitive and intelligent nature, her eloquent mannerisms, her undeniable femininity. Yet, he also sensed she was hiding something from the first moment he met her.

He wondered if it was simply misfortune that Claudia Denoit had gotten away under Jade's watch.

Bar had sent the accident report of Jade's car crash in New Jersey to Tolen's phone. He reviewed it on the cab ride to the airstrip. The information bothered him. Jade's claim of being run off the road after attending Phillip Cherrigan's funeral had not been substantiated by any witnesses, although the wreck had occurred on a barren two-lane highway. Jade had reported that a dark van with tinted windows had come alongside and forced her off the road into a ravine. The damage to her rental car confirmed a sideswipe. Scratches and dings to the front bumper and grill indicated damage as a result of plowing down a hill through underbrush and small trees. Yet, remarkably, Jade had come out of it unscathed except for some minor bruises.

The reality was Tolen had kept his destination to Switzerland a secret not from Diaz, but from Jade. His rising mistrust of her was also the reason he had planted a small tracking device in her PC bag before leaving the hotel.

Tolen sent a text message to Bar requesting Simon Anat's

address. She confirmed receipt and responded minutes later with the information. He also requested she find out if Claudia Denoit had been in Switzerland on the same day as the others last year.

The moment Tolen stepped aboard the airplane, Reba Zee addressed him in her usual bubbly tone. "Looks like we've got beautiful flying weather today."

The flight took three hours. Tolen slept the entire way. It might be his last opportunity to rest for some time. Shortly before landing, he changed into a charcoal gray suit and maroon silk tie.

They arrived at Zurich International Airport, and Tolen took a taxicab to the address Bar had furnished. Dietikon, Switzerland was less than ten miles southwest from the airport. The estate of Simon Anat was on the edge of the Honeret Forest.

Tolen considered what he knew about the billionaire. Fifty-six-year-old Anat, a lifelong bachelor, had always been a public figure until a year and a half ago, when he literally dropped out of sight. As far as anyone knew, he had remained at his residence all that time; not unlike Howard Hughes toward the end of his life when he had become a recluse and severely altered his appearance. Thus, Tolen thought, it was possible Simon Anat was undergoing the same type of transformation. The last time Tolen had seen Anat in *TIME* magazine, he appeared as the consummate professional: well groomed and immaculately tailored. If Hughes-like eccentricity had set in, there was no telling what the man might look like these days.

Simon Anat's sprawling estate was sequestered upon a rolling, tree-covered landscape. Tolen knew from the information Bar had provided that the mansion dated back to 1682 and was originally the location of a winery. The opulent grounds were a conglomerate of beautiful meadows with acres of old grape vines and lavish gardens. There were no less than six ornamental stone wells spread out on the property. High quarry stone walls ran horizontally from either end of the dwelling, obscuring the view of the back. The entire complex was guarded by a high, pronged iron fence, with signs bearing strong warnings that it was electrified.

With an inward shudder, Tolen reflected that electrocution was not something he ever wanted to experience again.

As they approached, Tolen admired the edifice. A proud contribution to Swiss architectural eloquence, the main structure of the estate was white stone with a brown tiled roof. From the road, the dwelling appeared to be as long as a football field with more windows than Tolen could count, each double glazed and fitted with a decorative awning. Spires loomed into the sky at each end, with another pair in the middle. A long, single-lane driveway ran from the road to the wrought-iron security gate and beyond, stretching to the house after a series of unnecessary curves.

Anat was a known art connoisseur. Although never confirmed, it was rumored he had a large temperature-controlled room on the second floor which contained over four billion dollars in paintings from such masters as Donatello, Giotto, Cimabue, and Raphael. Some conspiracy theorists suggested the Hungarian billionaire had somehow recovered stolen artwork from the World War II "Gold Train," the infamous 42-car freight train Nazis had loaded with gold, jewelry, gems, paintings, and an assortment of other valuables in 1944, all of which had been taken from Jews as the Soviet army advanced on Budapest, Hungary. Much of the stolen loot was never recovered. The fate of approximately 200 paintings seized from the train has never been determined, but U.S. restitution policy officially considered them "cultural assets" which should have been returned to their country of origin: Hungary. Some even contended Anat had the original of Raphael's *Portrait of a Young Man*, created circa 1515, which was speculated to be worth well over $100 million today.

Tolen had the taxi driver pull into the driveway but stop well before the security gate. He paid the driver and requested he wait, tipping the man handsomely. A guard in a sentry box regarded Tolen as he approached on foot.

"No one is allowed entry, sir," the guard, a burly man in his mid-thirties clad in a brown uniform, said in German.

Tolen arrived at the sentry box and responded in kind. "Tell Mr. Anat these two words: Gurkha and Sudarium."

"No, sir," the man responded brusquely. "Leave the property immediately." The guard stepped out from the box and laid a threatening hand on the pistol holstered at his right hip. With a flick, he undid the holster strap.

"I believe you'll find Mr. Anat wishes to speak with me," Tolen said calmly.

The guard drew his gun. In a flash, Tolen swung his arm up, knocking the weapon from the man's hand. At the same time, he withdrew his Springfield .45 and pressed it to the man's forehead. The guard's pistol clanged to the pavement a dozen feet away.

"Let's start again," Tolen said sedately. "I have a proposition for you. You get on the phone and tell Anat what I said, and I won't shoot you."

The German grumbled, but Tolen was certain he would comply. Few people have the courage to fight once the barrel of a pistol touches their head. The guard suddenly batted Tolen's arm away and grabbed him in a crushing bear hug, easily lifting Tolen's 225-pound frame off the ground. His gun also rattled on the driveway. Tolen's ribs were close to snapping when he raised both hands above his head and to the side, and boxed the other man's ears as hard as he could. The guard let out a feral yelp, dropped Tolen, and clutched at his ears in agony. Tolen took the opportunity to drive a fist into the bulky man's face. It only took one shot. The guard dropped his hands, staggered, and collapsed to the ground. Blood rolled from his broken nose as he lay groaning weakly.

Tolen stood, then stepped inside the sentry box and found the telephone.

"Tell Mr. Anat, *Gurkha* and *Sudarium*," he said to the male voice who answered in German at the other end.

The line went dead without a response. Tolen wondered if he might have to find his way inside the grounds by alternative methods. A minute later there was an electronic beep and the joined gates opened inward.

Tolen left the still-slumped guard and proceeded on foot up the driveway, turning once to ensure the taxi remained by the road. He passed between the spires and through an elaborate trellis onto a large portico. He approached a high, arched entryway with two massive oak doors. Before he had a chance to ring the bell, the doors parted.

Before him stood a man with deepset eyes, high cheekbones,

and dirty-blonde hair. His age was difficult to determine. Tolen placed him somewhere between his early thirties to mid-forties. He had a sullen expression, as if his responsibilities were so oppressive that they caused his face to droop. "Who are you?" the man asked sourly in German.

Tolen responded in English, "My name is Samuel Tolen. I'm an American CIA agent, and I have business with Simon Anat."

The man cocked his head arrogantly and spoke in English with a heavy German accent, "Not according to Mr. Anat."

Tolen stared at the man wordlessly.

"He has, however, consented to allow you an audience. I am Nicklaus Kappel, Mr. Anat's personal assistant." He did not offer a handshake. "Please follow me." Kappel stepped far back, allowing Tolen ample room to enter. He led Tolen through the vestibule, where Doric columns sailed up to the high ceiling and colorful tapestries draped the walls. A huge, elaborate Tiffany chandelier hung high overhead. The vestibule emptied into a long corridor where artwork adorned every wall. They passed statues of the Roman figures Romulus and Remus at the end of the hallway before it spilled into a copious living room with a box-beam ceiling. A fruity fragrance filled the air as they approached a deep kitchen with built-in cupboards and modern stainless steel appliances which seemed woefully out of place in the antiquated space.

Kappel opened a door in a sidewall. He led Tolen down a stony staircase. They arrived at a dark corridor with a stone floor and low ceiling. If not for the light somewhere ahead in the distance, they would have been immersed in complete darkness. The air was cool and dry with a musty, oaken smell. Tolen recognized the place as a wine cellar. They took the hallway a short distance to where it opened into a large, arched cellar with wooden wine racks crawling up every wall.

Sitting behind a quaint, wooden desk in the middle of the room was a clean-shaven, frail man with gaunt eyes and short, unruly silver hair. He wore a light-blue collared shirt buttoned up to his neck. The man silently watched them approach with searching brown eyes. He had a look of frustration, as if he might know Tolen, yet something was interfering with his recollection.

It took a moment for Tolen to realize the man was Simon Anat. The man's appearance had changed to the point where he was almost unrecognizable. *Just like Howard Hughes*, Tolen thought, *he's gone over the edge.*

There was a nondescript wooden chair before the desk. Kappel motioned for Tolen to take a seat then backed behind him a dozen feet where he stood quietly.

Tolen looked at Anat. The man was a weary shell of his former self. Tolen prepared himself, certain he was about to engage in a conversation with a man disconnected from reality. Who else would set up a desk in a wine cellar?

"And how is it that I know you, Mr. Tolen with the American CIA? Surely I would remember a man who is so fashionably dressed and handles himself with such bravado." Anat's voice was clear, his words thoughtful and concise, spoken in perfect English. Anat already knew who he was, but that was not what surprised Tolen. It was Anat's lucidity that was completely unexpected.

Tolen chose not to mince his words. He leaned back in the chair, folding his hands in his lap. "Gordon Nunnery recently died. How do you know the man?"

"I don't believe I do," Anat said with a subtle smile. He looked over Tolen's shoulder at his assistant. "Do I, Mr. Kappel?"

There was a hesitation. "He was...on the guest list for last year's event."

"So you do know him," Tolen pushed.

"I would venture to say we've met, but I don't really know the man. He was at the mansion once."

"What were the circumstances of his visit?"

Anat leaned in. His expression turned defensive. "What is your interest? You disable my guard and then call in using the words *Gurkha* and *Sodarian*. Speaking of Gurkha," Anat sat back and opened a desk drawer to the side. He retrieved a box, which he laid on top of the desk. "Best cigar ever made, in my opinion. Sadly, I find after 10 or 12 puffs, the flavor wanes. I recommend anyone who smokes a Gurkha stop at that point." He smiled. "I never smoke alone. I see so few visitors these days, and it's been a while since I've indulged. Will you join me?"

Tolen saw the hand-carved, camel bone box was, in fact, a box of Gurkha Black Dragons. *Ten or twelve puffs.* That explains why the cigar found in Nunnery's house was only partially smoked. "Thank you, but I respectfully decline."

Anat looked momentarily hurt. "Ah well, they're bad for the health anyway." He loosed a strained chuckle. Then, as if flipping a switch, his expression solidified. "Again, I ask: what is your interest in this Gordon Nunnery and what is a Sodarian?"

"Sudarium," Tolen corrected him. "It's a relic held in a church in Oviedo, Spain. It's purported to be a cloth that wrapped the face of Jesus Christ immediately following his crucifixion."

"You're not talking about the Shroud of Turin, are you?"

Tolen shook his head, no.

"Then I've never even heard of this Sudarium. As for Gordon Nunnery," Anat paused as if tentative about saying more, "he was part of an assembled group that was here for one day last year."

"Did this group also include Boyd Ramsey and Richard Mox?"

Anat again looked over Tolen's shoulder, obviously to get confirmation from Kappel. "Yes, they were here."

"There have been two recent murders," Tolen continued. "One was an archaeologist in Costa Rica, and the other a church security guard in Spain. A radical group calling themselves the 'True Sons of Light' claims responsibility for both deaths. This group has a self-prescribed charter of destroying relics supposedly tied to Christ. They contend His existence is a fable, and they wish to stop the charade by eliminating false artifacts. Gordon Nunnery and Richard Mox were somehow involved. The only connection between Nunnery, Mox, and Ramsey is that they were all in Switzerland for one day last year, and you've just confirmed all three were here at the mansion for some 'event.' I need to know the circumstances of this gathering."

Anat's eyes hardened. "You realize I've answered your questions so far because, frankly, I have nothing to hide. I've barely met these men and know nothing of a radical group or these two murders. I could easily send you on your way. We've already alerted the local authorities, and the guard you temporarily disabled is waiting upstairs in the kitchen heavily armed in case our conversation becomes uncivilized."

Tolen spoke in a low voice holding Anat's gaze. "Given the international flavor of these murders, Interpol is involved. If needed, I'll return with a search warrant and a squad of agents to go through your mansion. Or, you can give me the information I need, and I'll be on my way. I'm not here to disrupt your life, Mr. Anat. I'm simply gathering facts to enhance our investigation. I have no illusions that you would knowingly support the activities of a radical group, but I believe you unknowingly brought people together which may have spawned their activity."

Anat seemed to digest Tolen's words for a moment.

He watched Anat's body language carefully.

Anat relaxed and sat back in his chair. His next words surprised Tolen.

"Are you a religious man, Mr. Tolen?"

"Each man searches for his own truth."

"Yes, well put," Anat reached into the desk drawer again, this time fishing out a bottle of Bowmore Scotch and a small glass. The label was dried and peeling. It was apparently well aged.

"An 1850 bottle of Bowmore sold for 29,400 pounds at an auction about five years ago," Tolen commented after seeing the label.

Anat forced an impish smile. "I know."

Even Tolen was somewhat taken aback. This was a man of sublime taste who went after whatever he wanted.

Anat looked to Tolen. "I assume since you're on duty..."

"Thanks, but no thanks," Tolen waved a hand.

Anat continued. "Like most, my faith had been ingrained since childhood. Yet there comes a point in a man's life when he's faced with his own mortality," Anat paused, brushing the tip of his nose as if a stray hair had fallen across it. "Almost two years ago, I was diagnosed with a most unpleasant disease; a form of terminal cancer. I won't go into the particulars, but I was given roughly 18 months to two years to live. You can do the math. I'm already inside death's window," he said somberly. He paused and poured himself two fingers of Scotch. Without hesitation, he slammed back the liquid and returned the glass to the table.

Anat's words brought a chilling image of Tolen's own father lying in a coma at the Florida hospital.

"I spend a great amount of time in this wine cellar as a doctor has told me that the cool conditions may slow the growth of the cancer. Is it the truth? Who knows? But what have I got to lose?

"Several months after receiving the grim news, I made a decision. You see, there is one great mystery that science universally accepts we will never be able to solve: the age-old question of whether there is life after death. Religions tell you there is. Many believe the soul continues after death, but they have the same great crutch: belief. There is life after death because they *believe* there is. Yet there has never been one bit of evidence to prove our soul continues on in an afterlife.

"They point to the Bible as their proof, but the Bible is a book; a book whose chapters were assembled by men. It contains no more proof than the Egyptian Book of the Dead contains proof to assist the departed in the afterlife. These are texts contrived by man, not by gods."

Anat spoke faster now. "I want evidence: cold, hard, indisputable proof that there is, in fact, life after death. I want peace of mind when my time comes. I do not want some religious pundit telling me that my soul will go to heaven if I believe. I want to *know* my being will continue in the afterlife. I *have* to know." A passionate glow blazed in the man's eyes.

"Given my time constraint and my need for understanding, I decided to engage some of the world's finest professionals in their field. I assembled a group of archaeologists, mathematicians, philosophers, biologists, physicists, and men and women of various other disciplines at my estate last year and made them an offer. They had one task: prove the existence of an afterlife. I did not care how they did it, or who did it, but someone had to be prepared to show me conclusive evidence." His eyes saddened somewhat. His voice pleaded. "I want to know the truth, Mr. Tolen. I want to know what will happen to my soul when I leave this body."

"And you thought a philosopher might hold the key?" Tolen asked.

"Why not? It's a riddle mankind has been trying to solve since the beginning of time. If the biologists and physicists cannot, perhaps some of the deepest thinkers can. There is an answer. I know it. There has to be a way to prove it."

"What was the offer?" Tolen asked, his mind reeling.

"The one who could provide proof would get everything I own; approximately $30 billion, less a few million for me to live the rest of my days. Discretion was paramount. I was not looking for publicity, so one leak to the press, and the entire deal was off for everyone."

"How many were privy to this offer?"

"I solicited 500 people from around the globe. One hundred attended the gathering I held here at the mansion, and they learned my true intent as well as the rules of engagement at the meeting. This estate has 122 rooms, and they were put up for the night after I provided dinner and made the offer. They were sent on their way the next day. Each received one of my Gurkha Black Dragon cigars. I assume that is how you tied me to these people."

That explained why Bar had not discovered where Ramsey, Mox, and Nunnery had stayed in Switzerland. "You created a competition, pitting the participants against each other."

"I didn't care how they did it or what alliances they formed."

Thirty billion dollars was enough motivation to make even a passive archaeologist commit murder, Tolen thought. He took a moment to assimilate this new information before asking, "Surely, you must have known the temptation of such a huge reward would drive people to extremes…even murder. Don't you feel any responsibility for the mayhem which was sure to ensue?"

"What mayhem?" Anat looked genuinely surprised. "I never endorsed their actions; just offered the prize."

"And allowed them to make the decision of how the end justifies the means."

Anat's words turned malevolent. "You are not going to dirty my hands with your sanctimonious assertion I had something to do with the deaths of those people. Besides, CIA Agent Samuel Tolen, I certainly would not support a radical cause which tries to destroy artifacts. Quite the contrary, I am looking for proof of an afterlife, nothing more." He paused, biting his bottom lip. "This concludes our conversation. Good day, Agent Tolen."

CHAPTER 38

September 13. Thursday – 10:58 a.m. Dietikon, Switzerland

Nicklaus Kappel escorted Tolen from the building. Walking through the manor, they passed the German security guard in the kitchen. He had his head tilted back, sniffling. A female in a cook's uniform was tending to his bloody nose with a red-stained cloth. The guard glared and mumbled obscenities in German as Tolen passed them.

Just prior to departing, Tolen had asked Anat for a complete list of the participants at the meeting last year, but the man refused. Tolen did not argue. There was not enough time to vet the list anyway, and with the information Anat had provided him, he was beginning to formulate a new theory.

How Boyd Ramsey had garnered an invitation to the gathering last year, Anat would not say. Tolen suspected it had something to do with his analytic abilities, and the fact Ramsey was a bit of a renaissance man who also held degrees in Biology, Philosophy, and Asian Humanities. It was odd to think Ramsey would accept Anat's offer, although, even for an agnostic, $30 billion is one hell of a motivator.

Tolen discovered the taxi driver had been sent on his way. Therefore, Kappel arranged to have Tolen driven back to the airfield in one of Anat's limousines. To Tolen's surprise, Kappel climbed into the limousine with him and settled into the black leather seat far across the way. He had noticed Kappel's extreme body language. Every time the man was put in a situation where he drew close to someone else, he became nervous and backed away.

The man had an expansive personal space bubble. Tolen had never known anyone with such acute aphenphosmphobia.

Now, sitting across the way, Tolen saw the back of Kappel's right hand. There were a series of small circular scars.

"Have you worked for Mr. Anat long?" Tolen asked in German.

The German responded in English. "Thirteen years." He paused. "I want to apologize for my behavior when you came to the door. I was only doing my job."

"I understand," Tolen paused. "Mr. Kappel, were you included in the offer?"

"Call me Nicklaus, and no," he chuckled. "It doesn't matter, because it's an impossibility. The eternal question is answered for each of us only in due time. Just because you tempt scientists and doctors with an outrageous reward doesn't mean they'll be successful. I've even advised Mr. Anat of my opinion, but he refuses to listen."

"Does he normally take your advice?" Just then, Tolen's phone rang. He elected not to answer in front of Kappel.

"He's open to suggestions and heeds my input when he deems fit, but impending death makes rational men irrational. He follows his own counsel these days."

For the rest of the drive, Kappel remained quiet. When they reached the airfield, Tolen was dropped off and thanked Kappel for the lift.

It was a bright, clear morning, and the airstrip was bustling with activity. In the distance, he saw the Learjet and began walking toward it. He was consumed in thought about Simon Anat's bizarre offer and Nicklaus Kappel's comments regarding his boss when his phone rang.

"Hello, Bar."

"Hey, I've been trying to get hold of you. I've confirmed that Claudia Denoit from Reims, France, did fly into Switzerland on the same day as the others last year. She's a geophysicist, by the way. That's quite an eclectic group of professions all flying into Switzerland one day and out the next. Did you find out what they were all doing there?"

"Yes," he responded as he reached the stairs to the plane. He briefly explained Anat's condition and his offer for proof of an afterlife.

"Wow, didn't see that one coming," Bar exclaimed after Tolen finished. "Oh, I decided to check on the travel of some of the other people, specifically the victims, and guess what? Dr. Phillip Cherrigan was also there."

"In Switzerland?" Tolen's surprise was evident in his voice.

"Yep. According to records, he *and* his wife, Margaret, were there, but something seemed out of sync. I found a credit card receipt at a gas station in New Jersey for Margaret Cherrigan the night she was supposed to be with her husband in Europe, so I had Interpol send me surveillance video from the Swiss airport. Dr. Cherrigan can be seen walking away from the boarding gate with a woman. She looks very similar to his wife: long blonde hair, svelte figure, but it struck me that she was acting suspicious. I ran her image through the facial recognition database. Turns out it's not his wife after all. It's your buddy, Dr. Jade Mollur."

"Jade?"

"Also, it appears Dr. Mollur is broke. Dr. Cherrigan was funding their archaeological activities. Once he was murdered, his wife shut down her access to the funds. If you and Diaz hadn't come along, once she left that jail in New Jersey, she didn't have enough money to catch a cab. She's practically destitute."

Tolen had no response. He scaled the steps and entered the cabin of the Learjet. Reba Zee was sitting in one of the passenger seats reading a magazine. She waved at him and headed to the cockpit.

"Tolen, you there?"

"Yes, I'm here, Ms. Bar," he said, feeling deflated. "Anything on Boyd Ramsey?"

"No," she said flatly. "We know he flew into Spain in the summer. He didn't try to conceal his movements at all, but then he just disappeared. The next we know, his fingerprints are at the Cathedral de San Salvador crime scene where Javier Diaz was murdered and the Sudarium stolen, then at the Costa Rican murder scene of Dr. Phillip Cherrigan, then on the communiqué sent to the Spanish press. As we discussed, each instance had a fingerprint from the ring finger of his left hand."

"There's one more person I need you to check on: Nicklaus Kappel," Tolen spelled out the name for her. "He's Simon Anat's personal assistant. Give me his background and recent travel. I'm sure Anat has a private plane."

"Where are you headed now? We only have ten hours before the Sudarium will be declared stolen, and I guess it goes without saying Vakind is anxious for some good news."

"I'm returning to the Isle of Patmos."

After hanging up and informing Reba Zee of their next destination, Tolen considered his options. The news about Jade was disheartening. She and Dr. Cherrigan had obviously been in attendance at Simon Anat's gathering last year, which meant they were privy to the offer. That explained her fervor to continue the search even after Dr. Cherrigan's death. So much for altruistic, or even archaeological, reasons, he thought to himself, wondering if she had killed Cherrigan and tainted the crime scene with Ramsey's fingerprints. Even if she was not the murderer, she was obviously after the $30 billion, and Tolen had unknowingly been drawn into her hunt. Without Tolen and Diaz and the ability to travel at no cost on the CIA's private jet, Jade Mollur would still be in Morristown, New Jersey, sitting on a street corner. She probably staged the car crash to make it appear she was a victim of an attack by the 'True Sons of Light' in order to get their attention.

To Tolen's chagrin, it was painfully obvious that Dr. Jade Mollur was far from what she appeared to be.

Yet as pieces to the mystery slowly fell in place, greater and equally perplexing questions arose: how would the discovery of a cache of objects which belonged to Jesus Christ satisfy Simon Anat's proof of life after death? How did the 'True Sons of Light' and Boyd Ramsey fit into all this?

Still, the most frustrating question remained: where was the Sudarium, and what was the medical laboratory technician, Aaron Conin, doing with threads from the relic? Obviously, he had conducted, or planned to conduct, tests. The Sudarium was said to have the bloodstains of Christ on it. If Ramsey, or whoever hired him, was trying to confirm that the blood on the Sudarium belonged to Jesus, they would first need a conclusive sample to match with it, but none existed. Besides, Anat wanted indisputable proof of life after death, not confirmation that Jesus existed.

One thing was certain: he had found the motivational trigger. Thirty billion dollars would drive a man or woman to do many deviant things, including murder.

Also, the date discrepancy still had him completely baffled. Conin had a sample of the Sudarium on August 24th, six days before it was stolen from the church in Spain on August 30th.

The answer suddenly hit Tolen like a shot. *It didn't make sense because it wasn't possible!*

Tolen walked into the cabin where Reba Zee was checking the instrument panels and gauges.

"Change of plans," Tolen said. "I need to go to Oviedo, Spain."

"You're the boss!" Reba Zee declared happily, as if she enjoyed these sudden shifts in destination.

Tolen considered Diaz and Jade waiting for him back on the Isle of Patmos. Given Jade's level of deception, it was conceivable Diaz's life was in danger. He picked up his cell phone and called Diaz.

****

Diaz sat on the bed drumming his fingers on the top cover. He had lost patience hours ago.

Jade held a piece of paper as she paced from door to window and back again. She had been doing so continuously for the last 25 minutes. The paper contained the translated text from the roll in the second stone jar. She had been studying it and talking to herself for an hour, first at the table and now hastening back and forth across the room. Diaz thought he could see track marks in the carpet, and it was getting on his nerves.

When his cell phone rang, he answered it, not recognizing the international phone number. "Si?"

"Diaz, it's Tolen. Please answer me with 'yes' or 'no' responses: is Jade still there with you?"

"Where are you? We're losing valuable time."

"Diaz," Tolen's words hardened. "Don't say another word. Just listen to me."

There was a peculiar tone in the American's voice which caught Diaz's attention; something grave. He curtailed any further outbursts, waiting for Tolen to continue.

" 'Yes' or 'no' answers only," Tolen reiterated. "Are you the only one who can hear me at the moment?"

"Yes."

"Is Jade there with you?"

"Yes," Diaz responded. Out of the corner of his eye, he saw Jade giving him a curious stare. She had stopped pacing and was standing in the middle of the room.

"Two things: first, I understand your concern about our condensed time. I have a strong lead I'm following. Please contact the Cathedral of San Salvador and arrange for one of the docents or priests to show me the crime scene at the Cámara Santa. I'll be at the church in three hours."

Diaz did not like it, but he knew from Tolen's tone there was no use in arguing. "Si, Señor."

"Second, I've uncovered information that implies Dr. Mollur has not been completely truthful with us. I suggest you be on guard."

Surprised, Diaz cast a wary eye toward Jade then broke off the gaze before she noticed.

"Given what I've just told you, do not disclose my activities to Jade. Tell her I'll be back in a few hours. When you contact the church in Oviedo, do so without her knowledge. I don't want her to know where I'm going."

"I understand," Diaz said. The accusation that Dr. Jade Mollur was somehow involved was startling, and Diaz was still reeling from the news when the line went dead.

CHAPTER 39

September 13. Thursday – 2 p.m. Oviedo, Spain

Tolen approached the Cathedral of San Salvador, admiring the elegant structure with its towering stone bell tower. Clarín, the Spanish novelist, had described it with poetic precision when he referred to it as a "stone finger pointing to heaven."

He arrived at the central door of the cathedral. A robed priest shuffled past, turned, and asked in broken English if he were Samuel Tolen.

Tolen nodded.

"Uno minuto, por favor," the priest said, ducking back inside.

Tolen admired the craftsmanship of the relief of the Transfiguration on the door as he waited in the comfortable Spanish sunlight before the entryway.

Shortly, a man in a black cassock appeared at the doorway and stepped outside. He sported a crew cut of gray hair and had narrow, accommodating eyes. His wrinkled face signaled his advanced years. Tolen shook the man's proffered hand. "Mr. Tolen, I am Archbishop Juan Gustavo. Inspector Pascal Diaz asked me to show you the most unfortunate scene of the events which recently occurred at our magnificent church. I must insist we keep the visit brief. The Feast of the Cross starts at 9 a.m. tomorrow morning, and we have much to do to prepare. The Cuerpo Nacional de Policia has spent much time examining the Cámara Santa, and I suggest you seek them out for their details. I will allow you some time and try to answer any questions you may have."

Tolen nodded. "Thank you, Archbishop. I understand what an

inconvenience this is, but I think the time will serve both of our countries well. I will keep my visit short."

The Archbishop gave Tolen a subtle nod of agreement. There was an unspoken understanding of the ramifications if the Sudarium was not returned before the next morning's events began.

He led Tolen inside, and they strolled down the long center aisle. Given the Archbishop's advanced age, he was quite spry and moved with purpose. Today's work for the elderly man was far from perfunctory. Preparing for the start of the Feast of the Cross was surely one of the most hectic and trying days of the year for the Archbishop.

Tolen marveled at the architecture inside the cathedral. Massive columns shot upward to a vast arched ceiling with ornate images, occasionally interrupted by magnificent stained glass windows. The eight-sided dome in the center lifted to a staggering height. Carved figures and reliefs were almost everywhere he looked. Tolen had read that the Cathedral was classical Gothic at heart, but a litany of styles had been integrated into the church design since its original construction in the 8th century. Various influences were clearly visible in the cloisters, choir, naves, narthex, and ambulatory—everything from Pre-Romanesque to Baroque, and even Romanesque, exemplified by a collection of fabulous column-statues. It was almost like walking through centuries of historical architectural progression.

Beyond the nave and before the choir area, several priests busied themselves fussing over a tapestry that hung at the front of the main altar where the image of the Divine Savior was situated on a four-column baldacchino. Nearby, the images of the other prophets who took part in the Transfiguration story mentioned in the Gospel came into view. The altar was further surrounded by eight magnificent paintings depicting scenes from the life of Jesus Christ embedded within a complex array of decorative masonry. Above it all, the colorful Churrigueresque cupola towered into the air.

On one side of the altar, Tolen eyed two robed priests who were putting the final touches on a diorama. Tolen recognized the scene as Mary and Joseph tending to the baby Jesus in a thatched cradle. The revered couple was depicted by life-size mannequins replete with period clothing being arranged with care by the priests. Baby Jesus was a simple toy doll wrapped loosely in a small, off-colored blanket.

"In preparation for tomorrow's celebration," the Archbishop announced, obviously noticing Tolen's gaze.

More priests were milling about the transept on the left, before disappearing out of sight. Their voices stayed low, softly echoing in the vaulted chamber. The smell of freshly polished wood lingered in the still air. Tolen figured the pews had just been attended to for tomorrow's ceremony when thousands of people would converge on the cathedral and spill out into the side streets and avenues, having journeyed from nearby towns and distant lands to pay homage to the treasured and venerable holy relic: the very cloth that staunch believers say covered the bloodied face of Jesus Christ while He still hung upon the cross immediately after His crucifixion; the cloth that most believed was now tucked safely away in the Arca Santa in the adjoining Cámara Santa relic room.

Tolen suddenly felt an irrepressible urgency to find the Sudarium.

The Archbishop continued on, directing Tolen to an opening at the apse wall where steps led up to a small room. Light shined ahead on the length of the room, accentuating its rough stone-masonry walls and barrel-vaulted ceiling. To the sides, pilasters were adorned with carvings of the twelve Apostles, two set upon each of six pilasters.

At the end of the room, Archbishop Gustavo approached a second, overlapping room with a much lower barrel-vaulted ceiling. It was set apart from the first room by an archway where perpendicular iron bars and an iron-barred door prohibited access. Unlike the entry room, this secured room—which Tolen recognized as the Cámara Santa—was filled with artifacts.

The Archbishop stopped before the locked gate and turned to Tolen. "The Cámara Santa was built to house the holy relics obtained during the Asturian Monarchy: the Cross of Victory, Cross of Angels, Agatha Box," he said, sweeping his hand before him with a swish of his robe as he pivoted, "and, of course, there are also the reliquary items stored in the Arca Santa." He pointed to a large, black, oak reliquary chest in silver gilt adorned with repoussé in the center of the room. "This is where the Sudarium is usually—" He stopped himself. A pained expression crossed his eyes. "That is where it is stored."

"Had anyone else opened the chest recently before the theft?"

"No, Señor Tolen. The Sudarium is only put on display three times a year. The last time the chest was opened was on Good Friday."

"It's not periodically inventoried?"

"No, there is no need. The contents remain inside."

Tolen leaned forward and peered at the decorative chest. "Is the chest locked?"

"No, but the iron gate is kept closed and locked at all times."

Tolen knelt down and examined the keyhole. There were scratch marks where someone had clumsily picked the lock. "Who has the key to this door?" Tolen asked.

"I have a key in my office, and the local police have one. They confirmed after the crime that they still have their copy of the key, as do I."

"Do you keep your office locked?"

"Yes."

"Does anyone besides you have a key to your office?"

"Yes, the poor guard, Javier Diaz, did."

Tolen thought for a moment. "Where was his body found?"

"On the floor behind the chest. Father Carletta, who discovered Javier with that halberd buried in his chest, hasn't been the same since."

Tolen looked deep into the man's eyes. "Archbishop Gustavo, surely you are aware of the violence which will erupt tomorrow if the Sudarium is not returned in time. Is there any way to forestall the festivities, even if for only a few hours to buy us more time to locate it? Could a substitute be used in place of the Sudarium?" Tolen knew what he was suggesting equated to blasphemy. No matter how small the chance, he had to try.

The Archbishop's gaze turned icy. He spoke sternly. "The Feast of the Cross will proceed as it always has. God will be with us.

Everything we do is part of *His* plan."

There was a long pause.

"Thank you for your time, Archbishop Gustavo," Tolen said, shaking the man's hand. "I can see myself out."

The Archbishop wore an expression of surprise as if to say, *is that all you needed to see?*

Tolen left the Cámara Santa, passed through the main sanctuary, and left the building. He stepped out into the grassy courtyard where he was greeted by a mild wind and comfortable temperature. The sun was beaming into his face, and he placed his sunglasses on.

He walked to his rental car parked in the side lot, now armed with information which had turned his investigation in a new direction.

CHAPTER 40

September 13. Thursday – 2:57 p.m. Oviedo, Spain

Tolen contacted Bar and requested a residential address, which she provided. He found the single-story villa situated at the end of Calle Cristiana, a quiet street on the edge of Oviedo. The residence was secluded, at least a hundred yards away from the nearest dwelling; a house situated far from the road on a wooded lot.

It was the home of Javier Diaz.

Tolen no longer believed Javier Diaz was an unsuspecting victim of a malicious, premeditated murder and theft. He now had evidence suggesting the man might have been part of the theft and, most likely, had been double-crossed somewhere in the process. Unfortunately, Boyd Ramsey's attendance at Simon Anat's gathering suggested that the ex-CIA analyst was, indeed, deeply involved. Tolen theorized that Ramsey and Javier Diaz had formed an alliance intent on winning Simon Anat's $30 billion reward. Ramsey must have somehow believed the Sudarium held the key to satisfying the proof Anat sought. The fact that the Virginia lab tech, with whom Ramsey had been in contact, had thread samples of the Sudarium on August 24th meant they had access to the Sudarium at least a week prior to its known theft. To compound matters, there was still the mystery of how Jade factored into all this.

Tolen pulled into the long, gravel driveway after confirming the address on the mailbox. The yard was overgrown, but the exterior of the house was well kept. Tolen parked, left his coat in the car, and approached the front stoop. He was not sure what he was looking for, but similar to Aaron Conin's apartment, which had not been thoroughly searched since it was believed his murder had taken place on the street, Javier Diaz's house had been left out of the investigation since the homicide occurred in the church. With any luck, he might uncover some telltale evidence to help solve this ever-twisting riddle.

Using a compact tool kit he pulled from his pocket, Tolen picked the front door lock and entered the house. The stagnant air inside was warm. The decor was quaint, not particularly color coordinated, nor had it been dusted in a while. Sports and automotive magazines were heaped on an end table. Typical bachelor's house, Tolen thought.

He made his way into the kitchen. Dirty dishes were stacked in the sink where the sour smell of rancid food rose from the drain. There was a stain on the counter which appeared to be the result of a spill from tomato-based pasta sauce of some sort.

He passed through, into a dining room with a small round table and two chairs. A filing cabinet was on the left. It was unlocked, and he opened it. The first two drawers were empty. The bottom drawer contained folders in complete disarray; turned and twisted, some ripped off the metal runners. Papers were scattered everywhere. Tolen spent the next fifteen minutes sifting through them. It was all personal information: bank statements, receipts, car titles, insurance cards, etc. Tolen assembled the monthly bank statements from the last four years. The only one missing was the statement for the month of June two years ago.

Tolen drifted into the master bedroom. The bed was unmade; the adjoined master bathroom cluttered with toiletry items. He thumbed through the junk mail on the bureau and found nothing of interest.

He checked a second, then a third bedroom with the same results. Whatever secrets Javier was hiding, he had left no evidence behind. Or perhaps someone had already purged the place, as evidenced by the file folders being scrambled and disorganized.

He moved into the living room and den before he returned to the kitchen. He checked inside the refrigerator. Only a scant amount of food was tucked into the small freezer above the main storage unit. He meticulously went through each cupboard, yet still nothing of substance turned up.

Tolen eyed a pantry door across the way. He looked at it momentarily, then strolled over and turned the handle expecting to see a shallow recess containing shelves of food.

Instead, when he swung the door open he saw gaping darkness.

Thin wooden stair steps led down into a basement. Tolen looked around on the wall near the door, inside and out, for a light switch. He found none. He retrieved a pen light from his pocket and turned it on, aiming the small shaft of light down into the abyss. Eight feet below, the beam landed on a solid cement floor. He carefully negotiated the steps, holding onto a rickety wooden side rail. The air became damp and cooler as he descended. A rank, earthen smell pervaded.

He arrived at the base and found a hanging string. After a single tug, an exposed light bulb on the ceiling flickered on. Tolen turned his pen light off and returned it to his pocket.

The enclosure was small; no larger than the kitchen above. The walls were unfinished, revealing uncovered wall struts and electrical wiring. The bare cement floor was uneven and rough. The only object in the room was a white freezer at the far end. He headed over to it.

The chest freezer was a large, rectangular unit. He could hear a low whir of a motor that signified it was turned on and working. There was a smear of red at the lip where the gasket sealed the lid to the main body. Tolen flashed back to the pasta stain on the kitchen counter above. A disquieting thought ran through his mind: *What if the two stains were something other than spilled food?*

Tolen leaned forward to examine the red fluid, which had long ago dried. He stood upright and removed a pair of latex gloves from his pocket and put them on. After wrapping his fingers under the edge of the lid, he pulled up. With a *pop*, the lid broke free of the cold-air seal.

A light came on inside, illuminating the assortment of frozen foods. Like the filing cabinet, the contents were strewn about haphazardly. Boxes of vegetables, bags of poultry, bread and food of every ilk packed the freezer nearly to the brim. Chilly air lifted to Tolen's face. Steam left his mouth with each exhale.

It was only after several seconds of examining the contents that Tolen saw it.

An icy human head was wedged in the back left corner, facing him. The frosted face resembled an alabaster statue. The eyes were closed; the nose holes plugged with crystallization. The thin, off-colored lips had mutated into nothing more than a frozen horizontal cut in the lower half of the face. The cheeks were pressed out, locked in a bizarre position as if food was stuffed in both sides.

Even in this grisly state, Tolen recognized the face. It was Boyd Ramsey.

Damn.

With his gloved hands, he reached forward and pulled some of the frozen items away. It had first appeared the head was severed, floating atop the frozen goods, but it had only been an illusion. As he drew back the stiff bags and cold boxes, he saw the man's taut neck led down to clothed shoulders and chest. His body was intact, which was not much consolation.

He spotted Ramsey's left hand sticking up between two bags of frozen carrots. As he had morbidly expected, the ring finger had been severed at the first joint.

Tolen looked back at the permafrost face. Just below the neckline, Ramsey was clad in a dark, bulky shirt of some sort. He gently dug the food away. Strangely, a red light began to flash across the man's chest where he could now see a harness and vest had been secured. The flash speed escalated until it was nearly a steady red light.

Tolen's blood went cold. He recognized it in an instant: he had primed an explosive.

He willed himself not to panic. He had to find the source and disarm it quickly.

Tolen looked at the underside of the lid, expecting to see a wire connection which had armed the device when he raised it. Oddly, there was none, but he did see a thin insulated wire running from inside the freezer and curving over the back edge. From there, it dove behind the freezer and out of sight.

It appeared that opening the freezer was not what had armed the device, but Tolen was unsure exactly what had. Holding his feet in place, he looked down. He was surprised to find he was standing on a paper-thin, white rubber mat which blended almost seamlessly into the cement floor. He squatted, ensuring his feet remained in place. He spotted the tiny insulated wire again. It originated from underneath the freezer and slipped beneath the mat where he stood. Stepping on the mat had armed it. He was also certain it would detonate if he stepped off the mat. Weight-trip detonators were activated when weight was applied and then detonated when some percentage of the original weight—usually 20%—was removed.

His only chance was to displace his body weight with another object. He looked about in the empty room struggling to discard morbid thoughts of what would be left of him if the device went off.

Now he knew why the basement was barren. Whoever had set this trap had considered the countermove.

He had to come up with another plan. As gruesome as the thought was, he considered pulling Boyd Ramsey's body from the freezer and placing it on the mat, but that would surely entail removing the harness with the explosives, and he was reasonably sure doing so would trip the detonator.

Tolen pulled out his cell phone to call for help. Then he hesitated. If someone was smart enough to establish an arming device underneath a mat (and remove potential weight displacements from the room), they were smart enough to engage relay tracking of cell phone transmission signals as a secondary form of detonation. Hitting the *send* button would have the same effect as stepping off the mat. He deposited the phone back in his pocket feeling more and more defeated.

His father's words rang in his ears: *Defeat only grabs you by your feet and yanks you under water when you invite it to do so. Always tell defeat to hold its place at the muddy bottom while you enjoy success swimming across the surface.*

An idea struck him. He could use the weight of the freezer.

But there were inherent risks in doing so. If the sensor underneath the mat was complex, it might complicate the parameters for detonation. For example, if additional weight is added, it may re-establish this new combined weight as the top mark, and a 20% decline in this weight would detonate the explosive. So if he was able to lift the freezer and get a corner of it on the mat, once he stepped off, chances were it would still detonate. The positive side of such a scenario was that such a more complex trigger would have a lag time in order to re-establish a top weight and assess the 20% drop. That lag time could be a few seconds.

Would that be enough time to get up the stairs and clear of the basement?

Another problem was lifting the corner of the freezer onto the mat. With the freezer full of food and a corpse, there was no question it would be immensely heavy. If, once he raised it, he was not able to move it over onto the mat quickly and set it back down, the loss in weight would spell his doom. For him to be successful, he had to lift it, move it onto the mat, and drop it down in one motion, then sprint up the stairs. There would be no second chance.

It was a glum predicament, yet it appeared to be his only option. Time was running out, and he had to take action. Beads of perspiration sprouted across his forehead.

He looked up at the top of the stairs. Light was coming through from the kitchen where he had left the basement door open. At least he had that going for him.

Tolen closed the lid. He knelt down and reached underneath the freezer. The bottom edge was sharp. It was going to be painful. He steadied his resolve and took a deep breath, knowing it might be one of his last.

****

Maria Sanchez had just returned home on Calle Cristiana, navigating up the long, dirt driveway. She had been out buying groceries and exited the vehicle carrying an armload of bags. Alimerka had a sale on vegetables, and she had taken full advantage of it, practically filling her front and back seat. Now she was tasked with getting them into the house and put away. She awkwardly readjusted her purse onto her shoulder, struggling to hold the numerous bags. Content she had everything under control, she headed to the front door, realizing with chagrin she had already placed her keys back in her purse.

Just as Maria reached the porch, a tremendous explosion rocked the afternoon silence, violently shaking the air. She jumped, uttered a slight scream, and dropped everything she was holding. To the left, a monstrous fireball appeared over the trees, swirling red and yellow, and then mushroomed out as the awful sound reverberated in the distance. The repercussion left her ears ringing.

It took her a moment to gather her wits. The only thing in that direction was Javier Diaz's house.

She shook herself from her daze and found her purse several feet away. She fished out her cell phone, spilling most of the contents of her purse, and dialed 112 for Emergency Services.

CHAPTER 41

September 13. Thursday – 4:14 p.m. Isle of Patmos, Greece

Jade was pacing about the hotel room relentlessly.

"Why don't you have a seat?" Diaz said from the table. He kept his head down looking at the hotel guide on top of the desk.

She swept across the room, moving from wall to wall, not bothering to respond. There was something about the rolled parchment clue which nagged at her...something familiar. *God, lion, desert*...the words swirled in her mind.

This was a clue she felt certain Dr. Cherrigan, with his biblical archaeological background, could have solved, and it made her miss him that much more.

She involuntarily sucked in a breath and felt her chest shudder. Suddenly, she knew why the clue rang familiar. Everything came together as a memory from the past replayed. She looked at Diaz. "I've solved it! I know where the last jar and the cache are located!"

A firm series of knocks on the hotel room door startled her.

Diaz looked up at Jade, his finger pressed to his lips to silence her. He gently laid the guide book on the table and withdrew his pistol while silently motioning her to the bathroom.

There was another series of hard knocks.

Jade slipped into the bathroom and closed the door, leaving it slightly cracked so she could see out.

Diaz went to the door, staying to the left side. "Who is it?" he called.

No response.

Jade felt a chill.

Diaz looked at Jade and raised the Beretta 9mm. He slowly moved his free hand across the door and grabbed the door handle silently.

Jade had a very bad feeling.

He glanced back at her one last time. With a quick twist of the knob, he yanked the door inward.

****

Tolen watched from a sitting position in a nearby copse of trees as the rescue vehicles arrived. His ears were ringing, his body was battered, and his clothes were torn in several places. He had been successful in lifting the freezer onto the trigger mat and, as he hoped, when the unit recalculated the additional weight after he stepped off, it bought him several seconds to flee. He had just enough time to traverse the basement stairs and reach the kitchen before the charge on Boyd Ramsey's corpse detonated. He was propelled through the window into the yard where debris rained down upon him. Groggily, Tolen had dragged himself away from the burning building and into the sanctity of the woods.

Javier Diaz's house was now engulfed in fire. The flames shot high in the air, sending black smoke billowing upward into the blue Spanish sky. Firefighters had converged on the scene and were hurrying about setting up hoses and waterlines from a mobile tanker.

Tolen looked at the palms of his hands. There were bloody cut lines across each where the sharp underside of the freezer had bitten into the skin. He flexed his hands in pain. After a few minutes, he rose, gathered his wits, and moved farther into the woods to avoid being seen. A loud static noise indicated the emergency crews were now fully engaged, armed with flowing water hoses, their concentration focused on containing the blaze. It would be some time before they had the fire under control. Even then, the house would be destroyed, as would any remains of Boyd Ramsey not already disintegrated by the explosion.

Tolen continued to weave among the trees, circumventing the activity. He kept track of the sun's position to ensure he remained on course. Thankfully, the woods were thinned out as the lush summertime foliage had already died away, signaling the approach of autumn. With each step, Tolen felt a barrage of pain from a multitude of aches.

Minutes later, he reached the only other house he had seen on the road. A car was parked on a dirt driveway. Tolen limped up to the front porch. Tattered grocery bags and fresh vegetables were scattered everywhere: on the porch, down the steps, and on the ground. Tolen spotted a purse, its contents spilled out among the vegetables. A large metal ring held a series of keys. Car keys.

A minute later, Samuel Tolen was on the road headed back toward the airfield where Reba Zee was waiting. The ringing in his ears had subsided, and he was finally able to think with clarity. None of it made sense. He had confirmed Boyd Ramsey's fingerprints had been planted, but he had no idea why the man's body had been rigged as a trap.

The only certainty was that Dr. Jade Mollur appeared to be involved up to her neck.

Tolen pulled out his cell phone. Fortunately, it had survived virtually unscathed. He dialed Diaz's cell number with mounting concern for the inspector's well being.

It went unanswered. He redialed. Still no answer.

CHAPTER 42

September 13. Thursday – 4:12 p.m. Oviedo, Spain

16 hours 48 minutes until the start of the Feast of the Cross

"Bar," Tolen said as he neared the airfield. "Have you found out anything regarding Nicklaus Kappel?"

"What's going on? You sound...stressed."

"Let Vakind know I found Boyd Ramsey. He's dead and apparently has been dead for some time. I found him in the basement of Javier Diaz's house. His corpse was rigged with explosives which detonated."

"That's terrible! Are you okay?"

"Anything on Kappel?"

"Yeah...um...whatever instinct caused you to check on him appears to be well founded. He doesn't have a criminal background, but his sister, Cecily, is incarcerated in Haufmer Langstrafenanstalt, a German prison, and will be for a very long time, for armed robbery. The two are close in a creepy way. They were in foster homes in their teens after their father died. It seems they had an incestuous relationship. From what I've uncovered, Kappel is desperate to get Cecily out of jail. He testified as a character witness at her trial and his testimony vacillated from a crying tantrum to a fit of rage. He was only permitted to visit her, for the first time, this week. German prisons are not known for being corrupt, but with enough money I'm sure he could buy her way out. If he's after Anat's reward, there's your motive.

"Kappel also called the hotel on several occasions in Costa

Rica where Dr. Phillip Cherrigan and Dr. Jade Mollur stayed. Oh, and get this: Anat's private jet took off from Switzerland about the same time you and Reba Zee departed from Zurich International Airport en route to Oviedo, Spain."

"That's why he drove me to Zurich airport," Tolen said aloud, "he was also flying out." He paused. "Bar, can you track the movement of the plane?"

"No, not like I could if it was in the U.S. They filed a flight plan for a town in southern Switzerland, but they never landed there. I checked. If we had started tracking it by satellite the moment of departure, I could have followed it, but there's no way to know where it's going now."

"Can you tell if it's landed somewhere?" Tolen asked.

"If you have a destination I can confirm with the airport or airfield."

"Try the airfield on the Isle of Patmos."

"Give me a sec…"

Tolen could hear Tiffany Bar typing quickly.

"Whoa, Anat's jet *did* land on Patmos this afternoon; at an airstrip to the north of the one you used. The plane's already left the island, though. How did you know?"

A bad feeling settled in the pit of Samuel Tolen's stomach.

****

It was 8:32 p.m. when Reba Zee landed the jet on the well-lit runway at the Patmos airfield. Tolen had changed into a fresh set of clothes and tended to his assortment of cuts and scrapes. He had already ruled out involving the local authorities, since he was not willing to risk the entanglement of an investigation which would have taken hours to explain. Besides, the homing beacon he had secretly placed in Jade's PC bag clearly showed she was still in the hotel. With Bar's information that Jade and Dr. Cherrigan had been in contact with Nicklaus Kappel, it was apparent now that Jade and Kappel were working together. Given the inability to contact Pascal Diaz on either his cell phone or the hotel room phone, Tolen had a mounting concern for the inspector's safety.

261

Reba Zee arranged for a priority rental car to be waiting for Tolen when they touched down. He reached the hotel in less than twelve minutes toting a handheld digital display. The signal remained strong, signifying Jade was still in the room. He reached the fourth floor landing in less than a minute, deposited the digital display in his pocket, and drew his Springfield, checking the magazine to ensure he had a full seven-round clip with an eighth bullet set in the chamber. He eased up to the hotel room door and pressed his ear against it listening for any sound. An older European couple, speaking Italian, emerged in a hurry from a nearby room. They were bickering about where to go for dinner. Tolen calmly slipped the gun back into the holster underneath his coat and nonchalantly walked past them so as not to draw their attention. Once the couple was inside the elevator, and the pneumatic doors swished shut, he spun around and quickly returned to the door. Again he pressed his ear to the door but detected no sound coming from the room. He drew the Springfield once more.

There was no way to know how many would be inside. Since Anat's jet had already departed the isle, it appeared Kappel had come and gone, although there was a possibility he had remained behind with Jade. If Kappel was using Anat's plane without the billionaire's knowledge, he might have sent it back to Switzerland.

Tolen weighed his options. He had gone through multiple attack scenarios on the drive over. Considering the probability that Pascal Diaz was being held prisoner, this might very well turn into a hostage situation. The other possibility was that Pascal Diaz was already dead, and this was a trap. Jade knew Tolen would eventually return, especially if the phones went unanswered. For him to enter via the front door might be playing right into her hands, but there was no time for anything other than a direct approach. He would do so as cautiously as possible.

Checking to ensure the hallway was clear, Tolen knelt down. He shifted the automatic pistol to his left hand as he gently grasped the door handle with his right. He turned it so slowly it took nearly a minute to rotate the knob an inch. He had expected to feel a hard stop during the rotation. Surprisingly, the handle continued to turn. Spinning it another half inch, to his surprise, he found the door unlocked. He paused, concerned that at any moment the door would release inward and blatantly announce his arrival.

Tolen took a deep breath. He could wait no longer. With a quick turn, he thrust the door open, falling back against the hallway wall to the side of the door, bracing for gunfire or explosives to erupt from the room.

He was met with only silence.

The faint light from a table lamp limped into the hallway.

He waited several seconds, drew in a deep breath, and rounded the corner with his gun leveled, prepared to fire at the first sign of movement.

Instead, what he saw caused him to freeze in his tracks.

The naked corpse of a female was suspended on the wall upside down next to the bed. It was covered in a veil of impossibly ashen skin, with a ghastly face full of deep bruises and lacerations. The bloodshot eyes, encased in dark eye sockets, were open and void. The body more closely resembled a demonic creature, with its contrasting white skin and red eyes, than a human being. The woman's feet were bunched together near the ceiling, restrained by wire which disappeared into the wall. The body was vertical except for her arms which were extended perpendicular to either side and were also tied to the wall by wire which sunk beneath the surface. The victim's hair, although dark like Jade's, was long and had been pinned up on her head. Blood had pooled a foot below on the carpet.

Tolen moved to the bathroom, checked the shower, and returned to the bedroom to confirm the closet was empty. He then holstered his weapon and stepped up to the wall, kneeling down to get a closer look at the battered face. Only then did he recognize the lifeless features of the French woman, Claudia Denoit. On the blood-stained carpet below the body, he saw a tiny object no larger than a shirt button mired in the coagulated substance. It was the homing device he had placed in Jade's PC bag.

He pulled a plastic glove from his coat pocket and put it on. He touched the woman's arm and found it stiff. Rigor mortis had already begun to set in, indicating death had been more than three hours ago.

Tolen rose and retreated a few steps, still eyeing the wall.

The symbolism was obvious. The upside down position, the arms stretched out at shoulder level, the gathered feet. The morbid positioning of the woman's body resembled an inverted "T." It was reminiscent of the Apostle Peter who, when he learned he would be crucified on the cross, asked to be martyred upside down, stating he was not worthy to die upright in the manner of his Lord Jesus Christ.

Under normal circumstances, Tolen would have immediately notified local authorities of the crime, but these were not normal circumstances. He simply could not afford to get caught up in an investigation.

Tolen surveyed the rest of the room for any signs of a struggle, but all seemed in order. In fact, it had been completely vacated and thoroughly cleaned. Even the bed was made.

He looked to the table. The second stone jar was gone.

What had become of Pascal Diaz? The thought of the Spaniard's fate was disquieting. If Kappel and Jade were capable of the atrocity on the wall before him, there was no telling what they might have done with the inspector.

With this latest murder of Claudia Denoit, the charade continued. By staging another Apostle-style murder, Kappel and Jade had once again implicated the 'True Sons of Light,' a group that Tolen now knew to be fictitious. The "True Sons of Light" had been an elaborate creation invented so that Jade could stage an attempt on her life, draw the CIA's interest as a target, and continue the search for the cache of Jesus' earthly objects on the CIA's bankroll.

It sounded clean, but there were several gaping holes in this rationale which tugged at Tolen, such as what was being accomplished by continuing these murders, and what was the significance of intentionally involving highly skilled agents from a multitude of international intelligence agencies, including the CIA, in their nefarious activities. Forcing this elaborate union with the CIA was a hell of a risk, comparable to "inviting the fox to guard the henhouse," as Jaspar Tolen used to say. There must have been a pressing need to continue the search for the cache of Jesus' belongings which overruled the danger of drawing worldwide attention to their activities.

Tolen turned away from the wall, deep in thought. Obviously, Simon Anat's reward was the key. Tolen closed his eyes, willed himself to calmness, and allowed his mind to work. Events and dates of relevant activities, starting with Aaron Conin's murder on August 24th through the Sudarium's display tomorrow morning, tumbled through his thoughts. He mentally linked the chronological order of the events to players and clues they had uncovered along the way. Removing all preconceived assumptions of guilt, it all parlayed into an interconnected maze of motives, timing, and facts. He knew the truth was embedded within this tapestry of clues, still waiting to be solved. He could feel it. Still the answer eluded him. He opened his eyes.

Tolen was about to remove the plastic glove from his hand when he had an epiphany, and he stopped cold: what if the culprits needed the CIA's involvement and public attention for another reason?

He was roused from his thoughts by boisterous voices which quickly grew louder. Tolen recognized the accent and dialect as belonging to the older couple he had passed earlier in the hallway on their way to dinner. It seemed they had been unable to come to consensus on where to eat. Tolen looked to the door where the voices flowed. With chagrin, he realized he had been so caught up in the gruesome scene that he had failed to close the hotel room door behind him. Now, the Italian couple stood silently in the doorway, their mouths hanging open, their eyes transfixed in horror at the body pinned to the wall behind the dark man wearing a single plastic glove.

The woman released a blood-curdling scream. Tolen left the room in a hurry, pushing past the couple just as the man withdrew his cell phone and began punching buttons with a shaky finger. As Tolen reached the stairwell, he heard the Italian man speaking in broken English reporting a murder and then giving his description of the man fleeing the scene.

CHAPTER 43

September 13. Thursday – 12:14 p.m. Keene, California (9:14 p.m. Oviedo, Spain)

11 hours 46 minutes until the start of the Feast of the Cross

The tall Italian man, Esposito, stood inside the condemned fellowship hall. He picked up his cell phone from the table and called his contact in Oviedo, known to him only as The Prophet. The man's name was concealed so that even if the authorities apprehended Esposito or any of the 21 martyrs in the States, they would not be able to ascertain the true identity of the trigger man in Oviedo. The phone call was answered on the second ring.

"Have you seen the news?" Esposito asked before he heard a greeting.

"If you are referring to the elevated terror threat level by the U.S., then yes, I have." As always, The Prophet's voice was serious, focused.

"We must go forth with the strike. I can band our brethren earlier than planned, and we will make the journey now. The Americans have admitted their guilt with this action. They took the Sudarium and fear our retribution."

The Prophet's voice was directive. "Patience. There has been a reported attack of an American military installation in Kuwait. I have people checking the validity of this incident now. If we determine it to be a ruse to cover up the elevated terrorist warning, we will strike. I should know within minutes. I will call you." The phone line went dead.

Esposito looked to the closet. He could feel a festering hatred toward the Americans and their godless society. He was anxious to make the United States aware of the critical mistake that their Central Intelligence Agency had made in taking the Sudarium. It was time they paid the price for their smug actions.

God's relics are not to be desecrated by the godless.

Several uneasy minutes passed before Esposito's cell phone rang. It was The Prophet. "We have a man outside the American base in Kuwait. He has confirmed there was an explosion and a burning building on the U.S. installation. Sources on base are reporting casualties. This was the catalyst for the elevated terror alert. We will wait until the start of the Feast of the Cross at 9:00 a.m. tomorrow. As planned, I will send you a text message from the Cathedral of San Salvador the moment I confirm the Sudarium is missing."

"Understood." The Italian hung up. He was disappointed and agitated. They had identified prime targets, one that would strike at the underbelly of this atheist country. Whereas the radical Islamic terrorist attack of September 11, 2001 took the lives of less than 3,000; their actions would eclipse that total by *seventyfold*.

He ached for the attacks to begin.

Esposito wandered back to the table and sought out the King James Bible lying at the end. He opened to the scripture echoing in his mind. It had informally become their theme:

> *And said unto them, it is written. My house shall be called the house of prayer; but you have made it a den of thieves.*

Yes, the tall Italian thought with pleasure, *in the valley we will strike*.

CHAPTER 44

September 13. Thursday – 10:29 p.m. Isle of Patmos, Greece (9:29 p.m. Oviedo, Spain)

11 hours 31 minutes until the start of the Feast of the Cross

On the drive back to the Patmos airfield, Tolen felt a gnawing in his stomach as he recalled a critical piece of the Hebrew text found in the Costa Rican sphere.

The third jar marks the end of your journey, but all three will be needed.

The first jar was still onboard the plane in a locker. If Jade and Kappel were going after the cache, they would need it.

Tolen called Reba Zee on her cell phone. She did not pick up. His concern escalated.

Tolen arrived at the dark airfield within minutes. He brought the rental car to a screeching halt just outside the gate. He left the engine running and hurried through the gate, racing toward the lone jet on the tarmac. It was after ten, and traffic on the runway had gone quiet. The hatch door was open, and the ramp folded out as he had left it, but the plane's interior light had been doused.

Still in a sprint, Tolen quickly closed on the plane. In one fluid motion, he retrieved his Springfield from its holster. He had given Reba explicit directions to stay with the plane, and she always kept the interior lights on while on the ground.

Tolen reached the stairs, galloping up them in an instant. He was filled with an overwhelming sense of alarm as he knifed into the dark cabin, gun aimed ahead, primed for movement. The airfield lights cast a murky view inside, and he could see the cabin door ahead was open, yet there was no sign of life in the cockpit.

"Reba, where are you?" he called out.

In the shadows, he raced past the rows of seats, reached the cockpit, and flicked the master switch on the lighting control panel. The inside of the plane burst with light. Tolen returned to the cabin.

"Reba Zee!" he called out worriedly.

No response.

He looked to the bathroom door. It was closed. He slowly approached it, wary of an ambush. He turned the handle of the thin door, and it opened outward without any help. Tolen stepped back, gun raised. Reba Zee slumped out of the bathroom and onto the cabin floor, landing on her back with a thud, her head lolling toward him. The front of her unruly gray hair was smattered with wet blood where the center of her forehead had been pierced by a lone bullet hole. A trickle of blood had rolled down her nose and chin, effectively dividing her face in half. One eye was closed. The other pale eye stared up at him, eerily, as if she were giving him one last knowing wink.

There had been no attempt to emulate an Apostle-style death. Just cold-blooded murder.

Dazed, Tolen took several steps back and plopped into one of the passenger seats, never breaking his eyes away from Reba Zee's lifeless body. He absently laid the pistol in the seat beside him, his head spinning.

Tolen looked at the locker. It was partially ajar. It was a foregone conclusion at this point, but he nevertheless moved lackadaisically over to it, not even bothering to pick his gun up from the seat. Sure enough, the stone jar was missing. He returned to his seat where he slumped into a fog of confusion and despair.

The chirping of his cell phone brought his thoughts back into some semblance of order. The caller ID number was not familiar, but it was a local number.

"Hello."

"Who is this, please?" The man spoke in broken English.

"Who is asking?" Tolen countered.

"This is Hellenic Officer Nestor Bouboulis."

Tolen stiffened. The Hellenic police were the national police force of Greece. It was CIA protocol not to divulge association with the U.S. agency, especially when on assignment outside American borders. At the moment, Tolen was not even comfortable giving his name. He feared somehow that the police had already connected him with the murder of the French woman.

"I ask again, who is this?" the man pressed.

"This is Samuel Tolen," he said, reluctantly. "What can I do for you, Officer?" The only security cameras in the hotel had been in the lobby, and Tolen had skillfully avoided them as he had exited. Jade's room, where Claudia Denoit hung on the wall, had been paid for by Diaz's credit card. Tolen was mystified as to how the local police had found him so quickly.

"Mr. Tolen, we need to speak with you. What is your location on the isle?"

"What is this regarding, Officer Bouboulis? I have urgent business to attend to."

"Do you know a Spanish Inspector named Pascal Diaz with the…," Bouboulis paused, "Cuerpo Nacional de Policia?" The man continued without allowing Tolen a chance to answer. "It's a silly question. Well of course you do," he added with a disingenuous chuckle.

"Yes, we're working together."

"What kind of work?"

"Officer, I have a right to know why you're asking me these questions."

There was a moment of dead air. "We found his body at the base of the Monastery of St. John. His face had been smashed in by rocks until he was unconscious, and then he was pushed from the steeple where he fell to his death."

Damn, like the Apostle Matthew: thrown from a steeple and, when he survived the fall, beaten to death with stones. They had the order wrong but had still achieved the same grim result.

Bouboulis continued. "We found his cell phone. You were the last person who called him. I ask again. What is your location on the isle?"

Tolen remained silent.

"This is not a request you can deny," Bouboulis' tone grew aggressive. "Another body was just found at the hotel where you have been staying. Where are you?"

Tolen disconnected and turned his cell phone off, tossing it in the chair to the side where it clinked against his pistol.

He stood, found a white blanket in one of the side seats, and used it to cover Reba Zee. Tolen returned to the seat where he hung his head, tired and exhausted. In the last twelve hours, things had gone from bad to abysmal. He had nearly died in the explosion in Javier Diaz's basement. He had uncovered Jade's connection to Simon Anat's reward offer and, through sundry facts, revealed her deception and partnership with Nicklaus Kappel, billionaire Simon Anat's assistant.

Jade. The thought of her pained him. He had trusted her. More than that, it had become personal. He had been drawn to her, only to discover it had all been an act. He felt betrayed. There was now no doubt in his mind Jade had solved the clue and that she was on her way with Kappel to retrieve the cache of Jesus' artifacts at this very moment.

To compound matters, his pilot and friend, Reba Zee, had been murdered, as had his international partner, Pascal Diaz. Now, the Greek authorities wanted him for questioning in the homicide of Diaz. By association, he was their prime suspect, and to top it off, he still had no idea who had the Sudarium. If it was not returned to the Cathedral de San Salvador in Oviedo, Spain, in the morning, untold numbers of innocent Americans would die at the hands of terrorists seeking retribution.

The whole situation had turned impossibly dire. Tolen wondered if his own personal agenda had a hand in subverting the mission from the start, and he could not help but feel he had allowed things to go woefully off track.

Willing himself to action, Tolen removed a piece of paper from his pocket where he had scribbled the text from the Patmos jar upon it. He read it aloud:

> *Of the Father, Son, and Holy Ghost, only the Son is charged with holding the contents on high where the ancients knew no god but themselves in the desert.*

Travel from the north. As David faced the lion, you will face the lion incarnate. Aim at the one on the left and dig at his right foot. There you will gain entry to the Holiest of Highs. The third jar marks the end of your journey, but all three will be needed.

He still had no idea what the message meant. Tolen had never felt so defeated in his entire life.

****

Eleven-year-old Sam sat in the middle of a small Jon boat, fiddling with his shoestrings. His father was in the back, next to the 20-horsepower hand-tiller-driven Mercury motor. It was an early spring morning, and the sun had barely begun to crest the horizon. The air was calm, the water placid, mirroring the dark morning sky, which was interspersed with a red and yellow hue to the east. The familiar smell of the river—rugged but not unpleasant— draped the still air. The occasional calls of whippoorwills and bobwhites originated from unseen places along the bank. As usual, the morning was picturesque and tranquil.

Sam watched as Jaspar Tolen pitched his lure in a weed bed of eel grass and slowly wound it back in, ever patient, waiting for a largemouth bass to strike. Once near the boat, the man would lift the lure and cast again: pitch, wind, lift—over and over; not going too quickly, and never stopping. Jaspar held his gaze on the reflective surface of the water. To Sam, his father's concentration was epic.

Sam felt a deep sadness. His mother had passed away from a rare blood disease seven months before, and he missed her terribly. Some days were better than others. Today was not a good day, even though he loved to fish with his father and had looked forward to the outing. For some reason, the morning had brought a myriad of hurtful memories of his mother. Now, his rod lay propped against the gunwale with the lure dangling a foot over the water's surface.

Jaspar Tolen spoke in a hushed tone, "Hey, Sam, you know how many fish you'll catch with your bait out of the water?"

Sam looked up at his father. He tried to force a smile. "I've caught just as many as you have: none."

"So you're quittin'?"

"No, just taking a rest." A question was perched on the tip of his tongue; something he had wanted to ask his father for seven months, but the time had never seemed right. For some reason, he blurted it out without much thought. "Why did God take Mom from us? What did we do wrong?"

Jaspar Tolen's expression turned poignant. "Ah, Sam, we didn't do anything wrong. It just happened. There are no explanations; only manmade reasons and excuses, but none of them matter. He took her, and now He's caring for her. There is a plan to everything. We still get to hold her in our memories. You can never let the death of a loved one kill your spirit to live. It's human nature to mourn and remember, but it's just as important that we move on." His father offered a warm smile. "Your mother wants you to enjoy life, son, so fish. Catch a big one, and I'll cook it for dinner."

The words settled over Tolen like a comforting blanket. For the first time, he knew his father's compassion would hold them together.

"Hey, Sam…" Jaspar's eyes lit up, and his voice escalated. It was odd for the man's tone to be so loud. He made it a rule only to speak in low voices when on the water so as not to scare the fish away. "Hand me that can o' pickles."

"What?" Sam said, not understanding. There were no pickles in the boat. *What is he talking about?*

"Can o' pickles," Jaspar Tolen repeated. He smiled.

Suddenly it was dark. Sam could barely make out his father even though they were only several feet apart. Confusion reigned. "What's happening?"

"I've got to go now. It's been time for me to go."

"Wait! Father, where are you going?"

Tolen's eyes flew open. He awoke to the bright light of the airplane cabin, breathing heavily as he lay inclined in the seat. A single thought ran through his mind: *What happened to the fish?*

Samuel Tolen had had this same dream many times since his youth. The frequency had slowed down in his adult years, but still it replayed every now and then, although this was the first time he had the dream since his father had lapsed into a coma. Because it was a remembrance of a real-life event, like watching a home movie, the events and imagery had always been the same. Yet, this time, and this time only, the ending had changed. This was the first time Jaspar Tolen had asked the bizarre question about a can of pickles, and the landscape had faded to black. Normally, the ending followed the true event: Sam had picked up his rod, and on his first cast hooked a 6½-pound black bass. After a dutiful battle, he had landed the trophy fish to their mutual elation. It was a day Tolen would never forget; one firmly etched in his consciousness not only for the thrill of the catch but for the answer his father had given him about his mother's death.

Tolen sat up and looked at his watch. It was approaching 11 p.m. He was stunned he had fallen asleep in the first place, but thankfully it had only been for an hour. Thoughts of the dream left him stupefied and wondering why it had been different this time. He recalled the exact words his father had said to him in the dream: '*Hand me that can o'pickles.*'

Can o'pickles? It made no sense.

Tolen shook away the vision. He looked at his cell phone sitting in the seat beside him. If the local police were monitoring his phone, there was a chance they might be able to triangulate his position. Still, he had to chance it. He picked it up, turned it on, and called Tiffany Bar.

"Tolen, where have you been? I've been trying to call you for the last hour."

"Reba Zee is dead, as is Inspector Pascal Diaz."

There was an audible gasp on the other end of the line. "Oh my god," her words were filled with shock and bewilderment.

"I need you to stay focused, Bar," Tolen instructed her with compassionate authority. "What have you got for me?"

"Um...I can't believe...," Bar started off track, her emotions bleeding through the phone.

"Come on, Tiffany," he gently prodded, "what do you have?"

"Uh...yeah...Dr. Jade Mollur."

"What about her?"

Bar released a long, stabilizing exhale. Slowly, her words gained strength. "She...was with Dr. Cherrigan in Switzerland."

"You've already confirmed that information to me."

"Yes…no," she sounded momentarily confused, "there's more. The night they were there, she phoned him late. The cell tower she called from was 57 miles away from the town where Simon Anat's estate is located. Although they arrived together, they were in different locations that evening.

"Also, I correlated the phone calls from Nicklaus Kappel to Dr. Cherrigan's hotel room in Costa Rica. The calls were made when Dr. Mollur was away, out of the country.

"Lastly, and this may be big, we found a hidden file on Aaron Conin's laboratory PC."

"Related to the Sudarium?" Tolen asked hopefully.

"Two years ago, Javier Diaz had a paternity suit filed against him by an American woman who had traveled to Europe. Javier, it appears, came to the U.S. and paid Aaron Conin to fudge the results so he wouldn't have to pay child support."

"Interesting."

"You'll find this even more interesting."

After she explained, Tolen felt renewed. "Bar, where is Vakind?"

"He's in a lock-down meeting with President Fane and Homeland Security. They're monitoring for terrorist activity."

"Get on the next plane to Oviedo, Spain. You don't need to notify Vakind. I'll deal with him."

"By myself?" she asked, sounding reluctant.

"Yes." Tolen took the next few minutes to explain what he needed Bar to do.

When they hung up, he took some consolation in knowing Jade was innocent. Equally disheartening was the realization she was now a victim. The most likely scenario was that she had been taken against her will to help find the last stone jar and the cache of Jesus' objects, but she would only be kept alive as long as she was useful. On the phone with Analyst Bar, Tolen had made a decision, which was a calculated gamble. He had sent Bar after the Sudarium, while he went after Jade.

The only way to save Jade was to solve the clue from the second stone jar. Again he focused on the text. Seconds turned into minutes; minutes into an hour. It was now approaching midnight.

Tolen was wracking his brain to unravel the clue, and he finally decided to close his eyes and lean back into the jet cabin chair, attempting to relax and let his mind flow. Immediately, he thought back to the dream from earlier. What did pickles have to do with fishing? Pickles don't even come in cans. Still, there was something familiar about the phrase. "Can o' pickles…can o' pickles…can o' pickles," Tolen repeated out loud. He recognized the phrase, yet he did not. With his eyes still closed, he said the words aloud, faster this time, "Can o' pickles…can o' pickles…can o' pickles… can o' pickles."

He paused, suddenly understanding. "Can-o-pic! Canopic!"

He reread the Patmos jar text just to be sure. The clue, with its vague words, fell into place with precision. He pulled out a map and, to his elation, confirmed he had solved it.

He now knew exactly where Kappel and Jade were heading.

CHAPTER 45

September 14. Friday – 1:36 a.m. Isle of Patmos, Greece (12:36 a.m. Oviedo, Spain)

8 hours 24 minutes until the start of the Feast of the Cross

Tolen rose, closed the exterior door, and went into the cockpit. He had learned to fly on smaller planes and, although he had relieved Reba Zee on long trips once they were airborne, he had never piloted the Learjet through take off. His understanding was that the basics were the same for all planes.

He buckled into the seat and reviewed the instrument panel. Then he gazed outside. The tarmac ahead at the moment was quiet. The runway lights were on, streaking off into the distance. Even at this late hour, there were aircrafts still landing, mostly Cessnas and other small planes coming in after nighttime tours of the island.

Kappel had several hours' head start so there was no time to waste. He checked the fuel gauge and found it at three-quarters, which would be enough for him to get where he was going. He reached over to turn the radio on but refrained. Takeoff from the airfield would be unannounced. No need to hear the chatter of an excited air traffic controller once they realized what he was doing. Tolen checked the avionics, adjusted several of the settings, and hit the ignition.

Complete silence.

It was a deflating moment. He realized the plane had been sabotaged to prevent him from following them. He unbuckled and quickly made his way through the cabin, opened the exterior door, lowered the stairs, and exited the plane. In the distance, he saw the lights of a small plane arcing in for a landing on the adjacent runway.

Earlier, he had been too preoccupied to notice it, but now he detected the heavy smell of engine oil. He looked to the rear, at the cone of the Pratt & Whitney engine to that side, and saw fluid had gushed from the turbine, pooling on the tarmac. Whatever damage had been done, it was beyond a quick repair.

Just then, two white Citroen Xsaras with blue stripes and red flashing lights came screeching around the corner of a large hangar with their sirens blaring. The vehicles turned and drew a bead on the Learjet several hundred yards away.

The Hellenic police had found him.

Samuel Tolen broke into a full sprint toward the next runway. He cut across the wide swath of cracked pavement. Behind, he could hear the car engines momentarily ease, as they adjusted their angle of pursuit, then whined again as they were pushed to the limit.

They would overtake him quickly. If the police took him into custody, Jade would surely die. He had one chance. He changed direction.

The plane he had spotted coming in for a landing had just touched down at the far end of the airfield. He turned right and ran up the runway directly toward the aircraft. It was a small plane and would need roughly one-third mile to land…and take off. He tried to estimate the distance as he raced forward. It taxied toward Tolen at a high rate of speed; its lights nearly blinding him.

He glanced back to see one of the police cars stopped at the Learjet while the other slowed as it passed, then resumed speed, braking hard to the right once it hit the landing runway.

Tolen ran as fast as he could at the approaching plane, hoping he had estimated correctly. The siren behind him grew louder as the police car trundled over the cracked runway. Tolen identified the aircraft as a Cessna Corvalis 400. The surprised look on the pilot's face came into focus as the man and plane converged. Tolen heard the protesting brakes of the craft as the pilot bore down on them, waving his hands frantically, trying to get Tolen to get out of the way.

Instead, Tolen withdrew his Springfield and aimed it at the cockpit window. He arrived at the plane just as it came to a stop, the pilot staring wide-eyed at Tolen.

"Leave it running and get out of the plane!" Tolen yelled, aiming at the man through the glass.

The doors on both sides swung upward. The Greek pilot came out one side; a young Hispanic couple exited from the other, closing the door behind them.

"Run!" Tolen screamed at them. The threesome looked at the pistol briefly and then took off at a gallop.

Tolen did not turn to look for the police car. He knew it was bearing down on him. Instead, he climbed in the plane. Just as he was about to retract the door, he lost his grip on his pistol and it clanged against the side of the plane and skittered away on the pavement below. There was no time to retrieve it. He closed the door and gunned the engine. The police car skidded to a stop next to him. Out of the corner of his eye, he saw two uniformed officers jump from their vehicle with weapons drawn. He spun the craft around and began taxiing up the runway. The craft quickly gained speed. There was a series of blasts and metallic pops as the officers fired on him.

He desperately needed to pull out of range before they damaged the engine or hull. As the speed increased, the blasts faded in the distance, echoing faintly in the cabin. The officers continued to riddle the plane but with less consistency.

The farther the plane taxied, the worse the runway became. He had not noticed it in the larger Learjet, but in the Cessna, he felt every crack and pothole. The craft bounced along, increasing velocity. He had forced a shortened landing when he had engaged the pilot. Now he only hoped there was enough runway to take off.

Rising before him was a most unwelcome sight. In the darkness, a black swell of earth loomed ahead, lifting into the sky twice the height of the Petra: an unforgiving hill blocked his escape.

It was going to be close.

The runway ceased almost without warning. Tolen had just enough time to pull the nose up as the rows of track lights ended. The black mound of earth grew as he neared it. The plane struggled to lift, then, as if grabbing the air, it soared at a sharp angle. Tolen felt the pull of gravity as the aircraft lumbered upward steeply. Still climbing, the plane barely crested the rocky rise and reached up into the starlit sky.

He took a moment to wipe the perspiration from his forehead and exhale.

Tolen leveled the plane then dropped altitude, choosing to keep low in order to avoid radar detection. He set the destination coordinates, and the onboard navigation computer took over.

Soon he was flying low over the Mediterranean Sea heading southeast. Moonlight shimmered off the surface, stretching across the watery horizon. Flying time was going to be nearly two and one-half hours, so he set the automatic pilot and pulled out his cell phone.

"Vakind," the acting director answered.

"It's Tolen."

"Where the hell are you? We have eight hours before the Sudarium will be declared missing and the CIA blamed." There was a degree of concern Tolen seldom heard from the man.

"Bar is on her way to Oviedo. I don't believe the Sudarium ever left Spain. With any luck, she'll find it in time. I've given her exact instructions what to do when she gets there."

"Tiffany Bar? She's an analyst, Tolen. I understand you sending her to locations in the States to interview people, but she doesn't know field protocol. Is an operative accompanying her?"

"No, Morris. She's alone. There will surely be members of the Flagellants in and around the area, and at least one will be stationed at the Cathedral for the beginning of the service at 9:00 a.m. to communicate to whatever terrorist cell is waiting to strike. We can't draw attention that she's CIA. She speaks Spanish better than most Spaniards and knows the local dialect and colloquialisms for northern Spain. No one will suspect she's CIA. She'll blend in seamlessly. She was the only one I could send."

Vakind released a long exhale. He paused before continuing on a different tack. "I'm flying to California. A man was pulled over on the outskirts of LA this afternoon with an SUV full of explosives. It was three times the amount McVeigh was hauling in

Oklahoma City. In other words, enough to level several city blocks. We traced the dynamite back to a Canadian company robbed last week. The problem is that the amount we found in the SUV only represented five percent of the total theft. The suspect in custody is 42-year-old Nelson Whitacre, and he has openly confessed to being a U.S. member of the Flagellants but refuses to divulge any further information. He's being held in FBI custody. I'm on my way there to interrogate him. If we can get him to crack, we may learn the target before it's too late."

"Did President Fane elevate the terror alert?"

"Yes, but we staged an explosion and fire at one of our bases in Kuwait in case there were eyes on it. Then we sent a press release of casualties. It must have been convincing. There have been no attacks by the Flagellants so far."

Tolen responded, "Good, but I need some help. You may need to brief President Fane."

Tolen explained his situation and concluded the call. He sat back and tried to relax, which was nearly impossible given his sore muscles, abrasions, and overwhelming fatigue. He pulled a small drawer open beneath the seat and found a bottle of caffeine pills. He popped two. Like Reba Zee, the pilot had kept a stash of legal stimulants.

Damn, he was going to miss the woman, with her Texas drawl and bubbly personality. She did not deserve to die like that.

He cleared his mind. Now was not the time to lament her death. He willed himself to turn his thoughts to the clue from the Petra stone jar. It had completely confounded him until, miraculously, his dream had sparked an epiphany that involved his father asking him about a "can o' pickles." Tolen realized why the term sounded familiar. It was his subconscious poking at him, trying to get him to see the obvious. The strange design and shape of the two stone jars had looked reminiscent of something he could not quite place until the dream; until he realized the "can o' pickles" was his subconscious telling him "can-o-pic"…Canopic…as in "Canopic jars."

Canopic jars were used by the ancient Egyptians during the mummification process to store and preserve the viscera of their owner for the afterlife. All the viscera were not kept in a single Canopic jar, but rather each organ was placed in a jar of its own. There were four jars in all, each charged with the safekeeping of particular human organs: the stomach, intestines, lungs, and liver. A particular god was responsible for protecting a particular organ, and each jar represented one of the four directions: north, south, east, and west.

With this realization, everything had fallen into place. Each of the previous Hebrew text messages they discovered had referenced a 'direction of origin.' The Harvard stone sphere text had said, "Travel from the south." The text from the first jar in Costa Rica had said, "Travel from the west." Then the most recent text said, "Travel from the north." Plotting these points of origin on a world map, he discovered that each represented an extreme direction when compared to the others. Palmar Sur, Costa Rica, where the stone sphere was originally located before being moved to Harvard, was the southernmost point. Joseph of Arimathea's tomb was the westernmost. The Petra on the Isle of Patmos was the northernmost. By process of elimination, the next destination would be easternmost in relation to the other three plotted points.

Egypt fell right in the corridor of the easternmost plot of the other three locations to which they had already traveled.

Then there was the phrase "...*where the ancients knew no god but themselves in the desert.*"

The Pharaohs in Egypt were considered by their people to be living gods or deities.

As David faced the lion, you will face the lion incarnate.

Since the term "incarnate" meant personified in human form, "*lion incarnate*" was obviously a reference to the sphinx, which at one time had the body of a lion with a man's head.

Aim at the one on the left and dig at his right foot.

It was this last line which told Tolen exactly where he had to go in Egypt.

Tolen recalled Jade mentioning that prior to teaming with Dr. Cherrigan in Costa Rica, the man had been involved with the excavation of a tunnel in the basement of the Sonali Giza Hotel not far from the Giza Plateau. Tolen remembered reading about it at the time. The passageway into the tunnel had been discovered when several feet of the basement floor of the hotel collapsed. There had been photos attached to the article: an image of the site prior to the beginning of construction of the hotel in the 1960s. Interestingly, one of the pictures was a large stone carved from the bedrock. The Director of Antiquities had been unable to derive the origin or purpose of it. One young archaeologist had theorized it was the partial toe of a large monument, possibly even the scant surviving remnant of a second sphinx. Most rejected his theory, but Tolen had always thought it made sense for several reasons.

First, it was highly probable that there had been a second sphinx at one time. Early Egyptian artwork always showed paired sphinxes adorning the entranceways to mortuary temples, tombs, avenues, and city gates. It has long been an enigma that the Great Sphinx on the Giza Plateau was a lone fixture on the landscape.

Second, the sphinx on the Giza Plateau faced east, and Egyptian artwork and writings stipulated that if there were two sphinxes, they would face each other. Therefore, it stood to reason the second sphinx would be to the east, facing west, which correlated to the location of the hotel. Plus, the large piece of stone resembling a toe was facing west toward the Great Sphinx, just as would be expected.

"*Aim at the one on the left.*" Since no entrance to an underground cave had been discovered at the existing sphinx on the Giza Plateau, this meant the clue was referring to the second sphinx that no longer existed; the one Tolen believed had once risen proudly upon the bedrock where the Sonali Giza Hotel now stood.

CHAPTER 46

September 14. Friday – 4:05 a.m. Egyptian Time (3:05 a.m. Oviedo, Spain)

5 hours 55 minutes until the start of the Feast of the Cross

Tolen kept the Cessna low over the water, flying south by southeast and eventually reaching the Egyptian coastline. The landscape below was bathed in the glow of the moon. From there, it was only a hundred miles more to the Sonali Giza Hotel. Tolen had requested that Director Vakind speak with President Fane to arrange unencumbered access to Egyptian airspace and landing at an airstrip near the hotel. Egypt had a formidable air force; the largest of all the Arabic nations. They remained technologically up-to-date, and their pilots were highly skilled. If the president was unsuccessful in her diplomacy, Tolen was certain to be intercepted and shot down within minutes.

When five minutes elapsed, and he was still airborne, he released a quiet sigh of relief.

As fate would have it, just then two Dassault Mirage 2000s swooped in on either side of him like hawks cornering their prey.

Tolen could feel his chest tighten. There was no going back even if he wanted to try. He was at their mercy.

His cell phone rang. It was Vakind.

"Morris, I hope you have good news for me. I have some visitors."

"Those are your escorts. The president has spoken with the Egyptians, and they've consented to allow you access into the country, but you must follow them to the airfield of their choosing near Cairo. Do not deviate, Tolen. They've made it perfectly clear they'll shoot you down. Tune to Channel 10 if you need to communicate with them."

Tolen was thankful for the escort, but Egyptian interference was going to be problematic. They would try to accompany him, and that was simply unacceptable. If they knew he was going underground into an ancient, unexplored tunnel, the Egyptian Director of Antiquities would forbid it. He would need to break free from his escorts once on the ground.

Tolen flew inland, accompanied by the two Dassault Mirage 2000s for twelve minutes when the engines started to sputter. He checked avionics: there was plenty of fuel. The craft began to lose altitude, and one of the twin engines failed as a red warning light signaled its demise. He flicked off the light. The engine had most likely been damaged by gunfire from the Greek police. He could land on one engine, but he would be forced to slow his airspeed.

This gave him an idea.

He switched on the radio and turned to Channel 10.

"Mirage 2000, this is Samuel Tolen, over."

He waited for a response. None came.

"Egyptian Air Force, this is Samuel Tolen in the Cessna Corvalis. Please respond, over."

Still no response.

He repeated the call. Again, there was no response. He wondered if the radio had also been damaged in the ruckus on Patmos.

He tried once more.

"This is Egyptian Captain Khateeb. What is your request?" The Captain spoke English reasonably well.

"Captain Khateeb, I've lost one engine, and the second one is damaged. I don't know how much longer I can fly. Request permission to land immediately."

"We will be at the military airbase in ten minutes. You will land there."

"I don't believe you understand. The aircraft is damaged. I'm losing power. I must land immediately or risk crashing into one of the populated areas below."

There was a momentary pause, then, "Very well. There is an abandoned airfield north of Giza at latitude 30.094049, longitude 31.174393. Please proceed to there, land, and wait inside the airplane. I repeat, wait inside the airplane. Our people will meet you there."

Tolen finished typing the coordinates into the navigational computer. He was surprised to find out he was practically on top of the airfield. He made a subtle bank to the south. The two Dassault Mirage 2000s momentarily stayed with him then peeled off into the dark night without notice, their fiery thrusters slowly vanishing in the distance.

It was now a race. Tolen had to get the plane on the ground before the pilots were able to radio for the military escort to meet him there.

Even in the dark, Tolen could see the terrain below was a vast mass of flatland. He descended quickly. The moonlight provided enough light for him to make out the abandoned airfield. It had a long runway with two hangars at the far end. There were no runway landing lights, but avionics easily calculated the topography, and within minutes Tolen had the Cessna on the ground and parked near the first dark hangar. So far, he was the only one there.

The airfield was pitted at the edge of Giza, the town which separates the Giza Plateau—with its three famous pyramids—from the Nile. Tolen left the craft, passed through a rusty gate that threatened to collapse when he opened it, and began jogging toward civilization, in the direction of the Sonali Giza Hotel using the GPS coordinates on his iPhone. He crossed several hundred yards of sand before he reached the first building on the outskirts of town. As he ducked into the shadows of the dark structure, he saw the headlights of two vehicles approach the airfield from the west. The drone of the engines signified military jeeps. They were not going to be happy when they discovered he was gone.

CHAPTER 47

September 13. Friday – 7:19 p.m. Los Angeles, California (September 14. 4:19 a.m. Oviedo, Spain)

4 hours 41 minutes until the start of the Feast of the Cross

Vakind stood inside a small room next to FBI Special Agent Abel Connell. The two men were eyeing Nelson Whitacre through a two-way mirror. As usual, there was an air of reluctance any time the CIA and FBI were forced to work together. With time slipping away, Vakind was in no mood for posturing or interagency politics. And so far, at least, the FBI had been reasonably forthcoming since his arrival.

"We've had him in there for hours," Connell said. "Between the FBI and Homeland Security, we've interrogated him nearly nonstop. Everything's been captured on video. All the man will confess is that he is a member of the Flagellants, and they are about to 'bring order back to the United States of America.' Threats of imprisonment have had no effect."

Vakind nodded. "He was arrested on the edge of Los Angeles, driving into the city, correct?"

"Yes, on I-15. We don't want to create a panic, but we felt obligated to alert some of the larger parks and recreational areas in town of a possible terrorist attack. Based on their lack of sophistication as a terrorist group, the Flagellants would most likely go after a soft target—heavily populated—yet also something with symbolic significance. In this case, something with anti-religious significance."

Vakind nodded his head again in agreement.

"We have agents canvassing his house. We should know soon if they turn up anything."

Vakind had dealt with all types of terrorists, including some of the most deadly Islamic extremists, but he was not sure he had ever seen the type of morbid contentment Whitacre displayed. He smiled as if his world could not possibly get any better. He looked more like a man who had just won $100 million in the lottery than a man facing terrorist charges.

After reading the man's dossier, the acting director of the CIA was about to get his crack at interrogating Nelson Whitacre.

As Vakind was preparing to go in, Connell's cell phone rang, and he answered it. The FBI agent listened intently, replied with an affirmative, and then ended the call.

"A goodbye note was found in Whitacre's house." Connell looked at his smart phone screen. "They just emailed it to me. Here it is." He turned the display so that Vakind could read:

> *The heathens of America spurned us into action.*
> *By God's glory, 21 in the fertile valleys out of 28 world-*
> *wide will be destroyed.*
> *His wrath will be felt with a vengeance.*
> *Point all fingers at the American Central Intelligence*
> *Agency for their wicked deeds.*

Vakind reread the second line. "Any idea what '*21 in the fertile valleys out of 28 worldwide will be destroyed*' means?"

"No, our analysts are working on it." Connell gave Vakind a somber look. It was borderline remorseful. "My apologies, Director, but with this new information, I've been instructed to interview him again. You'll have to wait your turn while I contact our interrogator and get him back here."

Vakind wheeled on the FBI agent. "Connell, I don't give a damn about jurisdictional protocol at the moment. The FBI, Homeland Security, CIA; somebody needs to interrogate this man now, and we're losing time. I'm here and ready to go. I'm not going to risk the lives of untold numbers of Americans because of a pissing match."

Vakind did not wait for a response. He leaned forward and hit the 'record' button on a low panel. He left the room and circled the corner to the interrogation room door. He stepped through it just as he heard Connell calling someone on his cell phone.

"Mr. Whitacre, my name is Morris Vakind. I am the acting director of the CIA," he said, taking a seat on the other side of the table. Whitacre's feet were secured to the base of the chair and his cuffed hands lay casually on the table before him.

"You," Whitacre smirked, leaning forward, "you're exactly the man I was hoping to see, Mr. CIA, currently ranked as the most blasphemous organization on the face of God's earth."

"Interesting," Vakind said sedately, "I was at church last Sunday, and Father O'Hara didn't seem bothered I was there."

Whitacre's smile widened, his eyelids twitched over brown eyes, but his words were acidic. "The godless often hide behind deception."

Vakind leaned in. "We found your note at your house."

Whitacre settled back in his chair. He stared hard at Vakind with a renewed grin but did not speak. Vakind knew the man's smug demeanor was a testament to his twisted faith.

"I found it a bit vague," Vakind continued. "If you want the newspaper and the rest of the media to run with this, to make you a famous martyr, you blew it. '*21 in the fertile valleys out of 28 worldwide will be* destroyed'? It reads like bad poetry."

"Nice try. By the time it's printed, everyone will understand. It's only heathens such as yourself who can't understand it."

"I understand you allowed your wife, Shelly, to die."

Whitacre's eyes narrowed. His lips tightened together. He offered no rebuttal.

Vakind spoke nonchalantly. "My mother once had pneumonia. Unlike you, I took her to the hospital, and she recovered."

"God's will is not to be questioned. If He had wanted her to live, He would have cured her."

Vakind pushed the issue. "Didn't God also create the doctors, the men and women who could have cured Shelly? Didn't He create the people who engineered the medicines and drugs which save people's lives every day? Face it, Nelson. You didn't want your wife to live. You wanted her to die so you could go out in a blaze of glory. You're ready to hide behind your religious façade in order to perpetuate the ultimate swan song. Why, Whitacre? Why must tens of thousands die because you falsely blame the CIA for something that has not occurred?"

"Try 200,000 lives and billions of dollars in property damage!" Whitacre blurted out. His face had colored red, and he looked away, seemingly straining to keep quiet.

Vakind felt his blood chill. He knew the cache of munitions stolen from Canada had the capacity to do the sort of catastrophic damage to life and property Whitacre had just referenced. "Yet, you do so in God's name: murder innocent men, women, and children?"

"We did not start this!" Whitacre erupted, his yell nearly deafening as his hands balled into fists so tight that the blood drained from his knuckles. His face was a solid mass of red. "Those who gamble....," Whitacre paused, swallowed, and, remarkably, calmed before he continued. "Those who gamble with God's will know exactly who they are. They made their choice. Now, they will suffer their fate and become the CIA's martyrs. Trust me, Mr. CIA, they are *not* innocent people." Slowly, Whitacre forced a smile back to his face. With an exhale, he again relaxed in the chair.

Vakind rose and left the room. Connell was waiting for him, along with a short, burly, bald man who Vakind did not know. He assumed it was the LA branch chief of the FBI.

Connell remained quiet as his cohort tore into Vakind. "Director Vakind, you were not authorized for that interrogation. Your superiors will hear about this. You did nothing but exacerbate the situation."

"On the contrary, I believe he offered us a clue when he lost his composure. Let's go back through the video and see what we've got."

"You're no longer a part of this investigation," the bald man snapped. "You have no authority here."

Vakind fixed the man with his eyes and removed a card from his coat pocket. "We don't have time to dispute our professional differences, but feel free to take this card and call that number. It's to my current superior. She lives at 1600 Pennsylvania Avenue. When you're done, I'll be waiting to review the video with you."

CHAPTER 48

September 14. Friday – 5:28 a.m. Egyptian Time (4:28 a.m. Oviedo, Spain)

4 hours 32 minutes until the start of the Feast of the Cross

Samuel Tolen made his way through the quiet but well-lit streets of Giza. The air was hot and dry, as was to be expected at the end of summer. Tolen could feel the perspiration accumulating beneath his clothes as the first rivulet of sweat ran down his back.

To the west, the tops of the pyramids on the Giza plateau hovered over the skyline. Giza, along with the cities of Cairo, Helwan, and Shubra El-Kheima, form the Province of Greater Cairo. Giza is a thriving center of Egypt's culture, past and present, with a population approaching three million people. At this early morning hour, there was little going on as Tolen passed blocks and blocks of silent buildings, schools, and residential neighborhoods. He had considered hailing one of the black-and-white taxi cabs sitting near the intersections but thought better of it. Not only did he not have any Egyptian pounds, he was reluctant to leave any trail for the military to follow.

Instead, Tolen continued to make his way down the still streets and side roads, keeping to the shadows when he could, ever watchful of the few passing vehicles. By the time he arrived at the Sonali Giza Hotel, he was drenched in sweat. He took a moment at the side of the building to gather himself and straighten his clothing.

The hotel was no different than one he might find in Washington, DC; a mauve-colored edifice six stories high in the shape of an open book with a ramped entrance at the crux leading to the second floor.

Tolen strolled up the wide outside stairs to the sprawling landing which led to the entrance. He passed through, barely looking toward the check-in desk on the right or the concierge stand on the left. As he hoped, the employees at both stations paid him little attention. Tolen stepped inside the elevator and rode up a floor. He got off, found the stairwell at the far end of the hallway, and proceeded down past the first floor to an unmarked door at the bottom where the steps came to an end. The door was locked. He had recalled from the newspaper article that, once the archaeological site had been shut down, the hotel had sealed the door and left the area intact.

Tolen pulled a thin metal pick from his coat pocket and had the door unlocked within a minute. He stepped into a spacious, pitch-black room with a bare cement floor. He searched for a light switch but there was none. Instead, he withdrew a flashlight and switched it on. The room was the breadth and depth of a basketball court with an eight-foot ceiling. In the back right corner, he saw cement chunks, some weighing hundreds of pounds, unceremoniously stacked in a pile of rubble. He wandered toward it, using the flashlight as his guide. The humidity down here was stifling.

In the corner, there was a gaping, jagged hole in the floor where it had caved in. He stood over it and shined the flashlight down. A horizontal tunnel continued out of sight, ramping down at a slight angle. He carefully dropped down the side of the cavity, spilling rock fragments into the hole with him. He cringed as the loose rock pressed into the cuts on his hand.

As Tolen moved forward into the tunnel, he was forced to crouch down nearly a foot to avoid hitting the stone ceiling. The smell of sand and limestone was thick. His lungs burned as he inhaled the chalky substance.

The passageway continued to decline gradually. After no more than 75 feet, he saw a wall ahead where the tunnel ended. This is where the archaeologists had abandoned their exploration.

Tolen retreated back up the hallway scrutinizing the wall on the left as he went. Then, he examined the right wall. A dozen feet before the dead-end, at the base on the right, there was an outline chiseled into the limestone 30 inches wide and 18 inches tall. Tolen bent down to examine it. He gave it a shove, and the rock slid back several inches. Someone had carved it loose.

Tolen sat on the stone ground and gave it a push with his feet. The rectangular block regressed. Several more inward shoves, and he was able to drop onto his stomach where he used his hand to push inside beyond the width of the twelve-inch wall. He scooted through, his face brushing against the block as he stood. On the other side of the wall, he resealed the plug into the opening.

Tolen shined the flashlight ahead into the dark void. He was at the end of a passageway that seemed to continue on indefinitely. He started forward, walking briskly through the carved tunnel. The ceiling here was higher, and he no longer had to stoop. Unlike the previous tunnel, which sloped downward, the floor here seemed perfectly horizontal. He shed his jacket and empty holster, allowing them to fall to the stone floor. They were of no use to him.

Tolen thought back to an old prognostication. It had been the American prophet, Edgar Cayce, who foretold the discovery of a chamber beneath the right foot of the sphinx in 1932. Remarkably, his words had come true, just not at the Great Sphinx on the Giza Plateau.

CHAPTER 49

September 14. Friday – 6:16 a.m. Egyptian Time (5:16 a.m. Oviedo, Spain)

3 hours 44 minutes until the start of the Feast of the Cross

Finding his way through the tunnel was proving to be a long and arduous process. The problem did not lie in which direction to go. There was only the one tunnel, and it ran in a straight line. The problem was that it appeared endless. Tolen was sure he had already gone several miles. It was amazing that this long passageway flowed beneath a thriving city, and no one had any idea it was here. Also intriguing, Tolen thought, was the fact that, beyond the tunnel itself, there was nothing of interest—no hieroglyphs or inscriptions, no artifacts. It was clear to him this was merely an access point to whatever lay ahead.

Not for the first time, he wondered if he could really be closing in on a cache of objects which belonged to Jesus Christ.

Tolen continually probed ahead with his flashlight looking for any signs of movement or some deviation in the passageway which would signal its termination point. He was already hindered by having to approach from one direction with no place to hide, and losing his pistol at the Patmos airfield put him at a severe disadvantage. Still, he pressed on, concerned that as each minute passed, the chances of Jade's survival were slipping away.

The echoes of his footfalls returned to him softly from somewhere in the distance. Beyond that, there was silence. He desperately looked for clues to confirm they were down here.

His trek continued through the straight corridor. Another mile went by, and he grew impatient. At the risk of announcing his arrival, Tolen broke into a trot, stepping as lightly as possible upon the limestone floor. The strong stench of sand and limestone remained. Even as he ran, he scanned the walls looking for any signs they had come this way.

Perspiration was dripping from his face, and he was growing thirsty. He had not considered that the tunnel would lead such a great distance. On and on he ran, training the light ahead as best he could while his arms swung in rhythm to his pace. Because of the jostling, the beam shot into the nothingness of the long corridor, and his mind began playing tricks on him. On one occasion he saw a shadowy figure lurking ahead, only to find the apparition was a trick of the erratic light.

Now, as he raced ahead with growing concern, his muscles fighting through the fatigue, he saw a brown-and-white clump on the ground, caught in the flashes of the light. It resembled some sort of small woodland creature; a mouse perhaps. Common sense told him it was a mirage, just a trick of the light. Yet, the closer he drew to it, the more real it became. Then he was upon it, and he stopped his forward motion only at the last second. For a moment he stood over it, panting, as he aimed the flashlight beam down onto the still mass, trying to fathom what he was seeing. It was obviously no animal...or anything organic for that matter. He squatted, breathing hard.

It suddenly came into focus, and he picked it up. A brown patch with white medical tape wrapped around it. It was the dressing he had applied to Jade's wound.

She had left him a sign that she was somewhere up ahead.

Tolen experienced a resurgence of hope. He dropped the bandage and began running with newfound determination.

****

Vakind sat in a room watching the video of his interrogation with Nelson Whitacre. Beside him was the stocky, bald branch chief of the FBI, Jason Gerly, and Homeland Security Director,

Rachel McNulty. It had taken Gerly a while to calm after Vakind had violated protocol and interviewed the subject without FBI consent. Eventually, Vakind had reasoned him into acceptance and collaboration. It had not hurt when Gerly was made aware of Vakind's direct relationship with the president. Now, the threesome sat in the room committed to working together, even if the relationship was an uneasy one. The text from the goodbye note which Whitacre left had been distributed and was in the hands of analysts from all three agencies.

Vakind knew they had one distinct advantage. Unlike most terrorist attacks, they knew when the strike would occur: at midnight local time; 9 a.m. in Spain, less than three-and-a-half-hours from now. The problem was, they still did not know where.

"*21 in the fertile valleys out of 28 worldwide will be destroyed,*" McNulty, a middle-aged, demure woman with short, crimson hair, read from the message. "Twenty-eight what? What are there 28 of in the world which we have 21 of nearby?"

"Keep in mind, we still believe—and Whitacre's response during interrogation seems to support—it will be a soft target, heavily populated with civilians," Gerly added.

"Two hundred thousand, according to Whitacre," Vakind said. To lose any life to a terrorist attack was a tragedy, but this was a daunting number. If carried out, it would easily qualify as the most devastating terrorist strike in history.

"Disneyland?" McNulty offered.

"At midnight?" Gerly shot back. "It still doesn't solve the 21 out of 28 riddle." His face scrunched in thought and frustration. "Maybe the 'fertile valleys' refers to the vineyards in San Fernando, Sonoma, Napa Valley, and the like. There are many large wineries in southern California which could be targets."

Vakind shook his head. "It doesn't meet the criteria. There would not be two hundred thousand people at 21 wineries at midnight. Besides, Whitacre was stopped by local law enforcement while driving into Los Angeles. He wasn't headed to wine country. He was going into the city."

"Yeah, but he lives in LA," Gerly retorted sorely. His attitude suggested he took exception with Vakind shooting down his idea.

"Maybe he was driving home. Remember, he's been in custody for nearly ten hours. Hell, he could have gone home and still driven a long way in the time he had left until midnight tonight."

"It's possible," Vakind said, attempting to keep the peace, "but then why had he already written the farewell note if he was going back to his house?"

CHAPTER 50

September 14. Friday – 5:48 a.m. Oviedo, Spain

3 hours 12 minutes until the start of the Feast of the Cross

Tiffany Bar gazed out the airplane window at the dark surface of the Atlantic Ocean thirty thousand feet below. The horizon to the east was showing the first faint glow of morning light, coloring a line of clouds with an orange hue where the sun would soon peek through. The plane was due to land at Asturias Airport in Spain in one hour.

Reba Zee's death had severely rattled her. And then there was the murder of Inspector Pascal Diaz. She shook her head, determined to put these depressing thoughts aside. Bar had a job to do, and it was going to require her full concentration. She would have to leverage everything the CIA had taught her, every trick Tolen had let her in on, if she was to have even a slim chance of success. An odd combination of exhilaration and apprehension washed over her as she considered the task before her. She kept reminding herself Samuel Tolen had entrusted her with this job, so he was obviously confident she could do it.

The man is one of the best, she reminded herself. If he thinks I can do it, then I can.

Still, she was unable to fend off her anxiety.

****

With the knowledge he was on the right path, Tolen continued to jog ahead through the limestone tunnel. He estimated that, given his pace and the amount of elapsed time, he had covered in excess of five miles. He had no idea which direction he was heading, only that it was not east. If he were, he would have run into the Nile River by now.

On and on he went until he thought he saw a change in the tunnel ahead. He stopped, momentarily caught his breath, and listened for any sounds. When he heard none, he proceeded at a quick walk, guiding the light into the distance.

He considered that he might be nearing the single greatest archaeological site in mankind's history, yet that mattered little to him at this point. Whatever lay ahead, his main goal was to save Jade.

Suddenly, he saw an aberration in the tunnel ahead. He reached a wide set of descending steps the width of the tunnel. There were no more than a half dozen, and he moved down them slowly, cautiously, keeping the light aimed low. If they were nearby, it was going to be nearly impossible to surprise them. Without a gun in these tight quarters, his only option was to use the shadows to his advantage.

Tolen found himself in another passageway with openings ahead on each side. The first proved to be an intersecting tunnel to the right and left. Neither corridor appeared to reach more than 30 feet. He paused, again listening for any sound.

Tolen turned left and followed the tunnel, which was considerably thinner than the main artery. He came to an end wall and found the tunnel continued at a 90-degree angle to the right. He turned down it, watchful of everything around him. It only went a short distance before it ended, opening into a square room.

He retreated from the room and made his way back to the main tunnel, this time crossing over to the other tunnel branch. Instead of turning at a 90-degree angle and continuing, as the previous detour had, it ended at a square room twice the size of the one on the other side.

Tolen wiped the sweat from his forehead and took stock of the tunnels, once again returning to the main passageway where he continued on. Almost immediately on his right, there was another corridor. He paused, listened, then proceeded down it, where he followed the 90-degree left turn and walked into a large rectangular room with a high ceiling. This one was twice as big as the largest room he had encountered so far. He returned to the main passageway.

The entire labyrinth of rooms presented a curious layout, and Tolen was reminded of the burial chambers which had been discovered in the Valley of the Kings. He had a distinct feeling he was moving through the catacombs, possibly the mortuary chambers, of some ancient Egyptians whose tomb or tombs had been plundered long ago, evidenced by the lack of any content whatsoever. Conspicuously missing were any hieroglyphic cartouches, any declaration as to which Egyptian Pharaoh or royalty these rooms were fashioned to serve in the afterlife.

He proceeded ahead. On his left was a large opening that immediately led into yet another room; this one long and rectangular. Shining his flashlight within, he saw it was empty. He retreated and saw yet another opening on the left. He moved through a short hallway which spilled into another rectangular room.

This chamber caught him by surprise. It was unique in that it had steps leading to a seven-foot-wide perimeter ledge around the entire room, resulting in a quasi-second floor. The ceiling beyond was easily 25 feet from the base of the floor where he stood.

CHAPTER 51

September 14. Friday – 7:09 a.m. Egyptian Time (6:09 a.m. Oviedo, Spain)

2 hours 51 minutes until the start of the Feast of the Cross

Tolen retraced his steps back to the main tunnel. Ahead, the corridor ended at a four-sided pillar turned at an angle so that one edge faced him from the middle of the passageway. He approached it cautiously and found room to pass on either side. He eased around the pillar and through a doorway opening. The room he now stood in was massive, easily covering the total area of all the other rooms combined.

He pivoted the light up. At the back wall where he had entered, there was a ceiling of indistinguishable height. A lower ceiling began approximately ten feet out and covered the rest of the area ahead, effectively giving the room a second floor. He looked around for stairs but saw none. There appeared to be no way to reach this upper level.

The monstrous room also had one other unique feature. The long straight back wall where he stood connected at each end to two angled sidewalls which narrowed far ahead until they eventually came to a point.

Strangely, the room was in the shape of a massive triangle with the point at the farthest end ahead.

Movement to the side caused him to spin toward the back wall. He caught the faces of two people: the pleading look of Dr. Jade Mollur and the malevolent expression of Inspector Pascal Diaz.

"Jade, are you all right?" Tolen asked.

She nodded. Her haggard face was caked with dust.

"Si, at the moment she is fine," Diaz said. "Turn on the lanterns, Jade. Tolen, give me your weapon."

The room suddenly illuminated as Jade switched on a lantern.

"I'm unarmed." Tolen responded.

"Turn around, then lift up your pants legs," Diaz said. He had a pistol aimed at Jade's back.

Tolen did, proving to Diaz he had no gun.

Jade lowered the first electric lantern to the floor and picked up a second one. She turned it on and placed it on the ground. The brilliant light revealed just how white the walls were.

Diaz inclined his head at Tolen for a silent moment. "You don't seem surprised to see me, Señor."

"On the way to Patmos, I had Reba Zee sweep the jet for any electronic devices that might be tracking us, and it came up empty. Yet someone was communicating our movements to a third party, or should I say, Nicklaus Kappel. Once I determined Jade's innocence, it only left you as the mole."

Jade shot Tolen a hurt look as if to say, *what did I do to ever warrant suspicion?*

Tolen continued. "Also, you were in the Spanish Navy as a demolitions expert. You'd been on numerous deployments during your time in the military. You weren't seasick in Costa Rica. It was just an act so you could be alone below deck to communicate our position. Oh, and that weight-sensitive arming device in Javier's freezer wrapped around the corpse of Boyd Ramsey took some extensive explosives knowledge to pull off. Nice work, by the way."

"I see your little blonde analyst has been doing some research on me," Diaz said brashly.

"You killed a tourist or transient on the Isle of Patmos," Tolen went on, "and bashed his face in until he was unrecognizable and planted your credentials and cell phone on him. You knew the authorities would look to see the last call on the phone. It came from me. I'm guessing you also murdered Claudia Denoit in order to leave one last Apostle-style death for me to find. With both murders, you knew the police would canvas the island looking for me, which would buy yourself more time. How am I doing so far?"

"Very good work, Tolen, but obviously the Greek police were unable to detain you. Kappel killed your Texas pilot, and I retrieved the first stone jar from the plane. How did you get off Patmos and here so quickly without a pilot?" Diaz grinned slyly as he realized the answer to his own question. "Ah, you can pilot a plane. I did not account for this."

"Indulge me," Tolen retorted. "What was Boyd Ramsey's involvement? And when did you get involved with Simon Anat's reward?"

Diaz's smile turned lecherous. "I see you found out about the lucrative prize. I am truly impressed." He paused. "Your ex-CIA friend was one of the hundred or so who were originally privy to the offer. He had the idea to perform lab tests on the Sudarium, so he approached my brother and tried to bribe Javier to let him inside the cathedral to steal the Sudarium. Javier came to me to turn Ramsey in. I tracked Ramsey to a hotel in Oviedo, since I was curious about his intentions with the Sudarium. With proper motivation, Señor Ramsey told me of Anat's challenge and the reward."

"So that's when you got the idea to go after it yourself," Tolen cut in. "Did you kill Ramsey after you forced him to tell you how he planned to use the Sudarium threads to make a claim?"

Diaz did not respond. Guilty by silence.

Tolen went on. "Once you had the fibers, you needed someone discreet to test them. Tiffany Bar discovered that, several years ago, you accompanied Javier to the U.S. where he faced a paternity test from an American who had vacationed in Spain. Javier located a U.S. lab technician, Aaron Conin, and paid him off to get favorable results to disprove he was the father. That was why you took Javier's bank statement showing the $5,000 payment from his house. You didn't want anyone finding it and tying you and Javier to Conin.

"After obtaining the Sudarium, you contacted Conin using Boyd Ramsey's cell phone, and brought him some threads without disclosing their origin. I suspect Conin became suspicious, and you were forced to kill him on August 24th."

It was Diaz's turn to cut in. "Ramsey had a revolutionary idea of how to reconstitute the dried white blood cells from the Sudarium. He said the evidence of Jesus' divinity would be present within these cells. I found his notes on the reconstitution process and took them to Conin along with the thread samples."

"That's impossible." Tolen started, his mind churning. "Once dried, white blood cells are dead. They can't be reconstituted."

"So I've heard," Diaz said with a pressed smile. "Nevertheless, Conin took Ramsey's notes. At first, he was unsuccessful. After numerous attempts experimenting with different processes, he eventually succeeded. He brought the white blood cells back to life.

"The problem was, when he saw the results, he was a little too excited. I was forced to kill him at his apartment to keep him quiet. Unfortunately, he never divulged how he modified Ramsey's theory to reconstitute the white cells."

Tolen tried to digest Diaz's claim with considerable difficulty. What the man said simply was not possible.

"The next day, I went to Simon Anat to pitch my evidence, and show him the data from Conin's analysis. I couldn't explain how I was able to reconstitute the white blood cells, so Anat wouldn't listen to what I had to say. He wouldn't even review the data unless I could replicate the process in front of him, and of course I could not."

"What could the analysis of the white blood cells have possibly proven?" Jade asked.

Diaz smiled sardonically but did not respond.

"Is this when you formed an alliance with Anat's assistant, Nicklaus Kappel?" Tolen interjected.

Diaz arched his eyebrows. "Yes, all of the participants vying for Anat's prize were required to report their progress to Kappel. This made him the focal point of information, and Anat had precluded his assistant from being eligible for the prize, so he happily became my silent partner. Having a man on the inside increased my chances of success."

For a moment, no one spoke.

"The discrepancy in timing initially had me perplexed," Tolen said. "I couldn't figure out how you had samples from the Sudarium before it was stolen on August 30th. Then I found out the Oviedo police maintain a key to the Cámara Santa in their possession, and I assumed you *borrowed* it to gain entry. That's when I realized you had stolen the Sudarium earlier in the month. You knew the relic wasn't inventoried and wouldn't be viewed again until the start of the Feast of the Cross, so no one would know it was missing. Then you staged the Sudarium's *theft* on August 30th. I suspect this had something to do with your brother, Javier. Javier discovered the Sudarium was missing before anyone else, didn't he? You killed him to keep him quiet and were forced to make it look like a theft. The scrape marks around the keyhole of the iron gate in the Cámara Santa were made by the same tool as the marks on Aaron Conin's bathroom door. You did it with your pocketknife, but unlike with Conin, you weren't trying to get in, you were making it appear as if the lock had been picked."

Diaz visibly grimaced. "Javier knew where the archbishop kept the key to the Cámara Santa and had access to it. Unbeknownst to me or anyone else, at the end of each month, Javier used the key from the archbishop's office to inventory the relics behind the gate late at night. On the night of the 30th, he discovered the Sudarium was missing and, in a panic, called me. I went to the Cathedral to meet him. We had a discussion, and I admitted to Javier I had *borrowed* the Sudarium and promised I would put it back soon, but he would hear nothing of it. He threatened to turn me in. My own flesh and blood!"

"You stabbed him with your knife?"

"Yes, after we got into a fight."

"And the halberd?" Tolen asked.

"I called Kappel that night from the Cathedral. He advised me to make Javier's death appear more than a simple homicide; something unique. I went back and found the halberd in one of the dioramas. I embedded it in Javier's chest and left his body by the Arca Santa."

"And you also planted Boyd Ramsey's fingerprint?" Tolen added.

"Yes, this is when Kappel and I hatched a plan to blame Boyd Ramsey and make him the leader of an anti-religious fanatical group. Kappel was aware of Jade's and Dr. Cherrigan's search for a cache of Jesus' belongings. Kappel believed my blood analysis despite the fact I was unable to duplicate the reconstitution of the white blood cells. Based on this, he theorized it might be possible to get DNA from Jesus' personal effects to prove His divinity. Kappel went to Costa Rica, killed Cherrigan, and took his notes. After my convenient use of the halberd, Kappel got the idea to perpetuate the Apostle-style executions by beheading Cherrigan. Only when we read Cherrigan's notes did we discover with delight the unique item among the trove Cherrigan was after; something that would solidify our claim to Anat's billions."

Jade looked confused. "Cherrigan didn't know the possible contents. We never found a list."

"Oh, I'm afraid he did, Jade. Before the two of you joined forces and started your decryption of the Copper Scroll, Dr. Cherrigan had already discovered a clue on a cave wall outside of Jerusalem which alluded to the cache and itemized the contents. It was in one of the files on his PC."

He turned to Tolen as he continued. "We wanted the authorities to tie the two deaths: Javier in Spain and Cherrigan in Costa Rica."

"But you didn't want it to appear too obvious, so you only placed Ramsey's partial prints at each scene," Tolen added.

"*Si*," Diaz replied, "then we faked a communiqué by the 'True Sons of Light' to the Spanish authorities and planted a better fingerprint on the paper; one that would conclusively link the two crime scenes so there would be no doubt the threat was real. When the Spanish authorities failed to notify the press, I had to take action."

"So it was you who leaked the news to the press of the crime scene and the ex-CIA agent's alleged involvement, and you and Kappel invented the 'True Sons of Light' to turn up the heat and avert suspicion."

Diaz smiled, as if reveling in praise of the plan.

"Did you try to drive me off the road in New Jersey?" Jade asked. Her voice was weak, defeated, and she seemed exhausted.

"No, that was Kappel. That part of the plan worked to perfection. Kappel and I had Cherrigan's notes, but neither of us had the education or background to know how to proceed in the archaeological quest."

Tolen understood. "You weren't trying to kill Jade; you wanted the CIA's attention to be drawn to her. Afterward, you convinced Spanish officials to allow you to come to the States and assist with the investigation, knowing we'd bring Jade into our protection. You communicated our location at Harvard, Costa Rica, and Patmos to Kappel as we went. Kappel sent messages to the other participants who were after the reward, most likely embellishing our progress. This motivated people like Richard Mox, Gordon Nunnery, the unknown assailants at the Petra, and Claudia Denoit to try and stop us. Even though they weren't ready to make a claim to the prize, they didn't want anyone else to beat them to it. You orchestrated the attacks, knowing I would encourage us to continue the search for two reasons: one, to catch one of the members of the 'True Sons of Light' when they attacked us, and two, to find and protect the trove before this anti-religious group destroyed it."

For a moment, no one spoke, until Tolen finally broke the silence. "What are you hoping to find among the cache that will verify life-after-death?"

Diaz smiled but did not answer, instead announcing, "Now, I am about to make the most astonishing and lucrative discovery in the history of mankind while Mr. Kappel is retrieving the Sudarium."

Tolen did not hesitate. "I've already warned authorities about Kappel. They're tracking Anat's private plane, so they'll get him before he gets to the Sudarium." It was a lie, since Bar had been unable to track the plane. Tolen wanted to see if his suspicion was correct about the location of the Sudarium.

Diaz continued to smile. "Oh, I doubt it. Kappel had the luxury to be able to use Anat's private jet whenever he wished, but Anat would sometimes question Kappel about his travels, and we couldn't let the billionaire discover his true destination. The pilot flew the jet from Patmos without Kappel and returned to Switzerland. Kappel used other means of transportation to get to Spain to retrieve the Sudarium while Jade helped me continue the search by brilliantly solving the latest clue."

Diaz's admission that the Sudarium had never left Spain was encouraging. Now, if only Bar could find it in time.

"We found the third stone jar against this back wall," Jade motioned. "It was in plain sight, but there was no clue; nothing but a bag of frankincense. There was no rolled parchment, and there's nothing else in this room."

"Ah, correction," Diaz cut in, "nothing here that we can reach." He pointed to the roof above, which Tolen had noticed earlier. With the additional light, it was evident the ceiling covering most of the room was a platform with open space above it. "There is a second floor we must get to. It's the only place left we haven't examined."

Tolen again eyed the gap above where the back wall was separated from the platform. He estimated the lower ceiling to be 14 feet high. It would be impossible to reach without a ladder.

Joseph of Arimathea liked to make things hard.

"Enough of this discussion. Tolen, unless you want to see how Dr. Mollur looks with bullet holes, I suggest you find me a way to that second level."

CHAPTER 52

September 13. Thursday – 9:12 p.m. U.S. Pacific Time (September 14. 6:12 a.m. Oviedo, Spain)

2 hours 48 minutes until the start of the Feast of the Cross

The tall Italian man, Esposito, stood on the loading platform at the rear of the abandoned warehouse. A lantern cast pale light over his gaunt features. Before him, a horde of vehicles had amassed on the cracked cement pavement; 20 in all, each packed with a large payload of explosives. The drivers had all gathered, bunched in a group below him, their faint chatter rising into the air. Beyond the area, the desert stretched out, lost in the darkness of the cloud-covered night. Not far away, the noise of vehicles sailing past on the expressway could be heard.

As a light wind pushed across the carpet of sand and into his face, Esposito drew in a deep breath, admiring the visceral smell of God's earth. In the morning, he would watch the events on the news. The martyrs would have achieved a resounding victory against the vile government of the United States. The media would bring such focus, such attention, to the event that it would be felt to the very ends of the earth. Humanity was about to be changed, and he was leading the children of God to salvation. No longer would the misguided religions, the holier-than-thou men of cloth, question his cause. The true man of deliverance would be revealed to them. He was the second coming. Soon they would know. Soon they would understand.

The only blemish on his plan was, somewhere along the way,

one of the flock had become lost. The 21 had been reduced to 20, but that was inconsequential in the overall scheme of things. It was time to prepare his followers.

"We are God's catalyst for change!" he shouted abruptly.

The 20 people below fell silent. They looked up at Esposito, hanging on his every word.

"One of our brethren has abandoned us. He has opted to live with Satan. Still, we will carry out God's will," his tone suddenly quieted to a near whisper. "Our flagellation will be more than mere flesh wounds." Esposito paused, turning his lanky body, eyeing each individual separately from one end of the group to the other. His face suddenly contorted. A vein ballooned on his forehead which threatened to break the skin and his words erupted. "Our flagellation will be the ultimate absolution!"

There was rousing applause. He quieted the group with a wave of his hand.

He spoke softly. "You know the plan. We will receive our signal from The Prophet. Only when we have confirmation will you go through with your mission. God will give you the strength. He is everlasting, and so shall you be."

"He is everlasting!" the group shouted in reply.

"Please bow your head."

Twenty heads bowed at the same time; forty eyes closed.

Esposito looked over them. "Dear God, we are the enlightened. We understand Your will, and vow to carry out Your orders against the armies of evil. We ask that You welcome us into Your house once our earthly deed is done. We will never ask for anything more than to be in Your heavenly presence. Amen."

"Amen," came the collective response.

"Now go. Get into position. The midnight hour is quickly approaching. Talk to God. Tell him you are coming." *You may also want to give the devil a call and let him know that 200,000 sinners are on the way*, Esposito thought with inward bemusement.

The gathering dispersed, speaking in low murmurs. Esposito could hear some whispering Bible verses, others saying prayers, and still others beseeching God for strength as they made their way to their respective vehicles. Headlights came on, engines roared to life. A slow procession of cars, vans, and SUVs left the parking lot, circled around the abandoned warehouse, and returned to the highway like a long, blessed snake slithering across the earth toward its destiny.

It was glorious.

He was alone now, standing on the loading dock breathing in the still air. Esposito turned. The lights in the distance glowed brighter on the horizon than they had any right to. He imagined this was how Sodom and Gomorrah had appeared just before the godless cities burned, sparked by God's eternal flame.

Before tonight was done, the brilliance from the actions of the 20 would be unmatched. A new chapter in the Bible was about to be written.

CHAPTER 53

September 14. Friday – 7:52 a.m. Egyptian Time (6:52 a.m. Oviedo, Spain)

2 hours 8 minutes until the start of the Feast of the Cross

"What makes you think I can find a way to that second level?" Tolen asked.

Diaz returned with a scowl. "Because you're very resourceful," his tone hardened, "and I'm growing impatient."

"Have you searched this entire area?" Tolen asked, turning to address Jade.

She was valiantly trying to mask her fear. "Yes, there's nothing in this lower level; no images or clues."

Tolen thought for a moment. This entire underground complex was unique. Although it had many of the traits and features of Egyptian tombs, it had enough differences for him to realize it had been altered by someone long after the ancient Egyptians had constructed it. The modification had probably occurred during the first century of the Christian era, most likely by Joseph of Arimathea.

"Well?" Diaz prodded. "I suggest you look around. You are free to go anywhere you like, but if you don't return here within ten minutes, I will end Jade's life."

Diaz was expecting a miracle. The chance of Tolen figuring out a means to reach the upper floor in ten minutes was miniscule. Still, he reasoned Joseph of Arimathea would have provided a way. In fact, Tolen was sure of it. In each location, the first-century

Christian had orchestrated unique and challenging hurdles which had to be overcome, yet they were never insurmountable tasks.

Tolen wandered to the center of the triangular room after Diaz allowed him one of the electric lanterns. He turned in a circle, scanning the walls. He looked to the back wall where Diaz still had the pistol aimed at Jade. His eyes searched up the wall to the gap in the ceiling.

Tolen recalled one of his father's favorite sayings, *'When nothing seems right, look for an out-of-the-box solution.'*

Or in this case, Tolen thought to himself, an *out-of-the-triangle* solution.

He turned toward the other two. "Exactly where did you find the third stone jar?"

"Right there," Jade pointed to the wall at a spot several dozen feet to the right of the entrance to the tunnel. Tolen eyed the spot and started slowly toward it, moving his eyes up the wall as he neared Diaz and Jade. Diaz's body tightened as if he were fearful Tolen would attack. He grabbed Jade by the shoulder, backed her up, and pressed the barrel of the pistol hard into Jade's back. She winced in pain.

"Easy, Diaz," Tolen said, passing by and moving around the square stone pillar which stood before the main corridor of the tunnel. In the hallway, he turned right, into the room with the second-story ledge wrapped around the walls. He studied it for a moment, making a mental calculation before taking the stairs on the far side that led up. Once on the seven-foot-wide ledge, he walked along the back wall until he arrived at the right wall. The limestone was in pristine condition, and it only took a moment for him to find what he was searching for.

"Diaz!" he shouted. "In here!"

Diaz reached the room in an instant, hustling Jade in front of him. "What is it?" Diaz growled.

Tolen turned back toward the wall. "It's here. The Boswellia sacra. The tree whose extract creates frankincense." He guided his fingers along the limestone, sliding them up and over and then down again, each time in a straight line. "There's a thin crevice in the stone which forms the outline of a doorway."

Tolen thought for a second. He backed away, lowered his shoulder, and charged into the wall, slamming into it with force. A generous section of the wall collapsed inward. Pieces of the fractured stone could be heard landing far below in the adjacent room. Tolen looked through the aperture and saw he was level with the second floor ledge of the triangle room, separated by the ten-foot gap.

By now, Diaz had forced Jade up the steps, and they were standing a short distance away. "One room connects to the other," Jade reasoned aloud as she viewed the ledge of the triangle room through the opening Tolen had created.

"Well, it doesn't exactly connect," Tolen conceded.

There was an earthly groan, and the floor began to vibrate. Debris and dust rained down from the ceiling. Diaz's eyes went wide, and he seemed indecisive whether he should run or keep the gun on Jade. The rumbling stopped as quickly as it had begun. It was followed by a noise like a babbling brook which went on for several long seconds before the silence returned.

"What in God's name was that?" Diaz asked.

Tolen could only shrug. "Remember, our friend Joseph of Arimathea likes to leave traps."

"Go! Now!" Diaz barked at Tolen, waving the gun away from them. He forced Tolen to walk on the ledge circumnavigating the rectangular room to arrive at the steps from the other direction. Once Tolen began to descend, Diaz and Jade followed behind.

With Tolen in front by several yards, Jade was shoved ahead of Diaz so he could adequately keep both of them in his sight.

They returned to the main passageway, and Tolen took a right, away from the triangular room and toward the ascending staircase where he had first entered this complex series of rooms. The air was almost solid dust. Tolen coughed and covered his mouth trying to breathe. He heard Jade and Diaz hacking behind him.

The threesome saw it as soon as the light penetrated the white cloud. The corridor was now a solid wall of sand piled up to the ceiling. Somewhere in the belly of the long corridor, the earth had caved in, and a mountain of sand now blocked their only way out.

They were permanently sealed inside.

CHAPTER 54

September 14. Friday – 7:32 a.m. Oviedo, Spain

1 hour 28 minutes until the start of the Feast of the Cross

Bar sat in her rental car in the parking lot of a store just outside of Oviedo watching the sun rise over the bank of trees at the horizon. The store would not open for another hour. It was as inconspicuous a place as she could have hoped.

Within minutes, a second and then third car arrived, parking beside her. A driver exited each vehicle and climbed into the back seat of Bar's rental car. Bar had chosen an obscure location for a reason. Tolen had warned her not to reveal her status as a CIA staff member, since any such presence in or near Oviedo would be considered an admission of guilt, and the terrorists would strike against the U.S. earlier than planned. She had to maintain secrecy. These were the only two people who would know her true identity and purpose for being in the country.

The first man leaned forward, offering Bar a handshake as she swiveled to face the backseat. "I am Chief Inspector Carlos Nuñez," the man said in Spanish. Nuñez was in his mid-fifties with a thick head of salt-and-pepper hair and a fair complexion.

"It's a pleasure," Bar replied in the same language.

The second man wore a black cassock. "Thank you for coming, Archbishop Gustavo. I know this is a stressful time for you," she continued speaking in Spanish to the two men.

"Senorita, the Feast of the Cross begins in less than two hours."

"I assure you Archbishop, I will only take a few minutes of

your time. It was imperative we meet in a secluded place. We fear that if anyone knows I am with the CIA, the terrorist strike will occur immediately."

Archbishop Gustavo ran a nervous hand over his gray stubble of hair. The lines in his face seemed to be growing deeper with each passing second. "Please proceed," he said.

"Chief Inspector," Bar started, "did you uncover anything at Inspector Diaz's apartment?"

A troubled look crossed over Nuñez's face. "No, Señorita, we did not. I hope you know accusing the inspector is very disconcerting. Pascal Diaz is a tenured officer with the Cuerpo Nacional de Policia. He doesn't always follow protocol, but it's difficult to believe he'd steal the Sudarium and kill his own brother."

"I assure you Chief Inspector, we don't make this claim lightly. All evidence points to Diaz and a second man who have partnered in the crime. If they're successful, the reward for them is substantial. Chief Inspector, does Diaz own any other property where he might be hiding the Sudarium?"

"No."

"Any safe deposit boxes?"

The Chief Inspector shook his head no. "Not that we know of."

"Any place you can think of?"

Again he shook his head.

Bar felt frustration building. Nuñez was cooperating, but he was not offering any support. It was clear he resented the CIA making a claim that his man was responsible.

A cell phone chimed, and Nuñez pulled a phone from his coat pocket and answered.

"Chief Inspector Nuñez," he answered.

"I see," he said after a long delay.

There was nearly a minute more of silence. "Thank you," he said, and ended the call.

Sadness fell over Nuñez's eyes as he looked at Bar. "That was the coroner. Tissue samples were found at Javier Diaz's house after the explosion this afternoon. DNA tests matched it to your former CIA analyst, Boyd Ramsey. Also, we checked the key to the Cámara Santa maintained by the police as you suggested. All fingerprints had been wiped off of it. It seems," he exhaled, swallowed, and continued, "you may be right about Inspector Diaz."

"Did Diaz do anything suspicious in the time leading up to his trip to the U.S.?" Bar asked.

Nuñez seemed to regard Bar's question with more thought this time. "No, nothing I recall." A look of remembrance brushed the man's face. "Wait…there was one thing odd. I drove him to the airport the day he left for America. He had me stop along the way at the Asturias Province Cemetery to visit his family mausoleum. He said he wanted to see his father before he left the country."

"Why was that odd?"

"Pascal Diaz hated his father. Also, it was 30 minutes out of the way to the airport. I had never known him to visit there before."

"Was he carrying anything when he went inside?"

"Not that I recall, but he was wearing a long trench coat. I waited in the car. He was there only for a few minutes." He paused momentarily before rushing on. "I must go now. I am needed back at the office."

Bar felt a small ember of hope. She thanked the Chief Inspector for his time and turned toward the other man as Nuñez exited the car. "Archbishop, is there any way to stall the ceremony beyond 9:00 a.m.?"

The man's narrow eyes fixed her. "I am sorry. I have already explained to your partner, Agent Tolen, that delaying the Feast of the Cross is not an option. The service will proceed as planned. I received an edict from the Pope himself." He looked at Bar for a moment before he looked down. As if she had loosened his resolve, he held up an aged skeleton key. "Take this," he said. "It unlocks a trap door directly beneath the Arca Santa in the Cámara Santa. Alfonso II had it secretly installed when the Cámara Santa was constructed in the 9th century in case the building was captured by the enemy. It would have allowed a way to enter without being seen and reclaim the religious reliquary items within. I will have the priests slide the Arca Santa and its base forward in the room. There is a small ground-level grate on the north side wall of the Cámara Santa. It is very tiny, but I believe you can fit through. Once inside, go to the left until you come to the key hole in the floor above. This key will unlock the trap door. If you do retrieve the Sudarium, you will be able to return it without being seen."

She knew the Archbishop was no doubt violating a long-held church secret. Bar thanked him with a gracious nod of her head as she took the key. "I promise your secret is safe with me."

"To my knowledge, it's never been used," Archbishop Gustavo remarked.

Let's hope I get a chance to try it, Bar thought.

CHAPTER 55

September 14. Friday – 8:39 a.m. Egyptian Time (7:39 a.m. Oviedo, Spain)

1 hour 21 minutes until the start of the Feast of the Cross

They returned to the triangular room where Diaz forced Tolen to carry one lantern while he carried the other. There, they retrieved the three stone jars wrapped in cloth, which Jade was charged with carrying. They were awkward, but she kept a firm grip. They went back to the rectangular room and ascended the steps to the second level where Tolen had broken through the wall. For the next several minutes, Diaz had Tolen break out the rest of the doorway while he held Jade at gunpoint.

Once Tolen had broken away the last bit of stone with his hands and forged a doorway of considerable width, Jade studied the opening and beyond. The gulf between the ledge of the rectangular room and the second story of the triangular room would have been impossible to cross without the benefit of a running start. With the doorway opening next to a corner, they could back up the length of the rectangular room and race along the ledge. It would not be easy, but it should afford them sufficient speed to leap across the ten-foot gap.

Peering across, there appeared to be nothing on the second story of the triangular room. Yet she knew that would not stop Diaz.

"Tolen," Diaz said, moving Jade to the side out of the way of the opening, "hand Jade your lantern."

Jade lowered the stone jars to the floor and took the lantern from Tolen. She brushed his warm hand as they made the handoff, and he looked into her eyes with an apologetic stare. She was still taken aback by his comment earlier that he only realized Diaz's guilt after clearing Jade of any wrongdoing. The words had not only confused her, they had stung her heart. After all they had been through, how could he have doubted her?

"You will be the first one across," Diaz said to Tolen, backing Jade against the wall of the perpendicular ledge and out of the running lane.

Tolen nodded his understanding. He examined the opening briefly and seemed to measure the distance across with his eyes. He turned, walked along the ledge in the opposite direction until he had passed the staircase and reached the far wall. His pause was so subtle, Jade barely noticed it. She could feel her own heartbeat racing as he broke into a trot, accelerated into a full run, and vaulted into the air just as he reached the opening. It happened so fast, Jade and Diaz had no idea if he had made it until they heard a muffled noise. They quickly gathered before the opening with one of the lanterns and saw Tolen rise to a stand on the far platform of stone.

"You can make it," he said, bending over and breathing heavily as he looked directly at Jade.

"Move back," Diaz instructed Jade. She took half a dozen steps along the ledge and turned toward him. Diaz turned and shouted through the opening. "Catch this." He swung the electric lantern in his hand back and forth in practice before finally releasing it. Jade watched as it arced through the air and Tolen deftly caught it.

"Put it on the ground to your far right," Diaz ordered. Tolen complied.

Diaz moved to the side, picked up the three stone jars in the cloth and took them out one at a time. With Jade still standing back, Diaz yelled across, "I'm going to toss these to you one at a time. If you allow one of them to fall and break, I will kill Jade."

Tolen nodded his compliance.

Jade swallowed a hard lump.

With little fanfare, Diaz swung the first jar and heaved it across the chasm. Tolen caught it with ease.

Jade felt slightly better about her chances seeing how effortlessly the toss and catch had gone.

The second jar flew across at the same arc and Tolen again fielded it, laying it to the side with the first jar.

Diaz picked up the third jar. "This one *is* heavier," he whispered more to himself than for their benefit. Diaz seemed more cautious as he made several practice swings before releasing it with an unexpected grunt.

Jade's heart sunk. She could tell instantly that Diaz had made a poor throw. There was virtually no arc, as the stone jar sailed across like a soccer ball kicked in a line drive and well short of its target. Tolen's eyes flared and his body shifted awkwardly, sending a long shadow darting erratically to the side. He lost his footing and slammed down hard to his knees on the stone shelf, yet he somehow managed to field the jar, catching it in his stomach, then cradling it as he somersaulted forward, stopping inches short of tumbling off the ledge.

He rose slowly and pulled the intact stone jar from its secure position in his midsection. Without a word, he stood it to the side with the others.

"Nice catch, Señor," Diaz taunted. He turned to Jade. "Your turn."

Jade's pulse quickened. She hesitated.

"I can shoot you, if you prefer," he snarled.

The guttural tone of Diaz's voice spurned her into action. Across the way, she heard Tolen call out to her, "I'll catch you. You can do this, Jade."

Jade walked somberly along the edge to the far wall. She closed her eyes, willing herself to remain calm. In college, as a gymnast, she could have made a jump like this blindfolded. She could still do it, she told herself.

She opened her eyes. Diaz waited to the side of the doorway. Across the dark gap, Tolen stood perched near the edge of the second floor shelf. She knew the longer she waited, the worse her anxiety would tear at her. So she took a final deep breath and focused all her energies on speed, acceleration, and takeoff. She could do this. She *had* to do this.

Jade burst into a gallop and drove her legs as hard as she could.

Adrenaline kicked in, and she felt as if she were already gliding on air. She arrived at the opening in an instant, and, as her last step met the stone floor, she pushed off with all her might. She never looked down. Instead, she concentrated on Tolen as she closed on him in an instant. She flew into his chest, and the two tumbled backward onto the hard surface with Tolen absorbing most of the impact, breaking her fall. She quickly stood up, breathing hard, elated she had made it.

"Very good," Diaz called across from the other side. "Now, Tolen, catch this lantern."

Diaz threw it across, and Tolen caught it.

Jade, standing beside Tolen, turned discreetly to the side and whispered, "What are we going to do?"

"Nothing yet," Tolen said quietly.

His response took her off guard. She had been certain he was planning some sort of action.

"Now, I want you two to take one of the lanterns, but leave the other lantern there. Also, take the three stone jars. Do not break them, or I will kill both of you, Jade first. Move all the way back to the point in the walls behind you. I'll be able to see what you're doing. Do not turn the lights out."

Tolen and Jade did as instructed. Jade arranged the stone jars against the wall near the far point of the triangle.

"Any chance he won't make it across?" Jade said.

"We can only hope. With both lanterns over here, he'll be running in near darkness on the ledge over there."

Diaz evaporated from sight as they watched the opening in the distance. Moments later, his stocky body came hurling through the air, and he landed with a harsh smack. He pushed himself up quickly. Although he seemed somewhat dazed, he immediately withdrew the pistol and aimed it in the general direction of Tolen and Jade. Slowly, he grabbed the other lantern, walked the distance, and joined them at the apex.

"Jade, next to me now," he demanded. He leveled the gun on her once again. Then he turned to Tolen. "The next step in locating the treasure must be here. Find it. Now."

Tolen made no move, and Jade felt a swell of fear.

Diaz raised the pistol and pushed the barrel into Jade's temple. "Are we now having an issue with words?"

A tremble of fear ran up Jade's back.

Tolen lifted the lantern and turned. Wordlessly, he pointed to the converging point of the two sidewalls. Then he aimed his finger up, directing their attention to a cutout in the right stone wall about six feet high. It was a perfectly square, inset shelf, approximately five inches deep.

Diaz waved both Jade and Tolen out of the way. He moved to the cutout and stood on tiptoe.

From Jade's vantage point, it looked empty. Diaz confirmed it. "There's nothing here…" He settled back down and turned to face them, a smile spreading across his face. "…but there are three small circles at the base, spread out evenly. I believe we have arrived at the last doorway."

CHAPTER 56

September 14. Friday – 9:06 a.m. Egyptian Time (8:06 a.m. Oviedo, Spain)

54 minutes until the start of the Feast of the Cross

"Even a novice like me can tell the three stone jars are supposed to be placed upon the shelf, precisely on the three small circles," Diaz said as he reached for the first one.

Jade silently concurred. It was probably a trigger to another opening. That was why the text mentioned all three jars were needed.

Diaz arranged two jars on the inset shelf, then, keeping a watchful eye on Jade and Tolen, set the final stone jar atop the last circle. He stepped back.

Jade watched and listened with anticipation as she held up the lantern.

Nothing happened.

After a prolonged silence, Diaz huffed, "Why won't it work?" There was a desperate look in his eyes as he aimed the gun, targeting Tolen then Jade.

Something Tolen had said struck Jade. It was what he had noticed back at the hotel on Patmos. Even though the stone jars were the same dimensions, the weights varied. "They have to be placed in a specific order," she said.

Diaz nodded in agreement. "Ah, yes, Mr. Joseph of Arimathea, ever the puzzle-master. I'm guessing they need to be arranged in the order of discovery?"

Jade nodded. "I assume so."

It took Diaz a moment to rearrange as he had to check inside each jar for the contents. He reordered them left to right: myrrh, gold, and frankincense. He stepped away from the wall.

Still nothing happened. "What now?" he wheeled to Jade and Tolen. "What now!?"

"May we?" Tolen asked.

Diaz stepped aside, motioning Tolen and Jade to the wall in obvious frustration.

With Jade standing next to him, Tolen took the first jar and the third jar, and switched their positions. Jade had thought the same thing. Hebrew is written right to left. Diaz had set the jars in a left to right order.

The moment Tolen reseated the jars, there was a rumble and a stirring at the wall before them. Beneath the inset shelf, a section of the wall retracted away with a shuddering scrape, revealing a square opening approximately four feet tall and three feet wide. Jade bent down, using the lantern to peer into it, when she suddenly felt a hard shove which sent her off balance and through the opening, where she fell to the stone floor.

"No!" she heard Pascal Diaz shout behind her. There was a loud crack, a deafening blast, and Tolen came barreling through the opening a millisecond before the retracted stone door fell back into place. Tolen ended up sprawled on the floor next to Jade. The lantern had flown out of Jade's hand, but was thankfully still working a few feet away.

There was pounding on the stone door and muffled rants coming from Pascal Diaz on the other side.

"What happened?" she asked excitedly, pushing herself up into a sitting position.

Tolen stood, examining a fresh cut on his arm. "I pushed you through, knocked one of the stone jars to the ground, and dove inside. Diaz got off a shot but missed. As I had hoped, the moment one of the jars was moved, the door closed. I heard the jar shatter, so there's no way he can follow us."

Jade took the hand Tolen offered, stood, and said with a worried look, "But we're trapped on this side."

325

"We were trapped before. At least now we no longer have Diaz to contend with." He turned, lifted the lantern to an upright position, and raised it. The light revealed a straight, inclining corridor. "Our only chance of finding a way out is that way. Let's go."

The air was clammy, almost cold. The corridor was wide, approximately seven feet across and about the same height. The walls, ceiling, and floor were rough cut. Loose pieces of limestone made the footing treacherous, especially considering the grade they were traversing. The smell of stagnant air blended with a fragrance Jade recalled after a moment: cedar. The concept was absurd. Any wood locked in these catacombs would have decayed long ago, yet the aroma was palpable.

They walked slowly, always mindful of the ancient traps they had encountered at Joseph of Arimathea's tomb in Costa Rica, under the Petra on the Isla of Patmos, and here, where one tunnel had already caved in and become blocked with sand. Jade considered the deadly snares. For the first time, she realized a pattern: water in Costa Rica, fire on the Isle of Patmos, and sand here in the underground rooms in Egypt. Water, fire, and earth: three unique traps using elements of nature engineered to pose supreme challenges to anyone who ventured inside. The intricacies of Joseph of Arimathea's designs were nothing short of genius.

They reached a 90-degree left turn where the stone corridor continued to escalate at the same mild incline. Jade thought it odd but said nothing, following a half step behind Tolen. A few minutes later, they reached another 90-degree left turn. Now she was genuinely perplexed. "Where could this possibly lead? Shouldn't we have reached the surface by now?"

"Jade, I assume you solved the clue from the second stone jar just as I did. You realized '*where the ancients knew no god but themselves in the desert*' referred to Egyptian Pharaohs, and then you remembered Dr. Cherrigan's expedition in the tunnel below the hotel before he teamed with you last year."

She nodded. "Yes, but I never did figure out the first line: '*Of the Father, Son, and Holy Ghost, only the Son is charged with holding the contents on high.*' "

" '*Of the Father, Son, and Holy Ghost*' is a metaphor for the three pyramids on the Giza Plateau. The 'Father' is no doubt the Great Pyramid of Khufu, the 'Holy Ghost' equates to the second largest, the Pyramid of Khafre, and the 'son,' or Jesus, would represent the smallest of the three, the Pyramid of Menkaure. I believe that's where we are now."

She stopped and drew in a surprised breath. "You mean, we're... inside a pyramid? But none of the pyramids have mortuary tunnels which follow this pattern of incline with 90-degree turns."

"This isn't a mortuary tunnel. Not long ago, a French architect named Jean-Pierre Houdin used state-of-the-art computer modeling to create a 3-D image so he could explain a theory he had regarding how the pyramids were constructed. The long-held notion of a straight earthen ramp had been proven impractical. The approaching ramp would have been exceedingly long, over a mile in the case of the Great Pyramid, in order to achieve a subtle enough incline to allow laborers to haul the millions of two-ton limestone blocks up on rollers. In essence, construction of such an earthen ramp would have been a greater effort than actually building the pyramid. Houdin's contention was that a ramp was, in fact, used, but instead of approaching the pyramid from a distance in a straight line, the ascending ramp followed the sides of the pyramid at a seven-degree angle and was built from stone blocks as the pyramid went up, thus becoming part of the edifice. At the conclusion of the pyramid, the ramp corkscrewed its way to the top at right angles, following the sides of the pyramid like a staircase looping around and around. Then the builders enclosed the outer shell of the pyramid to conceal the ramp. Houdin theorized these ramps were still in place today, but Egyptian authorities never allowed him to test his theory. Satellite imagery was used to see inside solid objects for air cavities and appeared to show these inner ramps inside the Great Pyramid. I believe we've just proven Mr. Houdin's theory to be accurate."

She stopped in her tracks momentarily, soaking in the information. "How can you be sure we're in the Pyramid of Menkaure?"

"The two other larger pyramids were once completely cased in fine, white Turah limestone. If you look to the side, you'll see some pink granite. There, see?" Tolen came back to where Jade was standing and pointed to the right wall. Sure enough, a light pink hue could be seen.

"The pink granite is a tell-tale sign, unique to the Pyramid of Menkaure. Only the first fifteen meters of the pyramid were enclosed in the pink granite. Above that, like the other pyramids on the Giza Plateau, it was covered in the Turah limestone. The pink granite on the outside was stripped away in the early 1800s."

It was yet another jaw-dropping find, although Jade did not feel very elated about the discovery. Her concern with their predicament took precedence. If Tolen was right, the winding ramp would lead to the top of the pyramid. If the ancient Hebrew clues were telling the truth, somewhere ahead, they would find the cache of objects which once belonged to Jesus Christ. *The Holiest of Highs.* The phrase made complete sense now. The word "high" not only applied in the figurative, celestial sense, it had a literal meaning: somewhere near the top of the pyramid.

Yet even if they found the cache, the harsh reality was that they might not live to tell anyone about it. They were trapped with no way out. With no food or water, they would not last long. Nevertheless, she continued trudging forward, keeping up with Tolen's vigorous pace.

Jade examined the right wall as they went, occasionally spying remnants of the pink granite that had long ago served as the outer coating. Then, as Tolen had said, it disappeared, indicating they had risen above the 15-meter mark. It was difficult to believe they were now ascending above the Giza Plateau, but Tolen's logic made perfect sense.

"I don't suppose you know the height of this pyramid?" she asked.

"Sixty-two meters, or 215 feet," Tolen continued with barely a pause. "Why didn't you tell me about your relationship with Dr. Cherrigan?"

"What?" Jade blurted. Her voice cracked, and at that exact moment, she slipped on some of the loose limestone. She awkwardly regained her balance, feeling her face flush.

Tolen had stopped and turned to face her. His expression was reprimanding, his blue eyes piercing her.

"I...," she started to lie. She was going to deny what had happened between her and Phillip. It was morally wrong, not to mention a blemish on her professional resume, and she had hoped to sweep it under the rug with time. Instead, she took a deep breath and exhaled with slumping shoulders. "I didn't think disclosing the...relationship...was pertinent. Is that why you thought I was involved in some criminal activity?"

Tolen stared at Jade. She searched his face for sympathy and found none. He remained quiet, never breaking eye contact. She felt wounded by his unspoken disappointment. If she had any further thoughts of withholding secrets from him, they quickly dissolved. "It was a short affair," she threw her hands up and turned away, tears welling in her eyes. "God, I knew it was wrong. He was a married man, but it happened, okay? It continued for several months before I broke it off. I'm ashamed of what I did."

"Why did you wear a wig last year when you and Dr. Cherrigan went to Simon Anat's gathering in Switzerland?"

"How did you know...? Simon Anat's gathering? You mentioned Diaz vying for Simon Anat's reward...what did you mean?" She felt immense confusion.

"No lies, Jade. Only the truth." Tolen reached out with his free hand and grasped her shoulder.

"Okay, okay. Look, I did go with Phillip last year to Switzerland. We flew into Zurich, but you obviously already knew that. I wore a wig at Phillip's request. His wife is a blonde, and they had been there a few times. He asked me to wear the blond wig so as not to raise suspicions in case anyone he knew saw us, but I have no idea what you're talking about when you said *Simon Anat's gathering*. What gathering? Phillip was there for some business he didn't disclose to me. As a matter of fact, it was senseless for me to even make the trip. We spent a few hours together that afternoon after arriving in the hotel, then he left for a meeting in a nearby town where he stayed overnight. He never told me any of the details. We flew out the next morning when he returned."

Tolen looked unconvinced. "And you never asked him about his business there?"

"No, but obviously you're implying he met with the billionaire,

Simon Anat. Do you know why?"

Tolen explained Anat's gathering and the extravagant financial offer he had made to the participants. When he was done, Jade felt empty inside. Not only had the affair with Cherrigan been a horrific decision on her part, but the respected archaeologist, Dr. Phillip Cherrigan, had deceived her. He had withheld knowledge of the inventory list of Jesus' cache in order to go after Anat's reward, something she knew nothing about. She now recalled Cherrigan's sense of urgency to find the Costa Rica stone sphere after they had returned from Switzerland. It had struck her as odd. Now she understood. Cherrigan must have thought the cache of Jesus' belongings would somehow meet Anat's claim to the reward; a reward that, if achieved, he obviously had no intention of sharing with Jade. He had betrayed her, plain and simple. Like so many men tempted with money, Phillip had become nothing more than a greedy fortune hunter, and she suddenly found his memory distasteful.

After several seconds of silence, Tolen addressed her more gently. "Jade, as my father says, *each of us must undertake life's journeys for our own reasons*. Dr. Cherrigan was in search of a fortune. I believe you and I share a different goal." His tone was remarkably sympathetic now.

His warm words sent a cathartic wave through her. It felt good to have the facts in the open. She hoped there would be no more secrets between them.

CHAPTER 57

September 14. Friday – 8:09 a.m. Oviedo, Spain

51 minutes until the start of the Feast of the Cross

Archbishop Gustavo stood at the doorway of the Cathedral de San Salvador greeting people as they entered. As always, excitement built to a crescendo as the Feast of the Cross was about to commence. This service would be full, as would every service for the next seven days until Octave on September 21st. In all, hundreds of thousands would pass through these doors to behold the holy relic which once veiled Jesus' face.

Knowing the Sudarium was gone, possibly forever, left a hollow feeling in the pit of the Archbishop's stomach. If it were up to him, he would have forestalled the display at least 24 hours, but the Pope had been insistent. He declared it to be God's will that the Feast of the Cross, and all associated activities, proceed according to tradition.

It would be hard to display a relic that is no longer here, the Archbishop thought dejectedly.

More and more people crowded into the church. Unlike other years, though, the hallowed sanctuary had an unusual hush about it. There was a collective nervous anticipation which he could feel drifting up from the mass of people. According to the American CIA, there were religious fanatics in the congregation today, who were there to observe and report to their brethren if the Sudarium was not removed from the Arca Santa and unveiled at the beginning of the ceremony. The consequences would be dire, with deadly strikes against untold thousands of innocent people.

Gustavo could feel his stomach wrapping into knots. He prayed to God for strength to get him through this.

****

Bar called Chief Inspector Nunez and told him of her intent to search the cemetery where Diaz had stopped on the way to the airport five days ago. Nunez offered to send an officer to assist, but Bar declined. An officer might not allow Bar the latitude she required.

The Asturias Province Cemetery was a ten-minute drive to the southwest. Nunez gave her instructions where to find the Diaz family mausoleum on the grounds. Bar raced through the Spanish countryside, knowing time was quickly running out.

The cemetery was in the middle of the woods, spaced between several small towns. It was much smaller than Bar had anticipated, and she had no difficulty finding the free-standing mausoleum toward the back as Nunez had described. There were no other cars in sight, and as far as she could tell, she was the only one on the grounds.

Bar drove into the cemetery on a dirt path, parked in the grass next to the mausoleum, and exited the rental car. It was overcast, and the air felt damp, as if rain was approaching. A light wind blew from the south, carrying the aroma of newly turned earth. She shivered for no particular reason as she approached the door to the mausoleum.

She looked up at the building. The structure was simple, with no overt architectural style as far as she could tell, and no extravagant features. Lichen was caked on the flat stone walls, checkering the pale surface in gray and green. The final resting place of the working-class, she thought, for those with enough family money to afford a mausoleum, minus all the frills.

Bar stood at the entrance and tested the door. It was unlocked, so she pushed it inward on creaking hinges and took a step through the threshold, pausing just inside. The air was stale with the undeniable smell of death and decay.

Again she shivered, but this time, she knew why. The place was the epitome of creepiness.

She learned from Nunez that Pascal Diaz's father was Goyo Iago Diaz. Now, standing in the doorway, she saw twenty crypts before her in four tiers, each with five vaults across. The top row nearly touched the twelve-foot ceiling. Each vault was labeled with its occupant. Above, thick, interwoven spider webs erased the ceiling corners. More spider webs draped down along the walls.

"A four-story Days Inn for the dead," she mumbled to herself. "I hope he's near the bottom, or I'll never reach it."

Bar left the door open for the natural light. She made her way over to the stack of crypts, stirring dust with each step. She pulled a flashlight from her coat, as the farther in she went, the dimmer it became. The names were inscribed in the stone facing and had significantly aged, making them difficult to read. She was surprised to see the first marker indicated a Santos Diaz, 1712 - 1768. The Diaz family history in this area went way back.

Bar heard a creak and wheeled around. The wind had nudged the open door to its full extent, where it softly rolled back and forth before stopping.

"Just the wind, Tiff. Settle down," she said to herself, flicking a long bang over one ear. She patted her pistol in the pocket of her coat. She had almost left it in the car, but Tolen advised keeping it on her at all times.

She turned back and knelt, examining the names on the bottom row of crypts before moving to the second row. It was immediately apparent the Diazes were interred in order by date of death, right to left, bottom to top. This did not bode well for Bar. By the time she reached the last crypt on the second row, she was only up to the late 1800s. To view the third row, she had to aim the flashlight over her head and crane her neck while standing on tiptoe. The first two dates were into the 1900s, and she prayed she got to Diaz's father before the third row ended. She doubted she could read the fourth row of names, much less reach it.

Thankfully, she found Goyo Iago Diaz listed on the fourth crypt on the third row. She drifted back to the door and looked out over the cemetery grounds hoping to find something to stand on:

a ladder left on the grounds perhaps. Seeing nothing of use, Bar stepped back inside, staring up at Goyo Iago Diaz's tomb, thinking.

Her eyes wandered down to the crypt on the first row below Goyo Iago Diaz's, then up again at the third row crypt. She bent down to the third crypt in the first row. She drew in a deep breath and wished she had not. She coughed it out as the dust entered her lungs. "Just do it, Tiff," she urged herself. Bar grabbed the handle and pulled. The twenty-four-inch square stone door to the crypt resisted, then gave with a pop, swinging downward on a rusty hinge. There was a loud shrill, and a wad of fur bounced across her arm. Bar was so startled that she fell back with a yelp, backing all the way up to the side wall. The creature scampered out through the mausoleum door in a flash. She brushed frantically at her arm; her mind only now registering the animal as a large rat.

She began gasping for air. *Get a grip, Bar!*

Her knees momentarily wobbled as she stood, and she took a moment to center herself and focus before walking over to the open crypt. The stench which rose from it was ghastly. She expected to see a coffin that she could drag partially out and use as a step up. Instead, she saw the top of a partially crumbled, aged human skeleton succumbing to time. She shined the flashlight inside and saw the rest of the remains lying prone in the long cavity.

So much for that plan.

With the clock ticking, she renewed her determination and grabbed the handle of the crypt on the second tier below Goyo Iago Diaz. In case there were more rats, she stood to the side and pulled, immediately yanking her hand away as the door fell open. This time nothing emerged from within. She cautiously moved before the opening, examining the insides with her flashlight.

Another gruesome skull appeared, this one more intact than the first, but still losing form as pieces had flecked off. Deeper inside the container, the bones of the ribs, arms, torso, hips, and legs lay still, colored brown with age. Another awful smell clouded around her, and she tried her best to ignore it.

Now came the hard part. Bar stepped up, using the inside of the second level crypt as a platform to stand upon. She cringed as she felt the tip of her shoe bump against the decaying skull. She tried not to think about it. Then, she raised her second foot up to the recess and reached over her head, grabbing the handle to Goyo Iago Diaz's crypt to steady herself. There was no time to waste. She gripped the handle firmly and gave it a hearty tug, praying a rat would not drop onto her head.

The door released much more easily than the other two and swung downward. She heard tiny feet scurry away, and cringed. Nothing fell and silence returned.

She backed down to the floor, retreating to the door of the mausoleum. Bar shined her flashlight at an upward angle, trying to get a view inside the high open crypt. Archbishop Gustavo had advised her that the Sudarium was folded inside a silver-plated wooden box, twelve inches by six inches. Bar searched the opening. All she could see was the upper half of the skull of Goya Iago Diaz.

Immediately, Bar wondered if her instincts had been wrong. Why else would Pascal Diaz have stopped here on the way to the airport if not to hide the Sudarium before leaving for the States?

She moved from side to side, trying to better her vantage point. No matter where she went in the room, she could not see the base of the high crypt. She climbed back up, wedging her feet once again inside the second-tier crypt and grabbing the lip of the opening above. Blindly, she felt around, grimacing when her fingers touched the rough skull perched on the cusp, tipping it out of reach. She looked up and was mortified to see the skull falling toward her upturned face. She dodged her head to the side just in time as the skull barely missed her. It passed by her, plummeting to the stone floor where it landed with a morbid crunch.

Bar winced at the sound, but did not look down. She steadied herself, breathing heavily, yet trying to ignore what had just happened. While she kept one hand on the lip of the vault to support her awkward angle, the other continued to search around. In the right corner, she contacted something. At first she thought it was the stone wall, or worse, more of the skeleton, but then she tapped it with her fingernail and heard the faint click of metal. Excitedly, she strained to wrap her fingers around the edge of what felt like a small box lying flat. She gave it a tug, and it moved easily, scraping along the stone. She pulled it past the edge so that a portion was overhanging.

It had a silver casing. There was no doubt she had found the box containing the Sudarium of Oviedo, but she needed to determine if the contents were still inside.

Bar pulled the box from the ledge and found it remarkably light. She quickly climbed back down and placed the box on the stone floor of the crypt. She knelt beside it and opened the lid. It took a few seconds to pry loose.

"Yes!" she cried triumphantly, spying the venerable cloth.

She looked at her watch: 36 minutes before the Feast of the Cross began. That might give her just enough time to make it to the Cathedral de San Salvador and replace the Sudarium in the Arca Santa before it was retrieved for the opening ceremony.

She placed the lid securely back on the box and stood.

"First, the old gray-haired woman with the ridiculous accent on the Greek isle, now a little blonde-haired girl in Spain. Where does the CIA get their people from? The circus?" a man standing in the doorway chortled, holding a pistol pointed directly at Bar.

Bar started, her pulse racing. She spoke as calmly as she could in Spanish. "Who are you? What do you want?"

The terror of seeing a gun pointed at her was beyond anything she could have ever imagined. Her thoughts jumbled, and her brain froze. A few seconds skipped past, and slowly her mind thawed. She took the man in. He was of average build and height with dirty-blond hair. His accent was heavily German. He backed away from the door and into the corner, yet even in the dim light she recognized him from his picture: Nicklaus Kappel, Simon Anat's private assistant.

"Discard your weapon."

Bar began to reach into her right coat pocket.

"Stop!" Kappel yelled, adjusting the gun to her head. "Remove your coat instead."

Bar did so, shifting the Sudarium from one hand to the other in order to shed the garment, which she placed on the ground. There was a muted *clink* as her pistol impacted the stone floor through the cloth.

"Kick your coat away."

She complied, sending it against the wall, well out of reach.

"Put the Sudarium on the ground," he ordered.

What he had first said to her finally sunk in. '…old gray haired woman with the ridiculous accent.' *This is the man who murdered Reba Zee!* Bar's heart was pounding, and she tried to take a deep breath. She had to keep a clear head.

Kappel's voice turned venomous. "Put it down now, and I will make your death quick like the pilot's. Do anything stupid, and you will die slowly and painfully."

Deep within Tiffany Bar, a seething hatred began to take over. She stared hard at his face and searched her memory for what she knew about the man. A German, the man's only family was his sister, Cecily, with whom he had had an incestuous relationship. She was in jail. He also suffered from severe aphenphosmphobia—an acute fear of touching anyone. Slowly, a desperate plan formulated in her mind.

Bar bent down and placed the silver-plated box on the ground at her feet.

"Kick it to me," he demanded.

She did.

Never taking his eyes off her, Kappel bent down and grabbed the box. He stood upright. "That's a good little girl," he smirked. "Now, let's take a walk in the woods."

The words chilled Bar, and her thoughts raced. "I spoke to Cecily. She's enjoying jail."

Kappel's eyes turned menacing in an instant. "She would never say that!" he shouted.

Fighting her fear, Bar took a step toward the man. Kappel instinctively backed up a step. "Stop moving!"

"Cecily says it's wrong what you two did."

"You do not know Cecily!"

"Oh, but I do. Her boyfriend went to visit her just yesterday at Haufmer Langstrafenanstalt."

"No, she no longer talks to him!" Kappel's anger caused his hand to shake and his aim to veer. He acted as if he wanted to use his other hand to stabilize it, but holding the Sudarium prevented him from doing so.

Steeling her nerves, Bar stepped forward once again. "Cecily never wants to see you again."

Kappel tried to back up, but he found himself pressed into the corner. His face had reddened, and his eyes were darting about wildly. The gun was waving up and down, and he was unable to stop it.

Bar took a deep breath. It was now or never. She suddenly rushed him, turning her body sideways to make a smaller target. Kappel shook with frenzied eyes as she neared. He fired a shot, but it was off target. Bar reached him quickly, sending a balled fist into his face with as much force as she could muster. He recoiled, and the gun flew back against the wall and rattled to the floor. Kappel began to hyperventilate as Bar turned and dove for the weapon, which had slid a dozen feet away. She landed harshly on the stone where the pistol was just beyond her reach. As she pushed up on her hands and knees and scurried forward, a powerful grip clamped onto her ankle, drawing her backward. At the same time, an animalistic moan emanated from Kappel. Her knees smacked the stone, sending a harsh pain through her legs. Bar rolled over, kicking wildly, trying to free herself from his hold. He maintained his grip despite the fear and repulsion in his face from his phobia. Bar reached her hands over her head blindly, but was unable to find the pistol. She kicked again, catching Kappel in the chest. He withstood the blow with a grunt, then extracted a long knife from somewhere behind him. "I warned you!" he screamed, still shaking. She kicked with fervor as he raised the knife.

Bar knew she was about to die. She valiantly reached her hands over her head and, this time, barely grazed the cold metal of the pistol. With an agonizing reach which nearly pulled her arms out of her sockets, she extended and found the gun suddenly in her grasp.

Kappel scowled at Bar, launching the knife toward her midsection.

The blast in the confined room felt as if it shattered Bar's eardrums. In a daze, Nicklaus Kappel wavered above her, a fresh hole in the middle of his forehead filled with blood. A look of disbelief and horror covered his face. She sent a second bullet into his chest, and he fell across her, his lifeless body pinning her down. Bar gathered her strength and rolled the man away. She sat up, the gun trembling in her hand. Her entire body shook, and she leaned over to the other side and vomited until nothing more would come out.

CHAPTER 58

September 14. Friday – 9:30 a.m. Egyptian Time (8:30 a.m. Oviedo, Spain)

30 minutes until the start of the Feast of the Cross

Tolen put a hand on Jade's arm, and they both stopped their upward trek. "Have you considered the real probability that this third, and final, destination somewhere in the pyramid above will hold the physical remains of Jesus just as the other two locations entombed Joseph and the Apostles? If so, and we find Jesus' remains, it will be irrefutable evidence to *contradict* the resurrection story."

During their discovery of the Apostles in the cave system underneath the Petra on Patmos, Jade had wondered if the remains of Jesus might also be stored there. She had been relieved to find only the bodies of the twelve Apostles.

Jade took a half step closer, drawing within inches of him, chewing briefly on her bottom lip. "I don't have an answer to that," she began softly. "I know you're in search of the truth, but I discovered long ago that faith is not something given to you by organized religion or a book. Those views are far too restrictive, imposed by men claiming to represent the divine simply because they deem themselves the experts. I believe true spirituality is only achieved by looking within. I'm not going to try and change your mind regarding what you experienced when you were electrocuted. I'm an archaeologist. I deal exclusively in facts, so faith tends to be a hard concept for me to latch onto, but I also know within each of us is an undeniable power whose source cannot be quantified by science. It drives us and carries us through the day, determining our actions. It exalts our achievements and tugs at our heart strings when we've done wrong."

"You're talking about the human conscience."

"Yes, that unquantifiable part of us which makes us human: the ability to be compassionate, to care, to love, to feel grief, to be embarrassed, to forgive, to regret. Let's face it, when you break it down, the human body is just a machine. Mankind can build robots that can replicate nearly every movement we can make. Computer programs can be generated based on decision models to replicate thinking. But no one will ever be able to duplicate decision-making based on emotions, because emotions have no tangibility. I believe this emotional power, the human conscience, or whatever you want to call it, carries on in an enlightened state once the physical vessel has ceased. I have no proof, but I believe it in my heart to be true."

Tolen's expression was unreadable, and he did not respond. Instead, he looked at his watch. "Less than half an hour until the start of the Feast of the Cross. I hope Bar is having better luck than we are. Let's keep moving." Tolen continued up the ramp, the electric lantern lighting the empty corridor ahead.

Again they reached a corner and turned left. Although the incline was subtle, Jade felt the strain on her thighs and calf muscles. Fatigue could have overwhelmed her if she allowed it, but she pushed on, diverting her thoughts away from her weary body and concentrating on her footing as they continued to trudge across loose debris. Even with the cool temperatures, Jade was perspiring profusely.

Tolen set a brisk pace. Jade found herself growing exceedingly anxious to discover what awaited them at the end of the corridor. They reached the corners at an ever-increasing rate as each ramp, which aligned to the pyramid's sides, naturally reduced in length. Jade had lost count of the left turns as they spiraled up the pyramid. Their footfalls echoed ahead in the distance, and the footing became easier as the loose, gravelly debris thinned out. The smell of cedar lingered as they climbed. Jade knew the tunnel would end when it reached the summit. The fear of not finding a way out was temporarily overshadowed by the excitement as they neared the end of what might be the greatest archaeological quest of all time. It had been a grueling journey, fraught with danger from both modern-day and ancient influences. Miraculously, the clues had led them to places and formations which remained in existence 2,000 years later. In all that time, these locations had gone undiscovered. In a way, Jade felt she and Tolen had been destined to make this journey; their fates interlocked to solve one of mankind's greatest mysteries. Now the moment was drawing close when they would learn the truth: whether the texts in the stone jars had been some ancient ruse or valid instructions to a pivotal discovery in mankind's continual quest for knowledge.

Jade's sweaty skin tingled in anticipation as the passageway corners became even more frequent. She found herself pressing faster up the incline in order to keep up with Tolen. At the next left turn, the lantern light fell upon a solid stone wall.

They had reached a dead end.

Jade noticed the left wall. There were handholds hewn into the surface leading upward. Wordlessly, she pointed to it, and Tolen raised the lantern as the two looked up. A four-sided shaft, four feet by four feet, reached overhead. It continued maybe a half-dozen feet into the ceiling before it opened up.

Jade wiped her brow with the back of her wrist and noticed her entire arm was shaking. With great effort, she steadied it.

"Are you okay?" Tolen asked. They had crowded together to see up the tunnel, and his face was close to hers.

She looked up at him. Her pulse had quickened, and she felt her face flush. She was breathing heavily from the climb and spoke barely above a whisper. "It's up there. I can feel it."

"You first," Tolen said, motioning with his hand and stepping back to give her room.

She turned away from Tolen and faced the wall. She gripped the first handhold and hesitated. Everything they had gone through, all the clues they had decoded, and the thousands of miles they had traveled, had been a frantic rush to get here, yet now she felt such irrepressible trepidation that she spun back toward Tolen. Jade stared intently into his blue eyes. He must have read her unfiltered expression of doubt because he offered no words, only a look of compassion. It was exactly what she needed at that very moment. She smiled, feeling newfound resolve. Jade leaned forward and kissed him lightly on the lips. It was a quick, satisfying show of affection. She drew in a deep breath, turned, and began scaling the wall.

Jade heard Tolen following her as she reached the corridor ceiling and climbed beyond into the vertical shaft. He was forced to hold the electric lantern in one hand as he went, and it clanked off the wall with each new grip and step up. Because the light was muted, filtering up from below her, Jade moved slowly, ensuring she had a firm grip and foothold in each carved niche. She paused to look up. Only a few feet above, she could see where the tunnel opened up, but the area was still cast in gloom. It had to be the end room: *The Holiest of Highs.*

She could hear her heartbeat in her ears.

She scurried up, taking the last few handholds with reckless abandon, anxious to see the level above. She reached the opening and pulled herself up, momentarily sitting on the stone floor in the darkness. Tolen's light from below streamed upward, dancing across a low, narrow ceiling where flecks of stone twinkled back at her. A second later, he joined her, pulling himself up to the floor. If there had been any doubt before, the smell of cedar was undeniable here.

The light revealed a tight hallway with a low roof. Jade rose, keeping her head low. Tolen did the same, dipping his tall frame awkwardly. Jade touched the walls and found them polished smooth. She looked to the ceiling and floor, which had also been buffed to a smooth finish. "It's granite," she said excitedly. "It's exquisite!"

Ahead, the narrow hallway curved left out of sight. Jade took the lantern from Tolen's hand. He offered no resistance. Still bent over, Jade led them forward through the banking turn. As soon as the passageway straightened, the tunnel ended.

To Jade's amazement, they stood in a square room. The walls rose a dozen feet before giving way to a ceiling which peaked to a point in the center. This was the pinnacle room of the pyramid.

At the back wall, facing out, was a large stone coffin, not unlike an Egyptian sarcophagus. As with the walls and floor, it was also made of granite and sat upon a granite base. A fourth, small stone jar sat atop the coffin. There was a continuous ledge, similar to a bookshelf, which wrapped around all four walls at chest level. Upon it lay aged clothing precisely folded and arranged—sandals, robes, sashes—as well as ancient plates, pots, cups, and other cooking and eating utensils. Every inch of ledge on all four walls was covered with artifacts. In one corner of the ledge was a large metal chalice. The staggering thought that this might be the Holy Grail was quickly overshadowed by the last feature of the room, an object which caused Jade to become dizzy as she gazed upon it.

A large section of light-brown tree trunk rose near the back wall behind the head of the coffin. Three-quarters of the way up, a second thick section of tree intersected it, forming a large crucifix. A second, black cross was thrown against the wall behind it, the mirroring shadow caused by the lantern's light. Although not mentioned in the Bible, it has been suggested the cross upon which Jesus was crucified was erected from a tree indigenous to Israel: a Cedar of Lebanon.

She studied the lofty cross for a long minute, speechless. It rose to a height of more than twelve feet. The light brown wood was rough and, at the extremities of the arms and at the base, was saturated with dark blotches.

"Oh my God, it has blood stains!" she realized. Her thoughts whipped through her mind nearly out of control.

"Wood decays within months. Maybe years, but that's if it's treated," Tolen remarked.

Jade noticed a sense of wonderment in his voice. It seemed that he, too, was overwhelmed.

"It could not have lasted thousands of years. This should be nothing more than a pile of dust," Tolen whispered. Tolen passed by her and reached the coffin. With great delicacy, she watched him lift the small stone jar from the top. "A fourth Canopic jar."

Jade merely nodded. Frankly, of all the objects in the room to take in at that moment, the stone jar interested Jade the least. She walked slowly past Tolen to the free-standing cross. It was set into the stone floor about six inches away from the wall like a Christmas tree in a base. Only when she drew near did she spy the Hebrew writing on the wall to the side of the cross. It had been inscribed meticulously.

She placed her fingers on the smooth wall and moved them right to left as she read the text aloud unconsciously. "*It is finished. Jesus of Nazareth rests.*" Jade looked at the writing, then back to the cross, lifting her head to take in its grandeur. As if having an out of body experience, she saw her trembling hand reach forward and touch it. The wood was far from perfect; rough and splintered, yet pressing her finger to it invoked a feeling of reverence Jade had never thought possible. She felt a sensation of warmth and cold at the same time. In her pious state, she turned to Tolen.

He was holding the stone jar. He tilted the jar one way and then the other. "Jade, look at this."

She drew her hand away from the worn wood and headed over beside him. This fourth Canopic jar appeared smaller than the others. He handed her the vessel, and she attempted to remove the cap, but it wouldn't budge. "The cap won't come off?"

"It's sealed."

She examined the stone jar, tilting it from side to side as Tolen had. As she did, she could feel whatever was inside shift. There was a faint slosh. "It's...liquid."

Tolen nodded.

"Against the wall!" a surly voice bellowed from behind them.

Surprised, Jade spun in the direction of the sound. In doing so, she lost her grip on the stone jar, and it fell to the ground near Tolen's foot, shattering in a conglomeration of stone shards and viscous red fluid.

Holding his lantern in one hand, the pistol leveled at them in the other, Pascal Diaz glared at them. They had been so captivated with the room that neither of them had heard him approach via the narrow passageway. "Over there!" Diaz waved the pistol, directing them to his left, away from the coffin and cross. His agitation was evident.

Jade and Tolen obeyed, backing against the chest-high shelf. Jade's gaze was riveted on the red fluid pooled on the smooth floor. The stark realization struck her. The jar had held the blood of Christ, and it was fresh blood! This was what Diaz was after.

Diaz quickly moved to the shards of the stone jar and lifted a section of the small base still intact. He stood, and his worried expression quickly morphed into a smile of victory. Keeping the pistol trained on Tolen and Jade, Diaz removed a small vial from his pocket and, holding the vial in the hand with the gun, poured a small amount of blood from the broken stone vessel into the vial. Then he capped the vial and placed it in his pocket.

Jade understood. "Dr. Cherrigan knew the jar of blood was here."

"Cherrigan's notes stated that Jesus' mother, Mary, gathered the blood from the wound where the Roman guard stabbed Him with a spear while He was on the cross. Cherrigan surmised correctly that the blood might have elements which could confirm His divinity," Diaz said, "and now it's going to make me a fortune."

"How did you get past the sealed doorway in the triangular room?" Tolen asked.

"Señor, when you break a jar, break it thoroughly. The weight of the pieces will always equal the weight of the whole."

"Diaz," Jade said, her words reverent, her eyes alive again, "look at this place. We found it. These are the objects of Jesus Christ…His possessions, and this," she pointed to the back wall, "must be the wooden cross He was crucified upon." As her words died, Jade was suddenly aware of the one obvious object in the room both she and Tolen had ignored: the coffin. It was the one thing she had prayed would not be there.

CHAPTER 59

September 13. Thursday – 11:46 p.m. U.S. Pacific Time (September 14. 8:46 a.m. Oviedo, Spain)

14 minutes until the start of the Feast of the Cross

Connell entered the room at the FBI office and sat down at the computer. "I've got the video from the arresting officer's squad car." He punched a button, and a screen slowly scrolled from the ceiling as Gerly, McNulty, and Vakind looked on. A picture appeared. It was a black-and-white image shot from inside the squad car, aimed out through the windshield, focused on a green SUV pulling recklessly out of a gas station. The police car followed and came up behind the SUV as it approached the Interstate on-ramp heading east. The vehicle ahead hit the brake lights, then sped up and continued under the overpass and took the on-ramp to the west. The policeman followed the green SUV for another mile before pulling Whitacre over and discovering the explosives in the vehicle. Whitacre was arrested.

"Play that back from the beginning," Gerly requested.

Connell did. At the point where the squad car first came up behind the SUV after leaving the gas station, Gerly suddenly said, "Stop it there."

Vakind saw it as well. "Did the arresting officer see Whitacre come off the Interstate before he pulled into the gas station?"

"No," Connell responded. "He only noticed the SUV when it pulled out and then followed him west on the highway."

"I know what you're thinking. I saw it, too," McNulty said. "He

347

hit his brakes approaching the east on-ramp as if he was considering going in that direction."

The faces of all four people in the room suddenly arrived at the same conclusion.

Vakind voiced their consensus. "He wasn't originally travelling west toward Los Angeles. He had turned off the Interstate for gas and then went west only when he realized the police were tailing him. He had been heading *east* on I-15."

Gerly rose and walked over to a roadmap of the western United States on the near wall. He started at Los Angeles and ran his finger east out of the city on I-15. He slowly followed the interstate as it banked up and crossed the Nevada border.

He stopped when he arrived at Las Vegas. There was a collective inhale.

He turned to the others in the room. "Oh lord."

"Shit," Connell exclaimed, shaking his head, "it's Spanish. Depending on the translation, Las Vegas is Spanish for meadows, or, in some cases, *fertile valleys*!"

The room stirred with macabre anticipation. "Okay, we know the city," Vakind said in a settling voice, glancing at his watch. They had twelve minutes to go. "Does the phrase '21 out of 28' mean anything in the context of Las Vegas?"

"Twenty-one: blackjack?" McNulty offered.

The memory of Whitacre's response during the interrogation suddenly struck Vakind. Just as Whitacre had paused at the east on-ramp and then turned west when he saw the police officer following him, when Vakind had flustered him, his statement during questioning had followed the same change of direction: '*Those who gamble…*," Whitacre had paused before restating and continuing. '*Those who gamble with God's will, know exactly who they are.*'

Whitacre was not quoting some proverb from the Bible as Vakind originally thought. He was literally referring to those who gamble…in Las Vegas. "The target is the casinos, the hotels," Vakind said.

Connell looked up from the computer with a bleak stare. "I just did a search. Twenty-one out of the twenty-eight largest hotels in the world are in Las Vegas. MGM Grand, Luxor, Venetian,

Bellagio, Mandalay Bay...taking into account room capacity, employees at the hotels and casinos, and various patrons, there may be as many as 220,000 people in those combined hotels at midnight. It's the perfect target for religious zealots: Sin City."

****

Bar drove frantically through the Spanish streets until she was within several blocks of the Cathedral of San Salvador. Crowds of people were on the sidewalk, moving toward the cathedral. It was eleven minutes before 9 a.m. She grabbed her cell phone and dialed Vakind. He answered on the second ring.

"I've got the Sudarium!" Bar practically shouted into the device. "I'm close to the church now! The archbishop gave me a way to get into the Cámara Santa without being seen!"

Vakind's voice was steady, as always. "Ms. Bar, we've identified a threat to 21 hotels in Las Vegas. The potential casualty is nearly a quarter million people. There's no time to evacuate without causing pandemonium and alerting the terrorists. You have to get the Sudarium back to the Arca Santa in time. Terrorists will be monitoring the activity at the cathedral. You cannot be seen returning the Sudarium, and no one can know you're CIA. Understood?"

A minute later, Bar parked illegally along the street and sprang from the vehicle still two blocks away. Throngs of people were on the sidewalk. She wrapped the silver-covered box in a white shawl which she had brought with her aboard the plane. Using a handheld GPS, she determined the location of the Cámara Santa and moved quickly down the block, navigating around several buildings.

She felt a crushing urgency. She ducked around the corner and found that the alleyway to the north side of the Cámara Santa was empty. She located the ground-level grate and pulled it free, squeezing inside on her hands and knees.

The air underneath the Cámara Santa was stifling and foul. She used the flashlight as a guide and crawled across the dirt-covered ground, awkwardly toting the Sudarium in the box. Bar had studied the architectural layout and knew that the rectangular antechamber,

349

or *cella,* accounted for most of the square footage of the building adjoining the Cathedral de San Salvador. The overlapping Cámara Santa, where the religious relics were stored, was at the far end. She crawled her way to the end, sucking in dust. She found the trap door underneath the floor just as Archbishop Gustavo had advised she would. Bar withdrew the key from her pocket, inserted it into the overhead lock, and prayed the years had not rusted the locking mechanism. She tried to turn it, but there was no give. Her worst fears appeared confirmed: time and weather had rendered it inoperable. She continued to try anyway. On the fourth try, with a strenuous turn of the key, the lock finally sprang open to her excessive relief. She gave the trap door a shove, and it rose with a creak and flipped over out of sight. Light invaded the area. Bar wasted no time rising through the trap door and stepping up into the Cámara Santa, still carrying the silver box wrapped in the shawl.

Ahead, the arched gate separating the room from the *cella* was locked. She spied an assortment of reliquary items around her, but a long stone platform in front of the trap door where Archbishop Gustavo said the Arca Santa would be, was empty.

The elation of recovering the Sudarium was replaced by the deflated realization she was too late.

****

Esposito had remained at the abandoned warehouse on the outskirts of Las Vegas waiting for the stroke of midnight and confirmation from The Prophet in Oviedo that the Sudarium was missing. Once he received word, he would communicate to his people to proceed with the eradication of Las Vegas. Each of the 20 martyrs had confirmed they were in place with their vehicles primed with the explosives, either in the parking garage underneath each hotel or ready to ram their cars, trucks, and SUVs through the front entrances. Each disciple had taken a vow to carry out his or her assignment, and Esposito had no doubt each would see it through to completion.

Now the hour was fast approaching. The nighttime sky to the northeast was about to burst with the newfound light of God; far brighter than the scandalous city of sin had ever known.

CHAPTER 60

September 14. Thursday – 9:50 a.m. Egyptian Time (8:50 a.m. Oviedo, Spain)

10 minutes until the start of the Feast of the Cross

Diaz stepped farther into the chamber, taking in the various objects lining the shelves. "This is it?" he said with a sour tone. "Clothes, shoes, and robes? Where is the gold, the silver?"

Jade looked at him in confusion. "What gold and silver? What are you talking about? These are the objects which once belonged to Jesus…His clothes…the cross He was crucified upon. These are priceless artifacts. They will have a staggering impact on humanity!"

"They are of no consequence to me," Diaz sneered. "I assumed, based on the Copper Scroll, there would be valuables here."

Jade felt an overwhelming frustration. "There is nothing more valuable than the contents in this room. Don't you understand that?"

Diaz reached into his pocket and withdrew a folded sheaf of papers. "This is the most valuable thing in this room. This, and the sample of blood I now have in my possession."

Tolen understood. "Aaron Conin's findings; the test data on the Sudarium. What evidence did you find in the blood when the white cells were reconstituted?"

"The same results I will find in the sample in my pocket. Once we deliver the vial, the report, and the Sudarium to Anat, and he replicates the test results, Kappel and I will be very wealthy men,"

Diaz nodded vigorously, seemingly giddy with the thought of his upcoming riches.

"Please tell me," Tolen asked, his voice tentative. He felt a weakness he had not experienced since his mother had died. "What makes you believe you can prove life after death?"

Diaz only smiled. "I have proof of Jesus' divinity. That is all you need to know." He looked at Jade and silently motioned her toward him. She complied reluctantly.

"Now it's time for you to do me one last act, Señor Tolen. Find me a way out of this place. I believe you know by now the penalty for failure." He positioned the gun at the back of Jade's head, and she flinched.

"What does it matter?" Jade said dejectedly. "You're going to kill us both anyway." A tear trickled down her cheek.

"Well, if that's how you feel—"

"Why did you kill Javier?" Tolen cut him off. "What was the real reason?"

Diaz looked at Tolen, freezing him with his gaze. "I told you, it was an accident."

"What about the ramifications?"

Diaz crinkled his face, flexing his fingers around the gun. Jade raised her shoulders in a silent plea for Tolen not to aggravate the man. "What ramifications?"

"We're standing in a room with tangible objects which confirm the existence of Jesus. You have the evidence of an afterlife. You are a man of faith, Pascal, yet you murdered. You killed your brother, you killed Boyd Ramsey, and you killed Aaron Conin. Surely you realize you will be judged for your actions."

"There were...extenuating circumstances. Javier was an accident. Boyd Ramsey was a thief. He would have stolen the Sudarium and never returned it. It has always been my intention to make sure it is delivered back to the Cathedral de San Salvador. As for Aaron Conin, the man was greedy; after glory and money. He was not a good man. My actions against each were vindicated."

Tolen raised his eyebrows. "Greedy? Interesting. The same could be said of you."

Diaz creased his brow and his forehead darkened as he

repositioned the pistol at Jade's temple. "I will give millions to the church, charities, and orphanages; more than Simon Anat ever dreamed of giving away." He uttered his words as if desperate to land on the right combination of benevolence that would appease the guilt Tolen was churning up within him.

Tolen continued to push, shoving absolution out of Diaz's reach. "You're going to buy your way into heaven? How many times have we heard that from convicts and murderers?" A ghost of a smile crossed his lips.

Diaz's rage flared. "No, Señor, I am not going to buy my way into heaven! I will be a humble servant of God, as I have always been."

"Money changes people, Diaz," Tolen said, taking a casual step next to the coffin. "It always has, and it always will. You can throw money at charities, feed the poor, save the whales…make yourself feel good…but in the end, you will be judged as an evil man. No fortune can scour away the blood on your hands."

"It matters not!" Diaz screamed balefully. Jade shuddered, grabbing her ears as the sound reverberated in the enclosure. Diaz's hand holding the gun was now shaking in anger.

Tolen had hoped to infuriate Diaz to the point that the man would divert his attention from Jade to him. If he did, Tolen was going to take his chances and rush Diaz, but Diaz had not taken the bait. His anger was now endangering Jade.

Tolen noticed the wall behind Diaz above the shelf. There was a distinct outline. He studied it, trying to be inconspicuous. At that moment, he recalled a line of the text discovered inside the stone sphere:

Only the man who has patience, is meager, and holds faith will arrive safely.

Holds faith. Tolen now knew what he had to do if they were going to get out of here alive.

CHAPTER 61

September 14. Thursday – 8:58 a.m. Oviedo, Spain

2 minutes until the start of the Feast of the Cross

Bar desperately moved through the atrium into the narthex at the rear of the church concealing the silver box inside her shawl, pressing it to her chest as she threaded her way through a sea of people. A considerable distance away, near the altar, Archbishop Gustavo was wearing a worrisome frown and looked as if he had aged ten years since she had seen him in the backseat of her rental car only a short time ago. To the Archbishop's side, another priest was tending to something low and out of sight. The Arca Santa was perched behind, elevated on a stand with its lid open. To the side was a diorama of Mary and Joseph and a thatched cradle. The pews were jam-packed with people and a general hubbub arose into the rafters of the cathedral. Bar sensed a collective anticipation within the bustling congregation that was incongruent with the usual ceremony.

Archbishop Gustavo happened to look up. Bar pleadingly sought out his wizened eyes. He looked her way for a moment then turned to say something to the other priest. Dejectedly, she knew he had not noticed her. If she walked into the packed cathedral now carrying a suspicious looking object wrapped within her shawl, the terrorists would surely know something was going on and trigger the attacks in Las Vegas.

She had come so close; to within 70 feet of returning the Sudarium, but she might as well have been a continent away.

****

"Don't you want to know, Diaz?" Tolen spoke in a tranquil voice. His demeanor had softened.

"Know what? Enough of your talking. Find me a way out of here, or I'm going to put a bullet in her pretty little skull," Diaz's teeth were clenched as he spoke.

Jade cowered, looking to Tolen with a helpless, pleading gaze.

"You know, maybe these aren't the clothes of Jesus," Tolen continued as if Diaz had not spoken. "Maybe this isn't the cross He was said to have died upon. Then again, maybe it is." He turned slightly, pointing to the elevated coffin. "The answer is right here, Diaz. The Son of God, or a mere mortal? No man in 2,000 years has known the answer with conclusive, indisputable proof. Given your recent wrongdoings, you should hope He is lying inside this coffin, that His remains are no different from any other human's, that His words about heaven and hell are just the rants of ancient fictional writers. It would surely serve you better to know your vile earthly actions are not going to be judged by a higher power when you die."

There was a searching look in Pascal Diaz's eyes. "Find me a way out of here!" his voice boomed. "I swear to God, I'll kill her!"

"Can you imagine?" Tolen's blue eyes were alive. "One push of this stone lid, and we'll be the only people on earth to know the truth. Was He or wasn't He? Really, it's the only way to know if the sample of blood you have is authentic."

There was an indecisiveness which permeated Diaz's body language.

"*I* want to know," Tolen said. His voice turned supplicative. "If you're going to kill us anyway, allow me this one last request. I want to see if there's a body inside. Then, I swear, I'll find you a way out of here. Joseph of Arimathea was not trying to kill us when he built this place, so it's a certainty there's a way to escape. Allow me to open the lid and take one look inside, then I'll find you an exit."

There was a moment of silence. Diaz nodded his affirmation.

****

Leon Smith sat in his covered Ford pickup parked a half block away from the massive dark structure which looked more like one of the Seven Wonders of the World than an American hotel. A white light shot straight into the nighttime sky from the tip of the pyramid like a laser beam ascending into heaven, yet he knew that heaven had nothing to offer the people inside. Of that, Smith was sure. The Sphinx out front left no doubt in his mind that the entire complex was a damned tribute to the Middle East and their anti-Christian ways.

That just burned him up.

He had been taken aback by the gaudy opulence everywhere he looked. This was a town full of massive carnival-like buildings rising up around him and droves of people in the street, herding about like cattle as far as the eye could see. He could only imagine the sin and debauchery going on inside these buildings—the charlatans, the gamblers, the alcoholics, the harlots. How could parents even think about bringing their children to this city of ill repute?

Now, parked and waiting, Smith watched diligently as the hordes of people, the misguided flock of hardcore sinners, floated in and out of the colossal pyramid-shaped structure. Men, women, and children constantly flooded the sidewalk, passing the Sphinx and making their way along the palm-tree-flanked sidewalk. If he had had any reservations about his task tonight, they were now gone. Carnal sin had wrapped this town in its heathen grasp. Enough was enough.

With over 4,000 rooms, Smith had gladly assumed responsibility for taking down the third-largest hotel in town. He could almost visualize how the edifice would collapse inward when he rammed his truck through the front entrance and detonated his payload. He found solace in knowing he would receive God's heavenly welcome with the demise of this manmade indulgence.

This would be Leon Smith's first and last time in the lights, the glitz, and the money of Las Vegas; a town so dedicated to self-aggrandizement, it was hard to believe people could not see it for the evil it truly was. More than ever, he craved the moment when he could carry out his holy mission. Now, all he could do was to wait for Esposito's signal, which would come at any moment.

One thing was certain: once the Sudarium was confirmed missing, this pyramid—Luxor Hotel—would not make it four thousand years like that one in Egypt.

CHAPTER 62

September 14. Thursday – 9:00 a.m. Oviedo, Spain

Start of the Feast of the Cross

The Prophet sat in the first pew, not far from the pulpit. He occasionally turned to scan the congregation behind him, monitoring for any extraordinary activity which might signify the American CIA's presence. One hint they were here, and he would have his admission of guilt. The text message to Esposito to proceed with the strike was already typed into his phone. All he needed was to witness the Sudarium's absence from the church, and he would hit the *send* button.

He looked at his watch and smiled. It was time for the archbishop to display the sacred cloth.

The archbishop slowly ambled to the altar. A weighty hush fell over the crowd. The Prophet found the sadness in the man's eyes to be very revealing.

He is about to break the disappointing news of the Sudarium's theft.

Archbishop Gustavo spoke with a firm voice in his native language. "Before we begin the Feast of the Cross and remove the Sudarium from the Arca Santa, I've been asked to perform a baptism on a very ill child. The child is not expected to live until his first birthday. I have consented to do this as requested by his mother, Maria Rodriguez."

The Prophet looked about suspiciously. This was most unusual and went against the normal liturgy.

"Will Maria Rodriguez please bring the child to the altar?"

Members of the congregation began to turn and look around the large cathedral, as no one seemed to be coming forward. Several long seconds passed, and he caught the increasing murmur of people seated in the pews behind. The Prophet turned to see a small blonde-haired woman slowly walking down the nave from the narthex. She had the child wrapped in a white blanket of some sort, and kept it pinned tightly to her chest. There was a lethargic expression on the young mother's face.

Something about this seemed wrong. The Church was probably stalling with this baptism. They were only delaying the inevitable.

The Prophet watched the woman closely as she passed, but was unable to see the baby which remained strangely silent, wound in a cocoon of material. Something was surely amiss. He placed his hand in his coat pocket and pulled his phone out discreetly, holding it by his side in the pew, ready to send the message.

Señora Rodriguez reached the altar and handed the child to the archbishop. He cradled the bundled baby in his arms and turned away from the congregation. The other priest walked up to the altar and addressed the congregation. "This will be a short baptism due to the child's extreme medical condition. Archbishop Gustavo will perform the baptism of the child at the chalice near the ambulatory. It will be a private ceremony between the Archbishop, Maria Rodriguez, and Baby Carlos. Please bear with us. The Feast of the Cross will start momentarily."

The priest escorted Maria Rodriguez around the altar, where she joined the Archbishop and the baby. They were partly obscured from view behind the altar and pulpit. The Prophet watched as the Archbishop drew back the blanket and touched the water to the baby's head, which was below his line of sight. Even though his microphone had been turned off, The Prophet could hear the Archbishop speak the Latin words of the ceremony. When he had finished, he crossed himself and blessed the baby and the mother. Señora Rodriguez said a few words, thanking him with a somber nod.

While the mother's emotional reactions seemed natural given the baby's terminal condition, The Prophet was growing ever skeptical of these proceedings. Nothing was following protocol. Not only had the infant remained quiet during the entire baptism, he had not been exposed once to the congregation.

The ceremony ended with the second priest leading Señora Rodriguez and Baby Carlos back around the pulpit. The small, teary-eyed woman walked up the nave, slowly passing by The Prophet. He craned his head as she went by, and for the first time he clearly saw the ashen facial features of the baby, who appeared to be sound asleep. Then the mother clutched the baby to her chest and began sobbing as she slumped, struggling to walk. One of the female parishioners rose from her seat and gave the grief-stricken woman a hand, leading her back to the narthex. The congregation remained silent, momentarily lost in the young woman's sorrow.

Suddenly, The Prophet's attention was drawn back to the Archbishop who stood behind the altar, turned to the Arca Santa and then back to the altar as if mired in a loop of indecision. He looked down sheepishly, and turned on his microphone. He seemed tired. "It is customary to begin the Feast of the Cross with the display of the venerable Sudarium, the cloth that covered our Lord and Savior, Jesus Christ, after His execution on the cross, where He died for our sins." His words were melancholy.

The Prophet regripped the cell phone, looking down to ensure he had his finger poised above the send button. *Here it comes*, he thought. *No more delays.*

The Archbishop moved before the open reliquary chest. He spun to face the congregation with a slow, deliberate turn. He offered a reluctant gaze.

Get on with it. Admit that it's gone!

"There are some who believe it to be a false relic. There are some who would bring harm to innocent people if it was ever taken from this holy sanctuary, but that is not Jesus' message. He taught unconditional love. He taught forgiveness. Through His tears and His blood, we can be absolved of our sins." The archbishop lifted the silver-coated box from the Arca Santa. There was a satisfying gasp from the congregation. He turned, brought the silver box to the altar, and placed it down with care.

*It can't be…*The Prophet thought. *It must be empty. He's still* *stalling.*

The Archbishop opened the box. With his elderly eyes firmly affixed inside the box, he reached in and withdrew an aged cloth, with its bloodstains and lymph. He carefully unfolded it and held it up for all to see.

There was a joint adulation from the audience which grew into rousing applause as people stood, crossing themselves in the presence of the hallowed relic that had once touched the dying face of Jesus Christ.

The Prophet inhaled deeply and looked around at the mass of people chattering and staring in awe at the Sudarium of Oviedo. He exhaled. There was a mystical aura about the cloth that The Prophet could not deny, and he found himself satisfied to see it was exactly where it should be.

He leaned down in the pew while the others continued to stand in praise. He quickly typed a new text message and hit send:

The Sudarium is safe. For now, abort the attacks.

We will fight against godless tyranny another day.

So Sayeth The Prophet.

****

Outside, Tiffany Bar reached her rental car. She quickly climbed in and laid the Baby Jesus from the diorama, still wrapped in her shawl, in the passenger seat. Archbishop Gustavo had been brilliant. He had obviously seen her standing in the narthex and guessed she had recovered the Sudarium by the way she clutched the shawl to her chest. He had then gotten the idea to call for a baptism as a means to get her to the altar. It had taken Bar a moment to realize *she* was "Maria Rodriguez" after she saw the Archbishop's penetrating stare in her direction. From there, it was a matter of simple deception. Once Bar had gone behind the altar, as the other priest briefly addressed the congregation, the archbishop switched the silver box with the diorama Baby Jesus from the thatched cradle. As Bar returned back up the aisle, she feigned grief of her pretend child's impending demise and even allowed the congregation to get a view of the baby's face, since she knew the terrorist or terrorists in the crowd might be suspicious. Lucky, it seemed no one had noticed the face was that of a doll. In the meantime, with the congregation's attention diverted to her, Archbishop Gustavo had time to move the boxed Sudarium from the cradle into the Arca Santa, keeping his back to the crowd and the box in front of him so as not to be seen by anyone. She stayed inside the atrium just long enough to witness the display of the Sudarium and hear the crowd's jubilant reaction.

Bar started the car and headed for the airport. She called Director Vakind to advise him the Sudarium had been safely returned. He, in turn, confirmed no attacks had transpired.

She breathed a huge sigh of relief and satisfaction, while at the same time wondering what had become of Samuel Tolen.

CHAPTER 63

September 14. Thursday – 10:00 a.m. Egypt

"The lid will be moved aside," Diaz said, "but you will not look inside it, Señor Tolen."

Jade watched Tolen's reaction. "What do you mean?" The CIA operative seemed indignant.

Diaz swept his hand to the side, motioning Tolen to move away from the coffin. When Tolen remained stationary, Diaz lifted the pistol and fired a round into the air. The gunshot echoed harshly in the chamber. Jade winced, and Diaz pushed her to the side against the wall. She nearly lost her grip on the second lantern.

"Move!" Diaz shouted at Tolen, aiming the gun at him. "I am getting tired of this, and I will not say it again!"

Begrudgingly, Tolen pulled away from the coffin and joined Jade across the way at the wall. Jade could see the disillusionment in Tolen's eyes.

Diaz smiled when he saw how it pained Samuel Tolen. "Only I will know the truth," Diaz declared, placing the lantern on the stone floor. "Now, do not move from the wall." The Spanish inspector circled to the side of the coffin to ensure the other two remained in his peripheral vision. For a moment, he stood looking stoically at the unmarked stone lid. Then, he placed both hands on the lid near the front, not far from where the cross rose up from the floor. In one hand, he held the gun awkwardly as he prepared to push. Diaz looked up at the cross. The hallowed fixture rose high into the air above him, and he seemed to regard it for a few seconds.

"Put the lantern on the shelf," Tolen whispered to Jade.

She gave him a furtive glance, but she did as she was asked and lifted it to the ledge.

"Be ready to grab onto the ledge," he whispered.

The statement confused her, but she did not want to risk drawing Diaz's attention, so she remained quiet.

Diaz was suddenly staring Jade in the eyes. At first, she thought he had overheard Tolen, but the look was not accusatory. Instead, there was deep confusion in his eyes. Jade realized he was unsure what he was doing. Diaz was a man whose faith was on a precipice.

Jade only returned a cold, petulant stare. If he was seeking a kindred spirit who would convince him that belief needs no proof, he was out of luck.

Diaz dropped his eyes. Without further delay, he dipped his knees and backed up a foot for leverage. Then, with a forceful heave, he slid the front end of the stone lid halfway across the coffin at an angle. Eagerly, he turned, grabbed the lantern from the floor, and raised it next to the coffin.

His expression was unreadable, as blank as any expression Jade had ever witnessed.

The floor began to quiver, and quickly escalated to a violent shake. Diaz looked around in panic and confusion.

"Jade, the ledge!" Tolen shouted.

She and Tolen turned at the same moment, just as Jade felt the floor give way beneath her feet. She grasped for the ledge, catching it with both hands, knocking a pair of sandals off the shelf. They grazed her head and then were gone. Her body stretched out, feet dangling in the air. She saw Tolen hanging onto the ledge beside her. Jade looked down and was mortified to see nothing but vast darkness. A wave of nausea shot through her. If not for Tolen's instruction to place the lantern on the ledge, they would have been consumed in the blackness.

There were a series of agonizing cries. She turned her body with great difficulty. The entire floor of the chamber had collapsed, falling to some unknown depth. The coffin was gone, but the cross was standing tall, embedded in the last remaining cube of stone floor. On it, Pascal Diaz clung near the base, bear hugging the thick shaft of tree, screaming deliriously. He was slowly scaling the cross, trying to get high enough to reach the ledge several feet away. His clothes were tattered. His hands, face, and chest were bloodied, torn apart by vicious splinters of wood as he gripped each new hold, dragging himself up an inch at a time.

"Get on the ledge, Jade," Tolen said in a strained voice, suspended beside her.

Her arm muscles ached almost beyond human endurance, and she used every bit of strength she had left to lift her svelte body to the thin ledge, knocking clothes and other items off to make room for her feet. She could barely keep her balance. Jade tried to reach down and give Tolen a hand, but in doing so, she nearly lost her balance.

"No," Tolen said. He swallowed hard, sweat pouring off his face. "There's not enough room for me there. Look for the Christian Fish on the wall. Hurry."

"AHHHH! God have mercy!"

The scream by Pascal Diaz was inhuman. Jade saw that the man had almost reached the level of the shelf and was stretching a bloodied hand toward it. Even when he found a grasp, he seemed slow to pull himself up and toward it. Then, in horror, Jade realized the man had literally impaled himself as he had shimmied up the rough wood. Massive wooden splinters jutted into his face, through his neck, and into his body at almost every angle. One arm was so riddled with sharp, wooden spikes, it was as if it was nailed in place.

Jade looked back down at Tolen, clutching his arm, trying to stop him from falling as he fought to hang on.

"God, NO!" Diaz's feral yell echoed down the seemingly infinite, deep shaft below them. There was a torturous groan of stone, followed by a voluminous crack of wood. A second, louder crack caused Jade to look up. The massive cross began to lean, as the top fell in slow motion. Diaz frantically tried to tear his body free from the trunk of wood, stripping off more ragged clothes in the process. His skin was now more blood than flesh, and he wiggled like electricity was flowing through his body. Saliva and bile launched from his mouth. He turned his head toward Jade and Tolen even as the cross continued to tumble over. His splinter-covered face caused Jade to grimace. At that moment, the cross toppled over completely, the tip driving downward. The end, where Pascal Diaz's body was affixed, disappeared last as he gave one final howl of excruciating pain before disappearing in the darkness. His shrieks of anguish faded into nothingness, and the abyss swallowed up Inspector Pascal Diaz without remorse.

Jade turned back to Tolen. He grimaced, squeezing his eyes shut, trying to hold on.

"Jade," he whispered hoarsely as if expelling the last of his energy. "Ixthus…"

"The Fish?" She looked to the wall. It was right in front of her: the same image from the Costa Rican sphere in Boston. "What do I do?" she turned to Tolen desperately. "Tell me what to do?"

Tolen couldn't speak. His fingers had turned pale from the strain of his weight. He was starting to slip.

Jade looked around. *Ixthus…The Christian Fish….* she thought desperately. *Wait…it started our journey. Does it also end it?*

Jade looked on the wall around the image. There appeared to be no cutout where a door might retract. She began clearing off more of the cloth material, clothing, and sandals on the ledge. Suddenly, her hand found a solid object underneath a roll of material. She quickly shoved aside the items and saw a stone handle in the crux of the shelf and wall.

Please God, she prayed. Jade gave the handle a swift yank, nearly losing her balance on the narrow ledge.

To her side, a limestone block swiveled outward at one edge. A broad beam of sunlight shot into the chamber. She felt her spirits leap. "Hold on, Samuel," she urged him. Jade quickly scooted her body out through the opening, feet first, with her torso still on the ledge, aimed face down. She grabbed a hold of Tolen's arms. "You've got to help me pull you up," she said breathlessly. "I'm not strong enough to lift you."

Samuel Tolen was unresponsive. Exhaustion had set in. He was holding on by sheer will alone.

"Samuel!" she screamed. "Don't do this to me. Don't leave me."

Samuel Tolen raised his head and tried to hoist himself up, but faltered, nearly letting go as he fell back, arms extended with less of a grip on the stone ledge now.

"You can do this," she urged, fighting back the tears, struggling to keep a grasp on his arms. She bit her lip so hard, it began to bleed.

Again he looked up at her, sweat streaming down the sides of his cheeks.

She gazed into his deep blue eyes and saw they were clouded with his fatigue. He was on the verge of giving up.

"You can't quit! I need you!" she pleaded, tears welling in her eyes, a single drop rolling down her face.

For a moment, he remained motionless, and she feared he had lost the will to live. Then, as if moving in slow motion, he lifted a weary hand and grabbed onto Jade's shoulder. The ache of his grip was intense, but Jade refused to show any pain. He placed his other hand on her other shoulder. As if drawing on the last store of his waning reserves, he raised himself up, sliding his body up hers, inch by inch, grunting. With Herculean effort, he was able to get his chest onto the ledge, where he rested, nearly hyperventilating. Then, using his feet, he found a purchase on the ledge and lifted with a grimace, his arm muscles tied in thick, tortured knots, until he spilled next to Jade and collapsed.

He lay on the shelf, reaching halfway outside through the opening. Jade struggled to rouse herself from her own exhaustion and backed through the opening, squinting in the bright sunlight. She turned and helped drag Tolen outside. The two lay on one of the massive limestone blocks next to the opening. They were facing each other, and she opened her eyes to see him staring at her. She only had enough energy to offer a feeble smile as they both labored to catch their breath.

In a silent few minutes, they pushed up, sitting with their legs hanging off the edge, their breathing finally returning to normal. As they did, a scraping noise drew their attention behind them. They turned to see the limestone block swing back into place as if it had never been opened.

The pyramid was once again sealed.

Tolen turned to Jade. "Thank you," he said, still breathing heavily. His face was filthy and sweaty, his clothes tattered and grungy, his arms cut and bleeding in a dozen places.

Jade looked out over the plateau. The desert reached into the distance. To the side, the two larger pyramids stood in defiance of time. Tiny figures—tourists—were milling about below. Oddly, no one seemed to notice the two people who had just exited from the top of the Pyramid of Menkaure. The sunlight was hot, uncomfortably hot, even at this early morning hour, yet she smiled wanly. "You can buy me dinner, sir…after you clean up…actually, after we've both cleaned up." She paused. "By the way," she said between deep breaths, "how did you know the floor was going to fall when Diaz opened the coffin?"

"I didn't exactly," Tolen said, using his ragged shirt to wipe the perspiration from his face. "I knew something would happen. Remember the text, *'Only the man who has patience, is meager, and holds faith will arrive safely?'* Well, we were down to 'holds faith.' I assumed it meant the coffin was not to be opened. Anyone who *holds faith* wouldn't need to see if Jesus' body was inside. They would know it was not."

"You goaded him into doing it. You made him think you wanted to open it, when you really wanted him to push the lid aside."

"Do you think *He* was in there?" Jade asked, laying a gentle hand on Tolen's shoulder.

There was a long silence. "I think we'll never know. We'll also never know what laboratory results Aaron Conin discovered after running tests on the thread samples from the Sudarium. Whatever it was, Diaz was convinced he had proof of life after death. It makes you wonder what could possibly have been so conclusive."

Minutes later, they made their way slowly down the towering pyramid, cautiously traversing the large limestone blocks. When they reached the bottom, they were met by Egyptian soldiers carrying automatic weapons.

"Samuel Tolen?" a sergeant asked in English.

Tolen nodded his weary head. He had no fight left in him.

"We have orders to take you both into custody. Oh, and your president sent a message via our president. President Fane wanted you to know that 'it was returned in time,' whatever that means."

Tolen and Jade looked at each other and smiled. Then they were placed in handcuffs and led away.

****

At the local police station, Tolen and Jade were forced to change into prison uniforms. Several hours later, Vakind, working through the State Department and the British Embassy, freed Samuel Tolen and Dr. Jade Mollur. They were given fresh clothes. By mid afternoon, the two were on a plane to Washington, DC.

They both slept the entire way.

CHAPTER 64

September 18. Tuesday – 7:09 p.m. Washington, DC

Tolen hung up the phone. "I apologize, but that was Vakind. The FBI field office in Los Angeles has arrested an Italian named Nico Esposito in Keene, California. He was heading up the planned Las Vegas attacks by the Flagellants. All of the explosives were recovered in an old church in the valley. It seems Mr. Esposito is already positioning his legal defense, claiming to be the second coming of Christ and promising vengeance and retribution."

"Another one?" Dr. Jade Mollur smiled at him. She was sitting across the table in an elegant blue dress. The restaurant was bustling with patrons, yet Tolen had arranged for a quiet, secluded corner table. Her smile faded somewhat. "Samuel, do you really think Kappel and Diaz found evidence of life after death?"

"I don't know," Tolen shook his head. "Diaz believed he had proof in the white blood cells taken from the Sudarium. We may never know how or if Conin actually accomplished the feat of reconstituting the blood. When Diaz's apartment was searched, nothing of Boyd Ramsey's was found: no PC, no notes. If Conin solved the process using Ramsey's procedural directions, which still seems impossible, it may be years before someone is able to replicate it."

"You took a hell of a risk sending Tiffany Bar to Oviedo like that. You must have been certain she'd find the Sudarium."

"Bar came through. She had the advantage of her proficiency with the language which allowed her to blend in seamlessly. She was really the only logical choice; just as I was the only logical choice to come after you."

"Logic," Jade smiled. "A big part of your life hinges on logic, doesn't it?"

"Oh, I don't know," he smiled, taking a sip of his merlot. "I can be impetuous at times."

"I may make you prove it later," she gave him a beguiling smile.

Samuel Tolen thought he could get used to the look.

"Those three places we discovered, it's still mindboggling," Jade said, changing the subject. "As soon as I can, I'm going to go after funding to return to all three locations."

"Each will be wrought with physical challenges and politics. Costa Rica, Greece, and Egypt will be wary of allowing a foreigner complete access to these sites again, and considering most of the Costa Rican and Greek sites are now under water, I hope you scuba dive. Egypt will be far easier. You just have to dig through the miles of sand which caved into the main tunnel or find the one limestone block which swung out and make it happen again."

She sighed. "Okay, Mr. Tolen, I get your point. Nevertheless, I'm going to try. Want to join me?"

"Of course," he said, "but for now, you'll have to excuse me while I use the restroom." He stood, walked past a cluster of tables filled with patrons, and pushed through the restroom door.

He felt a jolt of pain to his head, and everything went black.

****

Samuel Tolen awoke in the back of a chauffeur-driven limousine. It took a moment for his head to clear. The last thing he remembered, he had gone to the restroom at the restaurant where he and Jade were having dinner in Washington, DC. Now, he was wearing a heavy winter coat.

He sat up as the driver, separated from him by a thick wall of Plexiglas, dutifully turned into a long drive and approached a small guardhouse. Tolen was startled when he realized where he was: at the gated entry of Simon Anat's estate.

He had no idea how he had gotten to Switzerland. Concerned, he felt for his gun and found an empty holster.

What the hell is going on?

At the guardhouse, the security guard with the crooked nose never said a word as he waved the long vehicle through. Through thick-tinted windows, he could see the guard scowling as the vehicle slowly rolled past.

At the top of the winding driveway, the limousine came to a halt. Tolen exited the vehicle and strolled toward the doorway of the mansion. It was a cold morning, and the sun had barely risen over the horizon. A swirling wind whipped across the grounds and penetrated the sheltered portico. Tolen drew his coat around him. As he reached the tiled entryway, he detected a faint smell of wood burning, probably from a fireplace somewhere deep inside the massive dwelling.

It was obvious that Simon Anat was anxious to speak with him in private, and he saw no reason to deny the man. His curiosity had gotten the better of him. Tolen knew he owed the man nothing. In fact, he felt utter contempt for what Anat had done. Many people had died as a direct result of the man's irresponsible actions. It had been his motivation of wealth which had fueled the murderous activities of others, and yet Anat had remained unscathed, easily washing his hands of any wrongdoing. Nothing legally could be tied to him, even though he was as guilty as if he had personally committed the atrocious acts of violence. The thought of Reba Zee's death angered Tolen as much as it had the day he discovered her body aboard the plane on the Isle of Patmos. This was probably the reason why Anat chose to disarm him, fearful he might try and exact some revenge.

Tolen's thoughts filled with the recent events. Dr. Jade Mollur had decided to remain in DC to assist with the lengthy report detailing their activities. With her help, they were able to tie up international protocols and put the paperwork to bed. Then the president had honored Tolen with dinner at the White House, which included a multitude of praise and thanks. This time, Tiffany Bar had accompanied him. President Fane was well aware of Bar's role in securing the safe return of the Sudarium. Then, just last night, or whenever it was he had been abducted, he and Jade had gone out for a romantic dinner. It was their first date. He had picked her up at her hotel room, and they had embraced in a passionate kiss even before leaving. Tolen could still see her standing there, her slender figure accentuated by her short blue dress, flashing her dazzling hazel eyes as she brushed her dark bangs aside with a warm smile. Her skin had been soft, her embrace exciting. She wore the same perfume, giving off the same alluring aroma, as the first time he met her at the jail in Morristown, New Jersey. He could no longer deny he felt something for her that he had not felt with a woman in a long time. He only hoped she had been left out of whatever game Anat was up to now.

The front door of the estate swung wide, and a rotund bald man in a light-colored suit waved Tolen inside. Instead of leading him down the long hallway and into the wine cellar as Kappel had done before, this time Tolen followed his portly escort up a spiral marble staircase with a polished mahogany banister. The clicking of their shoes echoed in the vaulted area. The smell of roasted fowl rose up through the mansion.

The steps emptied into a lengthy, carpeted hallway. The well-tailored escort, who had neither introduced himself nor said the first word, turned smartly on his heels and returned quickly down the staircase, leaving Tolen standing before a steel door. A security camera at the ceiling aimed down, panning slowly from side to side. Tolen heard an electronic hum and a buzz, then a sharp click. The steel door opened inward.

Tolen stepped inside. The visage took him by complete surprise. He was at one end of an excessively long, wide white corridor with a high, barrel-vaulted ceiling. Occasionally, columns rose up on either wall and arched against the ceiling forming a series of fused sections. The entire area was exceedingly well lit, and the temperature was several degrees cooler than the hallway. Paintings hung in rows on both sides, spanning into the distance. An instant familiarity registered, but it took Tolen a moment to recognize the place.

He was standing in the Grand Gallery in the Louvre, or rather it was an exquisite facsimile of the original, masterfully crafted in every detail. It fact, it was such a perfect replica, if Tolen had not known he was inside Simon Anat's estate in Switzerland, he would have thought he was standing inside the great structure in Paris.

Despite all its glitz and elegance, there was one noticeable difference from the original museum: the artwork. Where the Louvre contained such treasured artworks as Alexandros of Antioch's sculpture, *Venus de Milo*, and Leonardo da Vinci's *Mona Lisa*, Anat's gallery contained different, but equally magnificent, artwork. Tolen approached the first painting on the left wall. The colorful scene depicted two children playing in the middle of a sun-drenched wheat field. He was amazed, although not completely surprised, to recognize the signature of Giotto de Bondone, the famous Italian Renaissance painter. He had no doubt the painting was an original.

He looked further down the gallery and saw statues in the center of the corridor by such masters as Raphael and Donatello. Again, he was certain they were originals. He walked a dozen feet across the inlaid wooden floor to the other wall where a second painting took his breath away. He immediately recognized the picture: Raphael's *Portrait of a Young Man*.

Like the rest of the world, he had only seen pictures and reproductions of the original. The last time the masterpiece had been seen was in 1945. It seemed the rumors were true of Anat's acquisition of the stolen artwork by the Third Reich in the 1940s. Tolen stared in awe. It was hard to fathom he was looking at a piece of lost history valued at over $100 million.

His attention was pulled from the painting by the clattering of shoes across the wooden floor. He looked down the gallery to see Simon Anat, dressed meticulously in a Kiton suit, approaching. At his side was a second man with crew-cut gray hair, also wearing an expensive suit. Surprisingly, Tolen recognized the man as 74-year-old Walter Ganhaden. Ganhaden's net worth of $52 billion nearly doubled Anat's, landing the British real estate investor as the second richest man in the world. To Anat's other side was a well-proportioned woman in her late sixties, who moved gracefully. She sported short gray hair, a dark complexion, and green eyes set within a face which had obviously seen a few surgical tucks. She was none other than Shauna Veers, cosmetics billionaire from Brazil. He could not recall her standing among the wealthiest people, but he was certain she also ranked in the top ten.

Tolen felt an unsettling bewilderment as the threesome approached.

"So glad you could make it," Anat said with a smile. Oddly, he seemed surprisingly healthy.

"Anat, you didn't give me a choice," Tolen acknowledged somewhat begrudgingly. "What happened to Jade Mollur?"

"What happened?" Anat seemed surprised. "I'm not a barbarian, Mr. Tolen. We never touched Dr. Mollur, although she may be annoyed with the way you abandoned her in the restaurant." A fleeting grin passed over the man's face.

Tolen turned to Ms. Veers and took her proffered hand. "Ms. Veers, my name is Samuel Tolen."

Veers seemed to regard Tolen with a small amount of fascination. He sensed she was fixated on his blue eyes. "I see you know who I am. The pleasure is mine," the woman responded.

"Mr. Ganhaden," he continued, turning toward the other man.

Ganhaden stuck a lively hand in Tolen's and shook it vigorously. "Mr. Tolen. We've been anxiously awaiting your arrival."

"Anxiously?" Tolen nodded with a quizzical look, still a bit off balance with the situation. He felt like a pauper in a room of the rich and famous.

"What do you think?" Anat said, spreading his hands as if displaying the entire long room in one sweeping motion. "I have to admit, you're one of very few people we've ever permitted in this room."

"We?" Tolen remarked.

"This gallery holds our mutual collections," Ganhaden said. The man spoke with a crisp British accent, similar to Jade's yet different, with a strained proper intonation hinting at his elevated status.

"I expected to find you in the wine cellar," Tolen remarked turning back to Anat, "in environmental conditions which would benefit your health."

Anat laughed heartily. "Yes, I must apologize for all that showmanship. We were in the heart of the drama, and I couldn't resist playing the part for you."

"He's quite the actor," Veers added. Her Portuguese accent had been all but shed in the years residing in New York City.

A moment of confusion passed through Tolen before he finally grasped Anat's meaning. "You're not dying."

"Well, certainly some day," Anat mused.

Ganhaden's face broke into a smile. "Our fate is inevitable, Mr. Tolen. It's the one thing money can't change."

"But no," Anat continued, "I'm as healthy as any man you know."

"Then why? Why make the offer?" Tolen asked, his mind suddenly spinning with questions.

"Let's take a walk, Mr. Tolen, shall we?" Anat said, turning. Ganhaden and Veers did likewise, and Tolen strolled slowly beside the group as they proceeded up the gallery.

After a few seconds of silence, Anat began, "I've know Mr. Ganhaden and Ms. Veers for some time, and when we merged our private art collections here at the estate several years ago, we realized we had similar tastes for life's experiences."

"You didn't bring me here to show off your wares," Tolen said, feeling a renewed sense of contempt for the man.

"Quite," Anat responded, appraising Tolen as they moved. There was another moment of silence. "You won't appreciate this, Mr. Tolen, but simply put, we struggle to find new ways to... enjoy life. Call it eccentricity or whatever you like, but as some of the world's wealthiest people, we are constantly looking for new stimulations in which to indulge ourselves. Last year, the three of us sat down over dinner and discussed this very topic. We jokingly considered ideas to appease our carnal urges for excitement." Anat paused briefly as if distracted. Then he pointed to the right wall at a painting of a woman's face. "That's a Monet. See the swirling brush marks? It's one of my favorites."

Ganhaden continued Anat's thought. "Mr. Anat, Ms. Veers, and I formed a pact; a partnership to see who could come up with the most novel and creative way to amuse ourselves. We needed something unique to satisfy our thirst for adventure. We came up with the usual lists of activities: swimming with sharks, skydiving, running with the bulls, et cetera, but these were all too mundane, and frankly, a bit more than I care to try physically at 74 years of age."

This conversation had taken an unexpected twist, and Tolen found himself baffled by where it was going.

Anat picked up on the thread of the conversation. "Ultimately, we decided to do what we do best. We leveraged the one thing we had, and which most people in the world didn't."

"Money," Tolen said.

"Yes, money, Mr. Tolen," Anat said with a smirk. "We got the idea when a mutual acquaintance of ours passed away from a lingering illness. We thought, 'what if we offered a fortune to anyone who could prove the existence of life after death?' Would so-called professionals and scientists in varying fields of discipline be willing to take such an obscene challenge? Frankly, we had our reservations whether anyone would undertake the challenge, but as it turns out, mankind is as greedy as it appears. As daunting...no make that, as impossible...as the assignment we laid out was, over one hundred people took the bait. Can you believe it? Those idiots were so blinded by greed they failed to recognize the implausibility of our request. Life after death...what arrogance would lead someone to think they could substantiate such a concept? They would stand a better chance of discovering alien life or the existence of Nessie in the Scottish loch."

"Yet it was this insatiable greed," Ganhaden said, "that started a truly magnificent show. With Mr. Anat playing the role of the terminally ill billionaire desperate for knowledge of his continued existence after death, we gathered the masses, made the offer, and sat back to watch the events unfold."

The reality struck Tolen. "It was all nothing more than a game?"

"The term 'game' is somewhat roguish," Veers added with a high-pitched chuckle. "No one else could have pulled it off." Her tone was flippant.

"Obviously, Kappel had no knowledge of the charade," Tolen said as they continued their slow pace down the gallery. He could feel his anger stirring.

"Correct," Anat replied. "Like the others, he thought I was dying and believed the reward to be real. Kappel was in the perfect position. I had tasked him with monitoring the activities of the potential claimants. They were to check in with him as to their progress. His strategic alliance with Pascal Diaz was most surprising and, frankly, brilliant. In retrospect, it was one outcome we never saw coming. In many ways, it made the experience that much more intriguing. Pity to lose such good help, though."

Tolen considered the circular scars on the back of Kappel's hand which appeared to be the result of someone snuffing out a burning cigar: a clear sign of Anat's abuse. The two men had obviously felt no love loss toward each other. Tolen stopped and turned toward the three. "Do you take no moral accountability for what you've done?"

"What we did, my good man, was not illegal. We had no control over the ripple effect," Ganhaden added.

"What transpired surprised even us, Mr. Tolen," Veers added with a salacious smile.

Tolen's rage flared. "You stoked the fire of man's most deep-seated desire, and preyed upon the participants' greed. You offered the reward knowing full well what the ramifications could be. People would do anything to earn billions of dollars, including cold-blooded murder." He could visualize Reba Zee lying on the airplane cabin floor, sprawled in a puddle of her own blood. Tolen had discovered only after the fact that, besides the known deaths, many others had died in the pursuit of the prize. A physician in Amsterdam had his assistant purposely stop his heart so he could experience death. Unfortunately, the process went too long, and the doctor died. Another man attempted a form of transcendental fasting in the snow-covered Alps in order to obtain "spiritual oneness" and film the spirits which would appear around him. He froze to death with the video camera still in his hand. An occultist-turned-astronaut in China launched himself aboard a private rocket in hopes of filming heaven, which he believed to be masked just beyond the dark side of the moon. Other reports continued to roll in. To date, the CIA had associated 19 deaths with Anat's offer; rational people driven to irrational behavior for an outlandish monetary reward.

"Nevertheless, the legal system doesn't see it that way," Anat said sternly.

"So you flew me here to brag about your efforts? Why? What makes you think I won't kill you?"

"We did our research, Mr. Tolen," Veers said. "You're a prudent man who is not prone to excessive threats or unrestrained acts of aggression. Still, we temporarily took your weapon in case insanity set in."

"And just in case you still feel the need for violence," Ganhaden added, "Mr. Anat has a plethora of video cameras filming us at this very moment, some with very tight shots. Your career would be over, not to mention the fact that killing three billionaires would certainly land you in one of our finer European jails. Also, there are five heavily armed men waiting outside the steel door who will enter this room on a moment's notice."

"I bet Interpol would be very interested in your art collection. I'm sure the Hungarian government would not take too kindly that you have some of their most prized possessions," Tolen threatened.

Anat smiled stiffly. "You and I both know I have authorities in my pocket. With one phone call, I could throw up a wall of red tape which would prevent any search and seizure for months. By then, all Interpol would find is an ornate hallway with reproductions of paintings from the Louvre, but they'd never find a single original masterpiece. I've been doing this far too long, Mr. Tolen, not to have thought of every contingency."

Tolen knew Anat was right. They stopped in the middle of the corridor, and Tolen faced the three billionaires. "Then why am I here?"

Anat was the one who replied. "As I mentioned, Pascal Diaz made a claim that he had met our challenge."

"By the way, do you have any idea where the good Mr. Diaz is these days?" Ganhaden asked in a jovial tone.

Tolen glared at the man without responding.

"It's not important," Anat said dismissively, "but what is important is the information Pascal Diaz had in his possession. You see, he had contacted me in late August with a fascinating, if not fictitious, claim. He said he had a report based on an analysis of white blood cells reconstituted from the dried blood on the

Sudarium. Now, I have a minor in biology, Mr. Tolen, and I seem to recall that, once a white blood cell has dried, it dies, and no useful data can be gleaned from it. This would be especially true of the type of data required to substantiate Diaz's assertion that he could prove the divinity of Jesus Christ and therefore prove His teachings of heaven and an afterlife were true. At the time, I thought the man was crazy; just another religious zealot. I told him I wouldn't accept any of his information unless he could prove to me that he could reconstitute the white blood cells, which, of course, he was unable to do." He paused. Tolen suddenly felt an inward satisfaction growing.

"While I never examined the report in detail," Anat continued, "and Diaz took the only copy, I must confess, I've grown more and more curious about his claim."

It was Ms. Veers' turn to speak. "We're intrigued by the data Mr. Diaz possessed, and frankly, we believe you were made privy to this so-called proof."

"Surely, you understand our fascination," Ganhaden said, wiping his brow with a handkerchief. "My good man, we're willing to pay handsomely for the report, even given the ludicrousness of Diaz's claim."

"Pascal Diaz still has the report. Good luck finding him," Tolen said, turning away and heading back toward the door.

"We don't take this knowledge lightly," Anat called to him. "Every piece of artwork in here is yours if you provide the information we're asking for. This collection is valued at over six billion American dollars."

Tolen continued walking.

"I'll throw in the estate, too," Anat shouted as Tolen moved further away.

"And Mr. Ganhaden and I will each throw in an additional $5 billion," Shauna Veers said in a high voice with growing desperation.

Tolen paused and slowly turned. He looked to the threesome, each wearing an expression of twisted anticipation, waiting for him to succumb to their gluttonous offer of wealth. No longer were the three billionaires jovial, bantering with him in witty repartee.

They had become stoic, and desperation etched their faces. It was remarkable how the tables had suddenly turned. He now held the advantage.

Tolen looked around at the artwork, up at the ornate arched ceiling, and down the long hallway, as if appraising it all and taking in the grandeur. It was an exquisite collection. No, it was more than that. It was the most fantastic collection he had ever witnessed outside of the Louvre. He could not begin to fathom the history and prestige of the assembled artwork spread before him.

Tolen could hear his father's words: *Material things don't make the man. It's his actions that forever define him.*

"Sorry, lady and gentlemen. As you so aptly put it, the proof you seek is impossible to quantify. Your combined fortunes could not buy knowledge which was never meant for mankind. You'll just have to wait and see like the rest of us." He turned and continued toward the door.

"You're lying!" Anat screamed. "Pascal Diaz had the proof. Where is he? What did you do with the lab report?"

Tolen spun, locking on Anat. "Do you know about my father?"

"Yes," Anat said. "Jasper Tolen is lying in a coma in Florida. My sources tell me the man has a living will with a DNR stipulation, yet you haven't carried out his wishes. It appears you're struggling to let him go."

Tolen felt a clawing sadness. "That's right." He paused. "Don't you think if I had this proof you're asking for that I would let go? I would free the man's soul." Tolen lowered his voice, speaking slowly. "The proof you seek does not exist, and it never will."

With that, he turned. He reached the door, but it remained shut before him. In a moment, there was a buzz, a click, and it slowly swung open. Five armed men stood at the door blocking his way. Tolen turned and looked at Anat, Veers, and Ganhaden as they approached. They stopped when they reached him.

Anat started to say something, but hesitated. He waved a hand at the armed men, and they separated, allowing Tolen to pass. "My driver will return you to the airport. You're booked on the next flight back to DC. I believe Dr. Mollur will be happy to discover you're okay."

Tolen made his way down the spiraling staircase. He never looked back.

****

In the limousine, Samuel Tolen watched the last of Simon Anat's estate recede in the distance.

Much had transpired during the five days when he had teamed with Dr. Jade Mollur and Inspector Diaz and traveled the globe in search of the cache of Jesus' earthly objects and the Sudarium. It was an assignment he would never forget for both its triumphs and failures, when his own personal agenda had nearly undermined their success. Ultimately, it had turned out to be a sojourn of both duty and enlightenment.

Nothing would ease the pain of Reba Zee's death or the deaths of all the innocent people caught up in the deadly game orchestrated by the three billionaires, but Tolen was now able to take some solace in the fact that, with all their collective money, they could not obtain the one thing they craved.

For himself, he no longer needed the proof.

Now, in the back of the limousine approaching Zurich International Airport, Tolen considered Anat's comment about his father.

You haven't carried out his wishes. It appears you're struggling to let him go.

Tolen drew in a deep breath and exhaled.

The limousine pulled into the unloading area, and Tolen climbed out. The driver rolled down the window and held out a boarding pass to a flight destined for Washington, DC. He never said a word. Tolen took the ticket and proceeded inside the airport. Tolen glanced at the security area where passengers were congregated, slowly passing through into the concourse. Then he looked to the ticketing counter at the other end.

For whatever reason, at that moment, Samuel Tolen vividly recalled something his father had said to him in the dream as they were in the boat fishing. *"I've got to go, now. It's been time for me to go."*

Tolen moved to the ticketing counter. After standing in line a few minutes, he presented his boarding pass to the airline agent at the counter. "I'd like to exchange this for a ticket to Jacksonville, Florida, U.S.A."

EPILOGUE

September 19. Wednesday – 5:09 p.m. Cairo, Egypt

The following day, Egyptian First Lieutenant Ishaq el Sha'er was called down to the basement in the evidence collection area at the police station in Cairo. It was the end of his shift, and he was ready to go home, so he hoped to conduct whatever business was necessary and be on his way.

Manu Bustaniq, the warrant officer in charge of evidence collection, was waiting for him at the counter. "What do you want me to do with these?" Bustaniq said, holding up two large, opaque, sealed plastic bags.

To el Sha'er, they looked like two pillows. "What are they?"

"The clothes of the man and woman you arrested on the Giza Plateau last Friday morning: the American and the British woman. The major general had us give them fresh clothes."

"They were not charged with any crime. Have them burned."

"Yes, sir, but I would like to point out one thing," Bustaniq said, pulling apart the seal on one of the bags. He removed a pair of dark pants. He pointed to the cuff of one pant leg. "Were you aware of this?"

At first, he saw nothing but dark material. El Sha'er leaned in to take a closer look. Then he saw a single, wet drop. "It's some kind of fluid."

"I'm not sure, but I believe it's blood," Bustaniq said, a conspiratorial gleam in his eye. "It stayed fresh inside the sealed bag. Maybe we let the American go too quickly."

"There's not much we can do now," el Sha'er commented.

GARY WILLIAMS AND VICKY KNERLY

"Still, reseal the bag to keep it fresh and send it to Mr. Pakhom. I'd like to know if it is blood and who it may have belonged to."

****

Three days later, el Sha'er walked into the Yousev Laboratory. It was a private facility which performed forensic tests for the Cairo police.

"First Lieutenant el Sha'er, it is a pleasure to see you again," Mr. Pakhom, the chief technician, greeted him and led him to his office, closing the door behind them.

"Likewise, although I have to admit, I am a bit confused. I received a message to come here but received no clarification why."

"Please, have a seat," Pakhom pointed to a nearby chair as he took a seat at his desk. "It's in regard to the blood sample on the pants leg your warrant officer brought us several days ago. Was this evidence for an active case?" Pakhom's brow furrowed.

"Actually, no," el Sha'er saw no further need to elaborate.

"Ah, very good, very good. It had me worried," Pakhom nodded.

The man was acting most unusual. "Is there a problem with the sample?"

"Well, yes, it's been contaminated."

"Who contaminated it?"

"Ah, now *that* I have no idea," Pakhom chuckled. It was an uncomfortable laugh. "It was tampered with before it was delivered to our laboratory."

"What are you talking about?" el Sha'er felt ballooning frustration. "Tampered with in what way?"

"Please," Pakhom motioned with his hand toward a report on the desktop. He picked it up. "I believe someone is playing a joke on the police department, although I must confess, I don't know how they did it."

"Mr. Pakhom," el Sha'er said firmly. He was hovering on the edge of anger. "Tell me exactly what you're talking about."

"Well," Pakhom started, somewhat nervously, "the blood is most definitely human. It appears to have splattered on the man's

386

pant leg, but when we analyzed the chromosomes from the white blood cells, they are…wrong. There's no other way to describe it."

"How is it *wrong?*"

Pakhom continued. "It's an impossible, inconceivable combination. I personally ran the test four times to confirm the results." Pakhom was waving his hands in the air to exemplify his mystification. His breathing had become erratic and audible.

What is wrong with this man? el Sha'er thought. "I have no more time for games, Mr. Pakhom. Explain."

Pakhom drew in a deep breath and exhaled slowly. "Okay, I shall do my best. Are you familiar with human chromosomes?"

"Familiar, yes. An expert, no."

Pakhom sifted through the report until he found the information he was looking for as if to confirm the data one last time before saying it aloud. "Every human gene has 46 chromosomes: 23 from the mother and 23 from the father. The 23 from the mother are composed of 22 autosomes and an "X" sex chromosome. Likewise, the father gives each of us 22 autosomes and either an "X" or "Y" sex chromosome. With the mother's "X" chromosome, and depending on which chromosome is donated by the father, the result is a combination of either XX, which makes a person female, or XY, which makes them male. This is a fact. There can be no deviations."

This man is teaching me grade school biology, el Sha'er thought as he felt his frustration building again. "Get to the point."

"Well," Pakhom swallowed hard, "the white blood cells in this sample had a total of 24 chromosomes instead of 46. It included the usual 23 that came from the mother's side and then a "Y" sex chromosome. This "Y" sex chromosome resulted in the person being male, but because it lacked the other 22 autosomes, it suggests the man whose blood is on that pant leg was fathered from a source *other than a human male*. Or," Pakhom chuckled awkwardly, "*wasn't fathered at all*. Neither case, of course, is possible."

After Pakhom finished, el Sha'er nodded slowly and stood. "Now I understand. The sample is corrupt. You may dispose of it, Mr. Pakhom."

AUTHORS' NOTE'S

<u>The truth?</u>

While this is a work of fiction, many elements of the story—history, mysteries, and locations—are accurate. Here is a summation of the facts:

According to the Bible, Joseph of Arimathea, the man who gave up his newly built family tomb to house Christ's body after the resurrection, was a metals dealer and is thought by some scholars to have traveled a great distance from Israel. Some suggest he went as far as South America to trade his wares.

The Costa Rican stone spheres are as described in the story, with most located in and around the town of Palmar Sur. Since stone cannot be carbon dated, their origin is unknown. Some suggest they were made around 800 AD, but it is also possible they date back to the first century or earlier. The stones were carved from indigenous rock—which is not a mystery—but there is no record why they were created or why they continued to be carved by the native Costa Ricans over the centuries. There are currently two spheres on display in the U.S. as depicted in the story: at the Museum of the National Geographic Society in Washington, DC, and in the courtyard on the Harvard University campus near the Peabody Museum of Archaeology and Ethnography.

The Sudarium of Oviedo is a revered religious artifact residing in the Cathedral of San Salvador in a special room called the Cámara Santa, as described. The cloth is kept inside the Arca Santa, a reliquary chest, and only brought out for display three times a year: Good Friday, the beginning of the Feast of the

Cross on September 14th, and the end of the Feast of the Cross on September 21st. There is blood and lymph dried into the fabric. It has undergone analysis and testing, as has the Shroud of Turin, although the results have not always been released to the public. Both cloths contain blood type AB positive, a rare type, applicable to only five percent of the world's population.

The "Formacion Descartes Santa Elena" is a natural land formation on the coastline of Costa Rica on the Pacific Ocean side. It is within the Parque Nacional Santa Rosa (Santa Rosa National Park). The authors are unaware whether it leads to a recess or cave.

Reference to Jesus Christ is excluded in the tomes of most well-known historians during the first century, even those who lived in and around Israel. The most famous historian at that time, Flavius Josephus, does indeed mention Him in *Antiquities of the Jews* as a teacher who attracted a mass following and was revered after death, but the authenticity of an additional passage summarizing Christ's ministry and death by crucifixion has been questioned by scholars since the 17th century. The writing is a stark departure from Josephus' text, with words and phrases characteristic of the Christian style. Many scholars believe the text was inserted into Josephus' work hundreds of years after his death.

The Petra on the Greek Isle of Patmos exists. It was a refuge for hermits dating back to the early Christian era. It is speculated that, during John the Apostle's exile on Patmos, he frequented this large outcropping of earth situated at the end of the bay. As mentioned, the Petra has hewn steps, carved holes for holding candles, and a cistern.

According to the Bible, Joseph, Mary, and the Baby Jesus fled to Egypt during the "Massacre of the Innocents," when King Herod the Great decreed the execution of all first-born male children in Bethlehem in order to avoid being dethroned by a newborn King of the Jews foretold by the Magi. There is, indeed, no mention of Jesus Christ in the Bible from the age of 13 until He began teaching the Gospel at the age of 30. Some have suggested He returned to Egypt during that time, although no reasonable explanation has been proposed.

Many cultures, including the ones cited in the story, are said to have very similar legends to the account of Jesus Christ in the Bible. As pointed out, the Egyptian figure Horus was said to have been born on December 25th, performed miracles, was crucified, and was resurrected on the third day after death. Supposedly, the Horus story can be found in Egyptian writing dating back to 1500 BC. The notion that Horus and other deities had the same characteristics as Jesus Christ long before the Christian era, and thus became the basis for Jesus' story, is a highly debated topic.

The Copper Scroll of the Dead Sea Scrolls, as depicted in the story, is accurate. The metal scroll contains 64 lines of text, 63 of which are directions to buried treasure—hordes of gold and silver. Possibly because of the obscure references to landmarks which no longer exist, none of the gold and silver has ever been recovered. Other theories propose that the 63 locations of treasure never existed. Interestingly, the 64th line does, indeed, mention a second, duplicate scroll, which is said to contain more detailed information regarding the location of the treasures. The Copper Scroll is unique when compared to the rest of the Dead Sea Scrolls for the numerous reasons listed in the story, including the use of dialect and text which dramatically differs from the rest of the scrolls that were written on parchment and animal skins. Curiously, there are two or three Greek letters which follow seven of the 63 listings of treasures. No one has determined their meaning or why Greek letters would have been etched next to the Hebrew writing.

There was once a religious fanatical organization known as Flagellants. Their inception can be traced to 13th-century Italy. They were condemned by the Catholic Church as heretical. Their followers implemented public flagellation in their rituals. The sect reached its pinnacle of support during the Black Plague. While flagellation, also known as "Mortification of the Flesh," is sometimes practiced today, the Flagellants as a group do not exist to the authors' knowledge.

As stated in the story, there was a group called the "Sons of Light" in first-century Israel, who lived on the shores of the Dead Sea. They were also known as the Essenes and are considered by most scholars to be the authors of the Dead Sea Scrolls. The "True Sons of Light" is a fictitious group.

French architect Jean-Pierre Houdin theorized that the Great Pyramid in Egypt was built using an ascending ramp which followed the sides of the pyramid at a seven-degree angle, twisting around until it eventually reached the top. At the conclusion of the pyramid's construction, Houdin believes the builders encased the outer shell of the pyramid to conceal the ramp, which he postulates is still in place today.

The hotel referenced in the story, Sonali Giza Hotel, is fictitious. While there is a strong theory that a second sphinx once existed to form a matched pair with the Great Sphinx on the Giza Plateau, there is no evidence suggesting where it may have stood on the Egyptian landscape.

The German World War II "Gold Train" was as described in the story. Countless pieces of artwork were never recovered.

The ceremony of the Feast of the Cross in Oviedo, Spain, when the Sudarium is brought out for public display, was altered by the authors for purposes of the story.

As of this writing, Las Vegas, Nevada, in the USA, does indeed have 21 of the 28 largest hotels (based on number of rooms) in the world.

EVIL IN THE BEGINNING

In the riverside town of Green Cove Springs, Florida, the freshwater spring at the city park briefly turns blood-red, startling onlookers. Moments later, the last of the discolored water flows into the stream and empties into the river.

Only one man knows this event is a prelude to evil.

Dr. Curt Lohan and Scott Marks return in the sequel to *Death in the Beginning* when they discover a hidden cave near the St. Johns River. The cave contains remnants of an ancient cross-oceanic expedition by one of the most enigmatic civilizations that ever inhabited the Earth. As sinister characters emerge in the small town and people begin to disappear, the terrifying truth becomes evident: the magnificent archaeological site holds a dark secret that has been unleashed on the world.

ABOUT THE AUTHORS

Vicky Knerly is a native of Syracuse, New York, and currently resides on St. Simons Island, Georgia. She has two grown sons. Vicky earned a bachelor's degree in English and two masters' degrees, and she has won awards for her research-based writing. She currently works for a private university based in Melbourne, Florida, where she also teaches as an adjunct professor.

Gary Williams lives in Jacksonville, Florida, with his wife and children. He has a bachelor's degree in Business Marketing and writes full time. His hobbies include fishing, history and watching football.

In 2009, Gary and Vicky formally partnered as co-writers. Their debut novel, "Death in the Beginning," was published electronically November 2011 quickly followed by their second novel, "Three Keys to Murder." Look for "Evil in the Beginning" in 2013.

To leave a review of "Indisputable Proof" on Amazon US, please go to:
http://www.amazon.com/Indisputable-Proof-Gary-Williams-ebook/dp/B0094JF00I

Printed in Great Britain
by Amazon